THE
OBSIDIAN
CHAMBER

THE OBSIDIAN CHAMBER

A Pendergast Novel

DOUGLAS PRESTON & LINCOLN CHILD

GRAND CENTRAL
PUBLISHING

NEW YORK   BOSTON

Copyright © 2016 by Splendide Mendax, Inc. and Lincoln Child

Cover design by Flag.
Cover photographs from Getty Images: clouds by Riccardo Mantero; building by DEA PICTURE LIBRARY; landscape by Jay Fleming.
Cover copyright © 2016 by Hachette Book Group, Inc.

Grand Central Publishing
Hachette Book Group
1290 Avenue of the Americas, New York, NY 10104
grandcentralpublishing.com
twitter.com/grandcentralpub

First Edition: October 2016

Grand Central Publishing is a division of Hachette Book Group, Inc. The Grand Central Publishing name and logo is a trademark of Hachette Book Group, Inc.

The publisher is not responsible for websites (or their content) that are not owned by the publisher.

The Hachette Speakers Bureau provides a wide range of authors for speaking events. To find out more, go to www.hachettespeakersbureau.com or call (866) 376-6591.

Library of Congress Cataloging-in-Publication Data
Names: Preston, Douglas J., author. | Child, Lincoln, author.
Title: The obsidian chamber / Douglas Preston & Lincoln Child.
Description: First edition. | New York : Grand Central Publishing, 2016. | Series: Agent Pendergast series
Identifiers: LCCN 2016022192 | ISBN 9781455536917 (hardcover) | ISBN 9781455541676 (large print) | ISBN 9781478938941 (audio book) | ISBN 9781478935278 (audio download) | ISBN 9781455536900 (ebook)
Subjects: LCSH: Pendergast, Aloysius (Fictitious character)—Fiction. | Government investigators—Fiction. | BISAC: FICTION / Thrillers. | GSAFD: Mystery fiction.
Classification: LCC PS3566.R3982 O27 2016 | DDC 813/.54—dc23 LC record available at https://lccn.loc.gov/2016022192

ISBNs: 978-1-4555-3691-7 (hardcover), 978-1-4555-3690-0 (ebook), 978-1-4555-4150-8 (int'l), 978-1-4555-4167-6 (large print), 978-1-4555-7172-7 (B&N signed ed.), 978-1-4555-7173-4 (reg. signed ed.)

Printed in the United States of America

LSC-C

10   9   8   7   6   5   4   3   2   1

Lincoln Child dedicates this book to
his mother, Nancy

Douglas Preston dedicates this book to
Churchill Elangwe

Even in our sleep
pain which cannot forget
falls drop by drop upon the heart
until in our own despair
against our will
comes wisdom
through the awful grace of God.

PROLOGUE

November 8

Proctor eased open the double doors of the library to allow Mrs. Trask to pass through with a silver tray laden with a midmorning tea service.

The room was dim and hushed, lit only by the fire that guttered in the hearth. Before it, sitting in a wing chair, Proctor could see a motionless figure, indistinct in the faint light. Mrs. Trask walked over and placed the tray on a side table next to the chair.

"I thought you might like a cup of tea, Miss Greene," she said.

"No thank you, Mrs. Trask," came Constance's low voice.

"It's your favorite. Jasmine, first grade. I also brought you some madeleines. I baked them just this morning—I know how fond you are of them."

"I'm not particularly hungry," she answered. "Thank you for your trouble."

"Well, I'll just leave them here in case you change your mind." Mrs. Trask smiled maternally, turned, and headed for the library exit. By the time she reached Proctor, the smile had faded and the look on her face had grown worried once again.

"I'll only be gone a few days," she said to him in a low tone. "My sister should be home from the hospital by the weekend. Are you sure you'll be all right?"

Proctor nodded and watched her bustle her way back toward the kitchen before returning his gaze to the figure in the wing chair.

It had been over two weeks since Constance had come back to the mansion at 891 Riverside Drive. She had returned, grim and silent, without Agent Pendergast, and with no explanation of what had happened. Proctor—as Pendergast's chauffeur, ex-military subordinate, and general security factotum—felt that, in the agent's absence, it was his duty to help Constance through whatever she was dealing with. It had taken him time, patience, and effort to coax the story out of her. Even now, that story made little sense and he was unsure what really happened. What he did know, however, was that the vast house, lacking Pendergast's presence, had changed—changed utterly. And so, too, had Constance.

After returning alone from Exmouth, Massachusetts—where she had gone to assist Special Agent A. X. L. Pendergast on a private case—Constance had locked herself in her room for days, taking meals only with the greatest reluctance. When she at last emerged, she seemed a different person: gaunt, spectral. Proctor had always known her to be coolheaded, reserved, and self-possessed. But in the days that followed, she was by turns apathetic and suddenly full of restless energy, pacing about the halls and corridors as if looking for something. She abandoned all interest in the pastimes that had once possessed her: researching the Pendergast family ancestry, antiquarian studies, reading, and playing the harpsichord. After a few anxious visits from Lieutenant D'Agosta, Captain Laura Hayward, and Margo Green, she had refused to see anyone. She also appeared to be—Proctor could think of no better way to put it—on her guard. The only times she showed a spark of her old self was on the very rare occasions when the phone rang, or when Proctor brought the mail back from the post office box. Always, always, he knew, she was hoping for word from Pendergast. But there had been none.

A certain high-level entity in the FBI had arranged to keep the search for Pendergast, and the attendant official investigation, out of reach of the news media. Nevertheless, Proctor had taken it upon himself to gather all the information he could about his employer's disappearance. The search for the body, he learned, had lasted five days. Since the missing person was a federal agent, exceptional effort had been expended. Coast Guard cutters had searched the waters off Exmouth; local officers and National Guardsmen had combed the coastline from the New Hampshire border down to Cape Ann, looking for any sign—even so much as a shred of clothing. Divers had carefully examined rocks where the currents might have hung up a body, and the seafloor was scrutinized with sonar. But there had been nothing. The case remained officially open, but the unspoken conclusion was that Pendergast—gravely wounded in a fight, struggling against a vicious tidal current, weakened by the battering of the waves, and subjected to the fifty-degree water—had been swept out to sea and drowned, his body lost in the deeps. Just two days before, Pendergast's lawyer—a partner in one of the oldest and most discreet law firms in New York—had finally reached out to Pendergast's surviving son, Tristram, to give him the sad news of his father's disappearance.

Now Proctor approached and took a seat beside Constance. She glanced up at him as he sat down, giving him the faintest smile. Then her gaze returned to the fire. The flickering light cast dark shadows over her violet eyes and dark bobbed hair.

Since her return, Proctor had taken it upon himself to look after her, knowing that this was what his employer would have wanted. Her troubled state roused uncharacteristically protective feelings within him—ironic, because under normal circumstances Constance was the last person to seek protection from another. And yet, without saying it, she seemed glad of his attentions.

She straightened in her chair. "Proctor, I've decided to go below."

The abrupt announcement took him aback. "You mean—down *there*? Where you lived before?"

She said nothing.

"Why?"

"To...teach myself to accept the inevitable."

"Why can't you do that here, with us? You can't just go down there again."

She turned and stared at him with such intensity that he was taken aback. He realized it was hopeless to change her mind. Perhaps this meant she was finally accepting that Pendergast was gone—that was progress, of sorts. Perhaps.

Now she rose from her chair. "I'll write a note for Mrs. Trask, instructing what necessities to leave inside the service elevator. I'll take one hot meal each evening at eight. But nothing for the first two nights, please—I feel over-ministered-to at present. Besides, Mrs. Trask will be away, and I wouldn't want to discommode you."

Proctor rose as well. He took hold of her arm. "Constance, you must listen to me—"

She glanced down at his hand, and then up into his face with a look that prompted him to immediately release his grasp.

"Thank you, Proctor, for respecting my wishes."

Rising up on her toes, she surprised him again by lightly kissing his cheek. Then she turned, and—moving almost like a sleepwalker—headed to the far end of the library, where the service elevator was hidden behind a false set of bookcases. She swung open the twin bookcases, slipped inside the waiting elevator, closed it behind her—and was gone.

Proctor stared at the spot for a long moment. This was crazy. He shook his head and turned away. Once again, the absence of Pendergast was like a shadow cast over the mansion—and over him. He needed time to be alone, to think this through.

He walked out of the library, took a turn down the hall, opened a door that led into a carpeted hallway, and mounted a crooked staircase leading to the old servants' quarters. Gaining the third-floor landing, he walked down another corridor until he reached the door to his small apartment of rooms. He opened it, stepped inside, and closed it behind him.

He should have protested her plan more forcefully. With Pendergast gone, he was responsible for her. But he knew nothing he said would have made any difference. Long ago he'd learned that, while he could handle almost anyone, he was hopeless against her. In time, he mused, with his subtle encouragement, Constance would accept the reality of Pendergast's death—and rejoin the living…

A gloved hand whipped around from behind, seizing him around the rib cage and tightening with immense force.

Taken by surprise, Proctor nevertheless reacted instinctually with a sharp downward movement, attempting to throw the intruder off balance; but the man anticipated the reaction and thwarted it. Instantly Proctor felt the sting of a needle jabbed deep into his neck. He froze.

"Movement is inadvisable," came a strange, silky voice that Proctor, with profound shock, recognized.

He did not move. It stunned him that a man—any man—had gotten the drop on him. How was it possible? He had been preoccupied, inattentive. He would never forgive himself for this. Especially because *this* man, he knew, was Pendergast's greatest enemy.

"You're far better versed than I in the arts of physical combat," continued the smooth voice. "So I've taken the liberty of evening the odds. What you're feeling in your neck at the moment is, of course, a hypodermic needle. I have not yet depressed the plunger. The syringe contains a dose of sodium pentothal—a very large dose. I will ask you once, and once only: signal your acquiescence by relaxing your body. How you react now will determine whether you receive a dose that is merely anesthetizing . . . or lethal."

Proctor considered his options. He let his body slacken.

"Excellent," said the voice. "The name is Proctor, I seem to recall?"

Proctor remained silent. There would be an opportunity to reverse the situation; there was always an opportunity. He only had to think.

"I've been observing the family manor for some time now. The man of the house is away—permanently, it would seem. It's as depressing as a tomb. You might as well all be wearing crepe."

Proctor's mind raced through various scenarios. He must pick one and execute it. He needed time, just a little time, a few seconds at most . . .

"Not in the mood for a chat? Just as well. I have a great many things to do, and so I bid you: *good night.*"

As he felt the plunger slide home, Proctor realized his time was up—and that, to his vast surprise, he had failed.

I

Slowly, Proctor swam back up toward consciousness from inky depths. It was a long swim, and it seemed to take a long time. At last he opened his eyes. The lids felt heavy, and it was all he could do not to close them again. What had happened? For a moment he lay motionless, taking in his surroundings. Then he realized: he was on the floor of his sitting room.

His sitting room.

I have a great many things to do . . .

All of a sudden, everything came back to him in a mad rush. He struggled to rise; failed; tried again with still-greater effort, and this time managed to push himself to a sitting position. His body felt like a sack of meal.

He glanced at his watch. Eleven fifteen AM. He'd been out just over thirty minutes.

Thirty minutes. God only knew what might have transpired in that time.

I have a great many things to do . . .

With a heroic effort, Proctor staggered to his feet. The room rocked and he steadied himself against a table, shaking his head violently in an attempt to clear it. He paused just a moment, trying to collect both his physical and mental faculties. Then he opened the table's single drawer, pulled out a Glock 22, and stuffed it into his waistband.

The door to his set of rooms was open, the central hallway of the servants' quarters visible beyond. He made for the open doorway, steadied himself against its frame, then lurched down the hall like a drunken man. Reaching the narrow back staircase, he grasped the railing tightly and half walked, half staggered down two flights of stairs to the mansion's main floor. This effort, and the sense of extreme danger that enveloped him, combined to help sharpen his senses. He walked down a short corridor and opened the door at the end leading to the public rooms.

Here he paused, preparing to call for Mrs. Trask. Then he reconsidered. Announcing his presence was inadvisable. Besides, Mrs. Trask had in all probability already left to visit her ailing sister in Albany. And in any case she was not the person in greatest danger. That person was Constance.

Proctor stepped out onto the marble floor, preparing to enter the library, ride the elevator to the basement, and take whatever steps were necessary to protect her. But just outside the library he stopped again. He could see that, within, a table had been overturned, books and various papers spilling over the carpeting.

He glanced around quickly. To his right, the mansion's grand reception hall—its walls lined with cabinets full of strange displays—was a mess. A plinth had been knocked over, the ancient Etruscan cinerary urn previously displayed upon it shattered into pieces. The oversize vase of freshly cut flowers that always stood in the middle of the hall, its contents changed daily by Mrs. Trask, now lay broken on the marble floor, two dozen roses and lilies disarrayed in puddles of water. At the far end of the hall, at the doorway leading to the refectory gallery, one of the cabinet doors was wide open, canted to one side, half ripped from its hinges. It looked as if someone had grasped it in a frantic attempt to avoid being dragged away.

All too clearly, these were signs of a terrific struggle. And they led—from the library, across the reception hall—directly toward the mansion's front door. And the world beyond.

Proctor ran across the hall. In the long, narrow room beyond, he could see that the refectory table—at which, until recently, Constance had been occupied with researching the Pendergast family history—was a riot of disorder: books and papers strewn about, chairs knocked over, a laptop computer upended. And at the far end of the room, where a foyer led to the front hall, was something even more disturbing: the heavy front door—which was rarely unlocked, let alone opened—stood ajar, admitting brilliant late-morning sunlight.

As he took in these signs with mounting horror, Proctor heard—from beyond the open door—the muffled sound of a female voice, crying for help.

Ignoring the still-receding dizziness, he raced down the room, pulling the Glock from his waistband. He ran under an archway, through the front hall, then kicked the front door wide and paused under the porte cochere beyond to reconnoiter.

There, at the far end of the driveway, a Lincoln Navigator with smoked windows was idling, facing Riverside Drive. Its closest rear door was open. Just outside it was Constance Greene, her wrists bound behind her. She was facing away from him, struggling desperately; but there was no mistaking the bobbed cut of her hair and her olive Burberry trench coat. A man, also facing away from Proctor, had hold of her head and was just now pushing her violently into the rear seat and slamming the door behind her.

Proctor raised his gun and fired, but the man leapt over the car's hood and through the driver's door, the shot going just wide. Proctor's second shot ricocheted off the bulletproof glass, even as the car accelerated with a cloud of rubber and lurched onto Riverside Drive, the form of Constance, still struggling wildly, visible through the tinted rear window. The car roared down the avenue and out of range.

Just before the assailant had leapt into the car, he had turned toward Proctor, and their eyes had met. There could be no mistaking the man's features: his strange bichromatic eyes, the pale, chiseled face, the trim beard and ginger hair and look of cold cruelty…This was none other than Diogenes, Pendergast's brother and implacable enemy, whom they had all believed dead—killed by Constance more than three years previous.

Now he had reappeared. *And he had Constance.*

The look in Diogenes's eyes—the ferocity, the dark and perverse glitter of triumph—was so terrible that, for the briefest of moments, even the stoic Proctor was unmanned. But his paralysis lasted only a millisecond. Shaking off the dread and the sedative both, he took off after the car, running down the driveway and leaping over the trimmed border hedge with a single bound.

2

In his youth Proctor had been an exceptional runner—he'd set a record on the endurance course during his OSUT that still stood at Fort Benning, and he'd kept in peak condition ever since—and he pursued the Navigator at the top of his speed. It was now idling at a red light, a block and a half ahead. Proctor covered the distance in under fifteen seconds. Just as he neared the vehicle, the light turned green and the Navigator screeched ahead.

Planting his feet on the asphalt, Proctor aimed his Glock at the vehicle's rear tires and fired twice, first at the left, then at the right. The shots hit home, the rubber of both tires shivering from the impact. But even as he watched, they stiffened again with an explosive hiss. *Self-inflating.* The Navigator, Diogenes at the wheel, gunned around the vehicle ahead of it and accelerated up Riverside, weaving through traffic.

Now Proctor turned and raced back toward the mansion, stuffing the gun back into his waistband and pulling out his cell phone. He had only limited knowledge of Pendergast's contacts in the FBI and other federal agencies; besides, in this situation, calling the FBI would only slow things down. This was a matter for local police. He dialed 911.

"Nine-one-one emergency response," a cool female voice answered.

Reaching the mansion, Proctor ducked through the front door and raced through the public rooms to the rear of the structure. For security and confidentiality, his cell phone was linked to a false name and address, and he knew this information would already be appearing on the operator's screen. "This is Kenneth Lomax," Proctor said, using the cover name, as he opened a false wall panel in the back corridor and snatched up a special bug-out bag he had prepared for precisely such an emergency. "I've just witnessed a violent abduction."

"Location, please."

Proctor gave the location as he stuffed the Glock in the bag, along with extra magazines of ammo. "I saw this man dragging a woman out of a house by her hair, and she was screaming for help at the top of her lungs. He threw her into a car and drove away."

"Description?"

"Black Navigator with smoked windows, headed north on Riverside." He gave her the license plate number as he grabbed the bag and ran through the kitchen toward the garage, where Pendergast's '59 Rolls-Royce Silver Wraith was housed.

"Please stay on the line, sir. I'm dispatching units to intercept."

Firing up the engine, Proctor peeled out of the driveway and turned north onto Riverside Drive, laying ten feet of rubber across the asphalt as he accelerated, running first one, then a second red light. Traffic was thin and he could see ahead for about half a mile. Peering through the hazy light, he tried to make out the Navigator, and thought he could just see it ten blocks ahead.

Accelerating further, he dodged his way between taxis, then ran another light to the furious blatting of horns. He knew that, because it was a possible kidnapping, the 911 operator would notify the Detective Bureau after calling in the marked units. She would also want a lot more information from him. He tossed the cell phone into the passenger seat, line still open. Then he turned on the police radio installed under the dash.

He accelerated further still, blocks shooting past in a blur. He could no longer see the Navigator ahead, even at the straightaway just before Washington Heights. The man's most logical escape route would be the West Side Highway—but there were no entrances along this stretch of Riverside Drive North. He began to hear sirens; the police had responded quickly.

Suddenly, in his rearview mirror, he saw the Navigator shoot out onto Riverside Drive from 147th Street, heading *south*. Diogenes, he realized, had ducked into the one-way street in the wrong direction and turned around.

Lips compressed, Proctor sized up the traffic around him. Then he yanked the steering wheel sharply to the left. At the same time, he used the hand brake to lock the wheels, spinning the car around in a power slide. Another shriek of protesting horns and screeching of brakes from the surrounding traffic greeted this maneuver. He followed through the sliding turn, releasing the handbrake when the car completed a 180-degree rotation as he gunned the engine. The big car leapt forward. In the distance now, he could see flashing lights accompanying the wail of sirens.

Five blocks ahead, he could see the Navigator swinging right onto West 145th. That made no sense: 145th quickly dead-ended in the parking lot of Riverbank State Park, the green space built—ironically—atop a sewage treatment plant sandwiched between the Hudson River and the West Side Highway. Did Diogenes have a fast boat waiting on the river?

It was the work of half a minute to dodge through traffic and turn the Rolls sharply onto West 145th. But it was vital he understood what Diogenes intended before proceeding. He brought the car to an abrupt stop and, plucking a small but powerful pair of binoculars from his bag, surveyed the landscape ahead: first the road, then the parking lot and its adjoining service access lanes. There was no sign of any black Navigator. Where the hell had he gone?

Proctor replaced the binoculars. As he did so, he saw out of his peripheral vision a disturbance in the brush to his right. The shoulder banked away sharply here, angling down toward the north–south ribbon of the West Side Highway. Foliage and saplings looked freshly cut; there was a thin, dissipating pall of dust—and fresh tire marks gouged into the dirt.

Proctor raised the binoculars again. There, in the distance, was the Navigator, on the highway, moving north at high speed. He cursed. This set of maneuvers had again given Diogenes at least half a mile's lead.

Gunning the engine once more, he turned the Rolls off the road and made the lurching, precarious trip down the embankment and onto the highway, where he savagely merged into the oncoming traffic, then grabbed the cell phone off the passenger seat. "This is Kenneth Lomax. The suspect vehicle is now moving north on the West Side Highway, approaching the GWB."

"Sir," the operator asked, "how can you be sure?"

"Because I'm in pursuit."

"Don't follow it yourself, sir. Let the police handle the situation."

Proctor rarely raised his voice, but he did so at this moment. "Then get some goddamned heat on that vehicle, and get it *now*." He threw the phone back into the passenger seat, ignoring the responding chatter of the operator.

He raced up the West Side Highway as it banked around the Hudson River Greenway, rising and falling with the contour of the land. He pushed the Rolls to over a hundred miles an hour, but he knew that Diogenes would be doing the same. Ahead and above arched the long slender span of I-95 as it passed over the George Washington Bridge. The Navigator was no longer in sight. Had Diogenes taken the exit helix and headed for New Jersey, or Long Island, or Connecticut? Or had he stayed on the highway, over the last brief nubbin of Manhattan, and gone north into Westchester?

Proctor cursed again. He cycled through the police bands, heard the chatter of the marked units responding to the call to be alert for a black Lincoln Navigator with tinted windows heading north on the West Side Highway. Except that by now the Navigator—one way or another—would no longer be on the West Side Highway.

The chase was over.

3

E<small>XCEPT THAT IT</small> wasn't.

At the last possible moment, following his gut, Proctor took the exit for the bridge, shearing across three lanes of traffic, barely able to keep the Rolls under control as it negotiated the sharp, walled ramp. He chose the lower level of the bridge because of its reduced truck traffic and, hence, greater maneuverability and speed. Crackled reports over the police radio were calling in their useless, negative findings. On the seat beside him, the 911 operator's voice began to flutter above the threshold of hearing again. Proctor knew that, once the cops turned their attention away from the failed chase, the next person of interest would be himself. He did not have the time for unwanted questions or—worse—potential detainment. Reaching over, he picked up the cell phone, lowered his window, and tossed it out. He had other prepaid burner phones stowed in the bug-out bag.

Reaching the far side of the bridge and New Jersey, he slowed to seventy as he passed the eastbound toll plaza; he did not want to get pulled over for speeding at such a critical moment. He negotiated the tangle of diverging freeways and headed for the I-80 Express westbound. Fifteen minutes later, he took Exit 65 from the interstate, making for Teterboro Airport.

Proctor had surmised there were only two viable escape options open to Diogenes: to go to ground in some nearby safe house prearranged for the purpose, or to take Constance somewhere distant via private transportation. If Diogenes had gone to ground, it was too late to do anything about it. If he planned on taking her someplace far away, he could not risk staying in the Navigator. It would be impossible to drag a kidnap victim onto a commercial flight or some other form of public transportation—and his license plate was known. What remained as a destination was Teterboro: the closest airport capable of handling long-distance private aircraft.

He turned onto Industrial Avenue and pulled the Rolls over to the curb beside the airport's closest entrance. He scanned the line of nearby structures: the tower, a fire station, various FBO buildings. There was no sign of the Navigator, but that meant nothing: it could be already abandoned behind, or within, any of half a dozen hangars. Opening the driver's door, he stepped out and quickly scanned the runways for taxiing planes—there were none—then peered up at the sky. A jet was climbing away, its gear retracting as he watched. But the airspace over the tristate area was full of planes: there was no way to be certain Diogenes was on that particular one.

Not yet, at any rate.

Getting back into the Rolls, he retrieved the vehicle's laptop, accessed the Internet, and pulled up the diagram for Teterboro. Next, he checked the AirNav website for summary information on the airport: latitude and longitude, operational statistics, runway dimensions. Teterboro's two runways were both about seven thousand feet in length, capable of handling nearly any size plane. He noted that the airport serviced around 450 aircraft a day, of which 60 percent were general aviation. Now he scrolled down the web page until he reached the fixed-base operator information: data on ground handling, avionics service, aircraft charters. He committed all this information to memory.

Putting the Rolls into gear, he entered the airport proper and drove along the line of buildings until he reached one at the very head of runway 1. The building was a cavernous hangar with a large sign that read NORTH JERSEY FLIGHT TRAINING. Grabbing his bug-out bag, he jumped out of the car and ran toward the building. He glanced inside it briefly and continued past to the end of the runway itself. The flight school had half a dozen crappy Cessna 152s parked directly on the tarmac. In the closest one, he noticed, two people were sitting: evidently a pilot and a student, going over the flight plan for an upcoming lesson.

Fixing a worried look on his face, Proctor ran to the plane, waving at them to open their windows. The occupants looked out at him. From the expressions on their faces it was immediately evident who was the pilot and who was the student.

"Can you help me?" Proctor asked, pitching his voice high and querulous. "Did you just see a man and a woman get on a plane here?"

The men in the Cessna looked at each other.

"The woman would have been young, early twenties, dark hair. The man would have been tall, trim beard, scar on one cheek."

"Mister, you shouldn't be here without clearance," said the pilot.

Proctor directed his attention to the student: an older fellow who was clearly excited just to be sitting in the plane. "That was my boss," Proctor said breathlessly, waving the bag. "He forgot this. I can't reach him on his cell. It's vitally important, he needs information from the documents in here."

"Yes, I saw them," the student said. "They got on a plane maybe five minutes ago. It was waiting for them, right there, on the runway. The woman looked sick. She seemed to be staggering all over the place."

"What kind of a plane?" Proctor asked.

The pilot frowned. "Sir, we can't be giving—"

But the student, clearly an enthusiast, spoke over him. "It was a twin-engine jet. A Lear. Don't know the model."

"Yes," Proctor said. "A Lear. That's him, all right. Thank you so much, I'll try to find some way to contact him." The pilot opened his mouth to speak again, but before he could Proctor turned and jogged back past the flight school hangar.

In the Rolls once again, he pulled up the FlightAware website and, on the site's landing page, instructed it to track KTEB: the International Civil Aviation Organization code for Teterboro. This brought up a map of the tristate area, with Teterboro at its center, overlaid with the ghostly white shapes of tiny aircraft headed in various directions. Below the map were two panels: "Arrivals" and "Departures."

Proctor quickly scanned the "Departures" panel. It consisted of several lines of data, listed in reverse chronological order. Each line represented an aircraft that had left Teterboro during the past several hours, and it identified the plane's tail number, aircraft type, destination, time of departure, and estimated time of arrival.

The time was now 12:45 PM. From the information on the screen, Proctor could see that the most recent planes to depart Teterboro had left at 12:41, 12:32, and 12:29 PM. So only one plane had left the airport in the last five minutes.

He checked the aircraft type of the plane that had departed at twelve forty-one. Sure enough, it was listed as LJ45—a Learjet 45. It was headed for KOMA. A quick search identified this as the ICAO code for Eppley Airfield in Omaha, Nebraska.

The website listed the "Ident" or tail number as LN303P. Proctor clicked on this and a new window opened: a map showing the projected path of the flight from New Jersey to Nebraska. The little symbol representing the plane had a thin, short tail behind it leading from Teterboro: a dotted line, which zigged slightly in two places, headed westward ahead of the plane icon, showing the projected course. A row of data at one side of the screen told him the plane had a projected cruising speed of 420 knots, and that it was presently climbing at six thousand feet, heading for nineteen thousand.

With a click, Proctor closed the flight map window. He now knew two critical things: Diogenes and Constance had gotten on that Learjet, and Diogenes had filed a flight plan with the FAA for Nebraska. All IFR flights were required to file such plans; trying to fly without one would generate immediate and unwelcome scrutiny.

Scanning the "Arrivals" panel, he saw that the Learjet with tail number LN303P had landed at Teterboro only half an hour earlier. So it was not a local charter—Diogenes had used a "repositioned" charter from another airport in order to help cover his tracks.

Clever. But not quite clever enough. Because Diogenes had not thought, or known, to block his tail number from such civil aircraft tracking as FlightAware. And as a result, Proctor now knew precisely where he was headed.

But such knowledge was of limited use. Because with every passing minute, Diogenes was streaking away from him, toward Nebraska, at hundreds of miles per hour.

4

ACCORDING TO THE AirNav website he had checked earlier, Debon-Air Aviation Services was the only aircraft charter service currently operating directly on the Teterboro grounds. Driving along the row of FBO buildings, Proctor finally spotted the charter's sign; he parked in a space near the frosted-glass exterior door and then, killing the engine and grabbing his bag and laptop, he quickly exited the Rolls.

The interior of the charter service was like others he had seen, comfortable yet eminently functional: most charter operators were either ex-commercial pilots or ex-military. There were three desks, only one of which was occupied. Framed aviation posters hung on the walls. An open door at the back of the office led to what was evidently a filing room.

Proctor sized up the man behind the desk. He was about fifty, with short iron-gray hair and a muscular build. A nameplate on his desk read BOWMAN. He was looking back at Proctor, evidently assessing a prospective customer.

Proctor considered the situation. What he was about to request was unusual, and would normally take time—more time than he had—to arrange. He quickly but methodically weighed his options, following each decision tree to its logical conclusion. Then he took an empty seat before the desk, placing the computer on the floor and keeping the bug-out bag protectively cradled on his lap. "I need an immediate charter," he said.

The man blinked back at him. "Immediate," he repeated.

Proctor nodded.

"What's the rush?" the man asked. His expression, abruptly growing suspicious, asked the silent question: *Illegal?*

"Nothing like that," Proctor said. He had already determined that a degree of honesty was most likely to procure a successful outcome—honesty, followed up with other inducements. "It's a pursuit operation."

At this phrasing, the man perked up. He glanced afresh at Proctor—one military man to another. "Rangers?" he asked.

Proctor gestured vaguely with one hand. "Special forces." He glanced at a framed case on the wall behind Bowman. "Airborne?"

Bowman nodded. The look of suspicion had eased. "Why not go to the police?"

"It's a kidnapping intervention. Any involvement with the police might mean the death of the hostage. The kidnapper is both intelligent and extremely violent. Beyond that, it's a sensitive personal matter—and time is critical. I know the plane's tail number and destination. I've got to reach that destination before the objective vanishes."

Bowman nodded again, more slowly. "The destination?"

"Eppley Airfield, Omaha."

"Omaha," the man repeated. "You're looking at a lot of aviation fuel, friend. How long would the layover be?"

"No layover. It's a one-way trip."

"I'd still need to charge you for the empty return."

"Understood."

"Number of passengers?"

"You're looking at him."

A pause. "You realize that a last-minute charter like this—given the extra red tape and overhead—would come with a significant surcharge."

"No problem."

The man seemed to consider this a moment. Then he turned to a computer on his desk, began tapping keys. Proctor used the opportunity to open his own laptop and check the status of Diogenes's plane. The icon of LN303P was still arrowing westward. It was at twelve thousand feet, approaching its cruising speed.

"You're in luck," Bowman said. "We've got a plane available, a Pilatus PC-12. We've got a licensed pilot at the airport, too; he's over getting lunch now." The man dragged forward a calculator. "With fuel, ramp fees, landing fees, segment fees, per-diem, one-way fee, and a fifteen percent, ah, usage surcharge, that will be one thousand, two hundred per—"

"That won't work," Proctor interrupted.

The man eyed him. "Why not?"

"The PC-12 is a single turboprop. I need a jet."

"A jet."

"I'm pursuing a Learjet 45. I'll need something as fast or faster."

The suspicious look returned for a moment. Then Bowman glanced back at his computer. "We do have one plane available. A Gulfstream IV. But it won't be able to leave anytime soon."

"Why not?"

"I told you we had a pilot on hand. I didn't say anything about *two* pilots. You can't fly a jet like that alone." More tapping of keys. "I've got somebody on standby; I can get him here first thing in the morning. That is, if the additional cost of the Gulfstream won't be a problem—"

"Unacceptable."

The man went silent abruptly, staring at Proctor.

"I need to leave immediately," Proctor went on, in an even voice.

"And I told you that I can't have a copilot available until the morning."

Once again, Proctor considered his options. Violence was usually his first choice. However, under the circumstances it did not seem well advised: there were too many variables at play, too much security in and around the area; besides, he needed voluntary cooperation if he was going to succeed. "What would the normal fee for a round-trip to Omaha be on the Gulfstream IV?"

Once again, the man plied his calculator. "Three thousand, eight hundred per hour."

"So I'm guessing that—with a one-way flight time of about three hours—we're looking in the neighborhood of twenty-five thousand dollars."

"Sounds about right—" the man began, but shut up again when Proctor reached into his bag, pulled out several stacks of hundred-dollar bills, and placed them on the desk. "There's thirty thousand. Let's go."

The man stared at the neat piles of cash. "I just told you, I can't get a—"

"You're a licensed pilot, aren't you?" Proctor asked. With his chin, he indicated another framed item on the wall.

"Yes, but—"

Wordlessly, Proctor reached into the bag and took out another five thousand dollars, which he added to the pile. He was careful to leave the bag open, displaying many more stacks of hundred-dollar bills— almost half a million dollars, in total—along with a pair of Glock 22s.

The man looked from the money on the desk, to the bag, and then back to the desk. At last he picked up his phone, dialed. "Ray? We've got an emergency charter. Yes, right now. Omaha. No, it's an empty-leg. I'll be flying the left-hand seat. Get on back here. Now." He listened to chatter on the other end of the line for a minute. "Well, tell her to wait until tomorrow, damn it."

During this exchange, Proctor had once again taken the opportunity to monitor Diogenes's flight via FlightAware. To his surprise and dismay, he saw that—just moments ago—the plane had veered off its original course and was now on a heading of zero four zero. A glance at the flight information window on the right side of the screen showed a new destination: no longer KOMA, bur rather CYQX. Looking this up, Proctor determined that it was the code for Gander International Airport in Newfoundland.

So Diogenes had not been content merely to hire a repositioned charter for his escape from Teterboro. He had also, it seemed, made a midair FAA request for a new flight plan, diverting his plane from Omaha to Gander. Just to make sure he wasn't followed.

While Proctor was examining his laptop, Bowman had made a brief series of calls. "Okay," the man said, scooping up the piles of cash. "My pilot's on the way over, and we're fueling the plane now. I'll get a flight plan filed on DUATS and we can leave immediately—"

"There's been a change in destination," Proctor interrupted. "It's no longer Omaha. It's Gander, Newfoundland."

"Newfoundland?" Bowman frowned. "Just a minute. Now we're talking international, and—"

"It doesn't matter. The flight distance is shorter. I'll pay whatever's necessary." Proctor took another five grand out of his bag, waved it a moment, put it back. "Just do what you need to do. And let's get the fuck out of here."

This unexpected expletive, delivered in Proctor's standard monotone, seemed to be the most effective persuader of all. Bowman exhaled, then nodded slowly. "Give me a minute to make the preparations," he said in a strange tone that sounded half-pleased, half-deflated. "We'll be wheels-up in ten minutes."

5

The flight plan from Teterboro to Gander International covered eleven hundred miles on a nonstop path over Cape Ann, Massachusetts; Nova Scotia; and Newfoundland. Including time spent taxiing, taking off, and decelerating on the approach descent, estimated flying time was one hour and fifty-one minutes. It wasn't until one hour and thirty minutes into the flight that Proctor managed to speak with the Gander Air Traffic Control.

Proctor had satisfied himself that Gander was, in fact, Diogenes's destination. There had been no further deviations—in fact, his plane was now on final approach. Although Diogenes had gotten the initial jump, as a result of his brief deviation toward Omaha—and because the two jets were evenly matched in speed—he was now no more than half an hour ahead of Proctor. However, the Gulfstream's pilots, Bowman and another man named Ray Krisp, were sticklers for protocol—as, Proctor knew, were most professional pilots—and they had steadfastly refused to let him use their radio, no matter how much he'd offered in cash.

Finally, as the plane began its descent trajectory, Bowman picked up the radio after the handoff to Gander tower. "Gander, this is November Three Niner Seven Bravo at four thousand, five hundred with information X-ray inbound for landing," he said.

There was a crackle of static. "Niner Seven Bravo Squawk, four four five two, clear direct to runway three. Contact ground point nine."

"Clear to land runway three, Niner Seven Bravo," said Bowman, and moved to replace the mike. As he did, Proctor's hand shot out, grabbed it, and—stepping back out of the reach of the strapped-in pilots—pressed the TRANSMIT button.

"Gander ATC," he said. "An LJ45, repeat a Learjet 45, tail number LN303P, is just now landing on runway three. Hold that plane on the taxiway."

There was a brief silence over the radio. "This is Gander Control," came the voice. "Say again?"

"Hold Learjet, tail number LN303P," said Proctor. "Do not allow the passengers to deplane. There is a hostage on board."

Both Bowman and Krisp were in the process of unfastening their belts.

"Who is this speaking?" said the air traffic controller. "This is not a law enforcement frequency."

"I repeat: *there is a hostage on board that plane.* Notify the authorities."

"Any such request must be made through law enforcement channels. Do you copy, Three Niner Seven Bravo?"

Bowman was standing now, facing Proctor, his expression dark. Wordlessly, he put out his hand for the radio.

Proctor was about to speak into the radio again, but even as he did so he realized his attempt had failed. He'd run into a wall of Canadian bureaucracy—as he should have expected.

"Give me the radio," Bowman said.

Even as the pilot spoke, the radio squawked again. "Three Niner Seven Bravo, do you copy?"

"All you're going to do is get this aircraft seized," Bowman said. "Not the one you're pursuing. And get us all held for questioning."

Proctor hesitated. His eyes shifted toward his bug-out bag, slung over one of the front passenger seats.

"What are you going to do—shoot us?" Bowman said. "That's not going to get you anywhere but crashed. Now: give me the radio."

Wordlessly, Proctor handed it to him.

Quickly, Bowman raised it to his lips. "This is Three Niner Seven Bravo. Ignore that last. A passenger made his way into the cockpit."

The voice from Gander tower responded. "Roger that. Do you require assistance upon landing?"

Bowman looked at Proctor as he spoke. "Ah, that's a negative. Passenger's just a little tipsy. He's been locked out and the cockpit secured."

Bowman kept his eyes on Proctor as he put the radio back, took his seat once again. "That's your forty thousand bucks talking, pal," he said. "Otherwise, we'd turn you over to the cops for pulling a trick like that."

Proctor returned the stare. At last, he turned away and headed back to his seat. He had done all he could, and that last effort had been a mistake. His judgment was off. He was neither a cop nor a federal officer. He could not force the authorities to act, especially the authorities of a foreign country; and it was, he realized, foolish to have tried. He would have to deal with Diogenes himself—back on terra firma.

And he was capable of doing so. He'd come this far. Gander was the easternmost major airport on the North American continent, teetering on the edge of the Atlantic. The question now was this: was Newfoundland the ultimate destination of Diogenes? Or a mere waypoint to somewhere else? In many ways, Proctor inclined toward the former. It was a perfect destination—in the middle of nowhere, surrounded by a vast and empty landscape: an ideal place to go to ground. The Lear's limited range would make a transatlantic flight a dangerous stretch, at the very edge of possibility.

Once on the ground, Proctor would do what he did best: track down his prey. It might take a little time. But there would be no place for Diogenes to run now; no opportunity to make fresh arrangements. Proctor would press the chase too hard for that. His quarry was burdened with an unwilling, dangerous hostage. No, the pursuit would not be long—it was just a question of exactly how it would play out.

Of course, he realized he had no real proof Diogenes and Constance were on the Learjet: just the eyewitness at the Teterboro flight school. But the lack of potential escape routes, the repositioned charter, the abrupt change of destination in midair—it all smacked of Diogenes. Proctor's gut told him as much. Besides, it was the only lead he had.

These thoughts occupied him as the plane descended toward Gander's runway three. Out of the window, he watched a bleak, gray-green sprawl of vegetation give way to a wide strip of asphalt. There was a screech as the wheels touched down, then a roar as the engines went into reverse. As they decelerated down the runway, Proctor leaned in closer to the window, looking at the planes moving along the taxiways or parked at gates, searching for the Lear. It was nowhere in sight.

But then he saw something. Directly across the intersecting lanes of asphalt from the runway of his own decelerating plane, he saw two distant figures emerge from a hangar and walk toward a parked jet: a Bombardier Challenger, by the look of it. A plane that could easily manage transoceanic distances—and one he could not effectively pursue in his current charter. The first figure was a young woman in an olive trench coat, dark-haired head lowered. *Constance.* Immediately behind her, with one hand on her shoulder and another placed against her back, was a man. The man turned, glancing left and right...and even at distance Proctor could unmistakably make out the tall, thin figure, neatly trimmed beard, and ginger hair of Diogenes.

Constance was walking strangely, unwillingly: frog-marched, Proctor realized. No doubt Diogenes had a gun concealed in the hand that was pressed against her back.

A rush of adrenaline burned through his body and he turned from the window, but his plane was still decelerating—it would be minutes before he could manage even an emergency exit.

He turned back to the window. Now the two figures were climbing the steps into the passenger compartment of the Bombardier. At the very last moment before Constance disappeared into the darkness of the cabin, Proctor saw her begin to struggle; saw Diogenes—quick as lightning—reach into his coat, pull out a canvas bag, and slip it over her head...and then the door closed behind them and the abruptly violent tableau was obscured.

By the time his plane had taxied to a stop, the Bombardier was airborne.

6

DURING THE FLIGHT from Teterboro, Proctor had used part of the time to research the airport and town of Gander. In the 1940s, Gander International had been a critical refueling point for flights headed to the British Isles and beyond. Now, however, modern jets with far greater range had rendered this role obsolete. At present, Gander was used more frequently for emergency landings: transatlantic aircraft suffering from medical or mechanical problems. On 9/11, with U.S. airspace closed following the destruction of the Twin Towers, Gander had briefly played an important role in Operation Yellow Ribbon, receiving over three dozen re-routed flights in one day. Other than that, however, the airport was a relatively somnolent place, with military operations and cargo flights to Iceland the order of the day. The nearby town was flat, cold, and depressing: windswept and treeless, with a gray sky spitting snow.

As Proctor pondered what to do next, he hazarded a guess regarding something else about Gander. Because of its remote location and relative proximity to international destinations, it just might be a place where a certain kind of pilot could wash up: air force discharge, ex-airline, transient—a flyboy who, for a price, might be willing to consider unusual or even questionable service.

He was presently seated at a table in the Crosswinds bar, one of a series of ramshackle structures that perched, limpet-like, just beyond the terminals, runways, and FBO buildings of Gander. The place was empty save for him and the bartender. He glanced at his watch: almost four thirty PM. Diogenes had taken off just over thirty minutes before. He tried to ignore this fact as he took another sip of his Heineken and waited. He had spent the last half hour roaming the airport and its periphery, making discreet inquiries about just such a pilot, and he had finally been directed to this bar.

Once again, Diogenes was a step—perhaps two—ahead of him. He'd anticipated being followed to Gander, and had a fresh jet fueled and ready to take off as soon as he'd arrived—this time, on a transoceanic flight. His failure to block his tail number from civil aircraft tracking sites hadn't been a failure, after all—rather, he was so confident in his ability to elude capture that he simply hadn't bothered. Or perhaps he was enjoying the chase: it was typical of Diogenes to prefer an elaborate game to something less risky and more straightforward. Why else had he allowed him to live? The safe thing would have been to give him a killing dose of sodium pentothal—but, Proctor mused, that wouldn't have been as much fun. And surely by now Diogenes knew he was being pursued, perhaps as a result of Proctor's stupid—he saw that now—radio call to Gander tower. His response to the kidnapping of Constance was a catastrophic failure, perhaps the worst failure of his life; but he had to push that aside and get himself under control, to suppress the emotion and fury that was warping his judgment—and proceed with cold calculation.

Using his laptop, Proctor saw that the Bombardier had filed a flight plan to Shannon, Ireland. Given the fact that the plane was now well over the Atlantic and hadn't deviated from its initial plan, Proctor felt reasonably sure Shannon was the true destination. Proctor's two pilots from DebonAir Aviation Services would fly him no farther—no surprise, given that their aircraft did not have transatlantic range. They had practically tossed him out, threatening to alert the authorities if he didn't immediately pay up and deplane.

Proctor needed a different kind of pilot for the pursuit ahead, one with a looser interpretation of rules and regulations, if he was going to catch Diogenes. He had been given the name of just one such pilot, who would be arriving at any moment.

The image of Constance—the back of her head shaking violently as the bag had been pulled over it—came back to him. He took another swig of his beer, pushed the image away.

At that moment the establishment's front door opened and a man entered. He was relatively short—about five foot seven—but he carried himself with the confidence of somebody who had won his share of bar fights. He was in his early forties, with a large pompadour of gleaming black hair, and he wore a leather bomber jacket scuffed from decades of service. A thin scar ran from the edge of his left eye back to a capacious sideburn. He greeted the bartender as he took a stool at the bar.

Proctor looked him over carefully. This was the man he'd been told about.

Picking up his Heineken, his laptop, and his bag, he walked over and took a seat next to the man. As a scotch on the rocks was placed before him, Proctor put down a twenty. "That's on me," he told the bartender.

As the fellow nodded and walked off to break the bill, the man in the leather jacket looked over at him appraisingly. "Thanks, mate," he said in a working-class English accent.

"Roger Shapely?" Proctor said, draining his beer.

"That's right. And you are?"

"The name's Proctor." The bartender came back with the change and Proctor pointed at his own empty beer bottle. "I'm told you're a man who can take people places."

The appraising look deepened. "That depends."

"On what?"

"On who I'm taking, and where they're going."

"You'd be taking me. To Ireland."

The man named Shapely raised his eyebrows. "Ireland?"

The fresh beer arrived. Proctor nodded, took a swig.

"Wish I could help you out. But my plane's a Cessna Citation A/SP. Not equipped for hopping the pond." Shapely smiled ruefully.

"I know all about your plane. It's powered by two Pratt and Whitney JT15D turbofans, and it's been modified from the standard two-crew model to be flyable by a single pilot. It's also been modified—by you—to carry fewer passengers and extra fuel. Fuel enough to get you almost four thousand miles."

Shapely's eyes narrowed. "Somebody's been doing a lot of talking."

Proctor shrugged. "Hasn't gone farther than me."

Silence for a moment. Shapely took a sip of his scotch. He was clearly thinking—and sizing Proctor up. "What's the job—exactly?"

"Somebody left this airport forty minutes ago, bound for Shannon. He's got something I want. I need to go after him."

"You mean, chase him?"

"Yes."

"That's a bit of a lark, isn't it? If this is about drugs, count me out."

"Nothing like that."

Shapely pondered this. "What kind of bird we talking about?"

"Bombardier Challenger 300."

The man shook his head. "No good. Cruising speed's more than fifty miles per hour faster than my Citation."

"All the more reason to get a move on."

"I can't take you to Shannon." As Proctor looked up from his beer, he saw the pilot break into a sly smile. "But I can get you close. If we have a tailwind, that is: any headwind and we won't make it as far as the Irish coast. What do you weigh?"

"One seventy-five."

"Any cargo?"

Proctor pointed a thumb at his laptop and bag.

"Can't bring anything else. We'll need a full load of avgas for that kind of hop as it is." Shapely scratched his head, clearly doing a mental calculation. Then he leaned over in his seat, gazing out the window of the bar toward the airport's wind sock, just visible from their vantage point. "Look's like the wind's in our favor. Now it's just a question of money."

"I'll also need you to keep the flight off the books. Just in case Ireland's not our final stop."

"Round the world in eighty days, is it? Then it's not a question of money. It's a question of more money."

"Eight dollars a mile. Round-trip fare. If we leave right away."

Shapely paused, considering. "If you're some kind of cop, this is entrapment. You know that, don't you? You couldn't charge me with shit."

"No cop. Just somebody in need of a ride. And a pilot who doesn't ask questions."

Shapely drained his drink. "Twenty thousand, up front. Ten more when we get there."

Proctor saw that the bartender's back was turned. He opened his bag, removed several stacks of hundred-dollar bills, and passed them to the pilot. "Here's thirty."

The man fanned them quickly, then shoved them into the pocket of his coat. "I'm assuming you'd rather avoid customs, luggage or no luggage."

"Right."

Shapely nodded. Then he patted the pocket that contained the money. "Let me stow this somewhere, make a call or two to set things up on the far end. Meet me at North Gander Aviation in fifteen minutes. It's beside hangar four."

Then he stood up, gave Proctor a thumbs-up, and quickly exited the empty bar.

7

Shapely hadn't been exaggerating about the weight. All fixtures save for the two pilot's seats had been removed, and the entire passenger cabin retrofitted with additional avgas tanks. Flying without such niceties as FAA regulations made this charter somewhat less expensive than DebonAir had been, but it made it a lot less comfortable, too.

They took off a few minutes after five, Shapely logging the trip as a VFR sightseeing jaunt up to Twillingate so he wouldn't need to file a flight plan. Once out of sight of the airport, however, he turned the plane eastward, and within fifteen minutes they were over the Atlantic. Here, Shapely descended, flying low, only a few hundred feet above the waves. Despite the alarming altitude, he was clearly a skilled pilot, and one—apparently—with very few scruples about their ultimate destination, so long as the money was good. Proctor could not even begin to guess what kind of unusual business ventures would have required Shapely to make such interesting modifications to his plane. It was small and relatively old, one of the earlier turbofan business jets, and the cockpit was tight and uncomfortable. As they headed east over the ocean, moving out of local radar range, Shapely increased altitude to thirty-three thousand feet: to "save gas," he explained, with a hurried half a dozen words about atmospheric pressure. The sky turned indigo and then black as the sun set and they flew into the shadow of the turning earth.

Proctor made some calculations in his head. Their plane had a cruising speed just shy of 450 miles per hour; as Shapely had pointed out, Diogenes's Bombardier was capable of 500. The only thing they were evenly matched in, thanks to Shapely's modifications, was range. Given his plane's speed advantage, Proctor estimated Diogenes would reach Shannon Airport in seven hours of flying. It would take them eight and a half to reach the Irish coast. Shapely hadn't said why they couldn't land at Shannon; Proctor assumed it had to do with the near-guerrilla nature of their flight and the need to avoid customs. It didn't matter; given his head start, Diogenes would arrive in Ireland at least two and a half hours before them.

Proctor used his computer to check on the Bombardier's flight path again, then he shut the laptop, made himself as comfortable as possible, closed his eyes, and—with military discipline—tuned out the Celtic music that Shapely played incessantly over the aircraft's sound system. He tried not to think of the stormy Atlantic skimming by below him; tried not to think of that final image of Constance being forced into the waiting jet. Most of all, he tried not to speculate on what Diogenes had in store for her—because he knew with conviction that, whatever it was, it could not be good.

It was just after 5 AM local time when their plane once again reached land. Mere minutes later, they were landing at Connasheer Aerodrome, a private airport in the Aran Islands with a runway just long enough to accommodate the Citation. While Proctor consulted his laptop one more time, Shapely got out of the plane and went over to the FBO—the aerodrome's lone building—where he was met by the airport operator, apparently manning the facility alone. The two embraced, and from their warm chatter it appeared Shapely made this particular run with some frequency. The pilot returned to the plane a few minutes later, smiling broadly.

"My friend's brother runs a taxi service out of Inishmore," he said. "If you catch the Rossaveal ferry, you could be at Shannon in—"

"I'm not going to Shannon," Proctor said. "Not anymore."

Shapely went silent.

Proctor indicated his laptop. "The Bombardier refueled at Shannon and took off again."

"Headed where?"

Proctor hesitated a moment. "Mauritania. Allegedly."

Shapely frowned, standing motionless, the door to the pilot's cabin half-open. "Mauritania? Christ, mate, that's . . . what, West Africa?"

"West Central Africa. Two thousand two hundred miles."

Shapely passed a hand through his pompadour. "And you want me to . . . ?" He raised his bushy eyebrows.

"Yes."

"I don't know. Bloody Africa . . . I've had a couple of run-ins there I'm in no hurry to repeat."

"We'll just be refueling and taking off again. I'm pretty sure Mauritania may be just another waypoint for refueling the Challenger."

Shapely was still frowning. "Which airport?"

"Akjoujt. Tiny. Far from normal commercial lanes. The kind of place where they don't ask a lot of questions. Look—just another five and a half flying hours, give or take."

When Shapely said nothing further, Proctor reached into his bag, took out a handful of stacked bills. "I gave you thirty thousand for the flight from Gander." He waved the stack at Shapely. "Here's another thirty-five thousand. That will more than cover the Mauritania leg. And there's even more if we have to keep going."

Shapely stared at the money. Sixty-five thousand dollars—more, Proctor guessed, than the man would make in a year of whatever specialized kind of smuggling he dabbled in.

After a minute, the pilot sighed. "Bollocks," he muttered, holding out his hand for the second stack. "All right. All right. Let me gas up, check the engines, and eyeball my charts."

Within twenty minutes they were airborne once again and headed due south, over international waters, just skirting the west coast of Ireland. Shapely had taken a couple of small white pills from a plastic bottle, popped them into his mouth, and washed them down with a giant mug of coffee.

Now Proctor was once again examining his laptop. Despite the odds, he reflected, they were lucky in at least two ways. First, landing at Shannon had cost Diogenes time: time in customs; the refueling delays common at a large airport; probably a crew rotation. All this had shaved half an hour from his lead, cutting it back to just two hours. Second, the route to Mauritania was almost entirely over water. A straight shot to Akjoujt meant they would barely graze the westernmost tip of Portugal, avoiding Europe and all its potential in-flight complications. The only body of land they would pass over was Western Sahara, a disputed territory too preoccupied with its own troubles to pay any attention to their plane—so long, that is, as no engine problems or other mechanical trouble forced them to make an unscheduled landing.

Proctor knew next to nothing about Mauritania, save that the country consisted almost entirely of the ever-expanding Sahara desert and that it was racked by poverty, child labor, and even slavery. He could think of no reason why Diogenes would be heading for such a flyspeck of an airport, save one: a refueling stop. Shannon had obviously been such a stop: the Bombardier would have exhausted its fuel crossing the Atlantic. Clearly, Diogenes was not approaching his ultimate destination, whatever that might be, in a straight line: rather, the range of his aircraft was dictating his stops. And Proctor's aircraft tracking apps had specifically shown a "CL30"—code for a Bombardier Challenger 300—en route to Akjoujt from Ireland, with no deviation in flight plan.

Once they reached Akjoujt, however, Proctor knew that he would no longer be able to rely on the Internet to track Diogenes's movements. At such a tiny Mauritanian airport—an ideal stop for private planes in a hurry and with no interest in answering many questions—there would be ways around such formalities as the filing of flight plans. Proctor would have to make use of other methods to determine the man's ultimate destination—because he felt in his bones that Akjoujt would be the penultimate stop. Four hops in a Bombardier or Learjet was enough to reach almost any destination in the world—and Diogenes was already on his third leg.

They reached Akjoujt—a flat, hot, desolate place, dry as mummy dust, with the sun boring like a heat lamp out of the sky—not long after eleven. Proctor quickly located an airport official who spoke decent English and—for a hefty consideration—was only too happy to talk about the big, gleaming Bombardier that had landed there. Yes, it had stopped to refuel. Yes, it had taken off again. The man knew its final destination, because he had overheard one of the pilots mention it. The plane was headed for the Hosea Kutako Airport in Windhoek, Namibia.

Given his lead, and his faster aircraft, Diogenes should have been over three hours ahead of them…except for a circumstance that the airport official now related. The Bombardier had been delayed taking off from Akjoujt. The man didn't know what the reason was, exactly, except that the delay had to do with a problem involving one of the passengers. Ultimately, Diogenes's jet had lifted off for Namibia just ninety minutes before.

Proctor considered the possibility that Diogenes had bribed or lied to the man, providing him with a false destination. After all, there was no way he could track his quarry's plane any longer using normal technology. But his gut, which he always trusted, told him this man was speaking the truth. Besides, if Diogenes had already paid him to lie, the official wouldn't have charged Proctor so much money for so little information.

He climbed back into the Citation. "We're headed for Namibia," he told Shapely.

The man stared at him with red-rimmed eyes. "You're bullshitting me, right?"

"No."

"You know how far that is from here?"

"Yes. Three thousand, six hundred miles."

Scratching one of his sideburns, the pilot said, "That's nine more hours of flying time. I'll be a wreck."

"It's the last leg. You can sleep for a week once we get there."

"Do you know how many hours over the FAA maximum I am already, mate?"

"I didn't think trifles like FAA regulations concerned you." And Proctor gave his bag, and the cash it contained, a meaningful pat.

"Bloody hell." Shapely shook his head in disbelief. "Well, it's your funeral. I'm so fagged I'm likely to augur in, or fly us straight into a mountain." And with that, he popped a few more of the little white pills.

Hosea Kutako International Airport was large and—at quarter to eleven in the evening, local time—surprisingly busy. While nowhere

near as strict as an American or European facility, the tower had
questioned their lack of a flight plan, and Shapely had been forced
to come up with a complicated story involving a leaky gas tank,
trouble with his communications equipment, and a vulture's close
encounter with one of the jet intakes. Proctor had been surprised
the pilot was still capable of such a feat of imagination: he'd been
flying almost twenty-four hours straight now, and his jauntiness was
long gone.

"I'm a corpse, brother," he told Proctor as they turned off runway
26 and taxied toward the airport's lone terminal. "If you want to fly
any farther, you're going to have to grow wings."

"You've done well," Proctor said, glancing out the windscreen.
Then he froze. There, parked on the tarmac, was Diogenes's Challenger.

"Stop," he told Shapely.

"But—"

"Just *stop*." Diogenes reached into his bag, pulled out another few
stacks of hundred-dollar bills, quickly counted off forty thousand, and
tossed them at the pilot with a hurried thanks. Then he opened the
passenger door and was off, racing toward the parked jet even before
the Citation had rolled to a halt.

Three hours, he thought as he ran. *He's just three hours ahead of me.*

It had been an exhausting game of cat and mouse—from plane
to plane, over oceans, over continents, keeping on Diogenes's tail
despite all the man's stratagems. The Bombardier wasn't going anywhere—one of its engine cowlings was up, and the door to the
passenger cabin was open, the deplaning ladder still down. Diogenes
and Constance wouldn't be far, now. With any luck, they were still
in Windhoek.

With a little more luck, they might even still be at the airport—
perhaps in the arrival hall.

Reaching the jet, Proctor raced up the steps two at a time into the passenger cabin. It was empty, but the door to the cockpit was ajar. Inside, a man wearing a pilot's uniform was seated in the left-hand seat. He was scribbling something on a clipboard.

Proctor ducked into the cockpit, grabbed the man by his lapel, and bodily lifted him out of the chair. "Are you the pilot from Shannon?" he asked.

The man blinked at him in surprise. "What the hell—?"

Proctor tightened his grip on the collar, adding pressure to the man's neck. "Answer the question."

"I'm...I'm one of them," he said.

"The other?"

"He left the airport an hour ago. He already gave his statement. I gave mine, too."

"Statement?"

"About the tragedy." The pilot was recovering his self-possession. He was evidently American. "Who are you?"

"I'm asking the questions," Proctor said. "What tragedy? And who were your passengers?"

"There were two of them. A man and a woman."

"Names?"

"They wouldn't give us names."

"Describe them to me."

"The man was about your height. Slender. Closely trimmed beard. Strange eyes—one was a different color than the other." A pause. "He had a scar on one cheek."

"And the woman?"

"She was young, maybe early twenties. Dark hair. Pretty. Didn't get much of a look at her, actually. She was drunk."

"And that was it? Just the two?"

"Yes. At least...at first."

Proctor tightened his grip on the man's collar. "What do you mean—*at first*? What's this about a tragedy?"

The pilot hesitated. "Well...it was the young woman."

"What about her?" Proctor asked. *"What about the young woman?"*

The pilot looked down, then raised his eyes again to meet Proctor's gaze. "She died midflight."

8

Died?" Proctor said. "*Died?*" For a moment, a red curtain fell across his vision. An overwhelming desire to inflict extreme violence—such as he had felt only once or twice before in his life, during times of intense danger and physical duress—came over him. It took a supreme act of will not to crush the man's windpipe.

With the greatest effort, he mastered the urge. This man was simply an errand boy. There was something better the man could do than die: he could furnish information.

"Tell me what happened," Proctor said in a low voice.

The man swallowed painfully. His face was ashen and beaded with sweat, as if he sensed how much danger he was in. "I don't know much," he said. "I wish I could tell you more."

"*Tell* me what you *know*."

"He wouldn't let us out of the cockpit."

"Who wouldn't?"

"The man. The man who chartered the plane."

"The man with the scar?"

The pilot nodded.

"What else?"

The man swallowed again. "The trouble started after we landed in Akjoujt. I was taking a nap in the cockpit. Mark—the other pilot— woke me up. I saw another girl, a blonde, board the plane. After that, I heard cries, a heavy thump. That was when…" He paused. "*He* came in, told us to take off and stay in the cockpit until we landed here in Namibia. Gave us bed urinals, told us to use those if we needed to."

The pilot seemed to see something in Proctor's eyes, because the words that followed tumbled out in a rush. "Look, I didn't see anything. She walked onto the plane in Shannon on her own two feet. When we got here, she was wheeled out dead on a stretcher." A pause. "As we were landing, he…coached us. What to tell the officials, I mean. He said she'd had a lifelong history of heart trouble. Death at high altitude…it happens sometimes."

"And the blonde? Who is this blonde?"

"I don't know." The pilot moved his head. "Do you think you could ease off a little?"

Proctor eased his grip on the collar.

The pilot nodded through the cockpit windscreen. "There. That's the official who met the plane, interviewed our passenger."

He had indicated a short man in a uniform, perhaps sixty years of age. The man was standing beneath a set of lights by a terminal door, at the center of a small knot of people.

"He'd know more than anybody," the pilot said.

Proctor stared at the pilot—a long, hard stare. Then he pushed the man back down into his seat and quickly exited the jet.

As he walked toward the group, the man in question looked over at him. He had tired but kindly eyes, and his hair was very short, wiry, and pure white. Seeing Proctor, the others stepped away.

"*Goeienaand*," the man said.

"*Goeienaand*," Proctor replied. "*My naam is Proctor.*" He knew that, though the official language of Namibia was English, most people were more fluent in Afrikaans—a language that various classified ops had, in the past, given him some small facility with.

"*Praat Meneer Afrikaans?*" the man asked.

"*Ja, 'n bietjie. Praat Meneer Engels?*"

"Yes," the man said, switching to accented English.

"*Baie dankie.*" Proctor pointed over his shoulder, toward the Bombardier. "I'm here about the young woman who was taken off that plane."

"I am Masozi Shona. General manager." The official shook his head. "Sad. Very sad."

"What happened?" Proctor asked.

Shona stared at him. "Pray, what is your interest in the matter?"

Proctor hesitated a moment. "My daughter. It was my daughter on that plane."

The official's face, already serious, took on a mournful cast. "I am sorry. Very sorry. She is gone. Passed away on the flight."

Proctor had not slept—not really—in over thirty-six hours. Ever since speeding away from 891 Riverside Drive, he had been on high alert, under terrific anxiety. Now he felt something give way within him. He did not cry—he hadn't cried since he was six—but as he spoke, he felt his voice break and his eyes begin to fill. He let it happen, as it meshed with his cover. "Please. You must help me. I...I was following them. I got here too late. *Asseblief*—I need to know what happened. Do you understand? *I need to know.*"

The man named Shona took his arm. "I am very sorry. I will tell you all I know, which is very little."

"What...what happened to her body?"

"It was taken away, sir. By private transportation."

"What about the inquest? The medical examiner? Why wasn't she taken to a hospital—or a morgue?"

The man shook his head. "It was all arranged before landing. A doctor was called to meet the plane. He made the initial examination, signed the papers."

Proctor went silent.

The official shrugged with a look of sympathy. "You must understand. I am the general manager...but I am not in charge."

Proctor understood. This was not America. If enough money changed hands, protocols could be bypassed.

"But my daughter," Proctor heard himself say. "My little girl...Are you absolutely sure she's dead? How can I know if it really was her? Maybe it was someone else."

Hearing this, the man perked up slightly. "There is a way I can help you to be sure."

"Anything."

A hesitation. "It might not be easy for you."

Proctor waved this off.

"In that case, follow me."

The man led the way into the terminal, then passed through a set of swinging doors and down a rather shabby, official-looking hallway. Near the end of the hall, he opened one of the numerous doors and gestured for Proctor to step inside. The room contained desks and half a dozen video monitors with CPUs. Two men in short-sleeved shirts looked up as they stepped in. With a few curt words in Afrikaans, Shona ushered them out.

He glanced at Proctor in embarrassment. "Now I'm afraid I must ask you for...some consideration. It is not for myself, you understand, but—" and he nodded in the direction of the two men who had just left the security office.

"Of course." Proctor reached into his bag, took out a small sheaf of bills.

The man pocketed the money and gestured toward a nearby video screen. "There is not much."

He took a seat at the table and Proctor stood behind him. Despite the small size and disheveled condition of the room, the airport's surveillance setup was of relatively modern design. Shona drew up a keyboard, typed in a few commands, pulled a DVD out of the nearest computer, consulted a tray beside it, pulled out another DVD labeled in longhand with a red marker, and inserted it into the computer.

More typing, and then a grainy image appeared on the computer screen, along with a running timestamp. There was the Bombardier—Diogenes's plane. The passenger door was open, and the ladder was extended. Proctor watched as a man in a linen suit climbed the steps into the plane—evidently the doctor—followed by two uniformed orderlies. Quite some time passed, during which Shona sped up the playback. Then the doctor emerged, a sheaf of papers in his hand. He was followed by a young blonde woman that Diogenes didn't recognize. Even in the low-quality video, he could see the sharpness of her cheekbones, the paleness of her eyes. She was followed by the two orderlies, carrying, with some difficulty, a stretcher between them. There was a figure on the stretcher, covered with a sheet. Proctor watched, scarcely drawing breath, as the orderlies manhandled the stretcher down the steps from the passenger compartment. Just as they reached the bottom step, the first orderly slipped, and as he regained his footing the body on the stretcher shifted and the sheet slipped partway off the face.

"Freeze that!" Proctor cried out.

The frame froze. Proctor leaned in, staring, hardly able to believe what he saw. His world fell in upon him.

The frozen video—grainy, seamed by horizontal lines that slowly rose up the screen—could not be denied. The image was all too clear: the dark hair, the full lips, the violet eyes wide open, the once-beautiful face frozen in a rictus of death.

He sank into a nearby chair. He could no longer delude himself.

Constance was dead. She'd never suffered from heart trouble. She couldn't have died of natural causes on the plane; she'd been murdered. *Murdered.* And Diogenes was the murderer.

Vaguely, as if from far away, he realized the man was talking to him again.

"I am sorry," the official told him, wringing his hands with genuine angst. "Very sorry. But—you wanted to be certain."

"Yes," Proctor said, not looking at him. "Thank you. I...I need to find them, recover my daughter's body. They are bad people. Do you have any idea where they took the body?"

A hesitation. "They did not leave the airport with the hired doctor. This I know, because I watched the doctor depart. The circumstances were unusual, you see—even for here. They went to an establishment that leases automobiles—jeeps, trucks, vehicles for desert use. It is next to the airport, across from the Millennium Business Park. It is the only place open after dark. They put the stretcher in a waiting van and drove across the street."

Proctor leapt to his feet.

"It is very late now," the man said. "They are almost certainly closed—"

But he was speaking to an empty room. Proctor was gone.

9

THE WINDHOEK-DETMONK Automobile Agency—as it was advertised by two signs, one in Afrikaans and the other in English, along with the proprietor's name, Lazrus Keronda—was a two-acre lot located amid a sad-looking, business-zoned neighborhood on the main east–west highway just south of the airport. Despite the seediness of its signage, the rental agency was ringed by expensive sodium vapor lights that lit up the night, and a dozen vehicles could be seen through the security fence.

It was the only business still open, and as Proctor marched quickly across the four-lane highway—quiet at this late hour—the external lights began to snap off, one by one.

The temperature hovered at just around one hundred degrees, and the *Oosweer*—the hot wind that often blew in from the coast this time of year—showered him in fine sand as he walked. The low hills of Progress could barely be seen in the distance: ghost reflections of the lights from the city. He glanced at his watch: just past ten o'clock.

A short, pudgy man in rumpled shorts and a khaki shirt with buttoned pockets was pulling a chain-link gate across the main entrance to the dealership. Proctor gave him a brisk tap on the shoulder and the man turned, blinking against the blowing sand.

"Hoe gaan dit met jou?" he said, looking him up and down in the way of salesmen the world over.

"Baie goed, dankie," Proctor replied. "But let's talk in English."

Proctor prided himself in being an expert at reading people. Even now—dead tired, in deep shock, stricken to the core with grief and self-reproach—he could tell there was something wrong about this man. The nervous way he kept running one hand through his hair as the wind disarranged it; his habit of not meeting Proctor's eyes; the very tenor of his voice—all told Proctor that the man was dirty and intended to lie to him.

Now the salesman frowned. *"Ek vertaan nie,"* he said.

"Oh, you understand me just fine, Mr. Keronda." Proctor opened his bug-out bag, flashed a wad of cash.

"We are closed," the man said, switching abruptly to unaccented English.

"Let's talk in there." And Proctor pointed toward a small, dimly lighted shed in the middle of the lot that, it appeared, served as an office.

"We are—" the man began again, but Proctor gave him a shove that pulled his hand from the gate and sent him stumbling back in the direction of the office.

Inside the building, Proctor gently but firmly guided the man to a chair behind a battered desk, pushed him down into it, then took a seat in front. "I'll tell you just once," he said. "No games. I've run out of time and patience. You have information I need. Give it to me and you'll be rewarded."

The man patted at his hair again, wiped sand from his forehead. "I do not know anything."

"You had a customer here," Proctor said. "About ninety minutes ago."

The man shook his head. "There has been nobody," he said.

Proctor took a deep breath. "I'm asking politely. Next time I'll be rude."

"We have been closed for hours," the man said. "The only reason I am here so late is because I've been doing paperwork—"

The storm of emotions that had been slowly gathering within Proctor—frustration at the absurd dance Diogenes had led him on; self-loathing for his failure in ensuring Constance's well-being; staggering grief at the news of her death—came together in a white-hot implosion of rage. Yet externally he remained completely calm—save for the sudden, snake-like quickness with which he moved. Snatching a large letter opener off the desk, he brought it down into the man's left hand, shattering the trapezoid bone and burying the point half an inch into the scarred wood.

The man's eyes rolled white and he opened his mouth to scream. Proctor grabbed an oil-soaked rag off the floor and jammed it into his mouth. He clamped his powerful hand over the man's jaws, preventing him from crying out.

The man writhed, moaning through the rag. Blood began seeping around the edges of the letter opener and trickling through the fingers and onto the desk. Proctor kept the man in position for well over a minute before speaking again.

"When I take the rag out of your mouth," he said, "you're going to answer my questions. If you lie, I'll respond appropriately."

The man nodded. Proctor removed the sodden rag.

"As God is my judge," the man began again, "I have not seen anybody all—"

Proctor pulled a rusty, four-inch awl from among an adjacent workbench of tools, seized the man's free elbow, yanked the arm forward, slammed the right hand on the table, and stabbed the awl through it, pinning it to the table as well.

The man screamed in agony. "*Laat my met rus! Polisie!*"

"Nobody can hear you," said Proctor. With a short, sharp movement, he kicked the man's chair straight back from his desk. Affixed as he was to the table, the man fell forward off the chair, his knees hitting the floor, arms straight out in front of him, hands pinned to the table by the letter opener and the awl. He uttered another inchoate scream.

From his bag, Proctor pulled a blacked-out KA-Bar knife with a serrated edge. With two quick flicks of the blade, he cut through the man's belt and sliced away his zipper. And then he picked a heavy set of hose clamp pliers off the workbench. "Last chance," he said, hefting the pliers. "Your balls are next."

"*No!*" the man said as the pliers swung toward him. "*Yes!*" He was almost crying.

"Who came here tonight?"

He blubbered, gasping in panic, hardly able to get the words out. "A man. And...a woman."

"Describe them to me."

"The man was tall. He had a beard. And his eyes...different colors."

"And the woman?"

"Young. Yellow hair." The man gasped. "Please—it hurts!"

"Blond? Not dark-haired?"

"No, no. *Ahhh!*" Blood was pooling over the top of the table now.

"There was nobody else?"

"No. Just the two. And—and their cargo."

"What cargo?"

"It was..." The man gasped. "A coffin."

"Coffin?"

The man nodded desperately. "A big coffin. Refrigerated."

A refrigerated coffin. "What did they want?"

"They rented a Rover. A, a Land Rover."

"What else?"

"They asked for tie-downs. To lash the coffin into the bed of the Rover."

"Anything more?"

Sweat was pouring from the man's forehead, dripping from his nose, mingling with the blood on the table. "No. But they loaded their own supplies in with the coffin."

"What supplies?"

"Water. Petrol. Camping gear."

"How much petrol?"

He swallowed. "Dozen jerrycans, maybe more."

"Where did they get the supplies?"

The man shook his head. "They were in the van they arrived in."

The van. Shona, too, had mentioned a waiting van. It must have contained not only the petrol and water—but the refrigerated coffin, as well. Diogenes had planned even that—on the plane, if not before. At the thought, Proctor felt a shudder go through his frame.

But a van would not be well equipped for desert travel. A Land Rover, on the other hand, would.

"Did you see where they went?"

The salesman jerked his head. "East. They headed east, on the B6."

East. In the direction of Botswana—and the Kalahari Desert.

Proctor took firm hold of the letter opener. Then he yanked it away from the table, out of the man's hand. He did the same with the awl. Then, ripping the oily rag in two with his teeth, he quickly fashioned tourniquets and applied them to the hands.

"I need an all-terrain vehicle," he said. He glanced out toward the lot, where a variety of cars gleamed in the remaining sodium light; there was one Land Cruiser, tricked out for desert travel. "That Land Cruiser. How much?"

"Take it," the man said, weeping and cradling his mangled, bleeding hands. "Take it!"

"No, I'll rent it." Proctor did not want to be found with a stolen vehicle. "How much?"

"Nine thousand Namibian a week." The man forced himself back up into the chair, where he rocked back and forth, forearms crossed before him, making a low keening sound.

Proctor counted out fifteen hundred American dollars and tossed them on the bloody table. "That should cover it for two. Get me the paperwork and receipt. Make sure everything's in order." He tossed a hundred more dollars at the man. "That's to get some medical attention. Clean the place up. *And* keep your mouth shut—I don't want anybody thinking I've paid you a visit. If I'm bothered—by police, military—I'll come looking for you, and..." Instead of finishing the sentence, Proctor shifted his gaze to the pliers.

"No," the man whimpered.

Proctor looked at the office's watercooler. "I'll take that jug. Do you have more?"

"...Closet."

"Maps?"

"On the shelf."

"Extra jerrycans of petrol?"

The man fumbled a key from around his neck. "In the shed. Back of the lot."

Ten minutes later, Proctor was on the B6, driving east at high speed, heading for the border, with fifteen gallons of water, fifty extra gallons of petrol, and a full set of maps of southern Africa, from Namibia to Botswana.

10

Proctor had raced eastward on route B6 through Witvlei, then Gobabis, covering the two-hundred-plus-mile journey to the border crossing with Botswana in three hours. At the Mamuno border post a bit of money—strategically exchanged—had confirmed that the vehicle with the refrigerated coffin passed through less than two hours before, and for an additional sum Proctor had obtained a Botswanan visa on the spot. The process was swift and efficient, and in less than ten minutes he was once again on his way.

It was at this point that the chase—and Proctor's progress—slowed significantly.

The B6 ended at a north–south highway called the A3. The exchange was situated at the edge of the Kalahari Desert, vacant and free of any roadside businesses. From this point he could not be certain which way Diogenes had gone. Proctor chose the route north, toward a town called Ghanzi, primarily on the basis that it was the road less traveled. He felt confident Diogenes had not taken the A3 south. The man would not risk trying to bribe a coffin through South African border control: it was a stricter, less corrupt country, known for enforcing regulations. And it seemed logical, somehow, that Diogenes would head into the Kalahari Desert rather than away from it.

But for what purpose, he had no idea.

When Proctor reached Ghanzi, a bustling desert town, he realized something was amiss. It took many inquiries—he did not speak Setswanan—until he finally confirmed that the Land Rover had not passed through. Now he drove back along the A3, slowly and painstakingly, pondering where he'd gone wrong. He remained confident that Diogenes and the girl had turned north, rather than south—which meant that, along the way, his quarry had turned off the highway onto one of the sparse desert tracks that led deep into the Kalahari. But which one?

He tried one track after another as he headed back south. None showed any signs of tire tracks. At last, he pulled off the highway yet again to consult his maps. Although it was many hours from dawn, tremendous stored heat radiated off the asphalt in waves. Eastward lay the vast, untamed expanse of the Kalahari, populated only by sparse numbers of Bushmen and a scattering of isolated game camps for tourists. In the 250,000 square miles of desert, there was nothing else—no paved roads and no towns. He looked up from his map to gaze across the infinite, sand-colored plains, dotted with scrub and the occasional acacia tree, barely distinguishable in the moonlight.

But there *was* a town—of sorts—marked on the map. A settlement called New Xade, about sixty miles east, connected to the highway by a dirt road. Proctor sensed this was the road Diogenes must have taken; all the others he'd passed were not on the map and looked improvised and unreliable.

He backtracked to the New Xade turnoff: an unmarked, sandy track leading like an arrow into the darkness. Before he turned in, he pulled his Land Cruiser over to the shoulder again and got out. First he used a flashlight to examine his own tires, new Michelin XPSs, noting the distinctive tread. Then he went to the turnoff and, with the aid of the headlights, examined the sand—and there he saw the marks of a similar tread, turning off the road from the south and heading east. The tread was fresh, and no other car had turned off since.

Grimly energized, he drove eastward along the straight dirt road, toward the town of New Xade. Whether that was their final destination, or whether they were continuing on into the untracked desert, was something Proctor could not know for sure. But judging from the amount of water and petrol Diogenes had taken, he believed the man would be continuing on, deep into the Kalahari Desert, on a multiday journey, for reasons unknown—with Constance's corpse.

With Constance's corpse. The thought brought back a rush of emotion and incomprehension. Proctor could understand why Diogenes would murder Constance; after all, the woman had tried to murder him, and had—in the opinion of all in the know—succeeded. By killing Constance, Diogenes would exact the ultimate revenge on his hated brother, Pendergast. But what could Diogenes possibly want with her corpse? Why take such complicated and Byzantine steps to spirit it away, preserved by refrigeration, practically to the ends of the earth? Compounding the mystery, many, though probably not all, of these elaborate preparations had been carefully made in advance. Why? Diogenes had a sick fondness for elaborate and cruel mind games, but this was unfathomable.

Proctor sped along, the Land Cruiser trailing a gigantic corkscrew of dust. Darkness would only help him see the fleeing vehicle better from a distance. Besides, Diogenes would not leave the track, he felt sure; not, at least, until reaching New Xade. If Diogenes then continued on into the heart of the Kalahari, Proctor was prepared. He mentally reviewed the contents of his bug-out bag, to make sure he had all he needed:

2 Glock 9mms with extra clips
KA-Bar knife
Leatherman MUT Tactical
$300,000 in remaining cash
Compass
GPS with miniature solar panel
Flashlight
Binoculars
Burner phone
Crank-operated radio
Various passports
Mylar-coated space blanket
Bivvy bag
Ferrocerium fire striker
Enhanced first-aid kit
Water purification tablets
MREs
Fishing line and hook
Signal mirror
LED light with strobe
Needle and thread
"550" parachute cord
Camp stove with LPG fuel

With these supplies, he could survive a week or more in even this harsh environment. And with the extra petrol, the range of his vehicle was over a thousand miles. Diogenes was not going to escape him. Proctor was going to find him. And he was going to get answers to his questions—every single one.

11

In the blazing inferno of the Kalahari, Proctor stopped yet again to consult his map. Despite his long experience in desert ops, he was seriously taken aback by the vastness of this place. It wasn't lifeless, exactly; he had passed a number of game animals along the way, including oryx, wildebeest, and a family of giraffes. There was bunch grass, brush, and even the occasional tree. What unnerved him was the endless immensity of it: infinity made visible.

He stepped out of the vehicle and unfurled the map on the burning ground, weighing down the corners with stones. There wasn't a breath of wind, and the air around him trembled in the heat. He took out his GPS, turned it on, laid it upon the map, then watched while it slowly acquired satellites and gave him his location. He found it on the map, pondered what it meant.

New Xade was almost 150 miles behind him, and before lay another 250 miles of desert. But he knew he was on the right track—and this time, it hadn't taken long at all to confirm it. Diogenes's Land Rover had roared through New Xade at high speed, an event the entire village had noted. At the far end of town, where the dirt road finally petered out, the tire tracks remained sharp and clear. As he continued the pursuit, even with his occasional stops to consult the map, he seemed to be gaining on this target. He assumed this was because Diogenes was carrying a heavy, refrigerated coffin that, no doubt, impacted the performance and handling of the Land Rover.

Where the dirt road petered out, Diogenes's tracks had continued over wandering cattle paths, game trails, and a series of bone-dry riverbeds before finally going overland. The sandy desert floor captured a clear tire track, much helped by the lack of wind and the slanting morning light. Diogenes's vehicle had made a slow arc to the northeast, heading, as Proctor suspected, into the very heart of the Kalahari. They had come within the official boundary of the vast Kalahari Game Reserve, but this spot was far from where the safaris operated, the land being flat, arid, and without variety.

Now, looking at the map, he began to see where Diogenes might be headed: a place marked on his map as Deception Valley. It was indicated as a long, uncertain, shallow gorge with a dry riverbed at its center, ending in a place called Deception Pan, a huge dead lake. What the "deception" was, and what the place looked like in reality, Proctor could only guess.

His assumption was that Diogenes had killed Constance out of revenge. But then, why the refrigerated coffin? Why this incredibly remote place? Was it possible Constance had resisted and been accidentally killed in a struggle? The latter seemed possible, given her hatred of Diogenes and her ungovernable rages. And there had been that talk, back at Akjoujt airport, of an unknown delay caused by one of the passengers.

Deception Valley lay only twenty more miles to the northeast. The sun was now high in the horizon. Proctor wasn't bothered by this; the A/C in the Land Cruiser had been running well.

He got back into the Land Cruiser, put the vehicle in gear, and set off, following the tracks slowly and carefully. In an hour he saw a streak of acacia trees silhouetted along the horizon. As he approached them, he spied a low, wandering swale in the landscape: Deception Valley. The tracks entered the riverbed and continued on the sand, now sharp and distinct in the early-afternoon sun. He accelerated abruptly, going as fast as he dared, following the tracks, the vehicle swaying and fishtailing.

The riverbed expanded—and suddenly he was on the rock-hard clay surface of a dry lakebed: the Deception Pan. It was as vacant and level as a hundred-mile parking lot.

The tire tracks completely vanished.

With a curse, Proctor slammed on the brakes and got out. He examined the surface and could see, just barely, where Diogenes's vehicle had passed. But on the hard lakebed the track had suddenly grown almost invisible, and would now necessitate great care, skill, and time in tracking.

All too obviously, this had been carefully planned.

He got back in the Land Cruiser and began inching forward, peering intently through the windscreen at the lakebed. He could—just barely—see the faint marks of the tires, but he could go no faster than five miles an hour, and more than once he had to stop and reconnoiter. The vehicle had ceased going in a straight line; sometimes it would zigzag, or make a sharp turn, or even loop around and cross its own tracks.

Shortly before dark, Proctor stopped again to consult the map. Once again, he spread it out and took out his GPS. He discovered he was now in the center of the Deception Pan; his GPS showed Diogenes had led him this way and that, in a maddening set of circles and zigzags.

Suddenly he heard the engine of his Land Cruiser—which he had left running—hiccup; hiccup again; and then die.

He felt a sudden, sharp apprehension. The engine had not overheated; he had been watching it like a hawk and the air was already cooling fast. He got into the vehicle and turned the key.

The solenoid clicked but nothing else.

Now he felt real alarm. He told himself to calm down; with all the heat and dust, the battery terminals probably needed cleaning.

He popped the hood and peered inside; the terminals were dusty but not overly so. He quickly cleaned the terminals, connectors, and engine ground. He checked the battery with a brief short using a screwdriver and got a massive spark. The battery was still good.

Still, the Land Cruiser would not start.

With the vehicle in neutral, he used the screwdriver to bypass the starter relay solenoid and tested the starter.

No good.

This made no sense. How the hell had the starter died at just the same time as the engine?

He shone the light around the engine compartment. Everything looked normal, no leaks or loose wires or signs of sabotage.

Sabotage. Proctor glanced at his watch. The vehicle had died at 6 PM exactly. Coincidence? Probably: but an unnerving one nonetheless.

The sudden dying of the engine would have an explanation. Proctor knew cars. He would find it.

Four hours later, exhausted and maddened, Proctor sat down next to the vehicle, leaned against a wheel, calmed himself, and took stock. His thorough and minute inspection had convinced him of one thing: somehow, some way, the vehicle's main computer had been reprogrammed. It had been set to render the Land Cruiser absolutely inoperable at six PM—just as night fell. It was the one thing he had no chance of fixing. Not only would it require a sophisticated diagnostic computer to identify, it would also need the source code for the engine, which was proprietary and a closely guarded secret of the parent company.

Proctor considered his predicament. He had undergone a revelation of sorts. There was now no doubt that all of this had been carefully orchestrated: an absurdly complex plan to lure him to the ends of the earth—to the most godforsaken place on the planet . . . and strand him there.

The vehicle was useless; he would have to walk back to New Xade, now 175 miles behind him. He had food and plenty of water. He would walk at night. Quickly, he did the mental calculations. He had fifty-six pounds of water left, give or take. His water requirement would be a gallon a day: eight pounds of water. That equaled a seven-day supply. Twenty-five miles of walking a day to reach New Xade.

He had a sporting chance to survive this; to walk out of the desert alive. No doubt Diogenes knew that, too.

The real question was why Diogenes had set up this elaborate deception in the first place. And it was elaborate indeed: involving multiple chartered jets, feints and double blinds, a long vehicle chase. Along the way, some people he'd met had been duped; others, he felt sure, had provided paid "assistance." He was not sure what was true and what was false. Who had told him actual lies? The pilot of the Bombardier, the Land Rover salesman—Proctor felt certain of them. The rest had seen what Diogenes wanted them to see. But those two, he believed, were part of his plan. They had told lies to Proctor's face—even though they both, undoubtedly, realized the extreme danger they'd been in. Was it possible, actually possible, the car salesman had stuck to Diogenes's script—even after the treatment he'd received at Proctor's hands?

Then there was the question of Constance herself. Proctor had only once seen her face directly: in the security video of the Namibian airport. If Diogenes was capable of such a thorough deception in every other way, surely he could have misled Proctor there, too. It was un-likely...but it was possible. Was she dead or alive?

Why? *Why?* The incomprehensibility of it all filled Proctor with use-less rage.

Taking a deep breath, he recognized that he was at the extreme edge of exhaustion, almost to the point of sleep psychosis. He had been going flat-out for over sixty hours straight. He could do nothing more without sleep.

As he lay back in the cool of the night, he heard a swelling sound in the distance, a throbbing crescendo that he recognized as the roar of a large male lion. The roar was joined by another, and then another: a call and response. It was a coalition of young, aggressive males not old enough to have their own prides, roaring together to establish a bond in preparation for a hunt.

A cooperative hunt.

He would deal with that later. He closed his eyes and immediately fell into a deep and dreamless sleep.

12

ALTHOUGH A SETTING late-autumn sun gilded the west-facing Manhattan façades overlooking the Hudson River, the library of 891 Riverside was cloaked, as always, in perpetual dusk. The tall, iron-framed windows were locked and barred, and covered by heavy tapestries, richly embroidered. But now no fire crackled in the large fireplace; no lamps of antique Tiffany glass were lit against the gloom.

As afternoon turned to evening, and evening to night, the house remained perfectly silent, in watchful repose. No footsteps rang against the marble floor of the reception room; no fingers touched the keys of the Flemish virginal. No movement of any sort, in fact, could be detected—at least, none above the level of the subterranean.

Behind twin bookcases in the library, a private elevator led down to the basement. Here, a labyrinth of corridors, heavy with efflorescence and redolent of dust, led past a number of stone chambers, including one that gave every indication of being an operating room, apparently unused for some time. The passageways terminated in a small space with a low, vaulted ceiling. Into one wall, the Pendergast family crest had been carved: a lidless eye over two moons, one crescent, the other full, with a lion couchant, along with the Pendergast motto

LUCRUM, SANGUINEM: "To gain honor, blood." Manipulating the crest with the proper motion caused the stone wall to swing away, revealing a circular staircase, cut out of the living bedrock and spiraling down into further darkness. This in turn led to a sub-basement of almost unguessable extent. A central brick pathway led along an earthen floor, below Romanesque arches, past chamber after veiled chamber: burial vaults, storerooms, and collections of every imaginable sort. There were rows of chemicals in ancient glass bottles; rare minerals; insects large and small, with iridescent abdomens and desiccated antennae; Old Master paintings and medieval tapestries; illuminated manuscripts and incunabula; military uniforms and weapons; and a large collection of instruments of torture. This seemingly endless and almost uncatalogable trove was the cabinet of curiosities that had been assembled over many years and at great cost by Antoine Pendergast, Agent Pendergast's great-grand-uncle—more commonly known by his pseudonym, Enoch Leng.

About halfway down the length of this central corridor, an isolated room, hardly more than an alcove, stood to one side, containing a priceless collection of Japanese *Ukiyo-e* art: woodblock prints of seascapes; Mount Fuji, wreathed in clouds; courtesans playing the koto. The rear wall of the niche was covered by a large rice-paper depiction of the Okazaki Bridge from Hiroshige's *Fifty-Three Stations of the Tōkaidō*. Behind the print was the massive stone wall that formed part of the building's foundation.

An almost invisible detent in the stone, however, acted much like the crest farther above: when turned to the proper notch, it released a spring that caused a portion of the wall to swing back, in the fashion of a small door. This led to a narrow passage that debouched onto a round chamber, lit faintly by candles, from which three rooms fanned out in the shape of a cloverleaf. One was a small library, containing a writing desk surrounded by old oaken shelves full of leather-bound volumes. Another room was devoted to reflection and meditation, containing only a chair set before a single work of art. And leading off from the far end of the round chamber was the third space: a bedroom-bath suite. The entire composed a small apartment, deep underground, furnished in a spare but nonetheless exquisite style.

The bedroom was similar to the other two rooms: understated, yet somehow elegant in its very asceticism. The large bed had a satin coverlet with matching crimson pillows. One nightstand held a porcelain washbasin from the court of Louis XIV, the Sun King; another held a taper, set into a candlestick of Sheffield pewter.

The set of rooms was as silent and still as the house above, save for the soft, almost inaudible breathing of a person dozing beneath the satin coverlet.

That person was Constance Greene.

Now Constance woke. A light sleeper by long habit, she was fully awake at once. Switching on an electric lantern and blowing out the bedside candle, she consulted her watch: five minutes past eight. Strange, how time felt so different down here, below the beat of the city above: if she was not careful, the days would start blending together so quickly she might lose track of them.

Swinging her legs out of the bed and rising, she reached for a silk robe that hung on a nearby peg and wrapped it tightly around herself. Then she stood for a moment, quite still, reflecting—in the tradition of the monks of the Gsalrig Chongg monastery in Tibet, where she had been tutored—on her state of being and mind upon waking.

She was aware, first and foremost, of an emptiness—an emptiness that, she knew, would never leave her and could never be filled. Aloysius Pendergast was gone. She had finally acknowledged this fact; her decision to retreat to these subterranean chambers—and to quit, at least for a time, the world of the living—was her way of accepting his death. In times of stress, or danger, or great grief, she had always retreated to these quiet, subterranean spaces, known to almost no others. Pendergast had, in his reserved yet gentle way, cured her of this habit; taught her the beauty of the world beyond the Riverside Drive mansion; taught her to tolerate the companionship of her fellow creatures. But now Pendergast was no longer with her. When she realized this, she faced the only two courses of action open to her: retreating belowground, or making use of the vial of cyanide pills that she kept as insurance against the world. She chose the former. Not because she feared death—quite the opposite—but because she knew Aloysius would have been irrevocably disappointed in her if she took her life.

She passed out of the bedroom and into the small private library. A set of dishes from last night's dinner—her first since retreating to the sub-basement some days before—sat on one corner of the writing table. It appeared that Mrs. Trask had just returned from her sister's hospital stay, because dinner had been left in the elevator. Previously, Mrs. Trask's meals had almost always been simple and fresh. But the dinner she'd left in the elevator for Constance the night of her return had been anything but: saddle of veal with chanterelles, on a bed of roasted white asparagus with truffle coulis. The dessert had been a luscious slice of *clafoutis aux cerises*. While Mrs. Trask could be an excellent cook when the situation required it, Constance was surprised by the richness of the meal. It was not in keeping with the reasons she had taken up a solitary life underground—painful, private...and ascetic. Surely Mrs. Trask understood that. Such a gourmet meal, bordering on the decadent, seemed inappropriate. Perhaps it was just the housekeeper's way of affectionately announcing her return. It put Constance off—but at the same time, she had enjoyed the meal despite herself.

Gathering up the dishes and picking up a torch, Constance made her way out of her private chambers, down the narrow passage, through the secret doorway, and out into the sub-basement proper.

She moved gracefully and surely through the succession of rooms, knowing every inch of the collections and needing very little light.

More slowly now, she made her way through the last set of chambers to the staircase that spiraled up to the basement level. Reaching the top of the stairs, she walked through the dim corridors to the private elevator. She would open it, put in the dishes from last night's repast, and take back to her rooms the meal that she knew Mrs. Trask would have waiting there for her.

She pulled back the brass gate, opened the door, put yesterday's dishes inside, and turned to the fresh dinner arrayed on a silver tray, with a crisp linen tablecloth and elegant silver setting. The entrée was hidden beneath a silver dish cover. This was not surprising: Mrs. Trask's way of helping keep the meal warm. What was surprising was the bottle of wine that stood on the tray beside it, along with an elegant crystal wineglass.

As Constance regarded the bottle—it was a Pauillac, she saw, a Château Lynch-Bages 2006—she remembered the last time she had tasted a bottle of wine. It had been in Pendergast's room at the Captain Hull Inn, back in Exmouth. The memory caused her to flush deeply. Had Mrs. Trask somehow learned about that unfortunate and awkward event...?

But that was impossible. Still, on the heels of last night's epicurean offering, this expensive wine was puzzling. It was out of character for Mrs. Trask, who never took it upon herself to choose wines from Pendergast's extensive cellar, and who was far more likely to serve dinner accompanied by a bottle of mineral water and a pot of rose hip tea. Was this the housekeeper's way of trying to coax her back upstairs?

Constance was not ready for that—at least, not yet. Mrs. Trask was welcome to show her concern, but this was going a bit overboard, and if it continued she might have to write the housekeeper a note.

Picking up the silver tray, she made her way back downstairs and along the listening galleries to her set of rooms.

Entering her small library, she set down the wine and the glass and removed the cover from the dish. She stared. This evening's meal was simpler than the previous night's fare, but nevertheless far more extravagant: foie gras, pan-seared rare, with white truffles arranged over the buttery liver in papery, fragrant shavings. The dish was flanked by two minuscule carrots with their tops, dusted with fresh parsley—a droll culinary flourish that was a far cry from Mrs. Trask's usual hearty helping of vegetables.

Constance stared at the plate in puzzlement for a long time. Then she picked up the bottle of wine and looked at it intently.

As she replaced the bottle on the table, she realized something else was not right. Earlier in the day, before withdrawing to her bedroom for a nap, she had been writing in her journal—a habit she had developed years ago and from which she never deviated. Now, however, she saw that another volume had been placed atop the distinctive orange cover of her Rhodia notebook.

This was clearly a deliberate, calculated action. It couldn't have fallen from a nearby shelf and, indeed, the volume wasn't even one from her small private library, which had been lovingly hand-picked.

She turned it over in her hands. Stamped gilt lettering on the slender spine told her it was a copy of the poems of Catullus, in the original Latin.

Then she noticed something else. Slipped between two of the pages, like a place marker, lay a feather. She opened the book to the marked page and removed the feather, staring closely at it. This was not just any feather—but one of great peculiarity and distinction. Unless she was much mistaken, this was a feather from a Norfolk kaka: a large parrot, now extinct, last seen in the wild in the early nineteenth century. Its habitat had been limited to the trees and rocks of Norfolk and Phillip Islands, two tiny external territories of Australia, lost in the vast Pacific. The breathtakingly iridescent, almost cinnamon-colored throat feather she now held in her hand was unique to the Norfolk Island variety of the species.

She immediately knew where the feather came from. Stuffed specimens of the Norfolk kaka could be found in only a dozen places, including Amsterdam's Zoölogisch Museum and the Academy of Natural Sciences in Philadelphia. But there was also a specimen in Enoch Leng's cabinet of curiosities in that very basement, a male of unusual scarlet brilliance. The stuffed bird had been knocked over and damaged in the conflict that had taken place in the sub-basement two years before. She'd repaired it as best she could, but several of the feathers had remained missing.

Once again taking up the electric torch, she left her set of rooms and—gaining the central corridor—began walking in the opposite direction, until she reached a chamber devoted to stuffed animals. She quickly located the Norfolk kaka, set on a stand behind a rippled-glass case of mahogany.

The feather fit perfectly into a bare spot on the throat.

Back in her library, Constance glanced at the open book. The feather had been marking Poem 50.

Hesterno, Licini, die otiosi
multum lusimus in meis tabellis...

She mentally translated the lines.

Yesterday, Licinius, a day of leisure,
We played many games in my little notebooks...

Then she noticed that—at the very bottom of the page—a small notation had been made with an elegant hand, in violet ink. The ink looked remarkably fresh:

Beloved one, I offer this poem for you.

She recognized it as a loose translation of the poem's line 16: *hoc, iucunde, tibi poema feci.*

She turned the book over in her hands, amazed and perturbed. Where could this have come from? Could Proctor have brought it to her? But no—he would never presume to do any such thing, even if he thought it would ease her suffering. Besides, she was sure Proctor had never read a word of poetry in his life, Latin or otherwise. And in any case, he did not know of these secret rooms in which she'd taken residence.

With Pendergast dead, nobody knew of them.

She shook her head. Somebody had left her this book. Or was she starting to lose her mind? Maybe that was it; at times her grief was proving overpowering.

She opened the bottle of wine, poured out a glass, took a sip. Even to her, hardly a connoisseur, it was remarkably complex and interesting. She took another sip and sat down to her meal. But before commencing, she turned once again to the poem. She had read it before, of course, but not for years, and now—as she again translated the lines in her head—the poem seemed far more beautiful, more provocative, than she had remembered...and despite all, she read it through from beginning to end, slowly, with absorption and pleasure.

13

Constance woke to the sound of music. She sat up in bed and pushed the sheets to one side. She had been dreaming of music. But which piece? It had seemed full of longing, pathos, and unrequited passion.

She rose and passed out of the bedroom into her small library. These late-afternoon naps, she decided, would need to be curtailed. It was not at all her way, and she did not want them to become habitual. Such behavior—excessive or uncharacteristic sleeping—was, she suspected, a manifestation of her grief.

And yet grief was not, at the moment, what she felt—not precisely. She could not say exactly what mixture of emotions filled her, save that they were subtle and contradictory.

She had intended to spend the morning writing in her journal. Instead, she found herself translating and transcribing some of the poems of Catullus, and then—for some reason she could not quite fathom—several poems from Mallarmé's collection, *Poésies*. Mallarmé's style was notoriously difficult to translate effectively into English, and at last, growing fatigued, she turned her attention to music instead.

Since "going underground"—as she referred to it in her own mind—she had been listening to the string quartets of Shostakovich, in particular the third. The final movements always reminded her of Madeline Usher and the strange, cataleptic death-in-life fit that sealed her doom in Poe's story. In some ways Constance, too, had been feeling buried alive, like Madeline: living in self-enforced exile beneath the Manhattan streets. The restless, anxious dissonances of Shostakovich suited her mood; their grief mirrored her own.

But this afternoon, she had reached for Brahms instead of Shostakovich: the Piano Trios, to be precise. While they, too, were complex and philosophical, they were also lush, beautiful, and without the deep sadness of Shostakovich.

As she listened, a strange somnolence settled over her, and she had gone into her bedroom, intending just to lay her head on the pillow for ten minutes or so. But instead, three hours had passed: it was eight o'clock; and Mrs. Trask would have her daily meal waiting in the library elevator. Over the course of the day, rather than deciding to upbraid Mrs. Trask for the luxuriousness of the recent dinners, she had found herself wondering what the evening's tray would contain.

She gathered up the dishes from the previous night's meal, along with an electric torch and the half-empty bottle of wine, and went down the corridor to the secret entrance to her rooms. She pressed the unlocking trigger; the improvised stone door opened into the chamber full of Japanese woodblock prints—and then she froze in shock.

There—on the floor directly in front of her concealed doorway—sat a single flower in a cut-glass vase.

Constance released her grip, letting the silver tray, plates, and bottle drop to the floor with a crash. But it was not a reflexive movement of surprise—it was to free her hands in order to draw out the antique Italian stiletto she kept on her person at all times. Springing the blade, she shifted the beam of her torch from left to right, knife at the ready, as she peered around.

Empty. She stood there, the sense of shock giving way to a flood of anxious speculation. *Somebody* had been there—someone had penetrated her sanctum sanctorum.

Who was responsible for this intrusion? Who knew enough to access this most private, hidden, inaccessible of places... and what possible meaning could be ascribed to the flower?

She considered running to the stairs and ascending them as quickly as she could—leaving behind this dark sub-basement with its endless black chambers, grotesque collections, and innumerable places of concealment—to rush back to the library and the fire, back to Mrs. Trask and Proctor and the land of the living. But this impulse died quickly. Constance had never run from anything in her life. She sensed, furthermore, that she was in no immediate danger: the book of poems, the feather, the flower, were not the work of a villain. Somebody who wanted her dead could easily have killed her while she slept. Or poisoned her food. Or stabbed her as she traversed the galleries on her way to and from the elevator.

Her mind went back to the feather, marking the love poem; the fresh notation in the margin of the unfamiliar book. This was no caprice of her imagination: clearly, the person had already penetrated her secret rooms. The book, the feather, the flower—all this, it seemed to her, was a message. An eccentric message, no doubt—but a message that, though she did not understand it, had nothing of threat about it.

Constance stood quite still for about ten minutes. The shock had faded, followed by the sense of fear; but it took much longer for the uncomfortable sense that her privacy had been violated to ebb.

It did not ebb entirely.

Finally—leaving the broken plates and wine bottle on the floor, and securing a spare torch—she exited the room of Japanese prints and began a painstaking search of the sub-basement, collection by collection, room by room. She conducted her search in perfect silence, alert at all times for the faintest sound, the least glimmer of light.

She found nothing. The floor was either stone or hard-packed earth; no shoe or boot would leave an impression. Areas of dust did not seem recently disturbed. Nothing else was out of order that she could recall. The vast, shadowed-haunted galleries appeared as they always had.

Reaching at last the stairway leading upward, she stopped. If the person or persons had exited the sub-basement, there was no longer any point in continuing the search.

Now she returned to the entrance of her secret chamber, and the flower in its cut-glass vase. It was an orchid of the rarest beauty—but of a variety unknown to her. The exterior of the labellum was pure white, of an elongated shape. Inside it was pink, flushing almost red near the stamen.

Constance examined it for several minutes, her mind drifting over the various possibilities, none of which seemed likely, or even possible. Shaking her head, she cleaned up the broken glassware and crockery, piled it on the silver tray, and took it upstairs to the elevator, placing it inside for Mrs. Trask to collect. She removed the new tray with its covered dish—from which rose a heavenly aroma. Next to it, nestled in a silver bucket full of crushed ice and draped with a linen cloth, was a bottle of Perrier-Jouët Fleur de Champagne. She carried them back to the sub-basement. But instead of retreating as far as her private set of rooms, she stopped in the chamber that contained Enoch Leng's vast collection of dried flowers and other flora. Here, setting the tray and bucket on an ancient desk, she consulted several encyclopedic books on the subject, including a few devoted to orchids. While she worked, her eyes strayed to the bottle of champagne, and on impulse she slid it from the ice, popped the cork, and poured herself a small glass.

Despite a thorough search of the dusty tomes, she could find no match to the flower that had been left, apparently, for her. But these books were half a century old, and no doubt other orchids had been bred, or discovered, in the years since.

She continued on to her set of rooms, closing the stone door behind her. Entering the small library, she settled at her desk, poured herself another glass of champagne, and booted up her laptop that—thanks to a Wi-Fi repeater installed in the basement—had limited access to the Internet.

It was the work of fifteen minutes to find a precise match. The flower was a newly discovered species of Orchidaceae, native to the Himalayas. It had been collected along the Tibetan-Indian border.

And it had been named *Cattleya constanciana.*

Constance stared. This was madness. Had it been named after her? Impossible; it had to be mere coincidence. And yet, the location where it had been found…was *that* a coincidence, as well? It was not far from the Tibetan monastery where her child was currently living in hiding. And the orchid had been found, described, and named only six months before. But *who* had discovered it was not indicated.

She continued her research, finally coming across the original note in *The Orchid Review*, published by the Royal Horticultural Society. Under *Discoverer*, the name was rendered merely as *Anonymous.*

It *had* been named after her. There were too many coincidences; there could be no other explanation.

She turned off the laptop and sat very still. She should report this intrusion to Proctor. And yet—strange though it seemed—she did not wish to. He would not take it well, this invasion of the house under his watch. He was a blunt tool. This situation, whatever its precise nature might be, seemed to call for more finesse. She was confident in her ability to handle whatever might come her way. She did not lack for means of self-defense: she had overcome threats far worse than this. Her own natural tendency toward sudden and effective violence was her best protection. If only Aloysius were here; he would know what was going on.

Aloysius. She realized that almost an hour had passed without incessant thoughts of her guardian. And now, thinking of him did not summon forth the usual stab of grief. Maybe she was, at last, finally adjusting to his death.

No; she would not report this to Proctor. At least, not yet. She was in her element; she knew of a dozen other places within these vast subterranean vaults, places even more secret, to which she could retreat. And yet some sixth sense told her it would not be necessary. What had happened was an intrusion...but it did not feel like a *violation*. It felt like something else. She was not sure what, exactly...but in a most peculiar way, she sensed—in this time of alienation and terrible loneliness—that she was sharing a private exile with some sort of kindred spirit.

That night, when she at last retired, she was careful to put a steel door jammer against the inside of the stone wall that led out into the room of Japanese prints. She was just as careful to lock the deadbolt to her bedroom, and to keep her Maniago stiletto close by. But before doing these things, she brought the beautiful orchid, and its equally beautiful vase, into her chambers and placed them on one side of her writing desk.

14

CONSTANCE LOOKED UP from her journal.

What was it that had so suddenly caught her attention? A noise of some sort? She listened, but the sub-basement was as quiet as a tomb. A draft of air, perhaps? That was absurd; no breezes stirred in this ancient space, so far below the streets of Manhattan.

She sighed. It was nothing; she was simply restless and distracted. She glanced at her watch: ten minutes past two in the morning. Her eyes lingered on the watch with sadness. It was a ladies Rolex with a platinum jubilee band, and it had been a present from Pendergast the previous Christmas. It matched the timepiece he wore on his own wrist.

She shut the journal abruptly. It was impossible to escape the memory of Aloysius; everything reminded her of him.

She had woken half an hour before. Recently, and most uncharacteristically, her sleep patterns had become disturbed—waking in the middle of the night only to find herself unable to fall asleep again. Perhaps this accounted for the lethargy that had been stealing over her in recent afternoons, prompting the naps that, almost inevitably, had turned into prolonged dozes. But at least she couldn't blame the insomnia on recent events, Pendergast's death or the apparent intrusion into her sub-basement: she had been waking at unexpected hours since at least the beginning of their trip to Massachusetts. At that time, her nocturnal alertness had occasioned an important step forward in their investigation. Now it was simply an annoyance.

So she had risen from her wakeful bed and gone into her library to write in her journal. The normally soothing practice proved another frustration: the words just wouldn't come.

Her glance moved from the closed journal to the dishes from last night's dinner, piled on the silver tray. The meal had been a chilled one, almost as if Mrs. Trask had known that Constance would be too preoccupied to eat it directly: a brace of cold-water lobster tails, sauce rémoulade; quail eggs *au diable*...and, of course, a bottle of champagne, of which she had drunk far too much. She could feel it now, a gentle throbbing behind her temples.

Almost as if Mrs. Trask had known I would be too preoccupied to eat it directly...

A strange thought arose in Constance's mind: was it really Mrs. Trask who was preparing these dishes? But who else could it be? She would not have hired another chef, especially not on her own authority. Besides, the housekeeper jealously guarded her maternal role, always fussing, and would never allow anyone else to prepare food in the house.

Constance placed her fountain pen on the table. She was clearly out of sorts. It was probably due to the wine, which she was unused to drinking, along with the rich meals of late. She could, at least, put a stop to all that. And while she thought of it, it might be a good idea, after all, to speak to Proctor about her recent discoveries in the sub-basement.

Picking up her pen again, she reached into her desk, removed a single piece of cream-laid writing paper, and jotted a note:

Dear Mrs. Trask,

Thank you for your kind attentions of late. Your concern for my well-being is greatly appreciated. I would request, however, that you return to serving me simpler meals, without wine; the dishes you have prepared since your return from Albany have been delicious but, I fear, rather too rich for my taste.

If you could also do me the favor of telling Proctor that I desire to speak with him, I would be grateful. He can leave a note in the elevator, suggesting a convenient time.

Kind regards,
Constance

Folding the note in half, she rose from the desk; put on her silk dressing gown; and then, lighting a torch, picking up the tray holding the dishes and champagne bottle, and placing the note on top of them, walked down the short hallway.

She opened the door—then stopped short once again. This time, she did not drop the dishes or the bottle. Nor did she draw her stiletto. Instead, she carefully placed the tray to one side, patted her dressing gown to ensure the blade was at hand, and then shone the torch on the thing that had been placed outside her door.

It was a dirty, yellowed, rolled-up piece of silk, with Tibetan writing and a red handprint. She recognized it immediately as the reverse of a t'angka—a Tibetan Buddhist painting.

She picked it up and carried it to the library, where she spread it out. And then she gasped. It was of the most gorgeous appearance imaginable: a coruscation, a sunburst, of reds and golds and azures, with exquisitely delicate shading and perfection of detailing and clarity. She recognized it as a certain type of religious painting depicting

Avalokiteshvara, the Bodhisattva of Compassion, sitting upon a lotus throne, which in turn rested on the lunar disk. Avalokiteshvara was the god most revered in Tibet as sacrificing his own salvation to be reincarnated again and again on earth, in order to bring enlightenment to all living, suffering beings of the world.

Except that this depiction of Avalokiteshvara was not as a man, but a young boy. And the child's features, so exquisitely drawn, were identical, down to the fine whorls of hair and the characteristic droop of the eyelids…to those of her own son.

Constance had not seen her child—the child of herself and Diogenes Pendergast—in a year. The Tibetans had declared him a rinpoche, the nineteenth reincarnation of a revered Tibetan monk. He was hidden away in a monastery outside Dharamsala, India, safe from any interference by the Chinese. In this painting, the child was older than he had been when she last saw him. It could not have been done more than a few months before, at most…

Standing utterly still, she drank in the painted features. Despite the father, Constance could not help but feel a fierce maternal love—exacerbated by the fact that she could only visit him rarely. *So this is what he looks like now*, she thought, staring almost rapturously.

Whoever left this, she thought, *knows my innermost secrets. The existence of my child—and my child's identity.* The hint that had begun with the location of the newly discovered orchid, *Cattleya constanciana*, was now made plain.

Something else was becoming clear. This person was, without doubt, courting her. But who could it be? Who could possibly know so much about her? Did he know her other secrets, as well—her true age? Her relationship to Enoch Leng?

She felt certain that he did.

For a moment, she considered engaging in another fierce and thorough search of the sub-basement. But she dropped the idea; no doubt a fresh search would be as fruitless as the last.

She knelt, picked up her note to Mrs. Trask, tore it in two, then slipped it into the pocket of her robe. There was no longer any point in sending it—because she knew now that it was not the housekeeper who had been providing her with these exquisite meals and precious wines.

But who?

Diogenes.

She quickly dismissed this as the most ridiculous speculation imaginable. True, such a fey, whimsical, teasing courtship would have been typical of Diogenes Pendergast. But he was dead.

Wasn't he?

Constance shook her head. Of course he was dead. He had fallen into the terrible Sciara del Fuoco of the Stromboli volcano. She knew this, because she had struggled with him on the very lip of the abyss. She had pushed him herself, she had watched him fall—and had peered over the edge into the roaring winds to the smoking lava below. She was certain her revenge had been complete.

Besides, in life Aloysius's brother had had nothing but contempt for her—he'd made that abundantly clear. *You were a toy*, he had written: *a mystery easily solved; a dull box forced and found empty.*

Her hands clenched at the mere memory.

It wasn't Diogenes; that was impossible. It was someone else—someone who also knew her deepest secrets.

It came to her like a bolt of lightning. *He's alive*, she thought. *He didn't drown, after all. And he has returned to me.*

She was overwhelmed with a tidal wave of emotion. She felt almost crazy with hope, frantic with anticipation, her heart suddenly battering in her chest as if it would break free.

"Aloysius?" she cried into the darkness, her voice breaking, whether with laughter or weeping she didn't know. "Aloysius, come out and show yourself! I don't know why you're being so coy, but for God's sake please, *please* let me see you!"

But the only reply was her own voice, echoing faintly through the subterranean chambers of stone.

15

Rocky Filipov, captain of the F/V *Moneyball*, a sixty-five-foot converted trawler, turned his head and ejected a stream of brown tobacco juice onto the deck, where it joined a sticky layer of grease, diesel fuel, and rotten fish juice.

"It's simple," the crewman, Martin DeJesus, was saying. "It's taking too long. Just fucking shoot him, put him in a fish sack, weigh it down, and throw him overboard."

A cold wind blew across the deck of the *Moneyball*. It was a deep overcast night with no stars, and they were snugly berthed in Bailey's Hole, not far from the Canadian-U.S. border. The small group stood on the deck of the dark boat, and all Filipov could see of the others were the glowing tips of their cigarettes. There were no other lights; the *Moneyball* had extinguished its anchor and running lights, and even the red illumination of the pilothouse had been doused.

"I'm with Martin," came the heavy voice of Carl Miller, followed by a brightening of his cigarette; a loud exhale. "I don't want to keep him on board any longer—they're just stringing us along. Screw the swap. It's too risky."

"It's *not* risky," said the cook. "We can be in international waters inside of an hour. The next shipment is weeks away. Arsenault's a mate of ours; he's worth the trade."

"Yeah. Maybe. Then why aren't the feds playing ball?"

Captain Filipov listened to the back-and-forth. The crew needed to talk it out. Tensions had been rising in recent days. The crew that was still on board, minus the watch on deck, had gradually assembled in the lee of the pilothouse to hash it out once and for all. He hunched in the cold wind, leaned against the steel pilothouse wall, arms crossed.

"I think they're setting us up," said Juan Abreu, the ship's engineer.

"Doesn't matter," said the cook. "If we get even the least whiff of the thing going south, then we'll take off and dump the guy overboard. We'd still have that watch of his to sell."

The argument went on and on, until they all began repeating themselves. Filipov finally pushed himself from the wall, spat another stream, and spoke. "We've had the bastard on board almost three weeks. We've been trying to work this exchange for days now. It's a good plan—let's stick to the plan. Three more days—that's what we agreed. If the swap isn't completed by then, we do the DeJesus thing and dump him overboard."

He stopped and waited for the reactions. In the drug smuggling business, contrary to all the bullshit television shows, you needed to build a consensus. You couldn't just bust balls and think it was going to work.

"Fair enough," said the cook.

"Carl?" Filipov asked.

"Okay. Three more days."

"Martin?"

"Well, fuck, I'm willing to hang in another couple of days. But that's it."

A grudging agreement was reached and the group began to break up.

Captain Filipov caught the cook as he was heading back down into the galley. "I'd better try to keep the motherfucker alive. You got any more beef stew from dinner?"

"Sure."

Filipov collected a bowl of stew and a bottle of water and carried them down to the aft lazarette hold. The hatch had been left open, replaced with a grate for air. He shone a flashlight through the grate and saw the man in the same position as the last time, with one wrist handcuffed to an open-base horn cleat. He was wearing the same torn and filthy black suit they had found him in, covering a skeletal frame, hollow cheekbones, and bruised face. White-blond hair was plastered to the skull.

He opened the grate and descended into the hold, setting the bottle of water before the gaunt figure. He squatted and stared. The man's eyes were closed, but as Filipov looked at him they opened: silvery eyes that seemed to glitter with internal light.

"Brought you some food," Filipov said, gesturing to the bowl in his hand.

The man did not answer.

"What's taking your friends?" Filipov asked for the hundredth time. "They keep on stalling."

To his surprise, the man's eyes finally met his. It made him uneasy.

"You complain of the silence of my friends?"

"Right, exactly."

"In that case, I apologize on their behalf. But let me assure you that, when the time comes, they will be delighted to meet you. Although I fear that, on the off chance you survive the encounter, you'll wish you hadn't met *them*."

Filipov stared. It took him a moment to process this. "Big talk coming from some shit-encrusted piece of flotsam we dragged out of the drink."

The figure smiled with a mirthless and ghastly stretching of the lips.

"Okay." Filipov put down the bowl. "Here's your dinner." He started to go, then paused. "And here's your dessert." He turned back and kicked the man viciously in the gut. Then he climbed out of the hold and let the grate slam down behind him.

16

19 Days Earlier
October 25

Rᴏᴄᴋʏ Fɪʟɪᴘᴏᴠ sᴛᴏᴏᴅ at the helm of the F/V *Moneyball*, guiding it through a cross sea. The rising sun was just breaking through a dirty scrim of clouds on the eastern horizon, the remains of the storm that had swept through during the night. Off the port side of the vessel, the low dark shore of Crow Island slid past, and ahead Filipov could see the winking beam of the Exmouth Light, standing on a bluff with the keeper's house beside it, touched with gold by the rising sun—a fine sight. The crew not on watch were sleeping in the cabin below. Martin DeJesus was standing next to him in the pilothouse, drinking coffee, eating a stale doughnut and playing a game on his cell phone.

Filipov was in a dark mood. They had finished delivery of product to their contact in Maine. The trip from Canada had gone without a hitch. They were now sitting on seven figures of cash, locked up in the hold. And they had a month to kill before the next pickup and delivery. It should have been a moment of triumph... except for the problem of Arsenault.

The feds had picked him up with a suitcase of money from the Canadian job a week ago—a hundred grand, enough to pique their interest. No drugs, no evidence, just a shitload of money. Now they had Arsenault in custody, and Filipov had no doubt they were working on him. He hadn't cracked yet—otherwise they'd all have gone down. While he believed Arsenault would be a hard man to break, the guy did have a wife and two kids, and that was always a man's weakest point. Also, he was stupid—he should have laundered his share of the money along the lines Filipov had carefully worked out, rather than be caught with it on his person.

The other problem was that the crew had voted to take the boat to Boston and dock it for the month while they enjoyed the fruits of their labor. Filipov was not happy with the plan: he did not like the idea of the crew, suddenly rich, going into the city, spending money, getting drunk, hiring prostitutes, and—possibly—talking too much. After all, look what had happened to Arsenault, who'd opted to leave the boat early. But, realistically, he had to go along with it. He couldn't just say no after how hard they had worked on the delivery, the risks they'd taken, and how well they'd pulled it off. He simply had to trust them not to get into trouble.

For his part, he was going to spend the month quietly laundering as much of the drug money as he could through the successful antiquities gallery he owned on Newbury Street, eating out at fine restaurants with his several girlfriends, going to Bruins games, and adding a few rare bottles to his wine cellar.

"Whoa," said Filipov suddenly, staring forward into the choppy water. "You see that?" He throttled down.

DeJesus looked up from his game. "Holy shit, it's a floater."

Filipov briefly slid the throttle into reverse, slowing the boat's headway. The body was lying faceup, arms splayed, pale in death.

"Get a boat hook," he told DeJesus.

DeJesus exited the pilothouse, grabbed a boat hook, and went forward while Filipov maneuvered the *Moneyball* to a standstill, bringing it alongside the body. When he saw that DeJesus had snagged it he put the vessel in neutral and exited the pilothouse as well, joining DeJesus at the port rail.

Filipov stared down at the body. It was male, about forty, pale hair plastered to the skull, black suit, pale-gray skin. A watch gleamed on the left wrist.

"Bring it aft and haul it on board," Filipov told DeJesus.

"Are you shitting me? If we report this we're going to get all messed up with an investigation."

"Who said we're going to report anything? You see that watch? Looks like a Rolex."

DeJesus issued a low chuckle. "Rocky, you *always* looking for an angle."

"Ease him around to the stern and haul him in over the stern ramp."

Having lost its forward motion, the trawler was rolling pretty good, but DeJesus managed to pull the body aft and around the stern, then dragged it on board with the hook fixed to the floater's belt. The body slid easily up the stern ramp, draining water. Filipov knelt and grasped the wrist, turning it over.

"Look at this. Platinum Rolex President Sant Blanc. Worth forty grand at least." He unbuckled it and slipped it off, holding it up for DeJesus to see.

DeJesus took the watch and turned it over. "Fucking A, Cap. It's still running."

"Let's see what else he's got on him."

Filipov made a quick search of the body. No wallet, no keys, nothing in the pockets. A strange medallion around the neck that looked worthless, and a gold signet ring with an engraved crest or symbol on it. He tried to take it off, and finally had to force it free, breaking the knuckle as he did so.

He let the hand drop, examining the ring. The value was in the gold, of course: maybe three, four hundred bucks.

"What do we do now?" DeJesus said. "Dump it back? We sure don't want to be caught with a dead body on board."

Filipov stared at the body. He reached back toward it and grasped the wrist again. It was not as cold as it should be. In fact, it was slightly warm. He pressed his thumb into it, trying to find a pulse, but couldn't detect anything. He reached over to the neck and checked the carotid artery. Once again, he was startled at the warmth. As he pressed his index and middle fingers in, he picked up a faint throb. And now he could see the body was in fact breathing—very shallow, almost imperceptible breaths. He put his ear to the chest and picked up a faint gurgling wheeze, along with a slow feeble thump of the heart.

"He's alive," he said.

"All the more reason to dump him."

"Absolutely not."

Filipov found DeJesus staring at him with a blank look on his face, his bald crown surrounded by a tuft of black wiry hair, his hammy hand gripping the watch. DeJesus was a reliable man, but about as intelligent as a side of beef. "Martin, look. Here's a guy with a forty-thousand-dollar watch. We just saved his life. Now...don't you think there might be a money play in this situation?"

"Like what?"

"Go wake up the crew."

DeJesus went below, shaking his head, while Filipov grabbed a heavy wool blanket from a storage locker. He glanced around to make sure there were no other boats in sight, then hauled the man farther up the stern deck, laid the blanket down, and wrapped him tightly. He had to warm the guy up fast or he'd die anyway, of hypothermia. The water temperature was about fifty-five degrees, and according to the tables Filipov knew by heart, a healthy man in water like that had about ninety minutes of consciousness, then another hour before death, assuming he didn't drown first.

The guy wasn't worth a shit dead, but he might be worth a lot alive.

Once he'd wrapped the guy up, Filipov thought about what to do with him. If he came to, he'd be confused. Maybe cause trouble. Best to lock him in one of the holds. The aft lazarette, the biggest hold, would be the place; it had light and some electrical outlets high up into which they could plug a space heater.

Now the crew was coming out on deck, wiping the sleep out of their faces, gathering around the unconscious man. Filipov stood up and looked around. "Martin, show them the watch."

The watch went around to murmurs and nods.

"You can buy a Caddy for the price of that watch," said Filipov. "This man is loaded." He looked around. "It means giving up your Boston holiday, but there may be some serious money to be made here."

"Money?" asked Dwayne Smith, the first mate. "Like a reward?"

"Reward? Shit. No reward would be anything near what we might get if we handled this in another way."

"What other way?" Smith asked.

"Ransom."

17

Filipov stood at the lazarette hatch, staring down at the mystery man shackled to the cleat in the bottom of the hold. The man had been with them for ten days, but they knew as much about him now as they had when they'd hauled him on board. Which was nothing. The man appeared to be sleeping, but Filipov wasn't sure. For the first few days after they'd fished him from the water, he'd been sunken in a kind of deep stupor. That was to be expected after almost dying of hypothermia. They had taken good care of him, keeping him warm, feeding him broth when he was able to take it, bandaging his wounds and broken knuckle, making him comfortable. Then he had run a high fever for three days—again, nothing surprising in that. But the crew began to get nervous, worrying that if they were stopped by the Coast Guard and boarded it would be all over.

To minimize that possibility, Filipov had taken the *Moneyball* beyond the Schoodic Peninsula, deep into the wildest coastline in the United States: Downeast Maine, with its thousands of uninhabited islands, coves, and estuaries. Filipov knew the coast well, and he also knew the habits of the Coast Guard. For days now they had been meandering from gunkhole to gunkhole, keeping well out of the cruising and shipping lanes and moving only at night. But the atmosphere aboard ship had continued to sour, especially when, after the mystery man's fever cleared up and he seemed to be on the road to recovery, he still hadn't spoken: not a single word. It was almost as if he were brain-damaged—which was a possibility, after being almost drowned. But in the few times he'd had a chance to look into the man's silvery eyes, Filipov had seen an alert intelligence. He felt in his bones the guy was cognizant. So why wouldn't he talk? What had he been doing floating in the water? And what about his wounds? It almost looked like he'd been mauled by a bear, with long tearing scratches, lacerations, and bite marks.

It was damned unnerving to everyone on board.

Now the man was lying in his usual position, eyes closed. Filipov stared at him, his hand in his pocket, toying with the man's gold ring. He was sure the answer, or at least *some* answer, lay in the crest or symbol engraved in that ring. It was a strange emblem, showing a weird vertical cloud with a five-pointed star inside it, lightning bolt shooting down, striking a lidless cat's eye inside of which was the number 9 in place of the pupil. To Filipov it looked vaguely military. Smith, his first mate and the resident computer guru, had spent hours on the Internet looking for a match, without success. The same was true of the bizarre medallion around the man's neck, although that looked less official, almost familial or perhaps even medieval. Smith had also tried to get an Internet match on the man's face. That had failed, as well. The problem was the man had almost died and his face was so haggard and drawn that he probably didn't look enough like his former self for the software to find a match.

The key to this man's identity was that ring; Filipov was sure of it.

He stared at the man, his anger growing. The son of a bitch was holding out on them. Why?

He stepped into the hold and walked up to the man. He lay there, eyes closed, shackled to the cleat, asleep. Or rather, pretending to sleep. And even as Filipov stared, those eyes slowly opened, revealing two glittering silver coins with pinpoint black pupils. He looked more like a ghost than a human being.

Filipov leaned over him. "Who are you?"

Those eyes looked into his own, with what Filipov felt was a kind of insolence. The man had started out almost dead, but now Filipov was sure he must have recovered more than he was letting on.

"I'm going to dump your ass back in the ocean. How about that?"

To his surprise, the man spoke for the first time. The voice was barely more than a whisper. "The repetition of that threat is becoming tiresome."

Filipov was taken aback by the quiet smoothness of the voice, the southern accent, and the distinctly arrogant tone.

"So you *can* talk! I knew you were screwing with us. All right, now that you found your tongue: who are you?"

"The real question is, who are *you*? Ah, but never mind: I already know the answer."

"Oh yeah? So who am I then, you little prick?"

"You're the unluckiest man alive."

With a curse, Filipov kicked him in the ribs. But even with that, the man's expression never changed, those eyes never shifting from his own.

18

CAPTAIN FILIPOV STOOD at the chart table to the left of the helm, staring over Smith's shoulder as the man worked his laptop computer. He was explaining his latest failed attempt to match the engraving on the mystery man's ring with something on the Internet. "Whatever it is," Smith was saying, "it's not on the surface web, not on the dark net. I used the best image-matching software available. It ain't fucking there."

Filipov nodded, staring at the image on the screen: a photo they'd taken of the ring. The boat was lying off Bunker Cove, south of Great Spruce Island. It was a protected anchorage for a dirty night, the swell coming from the northeast, rain splattering the pilothouse windows.

"Want a beer?" Smith asked.

"Not right now."

Smith scraped the chair back and went below; a moment later he returned, a beer in one hand. He took a long swig.

"Whoever this asshole is," said Filipov, sitting down at the computer, "he wants to be anonymous. Why won't he tell us his name?"

"Yeah. Exactly."

He stared at the design. Weird cloud; lightning; cat's eye; nine. And suddenly an idea came to him. He winced at the obviousness of it. "A cat has nine lives."

"Yeah?"

"So this group, whatever it is, is all about survival. Nine lives."

"Okay." Smith took a pull from his beer.

"And this cloud. You ever see a cloud like that?"

"It's strange. Sort of like a thunderhead."

"Maybe it's not a cloud at all."

"So what is it, then?"

"A ghost."

Smith peered at the image of the ring on the screen, squinting, and then grunted. "Maybe."

Filipov took the real ring out of his pocket and looked at it, turning it in the dim light of the pilothouse. "Ghost. Star. Nine lives. Lightning. Okay. So the image isn't on the web. But perhaps a *description* of it is."

Filipov started Googling the words "ghost," "star," "nine lives," "lightning." And almost immediately he got a hit. It was a small article in an FBI newsletter, *Hall of Honor*, devoted to agents killed in the line of duty. It was dated three or four years back, and it described the funeral of a Special Agent Michael Decker, who had been killed "In the Line of Duty as the Result of an Adversarial Action." The article described the funeral and noted some of the attendees. Filipov read through it, then stopped at one passage:

In addition to the American flag, the coffin displayed the emblem of the elite Ghost Company to which Decker belonged—a ghost on a blue field, decorated with a star, throwing a thunderbolt at a cat's eye with the number nine as its pupil, symbolizing the nine lives that all members of the Ghost Company were alleged to have by virtue of their training, determination, and experience.

The Ghost Company was a highly secret, tight-knit, specialized descendant of the army's now-defunct "Blue Light" detachment, and was created specifically to operate in classified, highly dangerous, and at times unsanctioned theaters of engagement. The Ghost Company's window of service was relatively brief. "Blue Light" as a whole later developed into the 1st Special Forces Operational Detachment—Delta Force. Special Agent Decker was one of a small, decorated group of agents who joined the FBI after serving in the Ghost Company.

"Our mystery man below," said Filipov, "was in the military. Special forces."

Smith stared over his shoulder, breathing hard. "Fuck me," he said, pointing. "Look at this!"

The article sported a small photograph of a group of agents at the graveside. And there, standing with his hands folded, was a tall, pale man in a black suit. While his face was blurry and indistinct, everything about the figure matched the man in the hold—the paleness, the blond hair, the pale eyes and lean physique.

The caption named him as Special Agent A. X. L. Pendergast.

"Christ," Filipov breathed out. "He's a *fed*."

There was a silence, broken only by the pattering of rain on the windows.

"Well, that's it," said Smith. "We throw the motherfucker overboard."

"You really want to kill him?" asked Filipov.

"We're not killing him. We're just putting him back where we found him. Nature will do the rest. Who's gonna know? He'll wash up somewhere weeks from now and nothing will connect him to us. We sure as hell can't keep a fed on board."

Still Filipov said nothing. He was sorely tempted. The prick had really gotten under his skin. He opened a small cupboard below the chart table, removed a bottle of scotch, unscrewed the cap, and took a pull. He felt the liquid make its fiery way down his throat. It felt good. He took another.

"I say we go back offshore of Crow Island," Smith went on. "Dump him there. Not far from where he must've disappeared. No one'll connect us to him." He paused, then grasped the scotch bottle. "Mind?"

"That's pretty strong stuff for a Mormon," said Filipov.

"Lapsed," said Smith with a grin, sucking down a mouthful. "We put the watch back on him. And the ring. No evidence left behind."

As the scotch set his belly afire, Filipov could feel a remarkable clarity taking hold in his mind. He waited for Smith to talk himself out.

"Fuck the watch," Smith went on. "We can't take the risk. With Arsenault maybe about to talk, we can't take any risks at all."

"Arsenault," said Filipov.

"Yeah, Arsenault. I mean, if he talks, they're gonna be after us hammer and tongs. And if they find a kidnapped fed on board, the drug charges will be the least of our worries—"

"*Arsenault*," Filipov repeated.

Smith finally stopped talking. "What about him?"

"The feds have him."

"What I'm *saying*."

"So...we've got ourselves a fed."

Silence.

Filipov turned his gaze full on Smith. "We offer a trade. This man Pendergast for Arsenault."

"You fucking crazy? You want to pull that shit on the feds? We'll be dead so fast, you won't have time to finish pissing off the stern."

"Not if we go to ground. And I know just the place. Listen. The feds have no idea where he is. There's been nothing in the papers about it. They don't know he's on a boat, and besides, that would be the last place they'd look. As proof we have him, we'll send them the ring and amulet."

"This is crazy."

"If Arsenault cracks, it's over. We spend the rest of our lives in prison."

"You really think he's gonna crack?"

"I think it's possible. They've had him now…what? Almost a month?"

"But to kidnap a fed for an exchange…" Smith lapsed into silence.

"The beauty of it is that it's simple. The work is half-done: we already have him and nobody knows where we are. We'll drop one of the crew on shore with the ring and amulet. He'll mail it to the feds from, say, New York City. Our demand is simple: release Arsenault and give him a one-way ticket to Venezuela. When we hear from him, we set this Pendergast free. If not, Pendergast dies."

"Set him free? He's seen our faces."

"Good point. So when Arsenault's freed, *then* we put the fed back in the water. Where we found him." This idea gave Filipov a sense of satisfaction.

"Son of a bitch." Smith furrowed his brow. "I don't know. We kill a fed, they'll hunt us to the ends of the earth. This guy's elite. He's got friends."

"But we've got money. And a boat. It'll take awhile for them to piece it all together—and by the time they do, *if* they do, we'll be long gone. If Arsenault talks, we're going down anyway." He delivered the clincher. "It's a miracle this guy just fell into our laps. We'd be crazy not to take advantage of it."

Smith shook his head. "It just might work."

"It *will* work. Roust up the crew. I'm calling a meeting."

19

Filipov stood on the forward deck, breathing in the perfume that wafted from the great spruce boughs jutting from the trees growing out of the bluff just above and ahead of the boat. It was a calm, cold, sunny fall morning. All was going as planned.

The captain had discovered Bailey's Hole when he was a teenager running pot from Canada into the United States in a sixteen-foot Boston Whaler. He'd never told anyone else about the hole—ever. Not even when he began running Charlie from Phinneys Cove, Nova Scotia, to Fairy Head, Maine, on a succession of lobster boats and draggers. It was a perfect hiding place, and Filipov had saved it for a time when he really needed it.

That time had come.

Bailey's Hole lay on that wild stretch of coastline between Cutler and Lubec, not far from the Canadian border. It was a deep cut in the granite coastline, with sheer cliffs on three sides, overhung with giant spruce trees whose shaggy limbs provided cover from above. The northern side of the hole was actually undercut, the granite rock forming a sort of frozen wave of stone under which a boat could be hidden so completely as to be totally invisible. The few lobstermen who worked the area shunned the hole because of its wicked, fifteen-foot tides and jagged underwater terrain that ate their lobster traps and sliced their lines.

It had been no joke easing the *Moneyball* into Bailey's Hole. Filipov did it at slack tide, at night, when the currents had ceased and the surface was calm. There was no way to drop anchor: the ground would eat an anchor just as readily as a lobster trap, and in any case there wasn't enough swinging room to accommodate an anchored boat. Instead, Filipov had strung cables from both shores, wrapped around spruce trunks, leaving enough slack to allow the *Moneyball* to rise and fall with the tides.

It was a tricky operation that had taken half of the night. Filipov was happy with the result. They were well hidden along a wild shore, with the nearest town twelve miles away and the closest house at least eight. There were no roads and no trails anywhere nearby. The shore was part of a large piece of forestland owned by the Montrose Paper Mill, in Lubec. The only people who ever came out there were loggers... but there was no logging at this time of year.

On the way to Bailey's Hole, they had dropped off one of the most reliable and resourceful members of his crew, Dalca, with the ring and amulet and a wad of money. His mission was to go to New York City and mail the two items and a photograph of Pendergast, along with their demands and instructions, to the New York Field Office. Dalca would then disappear into the city, lie low, and await the outcome.

After dropping off Dalca on a lonely stretch of coast, Filipov had taken the *Moneyball* north to Bailey's Hole.

He had taken careful precautions. Long before reaching the hole, Filipov had ordered the boat's GPS and all cell phones to be turned off, their batteries removed. Anything that could be used to track them was shut down.

He'd considered the problem of communicating with the FBI.

There had to be a way to do it without betraying their position. Fortunately Smith, the first mate and computer guru, knew how to set up an untraceable, encrypted email system. Filipov himself understood a good deal about computers, and together he and Smith had worked it out. They used a program similar to Tor, but more advanced. Called BLUNT, it quadruple-encrypted all Internet communications using PGP and re-routed them through myriad computers around the globe, making it almost impossible to trace the signal back to its original IP. Within BLUNT he and Smith had set up a temporary, disposable email service called Insurgent Mail on the dark net, which was—so they believed—impregnable even to the NSA.

There was only one small problem with this setup: Bailey's Hole had no Internet connection.

Which meant that Smith had to get himself and his laptop computer to a place that *did* have an Internet connection in order to send and receive messages. That place, they had decided, would be the town of Cutler, a dozen miles down the coast. A motel in Cutler called Goderre's Downeaster offered free Wi-Fi. This is where Smith would go.

The *Moneyball* carried a launch that doubled as a life raft. It was an almost new Zodiac inflatable, nine feet, six inches, with a 9.8 Tohatsu four-stroke. In a calm sea with one person, the boat could plane along at a good twenty knots. But the seas between Bailey's Hole and Cutler were anything but calm, and twelve knots was about the max a man could make without being beaten to hell by the chop, and then only in good weather. In stormy weather—forget it.

They had to be careful. The coming and going of a small Zodiac in a harbor wouldn't merit a second glance, but seeing one tooling along the coast in open water *would* be noted—especially by fishermen who would think it pure insanity to be driving a small boat in late fall, on a rugged coastline known for its epic storms, currents, and tides. If they saw him, they'd want to know who the hell the crazy bastard was. Fishermen, Filipov knew well, were infamous gossips.

For all these reasons, Smith would have to come and go from Cutler at night, greatly increasing the danger of an accident. But there was no other way.

Despite taking painstaking care to set up a secure email system, Filipov knew it was more than likely that cell phones would be needed, too. It was entirely possible, for example, that Smith might at some point need to speak with Dalca in New York. And he knew enough about feds to expect them to insist, sooner or later, on communication by voice.

He had this covered, as well. On board the *Moneyball* were a couple of dozen GSM cell phones, prepaid minutes included, purchased with cash from a variety of foreign countries—very useful for conducting his kind of business. Filipov gave two to Dalca and four to Smith, with explicit instructions for Smith in particular: when speaking to the FBI, use a different phone for each call and keep the conversation short: a phone's cell ID could be triangulated in as little as thirty seconds. Smith, not the FBI, would be the one to initiate the calls. After completing a call, the battery would be taken out and the phone disabled so that it could not send "heartbeat" messages back to the cell network.

Filipov inhaled the pine-scented air again. Smith had left that night for Cutler, his laptop computer and burner phones securely wrapped in multiple layers of plastic against the salt spray of the ocean. Smith was not the mariner one might wish for a dangerous sea journey at night, and Filipov had briefed him carefully: he would hug the coast, keeping close to shore but well out of the surf zone. He would need a powerful spotlight, which he would turn off before entering the harbor.

Filipov had watched him go, heard the tinny engine as it faded into the darkness. It was a risk but, again, a necessary one. The plan had been put into action and there was no going back. They would hear nothing for three days, maybe four at most.

But it was a good plan. He had gone over it in his head a hundred times, and the crew had discussed it ad nauseam. Smith would check into Goderre's under the pretext of being a Mormon missionary. He was just young looking enough to pull it off. Not only that, but he—and indeed all of them—had brought along conservative suits: a crisp, expensive suit was an invaluable accessory in certain drug smuggling situations. Best of all, Smith *was* a Mormon, or had been until a gigantic lapsus, and he had in fact put in his year of missionary work. He knew how to talk the lingo.

Three days of silence. While in Cutler, Smith could not, of course, communicate with them. But Filipov had given him precise instructions on how to respond to a large variety of possibilities in his negotiations with the FBI. He was to stick to a basic message: if Arsenault wasn't in Venezuela in a week, the FBI agent would die. Simple.

In negotiations like this, Filipov knew, SOP was for the authorities to push for more time and ask for small things, gradually piling up requirements and requests, dragging things on and establishing dominance over the hostage takers. He wasn't going to fall into that trap. One week. If they hadn't heard from Arsenault via Skype, standing in front of the Simón Bolívar statue in Plaza Bolívar in Caracas, Venezuela—a venue that could never be faked—then they would take this fed son of a bitch out to sea, dump him, and leave the country. Of course, if they did hear from Arsenault they'd dump him anyway.

Filipov knew that bluffing the FBI did not work. He had to make up his own mind: to be determined, up front, without question, to follow through and do what he said he would, no matter what. The FBI negotiators were experts and would see through a bluff. If he showed the slightest weakness, the tiniest hesitation, the slightest accommodation to one of their demands, it would all be over.

Again, Smith had been carefully briefed on all this. He had strict orders. Filipov had confidence in him. It was perhaps an advantage that Smith could not communicate with them while in touch with the FBI: he had no choice but to stick to his guns. Meanwhile, it was important to keep Pendergast alive and healthy for the next seven days, in case the FBI demanded proof of life before releasing Arsenault.

As Filipov stood there, in morning light, with the sound of the wind sighing through the spruce branches over the boat, mingling with the regular cadence of the sea brushing the rocks, he decided there was no reason to tell the man below anything about what they were doing, what was going on. He would be dead in a week either way.

Filipov had one final annoyance. Two of the crew, DeJesus and Miller, had a special hatred of the FBI due to bad history. Neither one had truly gotten with the program. In the meeting, both had argued for tossing the FBI agent into the sea right away. They had voted against the plan of exchange and had gone off angry. That night, Filipov had caught both of them down in the hold, shitfaced, pissing on Pendergast to much raucous laughter, after having roughed him up pretty bad. Filipov had been annoyed, but there wasn't much he could do to punish them, beyond locking up the liquor. Fact was, he had to admit part of him was glad to see the arrogant bastard get taken down a notch. And quite a notch it was: they had left him unconscious. The captain needed to keep the peace, keep everyone together, for seven more days.

Filipov had been disturbed at the breakdown in discipline. But something else had troubled him even more: the look in the FBI agent's eyes as those two drunken idiots, cursing and laughing, had been draining their hosepipes all over him, just before DeJesus clocked him with a mooring hook. What Filipov had seen in those eyes was damned frightening.

20

SPECIAL AGENT IN Charge Rudy Spann ran a hand through his whiffle cut and stared at the evidence bag on his desk, inside of which gleamed a worn gold ring and a bizarre, partly melted medallion, along with a letter and envelope. He had mixed feelings about this case that had suddenly, and with such big noise, arrived on the doorstep of the New York Field Office of the FBI. An agent had been kidnapped. It wasn't just any agent, either, but A. X. L. Pendergast. Spann, who had only recently become SAC of the New York FO, did not know Pendergast well. But he had certainly heard the rumors. This Pendergast had a kind of special dispensation; he was a sort of agent-at-large, who picked and chose his own cases. Apparently he was enormously wealthy, accepting only a one-dollar annual stipend— a far cry from the salary normally earned by a GS-15, Step 10. Rumor had it that Pendergast was a maverick, even something of a rogue agent, who pushed the rules and was protected from above. Frankly, he was not well liked among the younger agents; they resented his freedom, his wealth, his elitist mannerisms. The old-timers in the office, on the other hand, held him in a kind of awe: a wary sort of respect. But nobody loved him; he was not a warm personality, he wasn't the kind to go out after work for a beer or hang out at the shooting range on weekends. For those reasons Spann had little to do with him directly, beyond providing the basic support of the field office. The agent rarely showed up at Federal Plaza.

But he was a federal agent. And if there was one thing that was absolute in the FBI, it was the loyalty and camaraderie that bound them together. If an agent was killed or under threat, the Bureau would move heaven and earth to get the perps.

For this reason, the kidnapping of Pendergast had caused an immediate furor; and it was Spann's case to win—or lose.

He glanced at his cell phone, lying on the table. The initial contact with the kidnappers would be in a few minutes, and he was determined to handle it with vigor. This was the kind of case that could make his career. Spann was apprehensive, but also stoked: he knew he was a damn good agent, he'd graduated at the top of his class at Quantico, and his career since had been stellar. At forty, he was one of the youngest SACs in the FBI, in the most important field office in the country. This was the sort of opportunity that came knocking only once. If he cleared this one—and he believed he could—the sky would be the limit.

Since the package had arrived that morning, he had exploded into action, dropping everything; he'd put together a small but powerful strike force, who would be arriving in minutes. He'd kept it small, elite, and nimble. An "agent down" was priority one. Whatever was needed—warrants, lab work, forensics, analysis, IT—would be done instantly, taking priority over every other case. He had already put out the word to all their labs, to ensure everyone was ready at a moment's notice.

His secretary announced the arrival of the strike force. He rose and went into the outer office, carrying the evidence bag. They all appeared at once: three men and one woman, all top-class agents, filing in the door, silent, grim. They took their places in the small seating area. Spann nodded to everyone and signaled his secretary for coffee; he strode to the end of the room and placed the evidence bag on the display table, below a whiteboard.

Just as he was about to begin speaking, the door opened again. Everyone stared in silent surprise. Spann did not know the new arrival personally, but the man was a legend in the FBI: Howard Longstreet, who bore the rather mysterious title of executive associate director for intelligence. The Directorate of Intelligence, which Longstreet oversaw, was rather far from Spann's own; although senior to Spann, he had no official supervisory role. Which was all well and good.

Longstreet cut a figure almost as eccentric as Agent Pendergast's, but in a different way: his hair was long and gray, his suits rumpled, his profile aquiline. His black eyes gleamed from underneath a deep, craggy brow. His voice was like a growl, and he was freakishly tall: six feet, seven inches. Perhaps as if to make up for it, or from a lifetime of ducking through doorways, he was bent ten degrees from the vertical, a posture very different from the ramrod military bearing common to the Bureau. Longstreet had a mellow, self-deprecating way of working that made him very popular with his subordinates. And, of course, there were the whispered rumors about his time in the legendary—some said mythical—Ghost Company. That, Spann suddenly realized, must be why he was there: the ring in the evidence bag indicated that Pendergast had been a member of the same unit.

Spann hesitated. "Director Longstreet, this is a surprise."

Longstreet turned his cliff-like face to him. He nodded toward an empty seat. "Do you mind if I join you?"

"Not at all."

Longstreet took a seat in the back, behind the others.

His sudden presence threw Spann off balance, but he recovered quickly. "Thank you all for coming," he said. "The ring and medallion are confirmed to be genuine. SA Pendergast's latents are on them: deliberately pressed there, it seems, to leave us no doubt that the unsubs have him. Exhaustive tests on the four items—ring, medallion, letter, envelope—have turned up no latents besides his. No DNA, fiber, hair—nothing."

He started the PowerPoint presentation with the press of a button. An envelope appeared on the screen. "This was postmarked at the General Post Office, 10001, at three PM yesterday. It was dropped in a post box around the corner and arrived this morning. Since today is Tuesday, it could have been dropped in the mailbox anytime Sunday or Monday up to three PM, as the first collection of the week in that box is at that time. The letter itself is dated Monday, but that means very little. There are no cameras on the mailbox itself, but plenty along the avenues and streets leading to it; all those are being reviewed."

He pressed on to the next image: a long windswept beach.

"This was where Agent Pendergast was last seen, at dawn, sixteen days ago. He was on extended leave, working a private case. I won't go into the details of that case because they almost certainly aren't relevant. He struggled on the beach with a deranged killer, and both were swept into the sea and disappeared. An exhaustive search turned up nothing. The water was fifty-five degrees, in which a man can live for about an hour. We believed he was dead until we received this package. So he was either picked up by a ship or washed up on a beach somewhere. In either case, those who discovered him—once they discovered his identity—have decided to use the agent as bait in a prisoner exchange. We're doing an exhaustive analysis of any ships that might have been in the area at the time, as well as of the tidal currents."

Another press of the button and a scanned copy of the letter appeared.

"The letter was typed on a computer with a fixed-pitch font and then photocopied multiple times to blur any telltale characteristics. Here it is."

To SAC Spann:

1. We have in our control SA Pendergast.

2. The enclosed objects removed from his person are proof.

3. We propose a trade: the FBI have a man named Arsenault in custody; you release him, we release Pendergast.

4. We assume you will require proof that Pendergast is alive. We will provide that proof through an email communication—see item 5.

5. We have set up a secure email address for communication. The email you receive will contain in the subject line the following random sequence, as proof it is from us: Lv5C#C&49!8u

6. You will release Arsenault from Sing Sing, where he is currently incarcerated, provide him with a passport and travel funds, and put him on a plane to Caracas, Venezuela.

7. We must hear from Arsenault by noon on the seventh day from the date of this letter. By that time, Arsenault must Skype us from Plaza Bolivar, Caracas, standing in front of the Bolivar statue, to confirm that he has been released and is a free man.

8. After that Skype call comes in, we will release Pendergast.

    9. If the Skype call does not come in, or if Arsenault
indicates he has been coerced, tortured, or abused in
any way—<u>Pendergast dies</u>.

    10. Any deviation from this nine-point letter will re-
sult in Pendergast's immediate death. The 7-day deadline
is absolute and non-negotiable.

"And here is the email we received today." Spann pressed a key and another slide came up: the photo of a man—Pendergast—looking shockingly emaciated but clearly alive, lying on a dirty piece of canvas. Next to him, unfolded, was a copy of *USA Today*, carrying yesterday's date. "We're throwing all our best IT resources into tracking that email address, but it looks like the setup is double-encrypted and probably untraceable."

Spann now went through the plan he had worked out for negotiating with the hostage takers. It was classic, based on the Bureau's—and his own—long experience with abduction and kidnapping situations. Don't agree; lowball the first offer; keep the perps continuously engaged; buy time with small requests. Wear them out, slowly remove their control—all the while tasking all the best agents with tracking them down.

He went through all this with the group, putting one agent in charge of each aspect of the investigation. He reserved the actual negotiations for himself.

"And in the end," he said, "we have a fallback: if this strategy doesn't work, we give in to their demands. We release Arsenault. And we get Pendergast back."

He paused and looked around, waiting for comments.

"Of course you know they're going to kill Pendergast regardless," said Longstreet in a low voice.

"Killing a federal agent would bring the death penalty down on them," Spann said. "Once their man is released, why take such an extreme step?"

"Because Pendergast would be the witness who would put them away for life."

A silence. Spann wondered how to respond. "Mr. Longstreet, these men are clearly not stupid."

At this, Longstreet unfolded himself from his chair in a sort of easygoing way, then strolled to the front of the room. "I'm sorry to be blunt, Agent Spann, but I believe this plan of yours will pretty much guarantee Pendergast's death."

Spann stared at Longstreet. "I respectfully disagree. This is classic, exhaustively researched and tested SOP."

"Which is *exactly* why it will fail." Longstreet turned easily toward the group. "Pendergast is on a boat. Drug smugglers, almost certainly. He got pulled from the water; they eventually realized who he was; and they cooked up this scheme. It is a *very* stupid scheme and these are *very* stupid people—although they clearly believe they are being very clever. That is why Pendergast is in such extreme danger. If they were smart, as you believe, your plan might work. But they are not. Whatever we do, they are going to dump the body and run."

"Drug smugglers?" Spann asked. How the hell did he know this?

"Arsenault is a drug smuggler. It stands to reason these are his colleagues. They're desperate to free him before he sings."

Longstreet was now strolling along, back and forth. "So what do we do?" He held up a spidery finger. "A: We stage a panic. We give in to all their demands immediately. We appear to do anything necessary to save our precious agent. We keep them engaged—as long as we're talking to them, Pendergast won't die." He held up a second finger. "B: We lean on Arsenault, *hammer* and *tongs*—but very quietly. Maybe he'll ID them. C: They're hiding in a boat somewhere, so we scour the Atlantic seaboard. D, and this is most important: We smoke them out. How? By bringing Arsenault down from Sing Sing to New York. I might add that this entire operation needs to be kept absolutely secret: not only from the press, but also from the NYPD and even compartmentalized within the FBI, limited to this team and a few of the top brass."

SAC Spann stood there, looking first at Longstreet and then at his strike force. They had focused their entire attention on Longstreet. Without anyone realizing it, just like that, Longstreet had taken over. Spann felt the slow burn of humiliation and anger.

21

In the subterranean vastness beneath 891 Riverside Drive, Constance Greene sat before a worktable in her small library, brow furrowed, violet eyes focused. All her attention was directed at what sat upon the worktable: an ancient Japanese vase with a simple ideogram baked into its glaze. Three sprigs from a miniature quince tree were tucked within, the flower buds shivering ever so slightly as she worked.

Over the last forty-eight hours—concerned about her own mental state—Constance had retreated into the spiritual and cerebral exercises that, she knew, would help maintain her emotional equanimity: that, and cultivating a perfect indifference to the outside world, a capacity that was at once both her pride and her defense. She had begun rising at four to meditate, contemplating the transcendental knot in a cord of gray silk that had been a gift from Tsering, an English-speaking monk of the Gsalrig Chongg monastery, where she had been taught the subtle intricacies of the Tibetan spiritual practice known as Chongg Ran. Through much training, she was able to attain *stong pa nyid*—the State of Pure Emptiness—within minutes, and she had maintained this trance-like meditative state for an hour each morning.

This, she'd been relieved to find, had helped calm her restlessness. She no longer felt drowsy in the afternoon, nor had she woken, abruptly, in the middle of the night.

It had helped in other ways as well.

Her unseen companion, suitor, whatever—she did not know precisely what to call him—had not made his presence known in these last forty-eight hours. If it weren't for the reality of the gifts he had left, he might have been a figment of her morbid imagination. Her meals, too, had grown simpler. While still more exotic and elegantly plated than the practical dishes normally favored by Mrs. Trask—the last had been wild chanterelle and hen of the woods raviolini—they were no longer luxurious. And neither of the last two dinners had been accompanied by wine.

She tried to give her mysterious companion as little thought as possible.

Now, more adjusted to her peculiar situation and aware of a growing reconciliation to the death of her guardian, she had turned back to one of her favorite activities: ikebana, the Japanese art of flower arrangement. It appealed to her not only for its antiquity, but also for its beauty and subtlety. The year before, in one of the alcoves in Enoch Leng's cabinet of curiosities, she had installed a four-hundred-watt phosphor grow light and, beneath it, had been cultivating a wooden rack of miniature trees: orange, apricot, and persimmon. She preferred the *shōka* style, employing as it did only three branches of a plant in each arrangement, symbolizing sky, earth, and being: a Buddhist philosophy that, she felt, dovetailed with the discipline of Chongg Ran.

She preferred to work with the branches of fruit trees, not only because of their beauty and impermanence, but also because their delicacy and unusual forms made them more difficult to master. She worked patiently, with exquisite care, keeping in mind the fragile nature of the blossoms. If she was happy with the final design, she would place it in the woodcut room, perhaps in an empty niche that sat opposite the t'angka of her son…

Suddenly she paused. Somewhere, echoing from the labyrinth of stone chambers outside her private set of rooms, came the evanescent sound of harpsichord music.

She sat up in her chair. This was no dream-music she was waking from: this music was playing in the here and now—within the sub-basement, very likely coming from the old music room.

She sat listening, her fragile equanimity suddenly in turmoil, beset by a surge of emotion. The music was lyrical, heartbreaking, played with ethereal sensitivity. Constance found it astonishingly beautiful.

Leaving her arrangement unfinished, Constance pulled off her white silk gloves and rose, stiletto in one hand, flashlight in the other. She kicked off her shoes to maintain silence in the stone corridors. Swiftly making her way to the central passage, she paused at the door, listening intently. There was no sense of another presence in the sub-basement, no scent or movement of air that was unfamiliar: only the distant, echoing music. It was not Aloysius—he could not play the harpsichord. And in any case her brief hope that he was still alive, she realized, had been only a foolish dream.

She felt no real fear. This unknown person, she now felt certain, was indeed wooing her—in his own eccentric way.

She turned to the right, toward the music room, again moving as swiftly as she dared to maintain silence. As she swept on, allowing the torch to lick only briefly over the brickwork ahead of her, the music grew in volume. She passed beneath half a dozen arches and through as many large rooms, each containing a specific collection of Enoch Leng's, until she made an abrupt left and stopped before two medieval tapestries depending from a stone lintel. The music room was just beyond.

The music stopped.

Throwing caution to the wind, she swept aside the tapestries and pointed her flashlight into the dark room, flashing the beam about, the hand holding the stiletto ready to stab at a moment's notice.

There was nobody. The room was empty. The crimson-colored harpsichord sitting in the middle of the room stood silent and alone.

She rushed over to it, wildly flashing the beam around, probing every dark corner and doorway. But the player had vanished. She placed her hand on the stool cushion; it was still warm.

"Who's there?" she called out. "Who was playing?"

Her voice echoed away into silence. She leaned on the instrument, her heart beating hard. The harpsichord was one of the finest instruments in the collection, once owned by Hungarian Countess Elizabeth Báthory, the sociopathic serial murderer who—according to legend—had bathed in the blood of virgins as a means to retain her youth. What stain or varnish had given the instrument its crimson hue had never been satisfactorily explained—although Constance had her own theories.

She sank down on the seat, still shining the light into the darkness. "Whoever is there, I beg you, reveal yourself."

No response. She waited, her fingers straying over the keys. The musical collection was the most curious of Enoch Leng's cabinets of curiosities. Leng was not interested in music for itself. Every item in this collection was here for a reason beyond the ability to produce sound: its association with violence and murder. The Stradivari violin held in a glass case on the far wall, for example, had been owned by Gabriel Antonioni, the infamous killer of 1790s Siena, who cut his victims' throats and then serenaded them as they died. Beside it was framed the silver trumpet, scarred and dented, that had been used to marshal Richard III's troops at the Battle of Bosworth Field—a grisly affair indeed.

Her eyes strayed to the harpsichord's music holder. Handwritten sheet music by an unidentified composer lay open on the rack. Curious, she placed the stiletto on the raised fallboard, within easy reach, touched the keys, and played a light arpeggio.

To the best of her knowledge, this instrument hadn't been played or serviced in many years. And yet, as her fingers glided over the keys, she found it was in perfect tune.

She turned her attention back to the music. It appeared to be a transcription of a piano concerto, adapted for solo harpsichord. At the top of the first page was a dedication, in what looked like the same hand that had notated the book of love poems: TO CONSTANCE GREENE. Only now did she realize that the handwriting looked faintly familiar.

Almost despite herself, she began to play. It took only a few measures to be certain: this was the same piece that she had woken to; the music that had disturbed her dreams; the music that had wafted so recently through the sub-basement halls. It was achingly beautiful without sentimentality. Its wistful, haunted strains reminded her of the long-forgotten piano concertos by the likes of Ignaz Brüll, Adolf von Henselt, Friedrich Kiel, and other obscure composers of the Romantic era.

Reaching the first-movement cadenza, she stopped. And then—as the sounds of the strings died away—she heard a voice echo from the antique shadows. It said one word—one word only.

"Constance."

22

CONSTANCE RECOGNIZED THE voice instantly. Snatching up the stiletto, she leapt up from the harpsichord stool, knocking it backward. Where had the voice come from? Feelings of humiliation, outrage, and violation mingled with surprise and homicidal anger.

He survived, she thought as she stood in the center of the room, torch darting from corner to corner, searching for his whereabouts. *Somehow, some way, he survived.*

"Show yourself," she hissed in a low voice.

Silence reigned. She stood there, trembling. So it *was* he who had so artfully contrived this tableau. And to think she had allowed herself to enjoy it. To think she had admired an orchid *he* had discovered—brought by him into her own most private of chambers. To think she had eaten, enjoyed, food prepared by *him*. A shudder of revulsion passed through limbs already quivering with rage. He'd been spying on her, stalking her. Watching her sleep.

The flashlight beam revealed the room to be empty—but there were several doors and numerous hanging tapestries. He was there. Laughing silently at her consternation.

If he wanted to play a game, she would give him one. She switched off the torch, plunging the sub-basement into darkness. He was, it seemed, familiar with these spaces, but he couldn't possibly know them as well as her.

In the dark, she would have the advantage.

She waited, gripping the stiletto, waited for him to speak again, to make a move, betray his location. The shame and horror of how she'd been toyed with continued to wash over her: those decadent meals he'd left, accompanied by wine... The poem with the feather of an extinct bird... His own little translation in the margin of the book... The new species of orchid, named after her... Not to mention that he had discovered the identity and location of her son—and then had a t'angka painting of him made for her.

My son... Anxiety lanced through her fury. What, exactly, was Diogenes doing—or worse, what might he already *have* done—with her son?

She would kill him. She'd failed once; she would not fail again. The basement collections were full of weapons and poisons, if it came to that. She might have the opportunity to better arm herself. But for now, the stiletto was exceedingly sharp and—if well handled—would be more than sufficient.

"Constance," the voice came again out of the darkness.

It echoed strangely, distorted by passageways of stone and muffled by tapestries. The very sound of it was gall and wormwood to her; it caused an inner fury that was as physical as it was emotional.

She dashed forward, in the blackness, toward the uncertain source of the sound, plunging her blade into one hanging tapestry, then another, stabbing and slashing. Again and again the blade was deflected by stone, depriving her of the satisfaction of feeling it sink into tissue. She continued around the dark room, knocking over instruments and stumbling over display cases, the only sound the ripping and tearing of her knife through the woven tapestries that, she was sure, concealed the hiding figure of Diogenes.

At last, the heat of her fury abated. She was acting like a madwoman; she was reacting exactly as Diogenes expected. She returned to the center of the room, breathing quietly. The room, like many in the sub-basement, had been built with stone air shafts to withdraw the unhealthy vapors from the subterranean space and disperse them into the upper air. He was using those stone shafts to confuse her. He could be anywhere.

"*Fils a putain!*" she said to the darkness. "*Del glouton souduiant!*"

"Constance." The voice came again from everywhere and nowhere. This time it had a mournful, but gentle, tone.

"I would tell you how much I hate you," she said, in a low voice, "except that one does not hate the dung beneath one's feet. One merely scrapes it off. I thought I had scraped you off. What a shame you survived. I do, however, take a certain consolation in the fact that you did not burn to death at Stromboli."

"How so?" came the voice.

"Now you can die a second death by my hand—and this time I can *watch you die in even greater agony.*"

As she had spoken, her voice rose in both pitch and volume. But now the red mist fell away, to be replaced by an icy calm. She would not give him the pleasure of hearing her betray any more hatred. He was unworthy of any expenditure of effort—save for the thrust of a blade. She would aim for the eyes, she decided; first one, then the other. *Out, vile jelly!* And then she would take her time. But first, she needed to wait for the moment to strike.

"What do you think of my composition?" Diogenes asked. "You played it beautifully, by the way. I hope I managed to catch some of the contrapuntal fire of Alkan, in one of his more conservative moods."

"It is unwise of you to bring up Alkan," Constance replied. "It will only make your end more painful."

There was a pause. And then: "You are right. That remark must have seemed—no, it *was*—insensitive. That was not my intention. That was my old self speaking. You have my apology."

On one level, Constance could not believe—simply could not comprehend—that she was speaking, *conversing*, with the man who had lied to her, seduced her for his own perverse ends, and then discarded her with such triumphant scorn and contempt. What was he doing here—and why? No doubt to humiliate her further.

Diogenes said nothing. The silence lengthened. Still she bided her time. "So Aloysius was right," she said. "He warned me to expect a confrontation: and now it has come. *Assume nothing*—those were his words. So that was you, in the tunnels beneath Oldham? That was you he saw, standing on the Exmouth dunes, watching us?"

Silence.

"And now your revenge upon your family is complete. Congratulations. Aloysius is dead—thanks to that *thing* you released. You think you are here to toy with me again. You think you can seduce me a second time, with your poetry and effete aesthetics and all the rest of your intellectual *ordure*. And then, when the moment is ripe, you'll slip the knife in—*again*."

"No, Constance."

She went on, "Except, *connard*, it is I who will slip in the knife: an emasculating slash. I cannot wait to see the look on your face when I do. I saw it once before, you know: on that day when I pushed you over the lip of the volcano. It was the surprised look of a man losing his manhood."

As she spoke, she felt the fury begin to rise again. She willed herself to stop talking, to let the cold composure return so that, when the chance arose, she wouldn't miss.

At last, Diogenes spoke again.

"I'm sorry, Constance, but you're wrong. Wrong about my actions—and utterly wrong about my motivations."

Constance did not reply. She was calm once again. And the hand that grasped the stiletto was ready to dart forward and thrust home at the slightest indication of sound or movement. The years spent in the dark spaces of this sub-basement had sharpened her senses like a cat's—odd it was taking so long for her eyes to accustom themselves to the blackness. She had been too long in the light.

"Let me assure you of one thing. I do not seek revenge on my brother or anyone else. No longer. Now my aim is different. Your hatred changed me. Your singular pursuit changed me. The volcano changed me. I'm a different man, transformed—*reformed*. The reason I am here, Constance, is because *you* are here."

Constance said nothing. His voice seemed to be getting stronger, as if he were edging closer. *Just a few steps more...a few steps more...*

"I will be honest with you. You deserve nothing less—and besides, your high intelligence would see through any deception. By the time I'm done, you *will* know I am telling the truth: I promise you that."

A brief pause.

"True: there was a time when I desperately wanted to see my brother suffer, as I had suffered as a child. Back then, I regarded you—forgive my bluntness—as merely a path to help destroy Aloysius. You see, Constance, *I didn't know you then.*"

In her stockinged feet, she took a slow step toward his voice. And another.

"I was horribly injured by the fall into La Sciara. During the months of recovery, I had a lot of time to think. I did harbor notions of revenge toward you. But then—and, Constance, it happened so suddenly it was like a veil being torn from a window—all of that changed. I recognized my anger for what it truly was: another emotion altogether. *My true feelings.*"

She maintained silence. Diogenes had used such words on her before. At the time, they'd had the effect he had desired. She had drunk them in like water thrown on a parched garden.

"Let me explain why I feel—for want of a better term—a reverence for you. First, you're the only person I've met who is my intellectual equal. And, perhaps, my emotional equal. Second: you bested me. I had to respect that. I made the mistake of toying with you, and you responded with the most astonishing vigor and singularity of purpose that I have ever seen in a human being. It *awed* me."

Another step forward.

"Reverence. And respect. There are few people on this earth that I respect, living or dead. You are one. And thanks to my ancestor Dr. Enoch Leng, you have led a long and rich life. His elixir kept you young for over a century. It was only with his death that you, like the rest of us, began to age normally. The upshot of this is that you sport more than six times my scholarship."

Diogenes laughed at this observation. But there was nothing snide or sarcastic in it: it was a light, self-effacing laugh.

"There is something else that I find most attractive about your long life span. You've *lived.* You are the one person whose thirst for knowledge, for revenge—and, if I may allude to something else as well, *passion*—has astonished me with its ferocity. Constance, I not only admire you, but I'm afraid of you. I realized this as I lay, recovering, in a small hut outside Ginostra, under the volcano, listening to the booming of Stromboli. It was humbling, because prior to that I feared nobody, man or woman. Now I do fear *one woman.*"

She slid another step forward in utter silence. She sensed he was there, mere feet from her. One more step and she could lunge...

"Which brings me to the other thing vital to understanding our connection: *you are the mother of my son.*"

In utter silence, she leapt forward and thrust the stiletto—into thin air.

"Ah, Constance. That saddens me. But I don't blame you."

Constance listened, motionless, in the dark. The voice had moved. Somehow he anticipated it. Or was he that close, after all? The echoes in the stone room, with its myriad doors and air shafts—combined with his low, soft voice—made it impossible to be sure.

"You see, Constance, I am convinced you are the one human being who, deep down, is capable of sharing my own peculiar view of life. Let's face it—we're misfits. We're misanthropes, cut from the same cloth."

It took Constance a moment to parse the meaning of what Diogenes had said. When she did, her grasp tightened on the stiletto.

"That is the crux of it," Diogenes went on. "I was blind; I didn't see. Now I do. We're alike in so very many ways. In others you are my superior. Is it any wonder, then, that my reverence for you has only grown?"

For a moment Constance thought that Diogenes would say more. But now the blackness around her became filled with silence—a silence that stretched on, and still on. Finally, she broke it herself.

"What have you done with Mrs. Trask?"

"Nothing. She remains in Albany, at the side of her sister—who is taking a little longer to recuperate than initially expected. Have no fear: it is not serious. And Mrs. Trask is easy in her mind, having received assurances that you are being well cared for here."

"Cared for? By Proctor, I suppose. I imagine you've murdered him."

"Proctor? He's not dead. He's rather preoccupied at the moment, though, on an unexpected trek across the Kalahari Desert."

The desert? Could he be telling the truth? Proctor would never leave the house defenseless while she was in residence. So much of what he was saying was shocking...and unbelievable.

"So then it's my son you're after."

"Constance," came the reproachful reply. "How can you say such a thing? It's true I did have...issues with my brother. But why would I wish to harm *our* child?"

"You're no father to him."

"Indeed I'm not. But that I hope will change. You saw the t'angka painting I had made of him. I went to India, by the way, to assure myself our child was being well cared for. He is: and he's a most remarkable boy." A pause. "As one would expect of our offspring."

"Our offspring. You once used much cruder terms to describe our liaison."

There was a pause. "How painfully I recall my unforgivable behavior. As a token of my true feelings, please take a look at the compartment beneath that harpsichord stool."

Constance hesitated a moment. Then she resolutely snapped on her torch, glanced around. While his voice was seemingly so close, he was still nowhere to be seen.

"The stool, my dear."

She opened the seat top. Inside was a photograph attached to some papers. She plucked it out, examined it closely.

"That was taken five weeks ago," came the disembodied voice. "He seemed very happy."

As Constance stared at the picture, the hand holding the torch trembled ever so slightly. It was without doubt a picture of her son, in a long silken robe, holding the hand of Tsering. They were standing in an archway framed by cork trees. He was gazing into the middle distance with the perfect seriousness of a gifted three-year-old. Staring at the picture, Constance was suddenly filled with an overwhelming sense of loneliness and yearning.

She glanced at the attached sheet. It was a note from his guardians at the monastery, addressed to her, affirming that the boy was safe and well and that he was already showing great promise. It was fixed with a special seal—a seal, she knew, that proved Diogenes had actually been there, and that the letter was genuine. How Diogenes had contrived such a visit with those most secretive and protective monks, Constance could not begin to imagine.

She placed the photo and letter on the harpsichord and switched off the torch, letting the darkness return. She could not allow this disgusting man to work on her feelings. "You were there," she said. "In Exmouth. You were spying on us."

"Yes," Diogenes replied. "It is true. I was there, along with Flavia, my—for want of a better term—assistant. You no doubt saw her: the young waitress in the Captain Hull restaurant who also worked part-time in the tea and curio store, A Taste of Exmouth."

"That girl? Flavia? Working for you?"

"I must admit to having a bit of a problem with her. She's a little too keen in performing her duties."

"I can only imagine those duties," said Constance.

When there was no response, she continued. "You released Morax. You set that cycle of violence into motion."

"You are correct. I did help that poor, abused creature escape his tormentors. I had no idea he would react the way he did. All I wanted was to sow a little confusion. Distract my brother. And thus allow myself...to get a closer glimpse of *you*."

Constance shook her head. She was beginning to lose her self-possession. She tried once again to marshal her anger. "Distract your brother? You *killed* your brother."

"No," came the voice, sorrowful once again. "There you are wrong. It does seem my brother is dead. But that was *never* my intention. I know a little of the feelings you two have, or had, for each other: forgive me, but I was quite relishing the competition. I'm sorry, it's crude of me to say so—it's a brotherly thing, you know."

"You..." Constance stopped. Another silence ensued. All her accusations, all her suspicions, all her objections, seemed to have been deflated, and with this deflation rose confusion.

"So... Why are you here? *Why?*" she stammered at last.

"Can it be that you still don't understand?" came the voice out of the velvety darkness. "My purpose in being here is quite simple. *I am in love with you, Constance.*"

23

At Goderre's Downeaster in Cutler, Maine, Dwayne Smith sat on the bed, eyeing the four burner phones arranged on the coverlet. Even with the window open and the heat turned down, he was sweating and anxious. Dalca had made contact with the FBI via email. The reaction had been surprising and gratifying. It was just as Filipov had predicted: the FBI seemed to be acceding to their demands, with only token threats and resistance. They would do just about anything to keep their man alive. This special agent was, clearly, a high-value asset.

Filipov had said the FBI would insist on talking to someone. They had. And that someone was Smith. It had all been arranged: he was to call this man named Longstreet at the New York FBI headquarters in five minutes on one of the burner phones. The thing that made him most nervous was the timing. The FBI, Filipov had explained, could triangulate a call in as little as thirty seconds. So he had twenty seconds to conduct this conversation. And then he had to hang up, disable and destroy the phone. Four phones: four twenty-second conversations.

Using his watch, he readied the timer for twenty seconds. As soon as its alarm went off, he'd pull the battery from the back of the burner phone, terminating the call. He picked up one of the burners—one was as good as another—and removed the battery cover. He opened his penknife and laid it on the coverlet, ready to jerk the battery out. Even a few seconds' delay in killing the phone might be fatal.

The appointed time had arrived. He dialed, at the same time starting the timer.

The call was answered immediately. "Longstreet," came the terse voice, and before Smith could even respond, the man went into his script. "We're going to do everything you want. But it's going to take us a couple of days to process and transfer Arsenault from Sing Sing to the Metropolitan Correctional Center, so we can get him to JFK airport for the flight to Caracas."

The Metropolitan Correctional Center. Ten fucking seconds left. "When are you moving him?"

"None of your business."

"Well it *is* my fucking business. You demanded that we talk. Now I have a demand of my own. Exactly *when* are you moving him? I want details or we kill Pendergast now."

A pause. Five seconds left.

"Tomorrow at—" a pause— "three thirty PM, the transport van from Sing Sing will be pulling into MCC, Cardinal Hayes entrance."

"Put Arsenault in the right-hand window."

"In return I want—"

The alarm went off. Smith shut off the phone, wedged the knife in, flipped out the battery. Then, working methodically, he opened the SIM card case, pulled out the card, and held it over an ashtray while he used a lighter to melt it into a small puddle of plastic and metal contacts. The room had a charming brick fireplace, where, later that evening, he would burn the phone as well, just to be safe.

He felt elated. This guy Longstreet had caved—and fast. Filipov was right: they really had the FBI by the balls. Amazing how easy it was, when you had one of their top guys. If it was some other schmuck, they wouldn't be playing so nice. And now, with the transfer to Manhattan, Dalca would be able to confirm with his own eyes if the FBI was just jerking their chain or serious about doing the deal.

24

THE SOFT ECHOES of this declaration by Diogenes slowly faded away, leaving the room in silence.

Constance was momentarily stunned. It had seemed sincere: a genuine confession of love. But she quickly shook off that impression. Diogenes had already humiliated her with his extraordinary capacity to lie, and this was merely a reprise.

Even as this thought went through her mind, she wondered: why would he even think he could succeed at such a charade again? Besides, Diogenes was incapable of love.

...I not only admire you, but I'm afraid of you.

...We're alike in so very many ways. In others you are my superior. Is it any wonder, then, that my reverence for you has only grown?

"If what you say is true," she said coldly, "then have the courage of that sentiment. Show yourself."

This was greeted by a moment of stillness. Then Constance heard the scritch of a match from behind. She whirled around. And there he was: standing in the tapestried entrance to the music collection, leaning, arms crossed, beside a newly lighted wall sconce holding a burning taper. He looked almost the same—the thin features, so like his brother and yet so different; the modeled chin, the well-formed pale lips, closely trimmed russet beard; and the strange, bicolored eyes, one green, the other cloudy whitish blue. The only difference was an ugly scar that now marred the otherwise chiseled perfection of his left cheek, traveling from hairline to jaw. An orchid boutonnière was tucked casually into a lapel of his jacket: she recognized it as *Cattleya constanciana*, the white-and-pink flower that had been named after her.

Constance stared, struck dumb by the abrupt appearance of this spectral figure out of her past. And then, quite suddenly, she leapt at him, swift as a bat, stiletto in one raised hand, aiming for his eyes.

But Diogenes had been expecting this. With a deft move, he ducked away from the blow; as her blade arm flashed past he grasped it in a grip of steel; then spun her toward him, pinning her other arm to her side, holding her in a tight embrace. The stiletto clattered to the floor.

She had forgotten how quick and strong he was.

She turned her face away from his, struggling furiously, fruitlessly.

"I'll release you," he said in a calm, steady voice, "if you'll hear me out. That's all I ask—that you hear me out. And then, if you still wish to kill me, so be it."

There was a moment of stasis. At last—mastering her anger—she nodded.

Letting go of one hand, Diogenes knelt to retrieve the stiletto. Constance thought briefly of kicking him in the face, but realized it would be hopeless: physically, she was overmastered.

She might as well let him speak.

Diogenes rose again. He released her other arm and stepped back.

She waited, flushed and breathing hard. He stood still now, in the light of the sconce, as if awaiting her reaction.

"You say you love me," she said after a moment. "How absurd for you to think I could possibly believe that."

"It's true," he said. "And I think you already know it—even if you can't admit it to yourself."

"And do you really think, after what you've done, that I'd reciprocate?"

Diogenes spread his hands. "Those in love are full of irrational hope."

"You mention the feelings I had for your brother. Why, then, should I have any interest in his inferior sibling—especially after the way you abused my innocence?"

This was said scornfully, sarcastically, with intent to wound. But Diogenes answered the question in the same mild, reasonable tones he had employed all along.

"I have no excuse. As I've said, my treatment of you was unforgivable."

"Then why seek forgiveness?"

"I don't seek your forgiveness. I seek your love. I was a different person then. And I paid for my sins—at your hands." He motioned, briefly, toward the scar on his cheek. "As for my being inferior to Aloysius, I can say only this: you and he would never have been happy together. Don't you realize that? He'd never love anyone after Helen."

"While you, on the other hand, would be an ideal partner."

"For you—*yes*."

"Thank you, but I have no interest in a union with a psychotic, misanthropic, imperfectly socialized killer."

At this, the faintest of smiles crossed his face. "We're both killers, Constance. As for being a misanthrope—is there not a similarity there, as well? And are not both of us *imperfectly socialized*? Perhaps it would be best if I simply described the future I envision for us. Then you can make your own judgment."

Constance started to make another cutting remark, but stifled it, feeling her responses were beginning to sound shrill.

"You're a creature of another era," Diogenes said.

"A *freak*, as you once called me."

Diogenes smiled wistfully, waved a hand as if to concede the point. "The simple fact is: you don't belong in the here and now. Oh, you've made valiant efforts to integrate yourself into the twenty-first century, into today's quotidian, vapid society—I know, because I've observed some of those efforts at a distance. But it hasn't been easy, has it? And at some level, you must have begun to wonder if such an effort is even worth it." He paused. "I don't belong in this time, either: for a very different reason. You couldn't help what happened to you— Enoch Leng intervened in your life, murdered your sister, took you under his . . . *care*. Just as you said, I, too, am imperfectly socialized. We are two peas in a pod."

At this trite observation, Constance frowned.

As he'd been speaking, Diogenes had been toying with the stiletto. Now he placed it on the harpsichord, took a step forward. "I own an island, Constance—a private island in the Florida Keys. It's west of No Name Key and northeast of Key West. It's not a big island, but it's a jewel. It is called Halcyon. I have a house there; a breezy mansion furnished with books and instruments and paintings; it offers both sunrise and sunset views; and it has been stocked with all the rare wines, champagnes, and delicacies you could ever wish for. I've been preparing this idyll over the years with painstaking, excessive care. It was to be a bastion; my last and final retreat from the world. But—as I was recovering in that hut in Ginostra—I realized that such a place, no matter how ideal, would be unbearably lonely without another per- son—the one, the *perfect* person—with whom to share it." He paused. "Need I name that person?"

Constance tried to formulate a reply, but found the words wouldn't come. She could smell his faint cologne. The unique and mysterious scent brought back a memory of that single night . . .

He took another step forward. "Halcyon would be our escape from a world that has no need for or interest in us. We could live out the forty or fifty years allotted to us, together, in mutual discovery, pleasure... and intellectual pursuits. There are certain problems of theoretical mathematics I should like to tackle, problems that have defied solution for centuries—such as the Riemann Hypothesis and the distribution of prime numbers. And I've always wanted to decipher the Phaistos Disc or work out a full translation of all the Etruscan inscriptions. These are of course massively difficult puzzles that would take decades to solve—if they can be solved at all. For me, Constance, it's the journey, not the destination. It's a journey we will make together. That we are *meant* to make together."

He fell silent. Constance said nothing. This was all too much, too quickly: the protestation of love; the vision of an intellectual utopia; the allure of a sanctuary from the world... despite herself, some of what he had said struck deep.

"And you, Constance, will have all the time in the world to undertake your own odyssey of the mind. Think of the projects *you* could complete. You might take up writing or painting. Or study a new instrument. I have a lovely Guarneri violin that would be yours to play. Think about it, Constance: we could live in absolute freedom from this dull and corrupt world, indulging our dearest pursuits and desires."

He stopped. In the silence, her mind raced.

Much of what he'd said about her was true. After he had so cruelly mistreated her, Constance had ceased to think of Diogenes as a person. He had been merely a focus of hatred, a monochromatic being whose only interest to her was in his death. What did she know about his history—his childhood? Very little. Aloysius had implied he'd been a curious, highly intelligent, withdrawn boy: a budding Captain Nemo, with his private library and arcane interests. Aloysius had also made very veiled references to a certain event: an event he refused to explain, but one that he felt tragically responsible for.

It was all too overwhelming…

Diogenes cleared his throat quietly, intruding on her thoughts. "There's something else that I must bring up. It will be painful; it will be personal—but it is of the greatest importance to your future." He paused again. "I know about your history. I know that my ancestor Enoch Leng devised an arcanum, a drug, that extended his life span. He tested that drug on you, and it proved successful. He became your first guardian. And as you know, Leng's arcanum required the murder of human beings and the harvesting of their cauda equina—the bundle of nerves at the base of the spine. Many years later, science and chemistry advanced to the point where Leng developed a second arcanum. This one was wholly synthetic. It no longer required the taking of human life to concoct."

He paused, taking another step forward. Constance remained rigid, listening.

"Here is what I must tell you: that second arcanum, the one he gave you for decades, was *imperfectly formulated.*"

Constance raised a hand to her mouth. Her lips moved, but no sound came.

"It worked for a time. You're living proof of that. But my research indicates that after a certain number of years, especially if one stops taking it—as you have—it would backfire. The person would start to age—*rapidly.*"

"Ridiculous," said Constance, finding her voice. "I haven't taken the arcanum since Enoch Leng's death five years ago. Naturally, I've aged—but only by those same five years."

"Constance, please don't delude yourself. You must have begun to notice the effects of accelerated aging. Especially…the *mental* effects."

"A lie," Constance said. But even as she spoke, she thought back to the changes she'd noticed in herself, minor problems that went back at least to her trip to Exmouth, if not before. Her insomnia; the occasional lassitude; a diminishment of her hyperacute senses. But more than that, she had become aware of a growing sense of distraction and restlessness that she seemed unable to shake. Much of this she'd blamed on the distress of losing Pendergast. And yet, if Diogenes was right: how terrible it would be to sit quietly in the empty mansion, feeling one's mind slipping away...

But no; this was just another one of Diogenes's baroque lies.

Again, his quiet voice intruded on her thoughts. "Here's the heart of the matter. Through a great deal of time and effort I've managed to accomplish two things. First, I've worked out Leng's formula for the *original* arcanum. This is the formula my brother believed he had burned the only surviving copy of. He was wrong; there was one other. I found it. It took longer than I'd care to admit, as well as unique knowledge of this house—but *I did it*. I did it for you. And then I was able to synthesize, *perfectly* synthesize, that formula, so its manufacture would not require ongoing human victims. I give this to you, my dear."

A brief silence descended. Again her head spun: it was all too much—too much. She felt overwhelmed; she could hardly stand. She glanced around, looking distractedly for a place to sit down; remembered who was standing before her; and with a great effort focused her attention once again on him.

"Of course, to do this I needed laboratories, scientists—and *money*. But that work is done. I have the new, synthetic formula. You don't need to age prematurely. You don't need to feel your mind tiptoeing into oblivion. After a brief course of treatment with my arcanum, your physiology will have stabilized; you can live out the rest of your life with no premature deterioration. We will both grow old together— normally. All I want from you is one word: yes."

But Constance said nothing.

Looking at her, a new urgency came over Diogenes's expression—as if, having said all this, he was afraid that she would refuse. His voice rose. "What kind of life are you going to have in this huge house, without my brother? Even if you do emerge from this self-imposed isolation, what kind of company do you think Proctor and Mrs. Trask will prove to be, year in and year out? Will they help you during the lonely decline you're destined to suffer…through no fault of your own?"

He fell silent. If what he said *was* true, Constance could picture the result all too clearly: a wasteland of boredom and ennui, sitting in the darkened library, moving between books and the harpsichord, while the well-meaning Proctor stood guard at the door and Mrs. Trask served her overcooked pasta. It would be nothing less than standing guard at her own death watch. The thought of losing her mental faculties was almost more than she could bear.

"All those years," Diogenes said, as if reading her mind. "All those years you spent under the tutelage of my great-grand-uncle Leng—what a shame to see such a mighty intelligence, such deep learning, go gentle into that good night."

He waited, looking at her intently, as if willing her to speak. But she remained silent.

At last, he sighed. "I'm so sorry. Please know that I've risked a great deal for you already. I would never force a choice on you. Once the course of treatment is complete and you found you were not truly happy with me and Halcyon, I wouldn't stand in the way of your leaving. I believe, I *know*, a beautiful and happy life awaits us there. But if you can't see past my terrible misdeeds and your own hatreds, if you can't believe that a love like mine can transform a man…I'll have to accept that."

And then, he turned away from her.

As he spoke these last words, Constance experienced a curious epiphany—one that had been bubbling up during their talk. Diogenes had treated her abominably. She had hated him with a fury that was almost beyond human. But it was also true that...she almost shuddered at the forbidden nature of the thought...here was the Pendergast she *could* have—a Pendergast who, perhaps, was more a kindred spirit to her than his brother could ever be. *If* Diogenes had truly changed.

He was slipping on a pair of gloves. She glanced over at the harpsichord, to where he had set down the stiletto. The weapon was still there. It would be the work of a second to snatch it up, bury it between his shoulder blades. Surely, he knew this as well as she did.

"I..." she began, then faltered. How could she possibly express the thought? But she said it: "I need time."

Diogenes whirled toward her, hope blossoming on his face—an expression so earnest Constance realized, with a shock, that it was impossible to feign. "Of course," he said. "I'll leave you now. You must be very tired. Take all the time you need." And he reached for her hand.

Slowly, self-consciously, she extended it.

He grasped her hand in his; turned it over in a slow, caressing motion; and planted a kiss in her palm. Then—as he drew back—he took the tip of her finger between his lips for the merest fraction of a second. It was like an electric shock to her entire body.

Then, with a smile and a short bow, he was gone.

25

ON A BACK street of one of the shabbier business districts in Katutura, Namibia—a Windhoek suburb whose name translates as "the place where people don't want to live"—stood a three-story residential building, sandwiched between a radio station and a garment factory. The building was seedy and in disrepair, its stucco exterior cracked and peeling, its tiny, lopsided balconies heavy with rust. Each floor was painted a different color—turquoise, yellow, gray—which, along with the mismatched windows and slapdash architectural details, gave the structure a bizarre, disquieted appearance. It was two in the afternoon, and every window was open in the vain hope of a cooling breeze.

Lazrus Keronda sat by the window of a two-room, barely furnished second-floor apartment. He was tucked back from the window, positioned strategically so that he could see the goings-on in the noisy street below while remaining unobserved himself. The restaurant on the floor below specialized in mopane worm crisps, softened in a stew of tomatoes, fried onion, turmeric, and green chilies. The pungent smoke from the steaming worms, wafting up, made his eyes water. But he would not take his gaze from the window.

He reached for a bottle of Tafel Lager—holding it loosely so that his injured hand would not protest—and took a long pull. The fresh, bitter taste of the beer helped a little. Maybe he was being overcautious. Still, it wouldn't do to take chances. Another three days, maybe two, and then it would be safe to leave town. He had a stepbrother who lived in Johannesburg; he could hunker down there, with the brother and his family, for a couple of months. And with the cash he'd received, he had enough money to start a new venture. The dealership had been deep in debt, it wasn't like he was losing anything by—

There was a faint sound behind him—the creak of a single floorboard—and he wheeled around.

"You!" he said. The beer bottle dropped from his hand and rolled away, unheeded, dribbling amber foam.

"Me," came a soft voice. And then a young woman stepped out from the shadows. She was in her midtwenties, with light-blond hair, blue eyes, and prominent cheekbones. She was dressed in black leggings and a denim shirt with the tails knotted around her midriff, revealing a flat, muscled abdomen and a navel pierced with a diamond ring. Despite the heat, her hands were covered in latex gloves.

Keronda jumped to his feet. He was immediately aware of the extremity of his situation. A hundred excuses came to mind; a hundred lies, distractions, apologies, justifications. Instead, he blundered: "How did you find me?"

"It wasn't easy." A fanny pack was fastened around her hips, and as she took another step closer to him—the motion as smooth and lithe as a panther's—it rose a little, then fell.

Keronda's mouth had turned instantly dry. What was it about this woman—this girl with the ridiculous piercing—that aroused such fear in him? She couldn't have been taller than five foot three, while he weighed at least twice what she did. And yet he was panicked. It was something about the coldness of those blue eyes—that, and the sly, cruel smile. He'd noticed these things the first time they'd met—and the memory had stayed with him ever since.

"You left the dealership," she said.

"I had to," he said. "I *had* to!"

"You were paid to stay. Instead you left the gate ajar, the office unlocked—and a lot of blood on your worktable. Now the police are interested."

"He hurt me. He threatened me." He held up his injured hand beseechingly.

"You were well paid to let him hurt you, let him threaten you—and then stick to the script we gave you."

Keronda was babbling now, almost crying. "And I did. I stuck to it! I told him what you wanted. Exactly as you said. I gave him the Land Cruiser. I made sure he took it."

"Then why did you run like a scared rabbit?"

Again he held up the bandaged hand. "Look what he did to me!"

As her blue eyes wandered over the bloody dressing, her smile deepened. "Quite the stigmata. But that still doesn't explain why you deviated from the plan. The plan you were paid a lot of money to keep to *exactly*." She stopped, as if to let the lesson sink in. "What did we tell you? Clean up any mess. Get treatment. Stay on the job. Business as usual. But what did you do instead? Leave a mess and run."

"*Look what he did to me!*" Keronda repeated, both hands up now.

"What do you think *we're* going to do?" was the silky response.

When there was no answer but a whimper, the girl shook her head sadly. "We promised you he wouldn't be back for at least a week, maybe never. You should have listened."

"I—" he began, then stopped. With a movement that seemed casual, almost desultory, and yet was terrifying in its speed, the girl reached into her fanny pack and drew out a knife. It was like no knife

Keronda had seen before: a multi-barbed blade, like four curved arrowheads in series, with a narrow, neon-green handle.

Seeing his terrified gaze on the weapon, her smile widened further. "Like the knife?" she asked. "It's called a Zombie Killer. I like it, too—especially the barbs. It's like the dick of a tomcat—hurts more coming out than going in. So they say."

"Dick?" Keronda repeated uncomprehendingly.

"Never mind." Then—with an even swifter movement—her hand darted forward and plunged the knife between his ribs. The blade was so sharp he barely felt the thrust but, looking down, he saw that it was buried to the hilt.

"I'm pretty good at anatomy," she said. "Almost as good as I am with a blade." She nodded at the handle. "If I'm not mistaken, that's just severed your phrenic artery. Not one of the major arteries—but you're still going to bleed out in five minutes, give or take."

She paused, surveying her handiwork. "Of course, you could always pull out the blade, put pressure on the wound—good luck with that—and call for an ambulance. If you did that right away, like this instant, I'd give you a fifty–fifty chance of pulling through. But I don't think you will. As I said: hurts more coming out than going in."

Keronda's only response was to sink back into his chair.

The girl nodded. "I thought so. Another nice thing about the Zombie Killer—it's cheap. You can leave one behind without regrets." She zipped up the fanny pack, tugged fastidiously at her gloves. "No parting words? In that case: have a nice day." And with that she turned on her heel and strode out of the apartment, leaving the front door wide.

26

DIOGENES PENDERGAST WAITED in a small, straight-backed chair in the little room at the top of the steps spiraling down to the sub-basement of 891 Riverside Drive. The door to the staircase stood open. He had set a taper into a wall sconce, and it threw a flickering, friendly light over the old stonework. At least, he hoped it was friendly; he knew very little about such things.

He had been careful not to place his chair directly before the door-way. He did not want to appear Cerberus-like: a threatening figure guarding the downward portal. He had worked hard to make sure everything about himself had been as friendly and unthreatening as possible. He was dressed simply in black wool pants and a black-and-gray tweed jacket... or so they appeared to him. He did not like tweed—it was itchy and unrefined—but it radiated sincerity, homi-ness, and affability.

Or at least—once again—he hoped it did.

These fragments I have shored against my ruins...

With an effort, he pushed this voice—a voice of the old Diogenes, which now and then came bubbling up unexpectedly, like methane in a tar pit—back down from whence it came. That was then; this was now. He was a changed man, a reformed man—and yet the Old Voice still returned in moments of extreme agitation, as now...or when, for whatever reason, his blood was roused...

He tried to focus on the tweed.

He had prided himself on his sophistication and worldliness for too long, despising the opinion of others. The only time he ever considered how others might view him was when he was engaged in social engineering. Or when, out of boredom or irritation, he deceived, punked, or trolled others for his private amusement. He was finding it difficult to show Constance the sense of vulnerability and affection that he genuinely felt for her. He was like a man who, having taken a vow of silence for half his life, suddenly tried to lift up his voice in song.

He adjusted his position in the chair. He'd had to drag it out of storage from one of the basement vaults, and its ancient silk-and-velvet cushions had been heavy with dust. As the creak of the chair subsided, he listened once again, his senses ready to capture the faintest sound, the least variation in air pressure, that would indicate her approach up the staircase that corkscrewed down into the sub-basement.

He glanced at his watch: quarter past ten in the morning. He had said good-bye to Constance a few minutes before midnight. He had been sitting here, waiting, for her—and for her response—ever since.

The degree of planning and money and time necessary to bring last evening's meeting to fruition—a meeting in which he could bare his soul, without fear of interruption—had been tremendous. But it would all be worthwhile—if only she said yes.

At another time, in another life, he could have found amusement in how well he'd pulled it all off. The handling of Proctor, for example, had been perfect: right down to Gander airfield, where he'd arranged things so that the devoted bodyguard would land just in time to see him force "Constance"—actually a disguised Flavia—into a waiting jet. Proctor had, of course, raced off to Ireland in pursuit...while he himself had immediately exited the Bombardier, boarded a different plane, and returned to New York. He'd been back in the city before seven o'clock, barely six hours after leaving it in the Navigator. Sending that alert, clever man on a wild goose chase to the ends of the earth had been a brilliant piece of work.

The refrigerated coffin had also, he felt, been an inspired touch. Proctor would not know what it meant—not that, in reality, it meant anything—but it would surely have put his imagination to work... and inspired him to the most extreme of measures.

He reminded himself that it was unseemly to take pride in what, for Proctor, must be the most mortifying experience of a lifetime. But the man was out of the way—inconvenienced but alive. Constance would never have forgiven him had he employed a more drastic solution.

Across the corridor from where he sat was the chamber that, in prior years, had served as Enoch Leng's operating room. From his vantage point, he could just make out the end of the operating table, fashioned out of an early martensitic-stainless-steel alloy. It was still polished to a brilliant sheen, and his own features looked back at him. They were splendid features, the scar adding a certain frisson to his chiseled face and heterochromic eyes. At least, he hoped that's what Constance would think.

You mention the feelings I had for your brother. Why, then, should I have any interest in his inferior sibling—especially after the way you abused my innocence?

...Why should these lines of hers, flung at him in anger just the night before, come back now to torment him? But he had always been an expert at tormenting himself, even more than at tormenting others. Self-torture was a skill Aloysius had taught him. Aloysius, who—while not smarter—was sufficiently older to have been always one math problem ahead of him, one novel better read, one inch taller, one blow stronger. With his disapproving sanctimoniousness and condescension, it was Aloysius who had driven his interests and pastimes underground, into more private and perverse avenues. And it was Aloysius who had triggered the Event, which ended all his hopes of a normal—

Diogenes clamped down hard on the inner torrent of words, realizing that his breathing had quickened and his heart was pounding in his chest. He calmed himself. His hatred for his brother was a just and good hatred. It could never be extinguished and now—with Aloysius's death—it could never be redressed. But a strange thing had happened: with his brother's demise, Diogenes's mind had cleared. He had become more certain than ever there was one person in the world who could in fact bring meaning, fulfillment, and joy into his life.

And that person was Constance Greene.

Lines from an old film came back to him unbidden: *That I should want you at all suddenly strikes me as the height of improbability. You're an improbable person, and so am I.* And that was how, in his first days after barely escaping the fury of the Stromboli volcano and its vomitus of lava...that was how he had looked upon his own budding passion for Constance.

Even now, the moment came back to him with the vividness of yesterday: that struggle on the terrible, forty-five-degree slope of the Sciara del Fuoco. It had not been a lava flow in the liquefied-stone sense of Hawaii, but rather a lava slope, a hellish rent in the earth half a mile across down which house-sized rocks, red-brown with heat, tumbled incessantly. The heat thrown off by the Slope of Fire created a rising hurricane of brimstone and ash: and it was this demonic wind that had saved his life. After Constance had hurled him from the edge of the slope, he had tumbled, not falling but ultimately rising in the heat-generated gusts, until he had been dashed against one side of the scorching chasm, wedged into a crevice, one side of his face sizzling where it touched the wall of superheated rock. In shock, he had managed to extricate himself, scramble over the lip, and—on all fours—make his way *farther* along the trail Constance had chased him up, skirting the actual cone of the volcano and eventually making his way down the far side to Ginostra. Ginostra, a village of some forty residents, accessible only by boat: a tiny nugget of the Sicilian past. And it was here where, fainting with the pain, he was taken in by a childless widow who lived in a cottage outside of town. She did not ask him how he came about his injuries; she did not seem to mind his request for utter secrecy; she appeared to be content to tend his wounds with what ancient liniments and tinctures were at her disposal. It was not until the day before he left that he found the true reason for her ministrations—she was mortally afraid of his *maloccio*, the evil bicolored eyes that, local legend held, would bring ruin upon her if she did not do everything in her power to help him.

He was laid up for weeks, his burns—the hardest of all pain to mitigate, even with modern medicines—causing him unendurable agony. And yet, while he was lying there enveloped in a universe of pain, all he could think about was, not hatred for Constance, but the equally unimaginable pleasure he had shared with her...for just one night.

At the time, he could hardly believe it. It seemed inexplicable, as though he was in thrall to the passions of a stranger. But his need for her, he now realized, was not improbable. In fact, it was inevitable— for all the reasons he had explained the night before. Her distaste for the base and servile world. Her unique depth of knowledge. Her remarkable beauty. Her appreciation for the manners, civilities, and courtliness of an earlier time—coupled most agreeably with a temperament purified, like the best steel, by heat and violence. She was a tigress, dressed tastefully in silk.

And she was a tigress in other ways, as well...It tormented him that he was so blinded by hatred of his brother that he'd viewed his successful seduction of her as a triumph over Aloysius. Only later, on his bed of pain, had he realized the night they spent together had been the most remarkable, exciting, raw, sublime, and pleasurable of his life. He sought hedonism like a penitent seeks a cilice—and yet nothing in his life came close to what he'd experienced upon igniting the passions of that woman, pent up for over a hundred years, inflaming that supple and hungry body . . . What a fool he had been to throw that away.

The rude, ancient medicines of the woman who had tended him had done little to help with the pain, but had done wonders to minimize the scarring. And two months later, he'd left Ginostra—with a new goal in his life . . .

He realized with a start that Constance stood before him. He had been so distracted that he had not heard her approach.

He rose quickly from the chair before recollecting it had been his intention to remain seated. "Constance," he breathed.

She was dressed in a simple, yet elegant, ivory dress. A half-moon of lace embroidery below the throat chastely covered, but could not conceal, a most admirable décolletage. The lines of the dress, shimmering like gossamer in the flickering candlelight, ran all the way to the floor, where they hid her feet in a gauzy gathering of fabric. She was looking back at him, regarding his evident discomfiture with an expression he could not quite read: a complex mixture of interest, circumspection, and—he thought and hoped—guarded tenderness.

"Yes," she said, in a quiet voice.

Diogenes raised one hand to the knot of his tie, fiddling with it unconsciously, uselessly. His mind was so disordered he couldn't respond.

"Yes," she repeated. "I'll retreat from the world with you. And . . . I'll take the arcanum."

She paused, awaiting a response. The shock of relief and delight that broke over Diogenes was so strong that it was not until this very moment he realized just how terrified he'd been that she would say no.

"Constance," he said again. It was the one word he could manage.

"But you must assure me of one thing," she said in her low, silky voice.

He waited.

"I need to know this arcanum truly works, and that its creation didn't involve harming any human being."

"It works, and no one has been harmed, I promise," he said, his voice hoarse.

She looked searchingly into his eyes for a long minute.

Almost without knowing what he was doing, he took her hand in both of his. "Thank you, Constance," he said. "Thank you. You can have no idea how happy this makes me." He was shocked to find himself blinking away tears of joy. "And you will soon learn just how happy I can make you, too. Halcyon is everything I've promised, and more."

Constance said nothing. She merely looked at him in that strange way of hers—appraising, expectant, inscrutable. Diogenes felt unmanned by this look that, paradoxically, was both titillating and intoxicating.

He kissed her hand. "There is one thing I should explain to you. As you might imagine, I have been forced to create, and maintain, a variety of identities. The identity under which I purchased Halcyon is named Petru Lupei. He is a Romanian count from the Carpathian mountains of Transylvania, where his family fled during the Soviet era. Most were caught and killed, but his father managed to bring out the family wealth, which Petru—he prefers to be called Peter—inherited as the sole son and last survivor of the House of Lupei. Their crumbling family castle is said to be adjacent to the estate of Count

Dracula." He smiled. "I enjoyed that touch. I made him a man of impeccable manners and taste, a beautiful dresser, witty and charming."

"Fascinating. But why are you telling me this?"

"Because on the way to the airport, I will have to take on the identity and appearance of Petru Lupei—and keep that identity until we reach Halcyon. Please don't be surprised at my temporary change of looks. On Halcyon, of course, I can be myself. But during the journey there, I would ask you to think of me as Petru Lupei, and to address me as Peter—to preserve my identity and ensure my safe passage."

"I understand."

"I knew that you would. And now, please excuse me. I have so much to do before we leave—which, if you like, could be as early as tonight."

"Tomorrow, if you don't mind," Constance said. "I'll need some time to pack and ... say good-bye to this life."

"Packing," Diogenes said, as if the thought was new to him. "Of course." He turned away; hesitated; turned back. "Ah, Constance you are so very beautiful—and I am so very happy!"

He vanished into the gloom of the basement corridor.

27

Proctor tried to rise, but only managed to haul himself to his knees. He checked the position of the sun, which was directly above, a white-hot disk. He had been unconscious for about an hour, he guessed. The rank smell of lion blood filled his nose. He shook his head, trying to clear it, and the world momentarily spun around. Bad idea. Steadying himself, he took several deep breaths and looked about. His pack lay in the sand a hundred yards off, where he had shed it during the lion attack. Near the pack lay the first dead lion, a sprawl of tawny fur. The second lion lay directly beside him, close enough to touch: stretched out, mouth open, eyes and tongue already alive with flies. A sticky, drying pool of blood soaked the sand around its chest.

His KA-Bar knife, covered with dried gore, lay beside him; he cleaned it by pushing it roughly into the sand several times, then slid it back into the scabbard on his belt.

Once again he tried to rise, but found he did not have the strength. Instead, he crawled across the sand, the heat burning his palms. When he gritted his teeth at the pain, sand crunched between them. He tried to spit it out but, through the fog of thirst and pain, he realized he had become severely dehydrated, his lips cracked, his tongue swollen, his eyes raw. There was water in the pack if he could only get to it.

Slowly, he made his way toward it and finally, with a gasp, reached out and seized it, sinking to the ground and pulling it toward him. He fumbled out the canteen and, taking great care not to spill a drop with his shaking hands, unscrewed the cap and took a long drink. The water was almost too hot. He forced himself to stop and wait, taking long breaths, letting that first drink settle. Five minutes passed and he took another drink. He could feel a small surge of energy and clarity returning. A third drink and that was it. If he didn't save the rest, he'd be dead in twenty-four hours.

The smell of the closer dead lion was overpowering. His .45 lay on the sand next to it. He crawled over and reached for it, then immediately let the weapon drop: the sun had rendered it too hot to pick up. He stared at it for a moment, trying to clear his head and think. He delved into his pack, removed a crank flashlight that had a hook at the end, hooked it through the trigger guard, and slid the gun into a side pocket, zipping it up.

A brief shadow passed over and he looked up, seeing that a column of vultures had formed and were circling lazily, waiting for him to either die or go away so they could feast on the dead lions. He thought, *You're welcome to the lions, but you ain't going to get me.*

Six hours to sunset. It would be suicide to travel in the heat of day; he had to remain where he was until it was dark. He could see, perhaps half a mile off, a lone acacia tree. He would need that shade—if he could only make it there.

The water he drank had given him strength. He grasped the pack again. He had already jettisoned everything in favor of water, save for the knife, gun, compass, map, and a couple of energy bars. But he couldn't eat now; that would only increase his thirst.

Struggling into a sitting position, he slid the straps of the pack over his shoulders. Now the trick was getting to his feet. Taking a few deep breaths, he summoned his mental strength and then, with a cry, stood up, staggering a bit but managing to steady himself.

One step at a time, one step at a time...

The two lions had separated and tracked him for the better part of three days, and in so doing had driven him from his planned route. The last day, he'd been forced to backtrack and circle so many times he had lost an exact knowledge of his position. Luckily the lions, being male and juvenile, were not good hunters. If they had been fully grown females, he would not have survived the attack. Even so, it had still taken a full magazine from his .45 to stop the first lion; but the second lion came on so fast he didn't have a chance to reload and he had been forced to kill it with the knife.

He had been mauled on the left shoulder and bitten on the calf, but what had almost done him in was the physical blow from the lion's final leap, which had hit him so hard he was knocked back unconscious. The lion was already fatally wounded with a knife thrust to the heart, blood pouring out. Proctor had initially woken with the hot, stinking lion partly covering him, surrounded by a pool of the lion's coagulating blood. He'd managed to drag himself out from under the beast before slipping into unconsciousness again.

Finally reaching the shade of the tree, he removed his pack and sank down, his back against the trunk, head swimming. One more taste of water? He removed the canteen, gave it a little shake. No—he would have to wait until sunset before taking another sip, which he hoped would give him the strength to walk through the night. If he could only reach the Mopipi road, a passing motorist would eventually find him.

Reluctantly, he took out his KA-Bar and sliced open his shredded pant leg, in order to have a look at the bite wound. A row of punctured teeth marks oozed dark blood. He had abandoned the medical kit; there would be no treating this until he got out. At least the bleeding had mostly stopped. His shoulder wound was in a similar condition, not good, but not immediately life threatening, either. Infection was the major concern, but that wouldn't set in for another twelve to twenty-four hours.

Once again, uninvited, the unbearable agony of his failure crept in, his every mistake and stupidity paraded before him.

Stop thinking. He lay back against the rough bark and closed his eyes.

He had to survive this. In fact, he *was* going to survive. He knew this for one very good reason: there was something he must do. Wherever Diogenes was, whatever his plan had been, Proctor was going to find him.

And kill him.

28

Rudy Spann sat in the small office on the fifth floor of the Metropolitan Correctional Center they had appropriated for the Pendergast operation. He was wearing a wireless headset. His men had set up a small tactical center in the office and were manning various video screens and audio feeds. He paced the floor behind them, occasionally stopping at the window to gaze down on the street below.

Setting up the stakeout had been a piece of cake. They didn't even need the special van, or teams positioned on rooftops and apartments. The street where the transfer would take place was around the back of the building, on Cardinal Hayes Place, a narrow lane overlooked by government buildings that no one could get into without clearance. So whoever came to make sure the Arsenault transfer took place was going to be on foot, on the street. It was a perfect place for the operation—maybe too perfect, as it might scare away whoever the kidnappers were sending to observe the transfer. They were relying on the stupidity of the kidnappers, and on this point at least Spann had come around to Longstreet's way of thinking. Anyone who kidnapped a federal agent was taking a big risk to begin with. They were overconfident, and that would be their downfall. The real danger was them panicking and Pendergast getting smoked.

Longstreet's setup, he had to admit, was extremely clever. And so it gnawed at him all the more that the man was about to bungle things so badly. Here they had a chance to take one of the kidnappers into custody—if he showed up—but Longstreet's orders had been specific: simply ID him and let him go about his business. That went against all the rules of apprehension Spann had learned at Quantico, and in his FBI experience that followed. Just letting the guy walk away— what the hell was that all about? Arsenault was proving a tough nut to crack. If it were up to him, he'd apprehend this cocksucker and exploit his initial confusion and fear, scare the shit out of him, and get him to talk. Kidnapping a federal agent? He'd be looking at life in prison without parole, if he was lucky, and to get out of that the guy would send his own grandmother down the river. He'd fold in twenty minutes, tell them where Pendergast was, and this business would be wrapped up by the end of the day. But no—Longstreet just wanted to ID the guy and let him walk.

And on top of it, Longstreet wasn't even there; he'd disappeared as he'd done before—gone for hours at a time—issuing his orders by phone or even sending encrypted emails from undisclosed locations. Who did he think he was, the damn vice president?

The guys manning the consoles were murmuring in their headsets to the rest of the team, which had staked out both ends of Cardinal Hayes, observing and videotaping everyone who came in or out. He listened to their terse, economical exchanges. These guys were professionals; Spann was proud of them.

He glanced at the clock. Three fifteen. The target would be arriving soon or not at all. It was a quiet afternoon, half an hour before the first government offices disgorged their workers. There were people walking back and forth, as always in Manhattan, but from his vantage point—and from the street-level camera feeds in front of him—they were pretty clearly not his man, or woman.

With Longstreet not there, Spann decided he was going to make a small adjustment to the plan. He wasn't going to let the guy just up and walk; he'd have him tailed. See where he went, where his hidey-hole was. After all, that wasn't actually contrary to Longstreet's orders.

He raised his mike and gave the order: *Tail the perp on foot. Two men only. Break off if he grabs a cab or calls an Uber.* A cab or Uber would be traceable later, so no need to follow. And if an accomplice picked him up in a car, so much the better—they could snag the plates and run them within five minutes.

Three twenty-five. And now he saw a man turn the corner at the Pearl Street end and come walking down the lane. He was dressed in a nice suit, hair slicked back, tan and fit. He looked like a Wall Street stockbroker or hedge fund jackass. Having spent much of his life downtown, Spann knew those guys: they walked fast, really fast. They knew where they were going and were the kind who worked out every day, ate quinoa and kale, and jogged twenty miles a week.

But this guy was walking slow—way too slow. He was pretending to stroll along, smelling the flowers. On the far sidewalk.

He was their guy, dawdling, making sure that the Arsenault transfer was made as promised. Spann didn't even have to say anything: the others had noticed him, too. He listened on his headset to their conversation.

"You see that guy?"

"Bingo."

"Zero in with the telephoto. Smile, you're on candid camera."

And right on schedule, the black maria turned in at Pearl Street, driving nice and slow. The man, still strolling along, looked up as it approached, trying to appear casual, trying to keep his movement to just a glance, but failing. He stared.

Oh, yeah. He saw his man: Spann could see it in his expression. It was like a gift from the gods.

The transport van passed the guy and made a slow and easy turn into the underground ramp leading to the security courtyard, then waited while the driver was checked; the big gates opened and the van disappeared.

Perfect.

And now he saw his own two guys go into action. One, who'd been sitting on a bench eating a shish kebab from a nearby food cart, tossed the stick in the trash and sauntered down the street. "Dog One following," the man murmured into his invisible wire.

On the near corner, as the perp went by, his second man, who'd been pretending to have trouble parallel parking his car, got out. "Dog Two following," he said.

The man took a right into St. Andrews Plaza, walking past the courthouse, and disappeared from Spann's field of view. Soon the two guys tailing him disappeared as well. The channel remained open.

"Perp crossing Foley Square, heading for Duane," came the voice of Dog One.

A moment later: "Left on Elk."

This was an odd route. What was going on?

A moment later: "Left on Reade. He's got a phone out. Looks like he's texting."

The guy was walking around the block. *Son of a bitch.* "Dog One?" Spann said into the headset. "He might have made you. Keep walking down Elk. Dog Two, take a left on Centre in front of him, going in his direction."

"Shit. He's running south on Centre toward Chambers."

Fuck. Somehow, he'd made the tail. "Take him down," Spann yelled into the headset. *"Take him down!* All units converge!"

The whole area was suddenly crawling with cops and in less than fifteen seconds it was over, the man was on his face, cuffed, on the pavement in front of Police Plaza.

"Hold him there, I'm coming down," Spann said. The tail had screwed up, but maybe this was better. In fact, it *was* better. This was exactly the outcome he'd wanted all along. They had their man and now he, personally, would break the son of a bitch. By the time Longstreet showed up, they'd have the info they needed and would already be planning the hostage rescue.

29

Filipov heard the whine of the Zodiac and came out on deck in time to see Smith come tearing into Bailey's Hole. It was five in the evening, not even sunset.

Smith came in too fast, didn't throttle back in time, and the Zodiac smacked up against the transom door.

"What the fuck?" Filipov said. "It's still daylight!"

"They picked up Dalca," Smith said, fumbling with the painter, cleating it and climbing across the slippery gunwale. Filipov opened the transom door and grabbed his hand, pulling him in.

"Dalca? How do you know?"

The rest of the crew was now crowding onto the aft deck.

Smith gasped for breath. "They grabbed him. It was a setup. He went down to make sure Arsenault was being transferred, but they'd staked out the street. They got him."

"*How* do you *know*?"

"He texted me—said he was being tailed."

"*Texted* you? He had his cell phone on him?"

"Yeah, one of the burner phones. I destroyed the phone he texted me on—I'm pretty sure it was within the twenty-second limit."

Filipov's head reeled. What a clusterfuck. It was over.

He mustered a calmness of voice that he did not feel. "I don't understand. What do you mean: a setup?"

"You told us not to trust the FBI—right? That's what you said. Not to take their word. So Dalca went down to witness the transfer. That FBI agent, Longstreet, said Arsenault was being transferred to the Metropolitan Correction Center to get him ready for the flight to Venezuela. I got the exact time of the transfer from Longstreet and passed it on to Dalca."

"And?"

"So Dalca went downtown, dressed like a Wall Street guy, to walk past on the sidewalk when the van arrived. To make sure Arsenault was in it." Smith spread his hands. "That's all."

Filipov stared at Smith as silence fell. For the first time, he realized what a terrible mistake it had been to rely on people like Smith and Dalca for something as risky as this. They were dumbass smugglers. They had fallen into a blindingly obvious trap. Dalca would eventually talk—*of course* he would. Maybe not right away, but soon enough. And with Dalca, they could get Arsenault to talk, too, pitting one against the other, doing the usual whoever-rats-first-gets-a-plea routine.

They were now fucked. He took a deep breath, doing his level best to quell his rising rage: there was no point, the damage was done, and he would need these men for what was to come. The only hope now was to get out of the country—fast.

He looked around at the crew. From the expression on their faces he could see that they all, in varying degrees, understood the situation. And he could also see they were starting to think about who was to blame.

"It's over," he said, making a supreme effort to keep his voice low and reassuring and waiting for the news to sink in. "We need to stick together and clean this up."

"This is fucked up," said DeJesus. "You *promised* us this would work." There was a chorus of low murmurs.

"We're no worse off than we were before," said Filipov calmly. "Arsenault was going to talk eventually anyway. Let's focus on what we need to do, going forward."

"Yeah, but whose idea was it to kidnap a federal agent? I mean, we are *fucked!*"

"Canada's right there. We've got money and passports. In twenty-four hours we'll be on a plane to wherever." He looked around. "The weather's clear. It's almost dark. We'll head across the Gulf of Maine. I know a secure cove near Yarmouth where we can ditch the boat. Yarmouth's got an international airport. We'll be out of the country tomorrow."

"I can't believe this," said DeJesus, stepping forward and jabbing a finger at Filipov. He spat on the deck. "*You* wanted to haul in the body. *You* came up with this scheme. *You* talked us into it! Well, I for one am *not* listening to your shit anymore."

"And your plan is—?"

"I'm taking the Zodiac. I'm outta here. And anyone who wants to come with me can do it." He began to turn.

"The Zodiac stays with the boat," said Filipov. He could hear in the tones of their voices, see in the looks in their eyes, that the crew was reaching a turning point. If he didn't do something fast, he might lose them.

Filipov reached out, grasped DeJesus by the shoulder. DeJesus spun around, furious, opening his mouth to spout some more bullshit, which was what Filipov anticipated. He already had his right hand on the butt of his .45, and he now yanked it out and shoved it into DeJesus's mouth.

The man struggled but Filipov pulled him closer. "You going to argue with this?"

DeJesus made an angry, inarticulate reply.

"Just nod your head yes or no. Don't think I'm bluffing." Filipov tightened his finger on the trigger. He would do it if he had to.

DeJesus saw the look in Filipov's eyes and stopped struggling. After a moment he gave a faint nod. Filipov relaxed his grip and drew back the gun.

Filipov looked around. "Anyone else want to sound off?"

Nobody did.

"What's done is done and we're balls to the wall. If we break up now, we're screwed. Understand, DeJesus?"

DeJesus gave him a dark look.

"Once we're out of Canada, we can go our separate ways. *But not until then.* And nobody stays in the U.S.: you'll get picked up for sure. We've all got money. We've got passports. They haven't ID'd us yet. There are dozens of no-extradition places to lie low in for a while— Cuba, Venezuela, Croatia, Montenegro, Cambodia."

He gave them all another searching look, and saw they were back with the program. He shoved his .45 into his belt.

"What about the fed?" Smith asked.

"He's the least of our problems. As soon as we're offshore, we kill him and dump the body." He glanced around. "Cut those cross cables, I'm taking the helm. Let's get the hell out of here."

30

Diogenes found Constance in her set of rooms on the second floor of the Riverside Drive mansion. A square-sided Louis Vuitton suitcase and a steamer trunk had been set up beside her bed. The suitcase, he saw, was already full of books, journals, incunabula, and a roll of what looked like old art canvases; the trunk was half filled with dresses, along with a few skirts and tops. Constance was facing away from him, very still, as if sculpted from marble. One hand was outstretched toward the open closet, pale fingers curling in midair. She was the very picture of indecision.

Diogenes's heart leapt into his mouth. This would make what he had to say even more difficult.

He cleared his throat, announcing his presence. Immediately Constance turned toward him. Her eyes flashed with a fleeting emotion, quickly suppressed.

"Forgive the intrusion," he said. "I merely wanted to tell you that all is ready. I have made the necessary preparations for our trip. Please tell me when I should call for you in the morning."

Constance paused. Her eyes strayed toward the open trunk. "Eight o'clock should suffice."

"Very good. Constance..." He hesitated. "Before I leave, I want you to hear a story. A true story about an evil man."

Constance raised an eyebrow quizzically, but said nothing.

"His name is Lucius Garey. Six years ago, on Christmas Eve, he broke into the house of a Jacksonville doctor, interrupting the family as they were singing carols around their tree. The doctor had two teenage daughters. Garey raped each daughter, in turn, while forcing the parents to watch at gunpoint. This was followed by the brutalization of the mother, once again with the entire family as witnesses. Finally, he shot the parents, then cut the throats of the two girls."

Constance spoke sharply. "Why in God's name are you telling me this?"

"Please bear with me. It took the authorities a month to catch Garey. A police officer was killed in the resulting confrontation. Garey was found guilty of five murders and sentenced to die. Before being placed on death row, however, he managed to strangle another prisoner to death with his bare hands."

He took a cautious step forward. "I've told you about Halcyon Key. I think you'll find it even more marvelous than I have painted it for you—especially once you're restored to your full youthful vigor. I've also told you about the arcanum. With a great deal of time, money, and research, I've been able to reformulate—almost—the old arcanum without resorting to the unfortunate necessity of extracting it from a human at the time of death."

"Almost?"

"There is a complication. In order to complete the work, I need to prepare the original formulation *one time only*."

"Why?"

"The explanation is complicated."

"That answer doesn't satisfy me at all. Are you saying you need to do an extraction from a human cauda equina?"

"Yes."

"Then you can obtain the cauda equina you need from a corpse."

Diogenes shook his head. "I'm afraid that wouldn't work. The cauda equina needs to be fresh, you see—extremely fresh. Obtained at the very moment of death. The medical researchers I've employed have all come to the same conclusion."

He saw a fury blaze across Constance's face. She spoke quietly, with a razor's edge to her voice. "You lied to me."

"What I promised was that no human being *has been harmed*. And that is true—no human being has. The fact is, my research would have been far easier, and less expensive, if I had taken human lives. But I knew you would object. And...I am no longer a killer."

"So you haven't taken a human life yet, but now you *will*. How contemptible."

"If you will let me explain, Constance. Please."

Constance stared at him, saying nothing.

"It's a life that would be taken anyway. You see, in three days, Lucius Garey will die by lethal injection, in a prison in southern Florida. He's exhausted all his appeals, and the governor will not commute. Garey is a sociopath who's expressed no remorse—on the contrary, he's bragged of how much he enjoyed it. This horrible man, this sadistic killer and rapist, will die *whether or not I lift a finger*."

He stopped, looking intently at Constance. She did not reply. That unreadable expression was once again on her face.

"Try to understand." Diogenes spoke more quickly now. "I need the cauda equina, *one* very fresh cauda equina, for the chemical synthesis necessary to re-create the improved formula. A drug can't be synthesized from nothing. You have to know its chemical structure. I need to have it analyzed and the chemical structure of certain compounds determined. We are talking about complex proteins and biochemical compounds that have millions of atoms within a single molecule, folded in complex ways. In the eighteen months I've had bio-chemists analyzing the problem, I've learned a great deal. As soon as I can obtain a sample of the original formulation, at long last my work will be done."

Still Constance said nothing. Diogenes was unnerved by the opacity of her expression.

"Constance, I beg you—think this through. It's a onetime process. After that, the synthesis of the arcanum will be free and clear. And no-body is being hurt: Garey is a dead man anyway."

"And just how do you plan to obtain this man's 'fresh' cauda equina?" Her voice was cold, cold.

"After an execution, a medical examiner must perform an autopsy. I will arrange to be that medical examiner. Once I have the cauda equina, I will extract what I need, bring the extraction to Halcyon, and biochemically synthesize it in the lab I've built there. Everything is prepared and in readiness—save for this. No more bodies needed. And you, my dear Constance, will get your youthful vitality, your health, restored in full. Please, Constance. *Please.*"

He fell silent, watching her very carefully. She remained still for what seemed an eternity, as if struggling with some inner conflict. Then—briefly, almost inaudibly—she said: "All right."

Relief flooded through him. "Thank you," he said. "Thank you for seeing the logic of the situation. I'll leave you to your packing. Until eight tomorrow morning, then."

And with a smile, he turned and left the room.

31

THE MIDNIGHT SEA was like rippled glass, with a quarter moon setting over the horizon—a perfect night for business like theirs. At the helm, Filipov glanced over at the chartplotter. He had taken a heading due south from Bailey's Hole, passing by the southern end of Machias Seal Island, avoiding the Grand Manan Banks and their flotilla of fishing boats. He was looking for water deeper than trawler depth, and according to the charts the Jordan Basin was the place for it. They were now fifty miles offshore, still in the U.S. exclusive zone but well outside the twelve-mile territorial limit. The radar indicated no boats, fishing or otherwise, as far as it could reach. This was one of the deepest parts of the continental shelf—and a notoriously poor fishing ground at that. The body would go to the bottom and never, ever reappear, not even in some bottom trawler's net.

Filipov throttled down, brought the boat in a circle, and backed the engine until they were stationary. They were within the Labrador Current, a sluggish, quarter-knot flow of very cold water coming down from the Labrador coast, with no wind and little swell. No point in putting out a sea anchor; the boat could drift.

The crew had gathered in the pilothouse, their faces illuminated in the dim-red light of the nighttime bridge. Filipov looked at Miller. The man had a special hatred of the FBI, and Filipov had decided to let him do the honors—along with Abreu, the engineer, who was built like a brick shithouse. That should keep them happy. When they had dispatched the fed and dumped him overboard, they would head to Canada. And then, just as soon as was humanly possible, Filipov would shake free of these losers and head to Macedonia, where his family was originally from and he still had relatives. He had plenty of money; he could lie low and see how things developed. But he wanted to make sure they all got out of Canada first, and that none of them balked and decided to try their luck staying in the States.

"Miller, Abreu," he said. "You two go below, get the fed, bring him up. Be careful—he's a dangerous one. Check your weapons."

"Why don't we just shoot the fucker down in the hold?" Miller asked.

"Leaving his blood and DNA everywhere and giving ourselves a ten-hour cleanup job? No: we lay out tarps on the aft deck and shoot him there, then we can wash everything out the scuppers with the raw water hose."

Miller and Abreu removed their weapons, checked them, racked in rounds, and stepped out into the darkness.

Filipov turned to Smith. "Dwayne, cut twenty feet of half-inch chain and spread some plastic tarps out on the aft deck. The rest of you, rack rounds; I don't want to take any chances with this guy. He looks like shit, but looks can be deceptive. Take positions along the gunnels."

He reached down to the breaker panel and flipped on all the night floods, bathing the working deck of the boat in dazzling light. Then he stepped out of the pilothouse, hooking the door open. Smith was already laying out the tarps, held down by lengths of chain. The lazarette hatch opened and Abreu emerged, hauling Pendergast up by his two handcuffed hands, with Miller shoving from below. The man could hardly walk; he looked practically dead already. Still, Filipov wasn't about to take any chances—he remembered the look he'd seen in the man's eyes.

"Everyone, keep your weapons at the ready. You two, dump him on the tarp."

Abreu half dragged the agent to where the tarps were laid out, then let him drop. He looked hideous, his face bruised from the recent beating. His eyes were slits, swollen like sooty holes in a lump of dough, blood crusted around the nose. His body flopped onto the tarp, his cuffed hands lying stretched out over his head.

"Let's get this over with," Filipov said. "Miller—you do it."

"With pleasure." Miller stepped over, right above the agent, raised his .45 in both hands, and aimed at the head. "Eat this, motherfucker."

At that moment the fed's eyes sprang open, sudden white spots in the black holes. Miller, startled, pulled the trigger, but the shot went wide as Miller simultaneously jerked sideways and fell. Filipov saw it as if in slow motion: the fed had swiped at Miller's ankle, sending it skidding out from under him on the slippery tarp; and as he was falling the man rose up in a smooth motion, his face suddenly charged with a demon-like intensity; he snagged the .45 from Miller's hand and shot him, then turned and fired at Abreu. It happened with incredible swiftness and yet, for Filipov, time seemed to have slowed into a kind of horrifying ballet. Pendergast kept rotating like a machine; firing next at the cook. One after the other, the tops of Abreu's and the cook's heads came off. Pendergast was swiftly moving on, swiveling toward Smith.

Filipov, shaking off his surprise and gathering his wits, began firing his own weapon, as did DeJesus. But they were caught off guard, panicked, firing too fast, and the fed evaded their fire by dropping and swinging sideways, scuttling to a place of cover behind the pilothouse.

Now Smith began firing as well, and the three of them engaged in a terrific, useless fusillade that Filipov could see was doing nothing but peppering the empty space where the man had just stood.

Realizing his exposure, Filipov scrambled back, taking cover behind the pilothouse, joined immediately by Smith and DeJesus. They crouched behind the steel wall, near the rail, and a momentary silence fell.

"He's on the other side of the pilothouse," said DeJesus. "I'm going over the top."

"No," said Filipov, breathing hard. "We need a plan."

"I've *got* a plan. I'm going over the top before he comes over on top onto *us*. That motherfucker killed my friend. He's going to run out of ammo; Miller's piece held seven plus one and he's shot three. I'm going to smoke his ass."

"He's too fast. It's just what I said: he's been faking. Give me a second to think this through—"

"*Fuck* thinking. I was special forces, I know what I'm doing. You and Smith go forward and come around the front—we'll squeeze him in a pincer movement. Get him to start firing. He'll go through his magazine—and then he's fucked."

Filipov saw the wisdom in the plan and stopped protesting. He watched DeJesus grasp the handhold at the edge of the pilothouse roof and, in one fast motion, pull himself up and over, on his belly, creeping forward.

DeJesus is right, he thought. *Take the high ground*. He motioned to Smith and they began creeping forward, crouching low. Where the pilothouse swept around to the helm windshields, he paused to listen. There was no sound at all. The fed was on the port side, no doubt taking cover around or behind the tied-down Zodiac. The three of them would draw his fire and he'd run out of ammo. They, on the other hand, had plenty of spare magazines.

He signaled to Smith to follow as he crept toward the corner. What was DeJesus doing? Strange that there was no sound.

And then it happened: a sudden, controlled burst of shooting, in groups of two. A pause, and then more shooting. *DeJesus*. He could hear the rounds hitting the Zodiac, hear the drum-like gasps of air as the pontoons were shot full of holes. The Zodiac was like butter to a .45 round—no cover at all. DeJesus was just going to riddle him. Or so Filipov hoped.

A third set of shots; DeJesus was on his third magazine.

Silence fell again. He crept forward. The man was dead, *had* to be, with DeJesus shooting down on him from above.

Just as he reached the far corner and crouched, hesitating, he heard a single shot; then a scream and a splash.

Silence again.

Filipov felt himself go cold all over. That scream had sounded like DeJesus. One shot?

With a jab behind he felt around for Smith. He signaled for him to turn around, and together they retreated to the other side of the pilot-house, crouching, breathing hard. Filipov had never been so frightened in his life. Smith looked equally spooked.

"What the fuck do we do?" Smith whispered, his voice cracking.

Filipov's mind was racing. They had to do something, and do it immediately. But for the life of him, he couldn't think what.

32

COME ON, FILIPOV told himself. *Think. Think.*

And then, suddenly, he knew what he had to do. He had to get the son of a bitch off guard.

Scuttle the boat. The water temperature was forty degrees. The bastard would fall unconscious and drown within fifteen minutes. If they could get into the cabin, they could pull on immersion suits, then scuttle. It was a steel boat; it would go down fast.

And when the boat went down, the EPIRB, the Emergency Position Indicating Radio Beacon, would pop free and—as it was designed to do when becoming submerged—send out its emergency beacon. The Coast Guard would be there in two hours. They would be rescued. Pendergast would be dead, the *Moneyball* and all its incriminating evidence would be at the bottom of the ocean—there would be nothing to get them convicted. Pendergast's corpse, if it was floating at all, would have been taken far away in the quarter-knot current. Just a freak boating accident.

The moon was setting. It would soon be pitch dark.

He grasped Smith's shoulder. "We go into the pilothouse. And down into the cabin."

Smith nodded. He was paralyzed with fear.

"Just follow my lead."

Another nod.

Filipov raised his weapon and fired at the Plexiglas window once, twice, popping it into slivers.

"In!"

Smith scrambled through the window frame and Filipov followed, half falling into the pilothouse and rushing down the companionway into the cabin. As Filipov swung the steel cabin door shut he saw a black shadow chasing them into the pilothouse; he dogged the hatch shut just as the fed threw himself against it.

They *had* taken him by surprise.

He heard the man try the hatch again. Filipov realized the first thing he would do was get on the VHF radio and broadcast an SOS—the wrong kind of SOS. Also, they were vulnerable through the portholes, which were too small to fit a man but could be fired through.

"Cover the portholes!" he barked.

He lunged forward, opened the breaker box, and grabbed a fistful of wires, yanking them loose in a shower of sparks. He then opened the battery compartment. There were four marine batteries: two main and two backup. He yanked open a tool drawer, pulled out a pair of rubber-handled snips, and, with more snapping of electricity, cut the positive cables—one, two, three, four.

The boat was plunged into darkness. So much for the VHF.

The EPIRB. Did the bastard realize all he needed to do was throw it in the water for it to go off, and get his SOS? Unless he was a sailor, he wouldn't know that. Filipov was banking on this ignorance.

He went to the emergency locker, threw it open, and pulled out two immersion suits, frantically putting one on and tossing the other one to Smith. He heard Smith yell, firing twice through one of the ceiling hatches.

"Put it on. I'll cover."

Smith grabbed it and began wrestling himself into it, while Filipov backed up against the hull. The portholes were covered, but the air hatches were not. It was dark and he saw a shadow moving fast by the ceiling air hatch; he fired, shattering it. And then it occurred to him: there was a second way into the cabin, through the forepeak hatch and anchor locker. It was the only hatch big enough to fit a person. If the fed knew it was there, they'd be in trouble. And there were two smaller hatches in the forepeak itself.

He scurried over to the forepeak and looked up at the two dark air hatches in the ceiling. The fed couldn't see down at them in the darkness, but there was enough ambient moonlight above that he could see the man if he peered in. He waited. Now he could hear movement, ever so quiet, along the side of the boat toward the bow. A slow footstep on the cabin roof; another; then another. Then he saw a faint shadow cover the hatch; he was ready and fired.

The hatch shattered, blown out. He waited, controlling his breathing, his heart pounding so violently he could hardly hear. Was he dead? Filipov knew in his gut that he wasn't. The way the fed had just risen up like that, those demonic, silvery eyes, the machine-like way he'd killed three people in less than as many seconds…

And then suddenly the fed's chalky face appeared in the shattered hatch, with that same contemptuous smile and a buttery comment: "Unluckiest man alive."

With a furious roar Filipov fired again and again at the porthole where the face had been, followed by clicks as he realized his magazine was empty. *The son of a bitch.*

Smith appeared next to him, dressed in the orange immersion suit. "What now?" He was terrified, waiting child-like for orders, freaked out by Filipov's loss of control.

He tried to get a grip. "Grab a sledgehammer out of the toolbox. We're going to break off the engine cooling intake at the hull."

Smith hesitated. "We'll sink."

"That's the fucking point."

"But—"

"The suits will save us. The fed will freeze. The EPIRB will be activated when the boat is scuttled and automatically call us a rescue."

Now Smith understood. He threw open the door to the engine compartment and undogged the broad hatch on the floor, exposing the intake valve.

"Wait. The cash." God, he'd almost forgotten. Filipov unlocked the storage compartment. There were six small waterproof gym bags, each with a share. He yanked them all out, slung three around his shoulder, gave the other three to Smith. "They'll float."

"But the Coast Guard will wonder—"

Fuck. "Why would they open them and do a search? We'll just say they're our clothing."

Smith nodded.

"Okay, now hit that intake valve. Hard."

Smith swung the sledge. It banged off the valve, the cooling pipe bending.

"Again!" The fed was like a fucking bat, flitting about, looking for a way in. He hadn't noticed the forepeak hatch yet. Nor had he deployed the EPIRB. So the man wasn't a sailor. Good.

Bang! Smith wielded the sledge. There was sudden spurting of water.

Bang!

Now Filipov heard a rushing sound. Smith backed out, dropping the sledgehammer. "Okay. It's coming in like a son of a bitch."

The water was boiling up like a gusher. It would be only a moment before it reached the floor of the cabin.

"We go out the forepeak hatch. Just get off the fucking boat and as far away as possible, out of range. He's only got four rounds left, and he'll soon have more important things to worry about than shooting us."

"Right."

Smith unlatched the anchor locker in the forepeak, pulled open the door, and crawled inside, over the anchor chain.

"Quietly," Filipov whispered. "Don't open it until I signal."

A nod. Smith reached up and undogged the hatch from below. Then he waited, looking to Filipov for the signal. It was so dark Filipov could barely see him. He eased himself in the locker, pressed up against Smith inside the small space.

"You lift me up. I'll turn and pull you up." Even as he said this, it occurred to Filipov that it would be mighty convenient for Smith to go down with the ship, leaving him the only survivor.

"Okay," Smith said.

"On three." He stepped into Smith's handhold.

"One, two, *three*." Smith stiffened and Filipov stepped up, throwing open the hatch, grasping the edges, and pulling himself out. He turned, slamming the hatch behind him.

A muffled cry came up. "What the fuck?"

Filipov raced for the gunnel, intending to dive into the sea; but something unexpected happened and he suddenly fell sprawling over the foredeck, his three bags of money scattering. Even before he could recover himself, he felt a foot press painfully against his back and the cold steel of a muzzle screwed violently into his ear.

A quiet voice said: "Take off your suit. Or die."

The forepeak hatch, which was operated from the bottom only, opened and Smith emerged. The gun muzzle went away, there was a single shot and a scream, and then the muzzle was jammed back into

Filipov's ear, more painfully than before. "I dislike having to repeat myself."

His pistol was underneath the suit, and if he could get to it...He fumbled with the zipper and began struggling to get it off, but then he remembered the magazine was empty. He stopped.

"Do continue undressing."

Filipov stared at him. The deck was already tilting. "But...we're sinking."

"You're stating the obvious. I need your suit."

Filipov hesitated and the fed fired the gun, the round hitting the deck so close to his ear that it sprayed him with cutting fiberglass.

"Okay. I'll take it off, I'll take it off!" He struggled out of it. He might have a chance when the fed was putting it on. It was damned awkward.

"Hands in sight, if you please," the fed said, dragging the suit toward himself. "Now lean forward, a little more, like that. Excellent!"

He smacked him across the temple with his gun.

When he woke, the fed was standing over him, fully dressed in the orange immersion suit, gun in his hand.

"Welcome back to the sinking ship," he said. "I'm sorry to say you are the one who's now going to die of hypothermia. Unless, of course, you know a way to stop the boat from going down. Without the suit you now have the proper incentive."

Filipov lay on the deck, staring up at him, head pounding. The deck was tilting sharply, the boat already a third under. "There...There *is* no way."

"Ah! What a pity."

"For God's sake, let me go below and get another suit for myself!"

A hesitation.

"It'll be cold-blooded murder if you let me freeze."

"Quite true," said the man, "and my conscience *is* rather tender. Very well. You may rise, but please don't try anything stupid. Get the suit and come back up without delay."

Filipov rose, almost fainting from the headache, sliding on the tilting deck, grasping handholds as he opened the forepeak hatch. He saw, to his horror, that it was already half full of water. He would have to swim down, in pitch darkness, to get another suit.

"The Zodiac?" he asked weakly.

"Riddled with holes, thanks to your enthusiastic friends."

Filipov suddenly felt overwhelmed with panic. There was only one way: dive in and feel his way to the suit locker.

"I...I have to dive in," he said.

"Be my guest."

Filipov lowered himself into the forepeak hatch. The water was up to his waist. The EPIRB would have been activated by now and the Coast Guard alerted and on their way, but he couldn't worry about that. He inhaled hard a few times, then held his breath and dove in.

The icy water was like a hammer to his body. Kicking down, he pulled himself through the forepeak door into the cabin, his eyes open—but all was pitch black. Already his lungs were bursting as he felt along the port side, trying to orient himself in the blackness. The current of the inflowing water pushed him to one side and he became disoriented, his diaphragm going into spasms. Realizing he had run out of breath, he reversed and swam back for the forepeak, but instead collided with a wall and suddenly surfaced in an air pocket at the top of the cabin. Gasping for breath, he desperately reoriented himself. The water was rising fast and the pocket was shrinking, the air rushing out with a moaning sound through the broken hatch in the ceiling. Fuck, the steel boat would go down any moment. He dove again, feeling along the sides of the cabin...and there it was. The suit locker! Still open. He fumbled inside, grabbed a handful of rubber, and hauled it out, resurfacing. But now there was only two feet of air left in the cabin. Fumbling with the suit, he tried to put it on in the water, but it was twisted and his hands were numb. He could hardly move his arms, he was so cold, and as he thrashed about the air pocket shrank further, the wheeze of air louder. And then, quite suddenly, he felt the boat shift hard, the air pocket disappeared, and he realized they were going down, down, into the deep cold Atlantic...

33

Lieutenant Vincent D'Agosta plopped the breakfast he'd just prepared—an egg white omelet with tarragon and cracked pepper—down on the kitchen table of the tidy two-bedroom he shared with Laura Hayward. He hated egg whites, but he'd learned that keeping himself slim—or what in his case counted as slim—required constant dieting and vigilance. Across the table, his wife was reading the latest issue of the *Journal of Forensic Science and Criminology* while enjoying her own meal: the quintessential New York breakfast sandwich of egg, bacon, and cheese on a buttered kaiser roll. No matter what she ate, she didn't seem to gain even an ounce. It was very depressing. He cut off a slice of his omelet, sighed, pushed it around the plate with his fork.

Hayward laid down her journal. "What's on your schedule today?"

D'Agosta speared the slice, popped it in his mouth. "Not much," he said, washing it down with a swallow of coffee. "Some mopping up. Paperwork on the Marten murder."

"You solved that one in record time. Must have made Singleton happy."

"He complimented me on my tie yesterday."

"That clothes horse? Impressive."

"Probably buttering me up just so he can dump another case on my desk. You watch."

Hayward smiled, went back to her journal.

D'Agosta went back to pushing the omelet around his plate. He was aware that Hayward, these last few weeks, had been careful to keep the tone of their conversations light. He was grateful for that. She knew how hard the news of Pendergast's disappearance and death by drowning had hit him. Although almost a month had gone by, he still felt an electric shock every time he thought of Pendergast being gone, which was too often. There had been reports of the FBI agent's death before, of course, but his friend had always soon reappeared, like the proverbial cat with nine lives. This time, though, it seemed his nine lives had run out. He felt guilty, as if he should have been there in that Massachusetts fishing village; as if his presence could somehow have changed the fateful course of events.

D'Agosta's cell phone went off, the "Who Let the Dogs Out" opening drowning out the noise of First Avenue traffic that floated up from street level. He pulled it from his jacket pocket and glanced at the screen: UNIDENTIFIED CALLER.

Hayward raised her eyebrows in mute inquiry.

"Anonymous. Probably that damned refinancing company again. They never give up." He hit the IGNORE button.

"Pretty obnoxious, calling before eight."

The phone rang again. UNIDENTIFIED CALLER. They looked at each other in silence until the ringing stopped.

D'Agosta put down his fork. "Bite of that sandwich?"

As he reached across the table, his phone rang a third time. UNIDENTIFIED CALLER. With a curse, he plucked it up and hit the ANSWER button. "Yeah?" he said harshly.

The reception was poor and full of static. "Vincent?" came the faint, crackly voice.

"Who is this?"

"Vincent, it is I."

D'Agosta felt his fingers curl tightly around the phone. The room suddenly felt dim and strange, as if he'd just stepped into a dream. "Pendergast?"

"Yes."

He tried to make his mouth form words, but all that came out was an incoherent splutter.

"Are you there, Vincent?"

"Pendergast—oh my God, I can't believe it! They said you were dead!"

Across the table, Hayward had lowered her journal and was staring.

The distorted voice of Pendergast began to speak again, but D'Agosta blurted over it: "What happened? Where have you been? Why didn't you—"

"Vincent!"

D'Agosta fell silent at the sharp tone.

"I need you to do something for me. It's of vital importance."

D'Agosta held the phone closer. "Yes. Anything."

"I haven't been able to reach anybody at my Riverside Drive residence: not Proctor, not Constance, not Mrs. Trask. I've tried the house phone and Proctor's cell, several times. Nothing. I am extremely disturbed. Vincent, please go there immediately, this instant, and report back to me. I can't be back in New York until tonight at the earliest."

"Of course."

"Do you have a pen?"

D'Agosta searched his jacket pockets, feeling Hayward's eyes on him. "Got it."

"Very good." Pendergast gave him the number of the cell phone.

"Now listen. On the left column outside the front door, five feet above the ground, you'll find a hidden compartment. Inside is a keyless entry pad. Enter the following code to disable the alarms and unlock the door: 315-514-17-804-18."

D'Agosta scrawled down the numbers. "Okay."

"Please hurry, Vincent. I am most concerned."

"I'll call you from the house. But I'd really like to know where you've been these last weeks—"

He realized he was talking to a dead phone: Pendergast had hung up.

"Vinnie—?" Laura began, then stopped. She said nothing more; she did not need to. D'Agosta could read conflicting emotions in her face; relief that Pendergast was alive, but concern about what it meant— and how the man might, yet again, draw D'Agosta into some fresh and dangerous case.

He reached across the table and squeezed her hand. "I know. I'll be careful."

Then D'Agosta rose, gave her a kiss, drained his cup, and hurriedly exited the apartment.

34

As he drove across town, D'Agosta just couldn't believe that anything was really amiss at the Pendergast mansion. He'd spoken with Proctor not three weeks earlier about the search for the missing agent, and he knew from personal experience that the reserved, taciturn chauffeur-*cum*-bodyguard was as capable and resourceful as any man could be. Nothing untoward was likely to go down on his watch. Mrs. Trask and Constance often didn't answer the phone, neither had cell phones, and Proctor kept strange hours.

He pulled the unmarked car into the porte cochere and got out. It was quarter past eight, and the big house looked asleep. A dark passenger van was idling at the curb, an UBER placard in its window, but that didn't necessarily mean anything: the driver could be on break or waiting for a fare in one of the adjoining buildings.

All was quiet; the only sound was the light ring of his heels against stone as he approached the front door. After a brief search he located the small hatch concealing the hidden entry pad, which sprang open when he pressed it. Pulling a folded piece of paper from his pocket, he entered the code. There was a muted click as the massive front door unlocked.

D'Agosta put his hand on the knob, turned it, pushed inward. With a whisper, the door opened. Ahead lay the front hall, and beyond it the long refectory, lying in the deeply woven shadows of early morning. Leaving the door open and walking into the refectory, he opened his mouth to call for Constance Greene, who—he imagined—was probably having a cup of tea in the library right about now.

Then, thinking better of it, he hesitated. Something about the oppressive silence of the place unsettled him.

And then he realized something. No lights had been turned on, and there were few external windows in this section of the mansion. He himself was a dark figure in a dark room. If Proctor saw him unexpectedly, without warning, a dim silhouette, the man might take some quick, precautionary measure that would prove unpleasant. He retreated to the shadows of a wall and considered the situation.

Should he have rung the doorbell? To the best of his recollection, there wasn't one—besides, if something was amiss, the last thing he wanted was to sound the alert.

He pulled out his cell phone, consulted the list of contacts, found Proctor's number, and dialed it. It rang eight times before cutting off; there was no voice mail.

D'Agosta shook his head. This was crazy; he was letting himself get the heebie-jeebies. He slipped the phone back into his jacket pocket and walked down the length of the refectory to the grand reception hall. This large and elegant space was somewhat better lit, and he stopped to take in the mellow glow of the wooden display cases that lined the walls, the various treasures ranged behind glass or seated upon decorous wall shelves. To his right stood the double doors that led into the library. He'd approach them, then announce his presence with a discreet knock.

As he walked across the marble floor, a man stepped into the room from a dark passage in the far wall. He was dressed in a dark-gray suit and carried an expensive, slab-sided suitcase in one hand. Even as D'Agosta took in the salient details—tall, slender, reddish hair, neatly trimmed Van Dyke beard—he felt himself freeze in shock and disbelief.

He knew this man; knew him, if not from the photographs and reconstructions Pendergast had shown to him, then from the clear resemblance to the man's brother. *It can't be*, he thought. *It's impossible.*

The man, obviously recognizing him as well, looked just as surprised, the expression quickly controlled. "Ah, the lieutenant," he said quietly, but with an unpleasant edge to his voice.

D'Agosta knew the voice, as well: it was a voice he had heard coming out of the semi-darkness of the Iron Clock, the railroad turntable far beneath the streets of Midtown Manhattan, during a tense confrontation almost four years ago.

Diogenes Pendergast.

All this flashed by in a single, incredulous heartbeat. Then the man began to move—but he was encumbered by the heavy case, which he dropped, and D'Agosta beat him to it. In a moment he had his gun out and pointed, dropping into a combat stance.

"Hands in sight," he said.

Slowly, Diogenes withdrew the hand that had been slipping under the lapel of his jacket, then raised his arms, stepping back into a beam of sunlight, which cut across his face, illuminating a scar on one cheek and his eyes: one silver, one green.

Now there was movement from the darkness behind Diogenes and Constance Greene came into view. She halted abruptly.

D'Agosta nodded to her. "Get behind me, Constance."

For an instant Constance did not move. Then, with absolute composure, she walked across the room, past Diogenes—his hands in the air—and moved behind D'Agosta.

"This is what's going to happen now," D'Agosta said, keeping the gun fixed on Diogenes. "I'm going to call for backup. And then we're just going to wait for it to arrive—the three of us. If you move your hands; if you move any part of your body; if you speak; if you so much as twitch, I'm going to put a bullet in your brain, and—"

There was a sudden explosion against the base of his skull. Brilliant white light flooded his vision—and then it turned to black as he collapsed to the floor.

For a moment Diogenes blinked at the tableau before him, and then at Constance, wearing an elegant fawn-colored dress and an old-fashioned but stylish hat, its veil pinned up. A handbag remained slung across one shoulder. As he looked at her, and what she had done to protect him, he felt an extraordinary swelling of emotion. He lowered his arms, recovering his equilibrium. "That was Ming dynasty," he said.

She stepped forward, gazing down at D'Agosta. The vase she'd just employed lay in shards across the lieutenant's motionless back.

"I never cared for the man," she murmured.

When Diogenes began to reach into his jacket, she spoke quickly. "He is no threat to us. And there's to be no taking of lives—remember?"

"But of course, my dear, I was only removing my handkerchief." He smiled, pulled it out, and dabbed his pale brow before tucking it back in. "Let me get the trunk and we'll be on our way."

He turned and disappeared into the dark interior of the mansion.

35

A COMMOTION IN his hospital room roused D'Agosta out of a narcotic torpor. He felt confused, in a fog. There was a faint but steady ringing in his ears and a dull headache at the back of his skull. The room swam as if underwater.

He tried to clear his head with a shake. Big mistake. With a groan, he lay carefully back, closing his eyes.

Voices were speaking: voices he recognized. He opened his eyes again, tried to blink away the confusion and the sedative. A large clock on the wall read five o'clock. *Christ, have I really been out all day?* Laura Hayward was sitting in a chair beside his bed. She now had a look on her face he recognized: a protective, hostile look, like a lioness guarding her mate.

"Vinnie!" she said, rising.

"Mmmm." He tried to speak, but his tongue wasn't working.

"Vincent, my friend."

The new voice came from the foot of the bed and—keeping his head still this time—D'Agosta swiveled his eyes in its direction. Special Agent Pendergast was sitting there. D'Agosta blinked some more, utterly shocked by his skeletal appearance, gray circles under his eyes, skin pale beneath the dirt, his face covered with raw cuts and bruises. He was dressed in an FBI windbreaker too large for his emaciated frame.

They made a fuss over him, even as he began to subside back into a half world of semiconsciousness. He lay there with his eyes closed, trying to focus on the conversation. Pendergast was speaking to Laura.

"The helicopter took me to the Downtown Manhattan Heliport," Pendergast was saying. "They told me what happened, and I came directly here. Was it you who found him?"

"When I couldn't reach him on his cell, I sent a black-and-white to your house. They found him on the floor of the reception hall, facedown, unconscious."

"I understand a large NYPD response has been mobilized."

"Are you kidding? With a woman kidnapped and an officer attacked? They've called out the cavalry."

D'Agosta found his voice again, his head clearing. "Pendergast!"

The FBI agent swiveled toward him. "How do you feel?"

"Never better. God, am I *glad* to see you..." He felt his voice choking up.

From his seat at the end of the bed, Pendergast waved this away impatiently.

"So...what happened?" D'Agosta managed.

"I've been...at sea. To make a long story short, the gentlemen who saved me from drowning decided to ransom me instead. I was held prisoner on their boat until it unfortunately sank. All irrelevant to the present situation. I wasn't myself when I sent you into danger. I'm truly sorry."

"Forget it," said D'Agosta.

A pause. "Can you tell me, please...what transpired?"

"Don't tire him out," Laura said.

Even through the pharmaceutical fog, D'Agosta could see that his friend was, most uncharacteristically, agitated and worried. He cleared his throat, struggled against the almost overwhelming feeling of fatigue. The doctor had told him he might experience amnesia, as well, but thankfully that had not happened—although the exact details of the morning were a little vague.

"I entered the house, using the key code you gave me. I walked into the reception hall just moments before...before Diogenes did."

At this Pendergast rose partway out of his chair. "*Diogenes*? Are you sure?"

"Yeah. He was coming from the rear of the house. I recognized him right away." D'Agosta paused to think. "He had a suitcase in one hand."

"And then?"

"He recognized me, too." D'Agosta swallowed. "I drew down on him. Then Constance came into the room."

Pendergast went even more pale. "Constance."

"I told her to take a protective position behind me. I was covering Diogenes, getting ready to call for backup, when I was clobbered on the back of my skull..." He stopped. "Next thing, I was waking up in an ambulance."

The look on Pendergast's hollow face was terrible to behold. "*Constance*," he said, as if to himself.

"It seems cut and dried enough," Laura said. "Diogenes had an accomplice Vinnie didn't see, who hit him from behind. We're dusting the broken vase presumably used as a weapon for fingerprints now."

"I thought Diogenes was dead," D'Agosta said.

"We all did," Pendergast said. He sat for a moment, very still. Then he spoke again. "How did Diogenes react when he saw you?"

"He was as surprised to see me as I was to see him."

"And Constance. Was she handcuffed? Restrained in any way?"

D'Agosta thought through the haze for a moment. "Not that I saw."

"How did she seem to you? Rebellious? Drugged? Coerced?"

"I never could read her. Um, sorry. She, she had a bag over one shoulder. Oh, and she was wearing a hat. I don't remember what it looked like."

"Did she struggle? Say anything?"

"Nothing. She got behind me when I asked her to. Didn't say a word."

"Did he have a weapon?"

The ringing in D'Agosta's ears was getting louder. "Nothing visible."

"I think maybe Vinnie's had enough," Laura said, with a note of finality.

Pendergast did not reply. His gaze seemed to go far away for a moment. Then he came back to the present again. The look on his face, the glitter in those silvery eyes, was as bad as D'Agosta had ever seen it.

He rose. "Vincent, I wish you a speedy recovery."

"You look pretty bad yourself," D'Agosta said. "Just saying."

"I'll get myself looked after. Captain Hayward?" He turned, gave her a curt nod, then swiveled to the door and walked quickly toward it. As he did, D'Agosta noticed—just before he drifted off once again—that underneath the FBI windbreaker, the agent was wearing a pair of filthy black trousers that had been sliced practically to ribbons.

36

Diogenes Pendergast, in his carefully curated identity as Petru Lupei, stepped out onto the private terrace of the tenth-floor suite of the Corcoran Hotel, then paused—as was his long habit—to scrutinize his surroundings with obsessive care. The Atlantic Ocean stretched from north to south in an unbroken line, its creamy breakers reflecting the pink of the evening clouds. The bustle of Miami's South Beach neighborhood surrounded the hotel on all sides, salsa music floating up to him on the freshening late-afternoon breeze. Nothing appeared amiss.

He probed his own sixth sense for danger, the internal psychic alarm he trusted more than anything else. It was quiescent.

Except for the sudden appearance of the NYPD lieutenant at Riverside Drive that morning—an event Diogenes, compulsive planner though he was, had been utterly unprepared for—everything had gone well. Even that unwelcome surprise turned out to have a silver lining: he had been gratified by how quickly, and without hesitation, Constance had acted to neutralize the threat.

He glanced over at her now, sitting on a deck chair, wearing a knee-length white skirt and a pale lemon-colored blouse, large-brimmed straw hat obscuring her face and dark glasses. One slender ankle was crossed over the other, and an iced glass of tart limeade sat on a nearby side table.

It was the outfit he had suggested she wear when they checked into the hotel. He had chosen this location—Ocean Drive, the very heart of the South Beach Art Deco District—because of how easy it was to hide in plain sight among the chic, flashy, self-absorbed crowds. And he had chosen this hotel not only for its elegance and comfort—it was the old Vanderbilt Arms, done over, as had been most of the hotels on Ocean Drive, in Streamline Moderne, although thankfully with a degree of restraint—but because it was large. A cruise ship full of German tourists had just arrived and was occupying the staff's full attention. He'd considered booking the penthouse, which occupied the hotel's entire top floor and came with four bedrooms, a seven-foot grand piano, and an infinity pool, but he'd decided that might attract attention. Instead, he'd settled for one of the dozen grand suites, with three bedrooms, rainfall showers, Frette linens, and cedar saunas. It seemed a good stepping-stone between the austerity of Constance's Riverside Drive rooms and the understated luxury of Halcyon.

Flying first-class to Miami had been straightforward. Thanks to the ironclad, unquestionable veracity of his Petru Lupei identity, it had not been necessary to "break his profile" for the flight. Everything was going according to plan—and yet, as he looked at Constance, he felt a tug of concern. Beneath the hat and behind the Bulgari sunglasses it was impossible to see her expression, but the stillness of her limbs, and the very way she was staring motionlessly out to sea, drink untouched, brought to mind the impenetrable stillness he'd noticed when he had watched her packing, preparing to take her final leave of 891 Riverside Drive.

Looking at her, he wondered if perhaps South Beach had been the right choice to stay during his harvesting of the cauda equina. After her ghastly, impoverished childhood, she had lived shut away from the world in the confines of the Riverside Drive mansion. Even after his brother had taken her under his wing, she had hardly ventured out into the world: only a few New York locations; Italy; England; New Orleans; and coastal Massachusetts. The gaudy Ocean Drive scene—all retro-chic neon and deco, steeped in preening narcissism—was perhaps even more outré than Las Vegas. Hiding in plain sight in such a trendy atmosphere had been part of the cover he'd chosen for them. But now he wondered if such a culture shock, coming as it did at a moment of galvanic change in Constance's life, might have been ill chosen.

Constance took a sip of her limeade.

"Constance?" he said gently.

She turned to look at him.

"I wonder if you would mind coming inside for just a moment. I thought it would be a good idea if I went over the arrangements I've made for the next few days."

After a moment, she rose. She appeared unsteady, because she placed one hand on the deck chair briefly before heading into the suite's salon. Taking a seat on an overstuffed sofa, she removed her hat, smoothed its brow, placed it on the arm of the sofa, then took off her sunglasses.

Diogenes was shocked. Inside, out of the glare of the sun, her face looked pallid and drawn, and her eyes dark, as if slightly bruised. Could this be the result of the flight, or the shock of leaving her home of so many years? No: these manifestations looked systemic, not emotional. Was it possible that—now she was no longer in denial of the physical degeneration caused by Leng's faulty elixir—she was succumbing to its effects? As he looked at her, pain and sympathy mingled with love.

"Are you all right?" he asked before considering his words.

She waved a hand. "A slight headache. It will pass."

He took a seat on a chair across from her. "Here's what will happen next. Lucius Garey is scheduled to die at nine PM tomorrow, in the Florida State Prison at Pahokee, about ninety miles northwest of here. The execution order has been signed and will not be rescinded. I'll take the place of the medical examiner, who at the last minute will be suddenly indisposed—nothing serious, I assure you, but an issue that will keep him from performing his duties. The body should be delivered to the M.E.'s office by about ten. I'll immediately remove and stabilize the cauda equina. Then I'll make the examination of the body, as required by law. I'll have to prepare a report and fill out the paperwork to have the body transferred to the next of kin. The incision I will make in the lower back will be small, and my report will give a medical reason for it. Nobody will be the wiser. Everything will be done by the book. My credentials and affiliation will pass muster."

He swept a hand around the room. "Over the next thirty-six hours, while I'm gone, I would strongly encourage you to remain in the suite. The less we show of ourselves, the better. I've done all I can to make this a comfortable retreat. Choose whichever of the three bedrooms pleases you most. There are books, music, and a video library at your disposal: I've laid in a set of the complete works of Yasujirō Ozu, by the way, and recommend them if you're not yet acquainted with his filmography. There's twenty-four-hour maid and butler service, of course, and a full menu for in-suite dining at your disposal. You'll find the refrigerator stocked with mineral water, fruit juices, and Dom Pérignon." He tapped a cell phone that sat on the glass tabletop between them. "Should you need anything at all, please call me anytime."

He stood up. "I should be back early the morning after tomorrow. My yacht is moored at South Beach Harbor. By that evening, we'll be at Halcyon. I'll have synthesized the arcanum—and you'll be on your way back to health." He glanced at his watch. "I have to leave in a moment. Is there anything else I can do for you, to make you more comfortable in my absence?"

"There's nothing, thank you."

"No meds? Muscle relaxants? Stimulants?"

She shook her head.

Suddenly, on impulse, he knelt before her and took her hand. "Constance, I make you a solemn promise: two days from now, we will already have begun our new life on my private island. *Our* private island. And I will devote myself entirely to your health and happiness."

He gently turned her hand over in his, kissed her palm. Constance smiled.

He rose again. "Remember: call me anytime. I love you."

And then he turned, picked up Petru Lupei's elegant malacca cane, and silently left the hotel suite.

37

At around the same time Diogenes was leaving the hotel suite, Pendergast—still dressed in the FBI windbreaker and ruined shirt and trousers—was entering his mansion at 891 Riverside Drive. Ignoring the crime scene tape set up across the reception hall, he stepped through and—after a quick reconnoiter—walked past the evidence tags and residual fingerprint dust into the library.

Nothing seemed out of place save for a letter that had been set on a side table: a letter, addressed to the house at which no mail was ever received, except via a post office box. The letter was from Mrs. Trask, addressed to Proctor.

Pendergast tore it open. The letter stated that, due to her sister's health, Mrs. Trask was forced to remain in Albany one or perhaps even two weeks longer than she had expected. She apologized, but she felt certain that looking after Constance would prove no imposition for Proctor.

Pendergast put the letter down. He remained motionless for a moment, listening to the empty house. Then, leaving the library, he made his way quickly through the upstairs area of the mansion, pausing first in Proctor's and then—at greater length—in Constance's sets of rooms.

The house appeared deserted. Proctor gave every indication of having left in a great hurry, and—judging by the very faint accumulation of dust over the surfaces of his furniture—had done so nine or ten days before. His bug-out bag was also missing.

Constance's rooms, too, appeared not to have been occupied recently, with the exception of what was clearly a hasty packing job.

Standing there in the gathering dark of her room, Pendergast slipped a cell phone from his pocket, then dialed a number in the Cleveland suburb of River Pointe. It was answered on the third ring. Pendergast waited through the requisite fifteen seconds of silence while the identification process was completed.

"Is this my own Secret Agent Man?" came the familiar, breathy voice at last, speaking from a room illuminated only by the glow of computer screens and a single candle, burning in the gable window. "It seems you've got yourself a new number. And a new phone, as well: iPhone 6s, based on the internal hashtag. Very nice."

"Mime, I need you to do something for me."

"Isn't that always the case? You never call just to chat anymore."

"It is most urgent."

"That's the way it always is, too." An exaggerated sigh. "Okay, what's on your mind?"

"You know my chauffeur, Proctor?"

"Of course. Ex-military, in your unit at one time if I'm not mistaken, first name—"

"Very good. He's gone missing from the Riverside mansion, as close as I can tell about ten days ago. I need you to track him down for me."

"Hey, that actually sounds like fun. And when I'm done, maybe you can do something for me? There's this new FBI toy that I've been coveting, a cellular duplexer that disguises—"

"Whatever you desire. Just find Proctor—and keep me informed. Thank you, Mime." And Pendergast slipped the phone back in his pocket. Then he glanced around one more time.

Despite the deserted look of the room, D'Agosta had seen Constance in the house just this morning—in the presence of Diogenes. D'Agosta had told him Diogenes was carrying a suitcase. And Constance had been wearing a hat. This was something she rarely did—and only when traveling.

Diogenes. That he had survived the plunge into the volcano at Stromboli seemed impossible. But he had nevertheless been in this very house that morning, and he could have only one possible motive: revenge. Revenge on Pendergast, and especially on Constance, who had pushed him into the volcano almost four years ago.

But something wasn't right. His questioning of D'Agosta that morning had raised certain discrepancies—curious, unsettling discrepancies that Pendergast found himself unable to account for.

He opened the door to Constance's walk-in closet. Although she had an extensive wardrobe, it was obvious to Pendergast that a number of items were missing.

He stood quietly, thinking. It had been twenty-four days since the struggle in Massachusetts when he'd been swept out to sea. Clearly, a lot must have transpired in his absence—and all of it troubling. Why would Proctor have left the house, abandoning Constance? This was the one thing the man would never, ever do. Where had he gone? Why hadn't he returned? Despite the request he'd made of Mime, Pendergast feared that Proctor might be dead at the hands of Diogenes. What had Constance been doing, alone, in the empty house?

But strangest of all: exactly what sort of scene had D'Agosta stumbled upon when he entered the mansion shortly after eight that very morning? His description of what transpired made little sense.

Two scenarios were possible. The first was that Diogenes had been caught in the act of abducting Constance for purposes of revenge, directed at her, or him, or both. But her demeanor, dress, and actions, as described by D'Agosta, didn't fit this scenario.

The second scenario...the one that best fit the facts...was too perverse, and too terrible, even to consider.

He broke his reverie suddenly, going into action. He dashed from the room and began an intense, methodical search of the mansion. He climbed up into the rambling attic and from there moved thoroughly and rapidly down through the house, looking for information, *any* information, that could help solve the riddle of the empty structure. His mind was fixated on the fact that, even now, the clock was ticking, ticking down to her unknown fate...

Sixteen hours later, he was in the sub-basement, sitting at the library worktable in Constance's small suite of rooms. He now understood a great deal: most significantly, that this was where she had been living for perhaps the past two weeks. Four items were ranged on the table before him: an orchid; a book of love poems by Catullus, with a marginal note in a handwriting all too familiar; a holograph sheet music score, dedicated to Constance; and a Tibetan t'angka painting, at whose center was the representation of a god-child whose features— once again—were disquietingly familiar.

Pendergast felt a numbness beyond anything he had experienced before. He had come to one conclusion: Constance had yielded to a subtle, inexorable, and beautifully executed campaign of courtship.

It was inconceivable that Constance, of all people, could be taken in, deceived, *won over* by such a campaign. And yet all the evidence suggested this is what had happened.

Pendergast had to admit to himself that, despite his unusual insight into the criminal side of human nature, he had frequently been at sea when it came to understanding women and the complexities of intimate relationships. And of all the women he had known, Constance, and her strong, violent passions, was the most enigmatic.

Pendergast looked around the room, his figure quiescent after hours of ceaseless activity, pale eyes glittering as they returned to the four items on the table. It still seemed impossible.

There was, he realized, one way to be sure. He removed the windbreaker and—without touching them—wrapped the sheet music and the book of Catullus poetry carefully inside it, then stood up and—after retrieving a hairbrush from Constance's bedroom—made his way back up to the main library.

Accessing a laptop computer hidden behind one of the wooden panels, he logged into the NYPD secure website and, accessing the fingerprint database, brought up a series of latents for Diogenes, which had been collected when his brother had been wanted for kidnapping and the theft of a diamond known as Lucifer's Heart.

With Diogenes's prints displayed on the laptop screen, he then retrieved a portable forensic fingerprinting kit and—using print powder and lifting tape—dusted the sheet music and the book of Catullus poetry. He was able to retrieve two different sets of latents. One of those sets belonged to Diogenes.

Constance Greene's fingerprints were in no database, official or otherwise. Turning to the hairbrush, Pendergast lifted samples of the lone sets of prints he found on it and examined them, comparing them with the other set of prints on the book and sheet music. They were a match. Proof that it was Diogenes, and no one else, who had courted Constance while Pendergast was prisoner aboard the drug smuggler's boat.

One other test remained. Pendergast felt afraid to undertake it.

He sat in the darkened library for a long time. Finally, accessing the NYPD database once again, he brought up the series of latents the police had lifted from the pieces of the Ming vase that had been smashed against the back of D'Agosta's head.

He knew the vase well. It was rare and fragile. Its impact might stun a man but not kill him. The NYPD photographs made it clear that the vase—lip, neck, handle, delicate body—had been shattered into a great many pieces. Only one part of the vase—the foot—was intact.

Pendergast brought up the suite of fingerprints lifted from the foot. Many prints had been found, but one set overlaid all the others— and the placement of those prints indicated that the last person who had taken up the vase had gripped it in a particular way: for use as a weapon.

Those prints belonged to Constance.

His hands slid off the laptop's keyboard and he shuddered. Constance had been courted by his brother. Knowing everything she knew about Diogenes, and despite the troubled history between them, she had succumbed and gone off with him. D'Agosta had interrupted their departure, and she'd knocked him senseless with a vase.

Unfamiliar emotions flooded through him: panic, confusion, horror—and underneath it, a sickening feeling of jealousy. He had to do something—immediately. But what? What was Constance doing at this moment? Was she still alive? Images, vile images, intruded themselves on his consciousness. Was she—God forbid—with his brother now, at this very moment? His thoughts went back to the unexpected confrontation with Constance he'd had in his room at the Exmouth inn. Had his awkward handling of that private moment somehow helped lead her into the arms of his hated brother?

Overwhelmed, Pendergast raised his hands to his head and—gripping at his white-blond hair—he uttered a cry: a cry of pain; shame; impotent fury... and overwhelming self-reproach. Whatever had happened in this house during his absence, one thing seemed clear. He himself was, at the very least, partially responsible for it.

There was no choice for the time being but to leave Proctor's fate to Mime. But Pendergast himself would find Constance—and when he did, he felt sure, he would find his brother.

And then he would make sure—absolutely sure—that this meeting would be the final one.

38

For many years, Diogenes Pendergast had scrupulously maintained four different and fully realized false identities. In certain ways, for him, they had actually *become* real, allowing him to become another person, but one that could act out various expressions or aspects of his complicated personality. Being able to slip into another identity was a kind of relief valve, a vacation from his own tortured and complicated self.

These personalities had been diverting to set up, develop, and curate. Creating a new identity in this digital age had at times proven a challenge, but once completed, maintaining the digital trail was easy. It required more than computer work, however: it required his physical presence. Keeping his doppelgängers up to date and busy, with visible and productive lives—and no suspicious gaps—took up a great deal of his time. That, along with establishing Halcyon, had provided the lion's share of his life's interest and amusement. Two of his identities had been "parked," for want of a better word, in the United States; the other was in Eastern Europe, where anonymity was easier to buy and maintain. This last identity he had recently allowed to go dormant, as it would no longer be necessary.

He had lost his favorite identity—that of Hugo Menzies, curator at the New York Museum of Natural History—during the events that culminated in the disaster atop the Stromboli volcano. He deeply regretted the loss: Menzies had been the first of his false identities and one that he had devoted enormous effort to maintaining, a distinguished staff member of a great museum. After Stromboli, of course, he had been forced to focus his attention for several months on merely clinging to life. But now, restored to health, he had been able to revisit the two remaining false identities and ensure they were intact, updated, and uncompromised—with suitable explanations for their absences during his recovery.

Petru Lupei was the remaining identity of longest standing. But the other identity would now prove of particular use to him. For the last eleven years, he had been (among other things) Dr. Walter Leyland, physician, living in Clewiston, Florida, on the southern shore of Lake Okeechobee. Clewiston was far enough away from such major population centers as Palm Beach and Miami to make his fiction easier to maintain. He had a deep knowledge of medicine as a result of his studies; Dr. Leyland was single, and he had a private practice catering to a limited number of wealthy clients; he spent most of his time abroad, donating his services to Médecins Sans Frontières—and as a result he was an infrequently seen, but respected, member of the Clewiston community. It had been remarkable, actually, how naively the professional community had accepted his bona fides at face value. More to the point, he had arranged a history of accreditation—medical school, a pathology residency, a forensic pathology fellowship—that allowed him to, under certain circumstances, act as a substitute consulting medical examiner for Hendry County.

His aim in doing so had been to get unfettered access to certain facilities, equipment, and drugs useful to his particular pursuits—disposing, for example, of dead bodies whose existence might otherwise prove troublesome. While he was no longer engaging in that hobby, the Dr. Walter Leyland avatar would nevertheless prove useful again now.

Florida state law allowed condemned inmates to choose the method of their death: electrocution or lethal injection. Lucius Garey had chosen the latter. This made things much easier for Diogenes.

It was quarter to eight in the evening when he approached the main gate of the Florida State Prison in Pahokee—flanked by rows of cheap cabbage palms—wearing a somber suit and the other elements of disguise—the salt-and-pepper hair, brown contact lenses, and cotton wadding in his cheeks—that went into bringing Walter Leyland, MD, to life. A physician's bag sat on the passenger seat beside him, and the scar on his cheek had been carefully erased by stage makeup. His beard was gone, of course, as both Petru Lupei and Dr. Leyland were clean-shaven. He showed his credentials to the guard, who checked them against a manifest on the computer terminal in his guardhouse.

"Welcome back, Dr. Leyland," the guard said. "Haven't seen you for some time."

"I've been abroad. Ebola epidemic."

The guard nodded, an uneasy look passing across his face. "Guess you know where to go, don't need me to show you—right, Doc?"

Diogenes did indeed know where to go.

One job of the Hendry County medical examiners was to examine the bodies of executed criminals and sign their death certificates. Another, rarer job for the M.E.'s was to administer lethal injections themselves, if the state executioner was unable to be on hand. Once, several years ago, when a prisoner on death row had exhausted his appeals and been scheduled to die, the county M.E., a Dr. Caulfeather, had asked Diogenes—at the time in residence at Clewiston in his Walter Leyland persona—to assist him in the death house as consulting medical examiner.

This was a development that Diogenes, in setting up the Leyland identity, had not considered. He had been only too happy to oblige, thanking the caprices of fortune for having dropped this attractive opportunity in his lap—one he could never have engineered for himself.

The experience had proven most interesting. It was the first time that Diogenes had legally participated in the death of another human being, with the encouragement and support of the state. Afterward, Diogenes had expressed his willingness to assist Dr. Caulfeather in the future, should his expertise be needed. In years that followed he had been involved in three additional executions, two of them directly.

Tonight, however, both the state executioner and Dr. Caulfeather had been unable to assist in the death of Lucius Garey. The executioner had been called away on a family emergency, and Dr. Caulfeather was experiencing the symptoms of appendicitis—both incidents engineered by Diogenes, of course. And so the Florida authorities, as always eager to proceed with an execution on schedule, had called upon the services of Dr. Walter Leyland.

Now he nosed the rented car into staff parking, then made his way through security into the prison proper. The death watch area was a separate structure off the death row block. It included within its walls the execution chamber, and security here was somewhat more relaxed than in the rest of the prison, given the fact that so many civilians—members of the press, families of the victim and condemned alike—had to pass through its gates. Diogenes had his credentials checked again at an internal barrier, then he was buzzed through first one, and then another, steel door. The lethal injection suite was to the right; the electric chair to the left. Diogenes chose the right-hand corridor.

Florida executions proceeded like clockwork. He checked his watch. By now, the condemned would have had his last meal; he would have been visited by the warden and, if he wished, a chaplain; and had his clothing removed and been dressed in a hospital gown.

Chances were that, at this very moment, the prison doctor, LeBronk, was attaching EKG leads to Lucius Garey's chest.

He walked past the two open doors of the witness observation area—the relatives representing the victims had a separate viewing room from the relatives of the condemned—and he noticed that, while the victims' room already held half a dozen people, the condemned man's viewing room was empty.

He stepped past a partition into a small room, the space from which the lethal injections were prepared. At the far end was a door leading into the execution chamber itself. The warden, two guards, some prison flunkies assigned to executions, and the prison doctor, LeBronk, were in the close, ill-smelling room.

The warden nodded at Diogenes. "Thank you for coming on short notice, Dr. Leyland."

Diogenes shook his hand. "Just doing my duty."

Dr. LeBronk mopped his perspiring brow with a handkerchief, then shook Diogenes's hand in turn. Like most in the Florida penal system, LeBronk believed in the death penalty with every fiber of his being. When it came to actually helping carry out the act, however, the man was wilting like a hothouse lily exposed to the sun.

"Most irregular," LeBronk said. "Our having no execution team available, I mean."

"Is the subject prepped?" Diogenes asked as he took a white lab coat from a row of pegs and slipped into it. From the moment the condemned prisoner left his cell for the last time, he or she became known as "the subject" for the rest of the proceedings.

LeBronk nodded.

"We don't normally allow executions to proceed with only a single team member," the warden said. "That's for the peace of mind of the execution team, you understand—not out of any consideration for the subject. But Dr. LeBronk, here, doesn't feel up to the task. I hope you

won't find this to be too . . . inconvenient," he continued, with a with-
ering glance at the prison doctor.

Diogenes understood the subtext of this. It was protocol for two
executioners to be on hand, each of whom would inject a deadly mixture of drugs into an IV tube. Only one of those tubes went into the
veins of the condemned, however; the other went into a disposable
bag. This way, those tasked with the execution could console themselves that they may not have actually killed another human being. It
was the psychology of the firing squad: one shooter would be given a
blank, the rest live ammunition.

"It won't be a problem," Diogenes said, careful to sound the correct
note of grim resolution, to keep any hint of eagerness from his voice.
He placed his medical bag on a nearby table. "Justice must be served.
And we all know how much the governor likes his executions to proceed on time. It would be inhumane—for everybody concerned—to
reschedule."

"My thoughts exactly." The warden nodded. "If you're ready, then,
we can proceed."

Diogenes glanced at his watch: eight thirty precisely. "I'm ready."

The warden turned and signaled to the guards, who exited the
room. They were going, Diogenes knew, to collect Lucius Garey and
bring him into the execution chamber.

39

Five minutes later, Garey was wheeled into the chamber by the guards. A spiritual adviser dressed in black, of generic affiliation, followed. The subject lay on a heavy stainless-steel gurney, restrained by wrist and ankle straps of thick leather. The heart monitor, Diogenes noticed, was already connected.

"You want a flunky to do the venipuncture?" Dr. LeBronk asked.

Diogenes shook his head. "Might as well go soup to nuts."

He stepped through the door into the execution chamber. The far wall was obscured by curtains. Garey craned his thick neck around to get a look at the agent of his impending death. He was a big bull of a man, his skull shaven, denim eyes small and pale and nearly expressionless, the skin of his arms, neck, and chest a mass of blurry blue prison tats. It was hard to tell what emotions he was experiencing: fear, anger, disbelief seemed to play across his face, one after the other.

Diogenes glanced around, refamiliarizing himself with the room, going through the upcoming procedure in his head. Reaching for a jar of cotton balls, he swabbed the inside of the man's right arm with alcohol.

The IV line ran from the drug administration room onto a rack that stood by the gurney. Diogenes tied a tourniquet, flicked the back of a fingernail against Garey's skin to get a good cubital vein. He had some difficulty due to needle scarring, but in short time found the vein and slid the IV needle home. Then he snapped off the tourniquet.

Garey watched the procedure without curiosity.

Diogenes went through the final preliminary steps, then withdrew from the gurney into the doorway of the drug administration room. Once he was out of sight, a modesty sheet was placed over Garey's gown and legs, extending as high as his midriff. Then the curtains on the far wall drew back with a faint whirring sound, exposing two large panels of one-way glass. Garey couldn't see the witnesses beyond, but they could see him.

There was a faint rasp over the loudspeaker system. "Silence in the witness area, please," came the voice of the warden. A brief pause. "Does the condemned have any last words?"

"Fuck you," said Garey. There was now nothing left on his face but anger. He spat in the direction of the one-way glass.

In the drug administration room, Diogenes signed paperwork handed him by the warden. He then checked the drug delivery apparatus, which consisted of a number of syringes, already prepped and loaded by trained prison flunkies. Instead of the usual two sets, tonight there was only one. Along with several other states, Florida used a combination of three drugs: a controversial cocktail that underwent frequent updating, based on the availability of the drugs. The intended result, however, never varied. The first drug would induce unconsciousness; the second would cause paralysis, halting respiration; and the third would stop the heart. They were always introduced serially.

Diogenes examined the drugs and dosages in the delivery system: one hundred milligrams of midazolam hydrochloride, followed by equally LD-excessive doses of vecuronium bromide and potassium chloride. He picked up the bulky, state-mandated execution forms and filled out the first of two sections, including his name, the name of the subject, his physician number, execution license serial number, and drugs to be administered.

"Five minutes," the warden said.

Diogenes broke the paper seals around the syringes, then fitted the syringes tightly into the three IV lines, one after the other. In the execution chamber, Garey was beginning to shout now: angry outbursts, mostly incoherent save for curses. Diogenes paid no attention as he turned on the cardiac monitor in order to observe the subject's heart rhythm. It was considerably elevated—as might be expected.

A death house guard stepped into the room.

"Final statement?" the warden asked wearily, going through the standard checklist.

"If you want to call it that, yes, sir," the guard answered.

"Governor's office?"

"Green light."

All was silent in the room save for Garey's expletives, louder now, filtering through the partially open door. The warden watched the wall clock tick slowly through one minute, then two. And then he turned to Diogenes. "The execution may commence," he said.

Diogenes nodded. Turning toward the first syringe, he injected the midazolam. The colorless liquid went down the IV tube, which snaked—along with several other tubes—through a small circular hole into the execution chamber.

"*Constance*," he whispered to himself, almost reverently.

At first, Garey's loud, harsh vocalizing remained unchanged. Then it grew slow and garbled. Within thirty seconds it was little more than a sporadic, incoherent mutter.

Diogenes depressed the second syringe, introducing the paralytic.

All eyes in the room were trained either on the partially open door to the execution chamber, or on the small observation window set into the nearby wall. Nobody noticed as Diogenes slipped one hand into the pocket of his lab coat, palmed another syringe he had already taken out of his medical bag and placed there, inserted its needle into the injection valve of the third catheter, and introduced its contents into the IV tube. Just as quickly, he replaced the now-empty syringe in his pocket.

This fourth, secret part of the lethal cocktail was one of Diogenes's own devising: a combination of sodium benzoate and ammonium sulfate, preservatives used—among other things—to keep meat fresh.

A moment later there were gasps in the room, followed by a series of murmurings.

"Look at him," said the death house guard. "He's flopping around like a fish. Never seen *that* before."

"It's almost as if he's in severe pain," said Dr. LeBronk, his voice strained.

"How's that possible?" The warden swore under his breath. Then he turned to Diogenes. "What's going on?"

"Nothing at my end. Everything's in order. I'm about to introduce the potassium chloride."

"Hurry," said the warden.

Slowly and carefully, Diogenes depressed the plunger of the third syringe, the contents of which would induce cardiac arrest and cause death. Given the unsanctioned chemicals introduced into his veins, the murderer was perhaps suffering more than was normally the case. Far more than normal, most likely. However, it was important that his harvest be as fresh as possible.

The plunger reached the hilt. Now it was just a matter of time. Diogenes watched the heart monitor begin to slow inexorably as, in the execution chamber, Lucius Garey struggled feebly, gargling and gasping for air, in evident torment despite the sedative and paralytic.

This is the way the world ends. This is the way the world ends. He took a deep, shuddering breath and pushed the Old Voice down. It took a full twelve minutes for cardiac activity to cease completely.

"Done," Diogenes said briskly, stepping back from the monitor.

The warden exchanged glances with the prison doctor. They were, Diogenes noticed, both ashen looking—the condemned had died an ugly, protracted, and painful death. He felt contempt for their weakness and hypocrisy.

The warden took a deep breath, mastering himself. "Very well," he said. "Dr. Leyland, would you please confirm that the subject has expired and sign the death certificate?"

Diogenes nodded. Stepping away from the monitor, he plucked a few items from his medical bag—replacing the empty syringe in it as he did so—then stepped into the execution chamber. The viewing curtain was closed once again: already, the family members were being escorted out by prison staff, and official witnesses would be signing documentation. He walked over to the corpse of Lucius Garey. The man, in his agony, had struggled mightily against the leather bonds, as abraded and bleeding skin at the wrists and ankles attested to. Diogenes plucked the needle from the cubital vein and disposed of it in medical waste. He shone a light into Garey's eyes and confirmed the pupils were fixed and dilated. After this, he did not look again at the face of the corpse: its unpleasant expression, including the fat protruding stub of a tongue—like an eggplant-colored Popsicle, papillae distinct and engorged as if from chelonitoxism—was offensive to him. Instead, he went methodically through the steps necessary to confirm death. He did a trapezius squeeze to ensure there was no pain reflex; observed the skin color; noted there were no signs of respiratory effort; felt the carotid artery for a pulse and found none. Using a stethoscope on the chest of the corpse, he listened carefully for respiration or a heart rhythm for two minutes. There was nothing; Lucius

Garey was as dead as a mackerel. He stepped back, then turned and walked quickly away from the body with relief: Garey had voided his bowels during the execution process.

He walked out of the chamber, gave his findings to the warden and LeBronk, then completed the official paperwork, concluding with the time and date. Everything was done now—everything, that was, save what was for him the most important step of all.

By now, he knew, a refrigerated van would be waiting in a small parking area outside the death house. He'd drive back to the M.E.'s office in advance of it. He shook hands with the warden and LeBronk in turn. They both still appeared a little shaken from Garey's protracted death. It amused Diogenes, on one level, that it had not occurred to either of them—or anyone else, for that matter—that the same doctor who'd administered the fatal cocktail of drugs to Garey would, rather unusually, also be the coroner who both pronounced the man dead and performed the postmortem. As a result, the unusual preservatives he had introduced would never be discovered in the deceased's bloodstream. Of course, he hadn't told Constance he was executioner as well as examiner—that would have distressed her unnecessarily.

Within five minutes he was out of the prison and headed toward LaBelle, county seat of Hendry County, where the M.E.'s office was located. He glanced southeast, in the direction of Miami. *While my little one, while my pretty one, sleeps.* In the trunk of his rental car—along with the beautiful suit, fast-acting hair coloring, and colored contact lenses of his Petru Lupei identity—was a special medical case, used in the transporting of organs or human tissue for such critical applications as transplants. At present, it was empty.

In an hour or so, he knew, it would be empty no longer.

40

Howard Longstreet's office on the twenty-third floor of 26 Federal Plaza was not at all like the usual FBI office, which was how Longstreet liked it. For one thing, it rarely if ever received visitors—the executive associate director for intelligence called on others; they did not call on him. For another, considering Longstreet's lofty position in the FBI, it was quite sparse. Longstreet eschewed the usual trophies, framed certificates or awards, and photograph of the sitting president normally found in such offices. There was not even a computer—Longstreet did his digital work elsewhere. Instead, there were three walls lined in books of every imaginable subject; a small table barely large enough for a tea service; and two wing chairs of cracked red leather.

Longstreet's thin and remarkably tall form lounged in one of the wing chairs. He was reading—alternately—from a confidential report in one hand and a copy of George Eliot's *Daniel Deronda* in the other. Now and then he stopped to take a sip from an iced beverage sitting on the table.

There was a faint knock on the door, then it opened a crack. "He's here, sir," came the voice of his private secretary.

"Send him in," Longstreet said.

The door opened wider and A. X. L. Pendergast entered the room. Now, two days after his rescue, his rather distracted face still bore the marks of numerous scrapes and abrasions, but he was once again wearing his trademark black suit.

"Aloysius," Longstreet said. "Good morning." He gestured to the empty chair—a little dusty from disuse—and Pendergast took a seat.

Longstreet gestured at his drink. "Care for an Arnold Palmer?"

"Thank you, no."

Longstreet took a sip of his own. "You've been busy."

"One could say that."

Those few people who knew Pendergast well would notice that he addressed Longstreet differently from the way he addressed others. There was somewhat less irony in his tone, and his normal air of remote detachment was tempered with something almost like deference. It was the vestigial effect, Longstreet knew, of being in the company of the man who had previously been one's superior officer.

"I want to thank you for my rescue," Pendergast said, "and for getting me back to New York so quickly."

Longstreet waved a dismissive hand. Then he sat forward and pinioned Pendergast with bright black eyes. "If you want to thank me, you can do so by answering a few questions—with the honesty that I've always expected and demanded of you."

Pendergast went a little still. "I'll answer however I can."

"Who brought you into the FBI?"

"You know who did: Michael Decker."

"Yes. Michael Decker." Longstreet ran a hand through his long gray hair. "My direct report, and your right-hand man, during our time in the Ghost Company. He saved your life twice during the later tactical ops, did he not?"

"Three times."

Longstreet raised an eyebrow as if in surprise, although in fact he already knew the answers to all these questions. "And what was the motto of the Ghost Company?"

"*Fidelitas usque ad mortem.*"

"Quite right. 'Loyalty unto death.' Mike was close to you, was he not?"

"He was like a brother to me."

"And he was like a son to me. After the Ghost Company, you were *both* like sons to me. And since his death, I've tried to take on his role so far as it pertains to you. I've done what I can to see you have free rein to work on the cases that most interest you—because, after all, that is what you're best at, and it would be a shame to waste or, God forbid, lose your services. I've also, on occasion, shielded you from the official wrath of the Bureau. So far as I could, of course; there were one or two occasions when not even I could help completely."

"I understand, H. And I've always been grateful."

"But it's Mike Decker's death I want to talk about right now." Longstreet took another sip of his drink.

Pendergast nodded slowly. Three years earlier, Decker had been found in his Washington, DC, home—murdered, with a bayonet pinning his head to his office chair.

"At first, there were some who suspected you as being the killer— I, of course, was never among them. Later it became clear it was your brother, Diogenes, who murdered Mike and tried to frame you for the job."

Longstreet peered into his drink. "Now here's where we get to the heart of the matter. A few months later, once you had been cleared of the false charges, you took me aside and said—not in these exact words, of course—'You didn't hear it from me, but my brother is dead.' When I asked you for proof, you went on to inform me that, while you had not seen the body with your own eyes, you had every proof necessary to confirm his death. You asked me to refrain from further investigation and to take your word for it. You further explained that you did not want me, your friend and mentor and erstwhile commanding officer, to waste countless hours conducting what would ultimately prove a fruitless chase. You suggested that, when the time was right, I should quietly bury Mike Decker's death among the cold cases. And so I did."

Longstreet sat forward a little further and laid a fingertip lightly on Pendergast's knee. "But therein lies the rub. After your disappearance from and apparent drowning near Exmouth, Massachusetts, we of course sent a field team to do a careful investigation. While we turned up no signs of you, either dead or alive, we did lift three prints—all from a wooden observation pier overlooking the town beach—that belonged to your brother. Diogenes."

Longstreet sat back and let this linger in the air for a moment before continuing.

"I kept the discovery silent. But you can imagine what went through my mind. As members of the Ghost Company—one of the smallest, most secret, most intensely loyal outfits in the military—we all took blood oaths to avenge any member who died at the hands of another. When you specifically told me your brother, Mike Decker's murderer, was dead, you were, in effect, asking me to put aside my blood oath. Now, years later, there is very good evidence that he was *not* dead, after all." He pinned Pendergast with his gaze. "What's going on, Aloysius? Did you lie to me, betray our common oath, because the killer was your brother?"

"No," Pendergast said immediately. "I thought he was dead. We all thought he was dead. *But he's not.*"

Longstreet remained still for a moment. Then he nodded, settling into his chair, waiting.

Pendergast's expression went far away. Then, after a few minutes, he roused himself.

"I'm going to have to share some history with you," he said. "Some very private family history. You mentioned that Diogenes tried to frame me for Mike Decker's murder—among others. For a while, he was successful, and I was imprisoned."

Pendergast went silent again for a moment. "I have a ward by the name of Constance Greene. She has the appearance of a woman in her early twenties. She also has a very difficult history that's not important now; what *is* important is that she is very fragile mentally and emotionally. She has a hair-trigger temper. Anything that threatens her or those few close to her is likely to precipitate a violent, even homicidal, response." He drew a deep breath. "When I was in prison, Diogenes seduced Constance and then discarded her with a cruel note suggesting that she kill herself rather than live with the shame. In response, Constance pursued Diogenes with single-minded fury. She chased him across Europe and finally caught up with him on the island of Stromboli. There, she threw him into the lava flow streaming down from the Stromboli volcano."

Longstreet's only reaction was to raise his bushy eyebrows.

"Both Constance and I believed Diogenes to be dead. And in the intervening years, there has been no reason for me to believe otherwise. Until my final days in Exmouth."

"He contacted you?" Longstreet asked.

"No. But I saw him, or thought I saw him, on one occasion—observing me from a distance. Later on, I came upon proof of his being in the vicinity. But before I could do anything about him, I was washed out to sea and held prisoner. And in the weeks since, it appears that—" Pendergast paused to compose himself— "Diogenes has managed to . . . *interfere* with Constance again."

"Interfere?"

"All evidence points to his having either kidnapped her, drugged her, or somehow Stockholm-syndromed her into becoming his accomplice. Whatever the case, they were seen leaving—escaping—my Riverside Drive residence together two mornings ago."

Longstreet frowned. "Stockholm syndrome would imply active participation on her part. Kidnapping would not. There's a big difference."

"The evidence suggests that Constance actively assisted in her abduction."

The office fell into silence. Longstreet tented his long, narrow fingers and rested his huge shaggy head on them. Pendergast remained motionless as a marble statue in the old wing chair. Many minutes passed. Finally, Pendergast cleared his throat.

"I'm sorry I didn't share these details with you before," he said. "They're painful. Mortifying. But...I need your help. I'm aware of the blood oath we took. Previously, my nerve failed me where Diogenes was concerned. But I now realize there is only one answer: my brother *must* die. We must work together to track him down and make sure he doesn't survive apprehension. It's as you say: we owe it to Mike Decker to make sure he's taken care of once and for all."

"And the young girl?" Longstreet asked. "Constance?"

"She must remain unharmed. We can sort out her involvement once Diogenes is dead."

Longstreet thought for just a moment. Then, silently, he extended his hand.

Just as silently, Pendergast shook it.

41

THE BOAT PARTED the cerulean water in a silky motion, the warm air riffling Constance's mahogany hair and playing over her long dress. She reclined on the turquoise-colored upholstered seat next to Diogenes, who was at the wheel. They had taken his yacht from South Beach Harbor to a place called Upper Sugarloaf Key. There, at a bungalow nestled among pines on the water, they had exchanged it for a smaller boat with a shallow draft. Diogenes had spoken of it in reverential tones: a nineteen-foot Chris Craft Racing Runabout built in 1950, which he'd had restored with new bookmatched sides, new decks, and a meticulously rebuilt engine. The boat's name, in gold leaf edged in black, was PHOENIX, with HALCYON KEY below.

Now, as they neared their destination, a change came over Diogenes. Not a voluble man to begin with, he had become more communicative, if not talkative. At the same time, his normally masked face had smoothed out and relaxed, his expression becoming almost dream-like—a most odd change from his normally acute, watchful mien. The wind stirred his short, ginger hair and his eyes were narrowed, looking ahead. As Petru Lupei, he had among other things covered his dead white eye with a colored contact lens, but she noticed that at some point he had removed it, bringing his eyes back to their heterochromic state, along with removing the dye from his hair. His Van Dyke was already starting to regrow. His whole way of moving, of speaking, seemed to have changed as well, physically becoming the Diogenes that she remembered from almost four years ago, but mentally different; not so hard-edged, not nearly so arrogant and acerbic.

"On the right," he said, his hand moving from the chromed wheel toward a cluster of tiny islands covered with palmettos, "are the keys called the Rattlesnake Lumps."

Constance gazed in their direction. The sun was low on the horizon to her left, a great yellow globe throwing a dazzling path across the water, painting the tiny islands in a golden light. Everywhere she looked there were low islands, uninhabited and wild. While she had never really thought much about the Florida Keys, the beauty and serenity of this place—and its tropical isolation—was something she never would have expected. The water was shallow—she could see the bottom zipping along below—but Diogenes handled the boat with sureness, apparently knowing the shallow, winding channels by heart.

"That little key to the left is called Happy Jack, and the one ahead is Pumpkin Key."

"And Halcyon?"

"Soon, my dear. Soon. That large key on the right, almost entirely mangrove, is called Johnston Key."

He turned the wheel and the boat eased left, bringing them toward the setting sun, passing Happy Jack on the left and Johnston on the right.

"And that, straight ahead, is Halcyon Key."

Beyond Johnston, silhouetted in gold, she saw a large island surrounded by four tiny humps. As the boat approached, a long beach came into view, with a low, sandy bluff at one end, and beside it the white rooflines of a large house. Mangroves extended across the lower two-thirds of the island. The islets were also clusters of mangroves, some with tiny beaches at the seaward end. A long pier extended from the key, with a little wooden gazebo at its terminus.

Diogenes brought the boat in smoothly to where the dock made an L. He threw out a couple of fenders, reversed the engine for a moment, and the boat came to rest. He killed the engine, hopped out, tied up, and held out his hand. She grasped it and stepped out on the weathered pier.

"Welcome," Diogenes said. He reached into the rear cockpit of the boat and pulled out her things. "Do I dare say, welcome home?"

Constance paused a moment on the pier and breathed in. The air was rich and fragrant with the sea, and the sun was just setting into the palms that fringed the beach. To her right she could make out, beyond the scattering of more uninhabited keys, the great expanse of the Gulf.

Two awkward pelicans sat on posts side by side at the far end of the pier.

"You are rather quiet, my dear."

"This is all very new to me." She inhaled, braced herself, tried to shake the feeling of being a stranger; of venturing into unknown and dangerous territory. She wondered, briefly, if she hadn't made the biggest mistake of her life and would come to regret it bitterly. But no: she had to forge ahead and not look back.

"Tell me about the island," she asked.

"Halcyon Key is about nine acres in extent," said Diogenes, strolling along the dock with her luggage in his hands. "Six of that is mangrove and the rest palm trees, sandy beaches, and that bluff, there, which is unusual for the Keys."

As they walked down the pier, the two pelicans raised their wings and flapped heavily away. Reaching the end of the pier, Constance followed Diogenes along a wooden walkway above the beach, through a cluster of mangroves, which suddenly opened into a wide area covered with sugary sand, shaded by numerous royal palms rising above lush gardens. In the middle of this open area stood a large, two-story Victorian house painted white, with wraparound verandas on both floors and a square tower rising at one end. It was a sprawling, airy house, the roof peaks and gables shining in the light of the setting sun.

"It was built in 1893 by a wealthy Bostonian," said Diogenes, "who retired here with his wife. They had romantic ideas of turning it into an inn, but once here they found it unrealistic and lonely and soon left. After that it had a string of impecunious owners and went downhill— until I bought it twenty years ago and had it restored to its original splendor. We're surrounded on all sides by the Great White Heron National Wildlife Refuge. This key with its house was grandfathered in when the refuge was created."

"I don't see any boats around."

"The water's too shallow, and the channels too tricky, for most motorboats. You'll see kayakers in the warmer seasons, though."

"It is beautiful," she murmured.

"Come." He led her up the stairs and onto the broad veranda, which looked out over the lush gardens to a wall of mangroves. He opened the door for her and she stepped inside. A front hall with walnut wainscoting led to a staircase, with a living room on the right and a library on the left, each with large fireplaces, Persian rugs, and two Venetian chandeliers. The house smelled pleasantly of polish, beeswax, and potpourri.

She felt his eyes on her, awaiting her reaction. When she said nothing, he continued: "I'd like to introduce you to my factotum."

She looked at him sharply. "You have help?"

"Yes." He turned. "Mr. Gurumarra?"

A man silently appeared, as if out of nowhere. He was very tall and slender, with very dark skin, an extremely wrinkled face, and a head of tight white hair. It was impossible to guess how old he was; he seemed timeless.

"Mr. Gurumarra, this is Miss Greene, who is the new resident of Halcyon Key."

The man stepped forward and shook her hand with his own, which was dry and cool. "Pleased to meet you, Miss Greene." He spoke very formally, with an Australian accent.

"I'm pleased to meet you as well, Mr. Gurumarra," said Constance.

"Mr. Gurumarra is from Queensland. He is Aborigine. Whatever you need, he can fix it here or bring it to the island for you. I suspect you will be needing a new wardrobe appropriate to the warm climate. If you put together a list, Mr. Gurumarra will take care of it."

"Thank you."

The man seemed to melt silently back into the shadowed corridor.

"He has been with me ever since I bought the island," said Diogenes. "His discretion is absolute. He does not cook—that is my domain—but he keeps the house in order, shops, and handles all the little details of life that I find so irksome."

"Where does he live?"

"The gardener's cottage, through the buttonwood grove across the beach." He took her hand, briefly, and led her around to the back staircase. "You probably want to refresh yourself after our journey. Let me show you to your rooms."

She followed him up the stairs. They arrived at a second-floor sitting room that faced the veranda in the back of the house. From here there was a spectacular view northward, past keys fringing the Gulf and to the great expanse of water beyond. The sun was now touching the horizon and sinking fast. The windows were open and a breeze from the sea billowed the lace curtains and flowed through, keeping the room cool.

"You have your own wing," said Diogenes. "Three bedrooms and a sitting room at your disposal, fireplace, and kitchenette. Accessible by the back stairs. Very private."

"And where do you sleep?"

"In the front wing." He hesitated. "The arrangements are, of course, flexible and can be allowed to...evolve."

Constance understood his meaning quite well.

He set down her suitcase and trunk. "I'll leave you to choose your room and get settled. I'll meet you in the library for a drink. Would champagne be suitable?"

That queer feeling of strangeness was almost overpowering. She wondered if she really had the spine to go through with this.

"Thank you, Peter."

He smiled and took her hand. "On Halcyon, it's Diogenes. I am myself. There's only family here." He paused. "And speaking of family, we should—at some point—discuss what to do about ours."

"Excuse me?"

"My dear, there's our son to consider. And, then, of course, there is my brother's child. Tristram. I want all my blood relatives well taken care of."

Constance hesitated. "My, I mean our, son is in the care of the monks of Gsalrig Chongg. I can think of no better place for him."

"And I agree. For now. Circumstances might change."

"As for Tristram, he's been told of his father's disappearance and I suppose, when his death becomes official, he'll learn of it. He's fine for now in boarding school, but perhaps we can become his guardians when appropriate."

"An ideal plan. I know so very little about my brother's sole remaining son—I look forward to a deeper acquaintance. But for now, adieu." He began to carry her hand to his lips but she gently removed it. He did not seem to mind. "In the library, at six."

He left, and she stood in the sitting area, looking out to sea. The sun had now vanished below the limn of the sea and a warm twilight seemed to rise up from the ocean.

Wandering through the three rooms at her disposal, she picked the one facing east—with a view of an archipelago of tiny uninhabited keys—to take advantage of the rising sun. It did not take her long to unpack. None of her clothes were the slightest bit suitable for Florida. She had taken so relatively little from the Riverside Drive mansion, and no keepsake or memento of Aloysius—that would only cause her pain.

She entered the library at six, pausing in the doorway, her breath taken away.

Diogenes, sitting in a wing chair by a small fire, rose. "I've worked hard to make the room agreeable to you. It's the heart of the house."

Constance took a step inside. It was a sumptuous space, two stories high. The floor was spread with Persian rugs, the walls crowded with bookshelves, with an oak library ladder on brass rails and a red marble fireplace. Instead of books, one wall was covered with small paintings, crowded together in the nineteenth-century atelier style. A gorgeous painted and inlaid harpsichord dominated a far corner.

"What a beauty," Constance murmured, approaching the instrument.

"The harpsichord is by the Florentine builder Vincenzo Sodi, 1780. Double tongue jacks with soft and hard leather plectra in the manner of the Cembalo Angelico. A lovely tone."

"I look forward to playing it."

"And you will find on the shelves all your favorite books, in rare editions, with many, many new titles for you to discover: titles of beauty and whimsy, such as Verga's *Livre de Prierès* in vellum, the closest thing one can find to a nineteenth-century illuminated manuscript;

or Teague and Rede's exquisitely rare set of colored woodcuts, *Night Fall in the Ti-Tree*. Just to name two. Ah, and the paintings! As you have probably discerned already, they're by Bronzino, Pontormo, Jan van Eyck, Pieter Bruegel the Elder, and Paul Klee."

Diogenes pirouetted almost like a dancer, gesturing this way and that.

"In the other corner you'll find an array of musical instruments. And in those cupboards are games, cards, and puzzles; chess and go. That construction in the other corner is an Edwardian dollhouse."

It was huge and intricate, of almost magical workmanship. She went over to it. It was exquisite, precisely the thing she would have loved above all else to own as a young girl, and as she examined it her feelings of uncertainty and physical enervation faded. She could not help but be enchanted.

"Come, let us enjoy the champagne."

He ushered her to a chair before the fire. With the setting of the sun, the evening had become slightly cool. The feeling of surrealness overwhelmed her again, seeing him sitting in a leather wing chair, smiling in domestic content as he removed a bottle of champagne from a silver ice bucket and poured two glasses, offering one to her.

"Nineteen ninety-five Clos d'Ambonnay, by Krug," said Diogenes, raising his glass and touching the rim to hers.

"Good champagne is wasted on me."

"Only until you develop your taste."

She sipped, marveling at its flavor.

"Tomorrow I'll show you the rest of the island. But for now, this is for you." He took out a small wrapped box from his jacket pocket, with a ribbon tied around it, and gave it to her.

She took it and removed the wrapping, revealing a plain sandalwood box. Unlatching it, she opened it—to find, nestled in velvet, an IV bag, filled with a faintly roseate liquid.

"What's this?"

"The arcanum. The elixir. For you, Constance. Especially and only for you."

She gazed into the liquid. "And how do I take it?"

"By infusion."

"You mean, intravenously?"

"Yes."

"When?"

"Whenever you like. Tomorrow, perhaps?"

She stared at the box. "I'll take it now."

"You mean, *right* now?"

"Yes. While we drink the champagne."

"That's what I love about you, Constance. No hesitation!" Diogenes rose, walked over to a tall, narrow closet, opened its door, and rolled out a gleaming, brand-new IV rack on a trolley, with all the associated equipment.

Constance felt a faint sense of alarm. This was indeed crossing the Rubicon.

"The infusion takes about an hour."

He positioned the rack by her chair, plugged in the electronic pump and monitor, fussed with the tubes and valves.

"Roll up your right sleeve, my dear."

Suddenly Constance had a thought: a very dark thought. Was all this a charade? Was she being played once again? Maybe Diogenes's love for her was a sham; maybe this was some insanely intricate plot to deliver into her veins some poisonous or deforming drug. But as quickly as this thought came, she dismissed it: no one, not even Diogenes, could pull off a deception as profound as that. And she felt certain she would have sensed something wrong. She rolled up her sleeve.

His warm fingers took the arm, gently palpated it, strapped a rubber tourniquet around. "No need to look."

She looked anyway as he expertly inserted the needle. Diogenes hung the bag on the rack, turned the stopcock—and she turned back to watch as the violet liquid crept down the tube toward her arm.

42

THE MAIN STREET of Exmouth, Massachusetts, looked far different to-day from the last time Pendergast had seen it in sunlight. That had been—he thought a moment—twenty-eight days ago. On that day, the entire population of the town had been assembled before the po-lice station, spilling down side streets, and the mood had been one of relief and joy: the cloud that had lingered over the town had vanished; the recent murders, and the vestiges of an old, poisonous past, had both been resolved. But now the police station was quiet and dark: a temporary National Guard barracks had been erected beside it until the shattered town could re-form itself and a new chief of police be appointed.

The main street itself still appeared at first glance to be a typical working-class New England fishing village…until one looked closely. Then the differences became apparent: the boarded-up windows; the numerous FOR SALE signs; the empty shopfronts. It would be years be-fore the town returned to normal—if, indeed, it ever did.

Back in New York, Pendergast knew, Howard Longstreet was—in his quiet way—bringing all the massive resources at his disposal to bear on the single question: where had Diogenes vanished to? Favors were being called in, sister agencies were being queried, even NSA domestic surveillance was being tapped. Nothing, however, had yet surfaced. And so Pendergast had journeyed to Exmouth: the last place he'd seen his brother before he himself had been swept out to sea.

He had spent the morning speaking with several of Exmouth's inhabitants, sharing joint memories with some and asking vague, indirect questions of others. Now he continued driving down Main, glancing this way and that. Here, he saw, was the corner from which he and Constance had watched the festivities on that final day. *Constance.* Pendergast held her image in his mind for a moment, then forced it away. Feelings of restlessness, doubt, and guilt were threatening to impair his judgment. It was vital that he keep his speculations as to her motives at bay.

At the far end of the business district, Pendergast paused long enough to glance at the rambling Victorian sea captain's house that had, until recently, been the Captain Hull Inn. The Inn's cheery signboard was now gone, replaced by a large, monochromatic sign bearing the name of the R. J. Mayfield Corporation and heralding the building's imminent destruction, to be replaced by Exmouth Harbour Village, a series of "starter condos, with ocean views, priced to sell." If, in the wake of tragedy, the town was ultimately unable to return to its roots as a fishing village, it could always become just another middlebrow vacation destination.

Nosing the big Rolls away, Pendergast turned onto Dune Road, driving slowly in order to check the numbers on the mailboxes. When he reached number 3, he stopped. The house was typical of the region: a small Cape Cod of weathered shingles, with a white picket fence around it and a small, carefully tended yard.

As he examined the house, his cell phone rang. He pulled it from his jacket. "Yes?"

"Secret Agent Man!" came the voice from River Pointe, Ohio.

"Yes, Mime?"

"Calling to give you an update. It seems that chauffeur of yours has been doing some serious traveling of his own. On November eighth, he chartered a private jet from Teterboro Airport, with no advance notice, using DebonAir Aviation. Final destination, Gander, Newfoundland. Well, that was the final destination of the charter, anyway—by poking through some private email exchanges between the DebonAir employees, I've learned your chauffeur wasn't exactly a model passenger."

"Is Proctor still in the Gander area?"

"Can't find a trace of him. Not in the motels, not in the surrounding hamlets—nothing. That's why I'm guessing Gander might not have been his last stop."

"But Gander is essentially the eastern tip of North America."

"Score one for our team! Roll the dice and play some Monopoly: where could your boy be headed?"

"Europe?" Pendergast asked softly.

"A possibility."

"Keep on it, Mime. Use all available resources—national and international."

"Oh, I will. International are actually better—I have lots of like-minded friends over there. And don't forget: the meter's running. I'll check in when I know more."

The line went dead. Pendergast thoughtfully replaced the phone in his pocket. He was relieved Proctor was likely alive. Once again, he had to consciously force himself to leave finding Proctor to Mime. He had to focus all his energy on the present mystery.

He sat very still, controlling his breathing, consciously lowering his heartbeat, establishing a mind-set. Then he opened the car door, walked up to the house, and knocked.

It was answered by a short, heavyset man in his late fifties, with a thin comb-over of mouse-brown hair, beady eyes, and what appeared to be an expression of permanent suspicion on his face. He looked Pendergast up and down. "Yes?"

"Thank you, I will come inside. It's rather chilly out here." And Pendergast slipped past the man and into a neat living room, with nautical prints on the walls and a hooked rug on the floor.

"Just a minute," the man protested. "I didn't—"

"Abner Knott, isn't it?" Pendergast said, helping himself to a chair set before a low fire burning on the grate. "I heard your name mentioned in town."

"And I know about you, too," Knott said, his little pig eyes looking Pendergast up and down. "You're that FBI man that was in town last month."

"How clever of you to recognize me. If you'll be so kind as to answer a few questions, I won't take up more than a minute or two of your time."

Knott walked up to a chair across from Pendergast, but he did not sit down. He stood there staring, arms folded over his chest.

"It's my understanding you have three cottages to rent, here on Dune Road." Pendergast had learned this—and much more—from his quiet inquiries in town that morning. He had also learned that Abner Knott was thoroughly disliked by the local citizenry. He was considered miserly and churlish, and held in almost as low esteem as R. J. Mayfield—the real estate developer undertaking the destruction of the Captain Hull Inn, and whose cheap, shabby condos were fast becoming the scourge of Cape Ann and points north.

"I own three cottages. It's no secret. Inherited two from my parents, and built the third one myself on a piece of adjoining land."

"Thank you. I also understand that during October, two of those cottages were empty—not surprising, being out of season—but the third was occupied. It was only occupied for about two weeks, however, which was unusual, since I understand you rent your cottages by the month."

"Who's been talking about me?" Knott asked.

Pendergast shrugged. "You know how few secrets there are in a small town like Exmouth. In any case, I'm interested in the temporary lodger in your cabin. Could you tell me about him?"

Knott's expression had become more and more truculent as Pendergast spoke. "No, I can't tell you anything about him."

"Why is that, pray?"

"Because my renters' business is their own, and I don't like to spread it around. Especially not to you."

Pendergast looked surprised. "Me?"

"You. It wasn't until you arrived in town that all our troubles started."

"Indeed?"

"Well, that's how I saw it. Saw it then, and see it today. So if it's all the same to you, I'll ask you to kindly vacate my premises—*and* my property. Unless you have some sort of warrant."

The man waited, arms crossed.

"Mr. Knott," Pendergast said after a moment. "It's odd you should mention a warrant. You might be unaware of this, but my sudden departure from Exmouth has resulted in a rather large FBI operation. After what I've learned here today, I could have just such a warrant— and within forty-eight hours."

Knott's expression grew, if anything, more truculent. "Go ahead."

Pendergast seemed to digest this a moment.

"The door's over there."

But Pendergast made no move to stand up. "So you refuse to answer my questions without a warrant?"

"I said as much, didn't I?"

"Yes, you did. You also said I was the cause of the town's troubles."

And here, Pendergast looked squarely at the short man standing before him. "But it hasn't all been trouble—has it?"

Knott frowned. "What do you mean?"

"This real estate developer, R. J. Mayfield. Most of the town is very unhappy he's planning to build condos in Exmouth—tearing down the Inn and erecting an eyesore in its place."

"I wouldn't know about that," Knott said.

"But then, there are a few who feel quite differently: those people who are eager to sell land to the Mayfield Corporation. Phase two of the Exmouth Harbour Village—still in the development stages, of course—will take up some of the coastline south of the old Inn."

Knott was silent.

"And that would include your cottages. It seems, Mr. Knott, that you stand to earn a pretty penny from Exmouth Harbour Village—a lucky thing, given how the rest of the town is faring."

"What of it?" Knott said. "A man has a right to make money."

"It's just that the scuttlebutt is your section of coastline is sand and limestone that, if speculation is true, has been eaten away by receding groundwater over the last century—meaning the odd sinkhole might open up somewhere at any minute. I'll bet that's something you don't tell your renters, do you?"

"Just gossip," said Knott.

Pendergast reached into his suit coat and removed an envelope. "The Tufts geologist who prepared this report back in 1956... Was he a gossip? I wonder what would happen if this were to fall into the hands of Mayfield? Say, this very afternoon?"

Knott's jaw dropped. "You—"

"Oh, he'd no doubt learn of it eventually—surveys, engineering studies, and the like. But this way, he'd learn about it *before* he has a contract with you." Pendergast shook his head. "And then, Mr. Knott, your luck would change—very fast." He paused. "You see, between ourselves I'd really much prefer not to have to wait forty-eight hours to obtain that warrant."

There was a long, freezing silence.

"What do you want to know?" Knott asked in a very low voice.

Pendergast settled back and made himself comfortable in the chair, taking his time, removing a notebook, turning the pages to find a blank one. "When did your lodger take possession of the cottage?"

"Three or four days after you came into town."

"Did he ask for a particular cottage?"

"Yes. The one with the best view of Skullcrusher Rocks."

"And when did he leave?"

"The day after the—" Knott stopped abruptly, and his mouth worked silently for a few seconds. "The day after everything went to hell," he finally said, lowering his eyes.

"Is this the man?" And Pendergast held out a police photo of Diogenes.

"No."

"Take a closer look."

Knott leaned in, squinting at the picture. "It really doesn't look like him."

Pendergast was not surprised. "This renter. Did he tell you why he was here?"

"Don't know. You'd have to ask his lady friend."

"Lady friend?"

"The one who lived with him."

A terrible feeling suddenly overwhelmed Pendergast. *Is it even possible...?* No, it wasn't; he had to get a better grip on himself.

"Could you please describe the woman?"

"Blond. Young. Short. Athletic."

"What can you tell me about her?"

"Got a couple jobs in town. Before the two left so suddenly, that is."

"What jobs were those?"

"Waitress in the Chart Room. Also worked part-time as an assistant in that tourist shop, A Taste of Exmouth."

For a moment, Pendergast went quite still. He knew this woman by sight—quite well, in fact. She had waited on him more than once at the Inn. So Diogenes had an accomplice—an assistant—a helper? This had never occurred to him before.

He was roused by Knott shifting irritably before him. "Anything else?" the man said.

"Just one more thing. I'd like to spend an hour or two in the cottage they rented—alone and undisturbed."

When Knott didn't move, Pendergast extended a hand, palm upward, in anticipation of receiving the key. "Thank you," he said. "You've been most helpful."

43

Constance rose just before dawn, in time to watch the sun burst over the distant sea horizon and climb into a clear blue sky. She slept with the windows open, and it had been a cool night. She shed her nightdress and felt the sun on her body, warm and inviting. Turning, she went into the bathroom. It was spacious and white, with an old-fashioned slipper tub and a shower. She ran the water in the tub and went back into the bedroom, arranging a few of her possessions on the bureau. The infusion had been disappointingly uneventful, and she felt no different this morning than she had before. But Diogenes had warned her it might take a day or two to feel the effects, which he assured her would be quite dramatic, invigorating, and energizing.

When she emerged from the bath, she could smell coffee brewing. She descended the back stairs, which ended in a small hallway leading to the conservatory; a short walk brought her to the kitchen. Diogenes was seated at a table in a breakfast nook, in a bow window looking out over the gardens. His lean frame was wrapped in an elegant silk morning gown, his ginger hair combed back; he looked fresh, trim, self-assured, and attractive. The likeness to his dead brother was undeniable. The bicolored eyes added an almost dashing touch. Again she had that queer feeling of strangeness, as if she'd fallen out of her own life and onto an alien planet.

"What will you have for breakfast?" he asked.

"Do you have kippers?"

"Indeed we do."

"Well, then, if it isn't too much trouble, kippers, two soft-boiled eggs, rashers, and toast."

"A hearty breakfast. I approve. Coffee or espresso?"

"Espresso, thank you."

He brought her a demitasse and busied himself at the stove while she drank the coffee. Her breakfast was soon placed in front of her, and he served himself the same. They ate in silence. Diogenes was one of those rare people, Constance thought, who was not disturbed or made anxious by long silences. For this she was grateful. A talker would have been intolerable.

At last, Diogenes put down his empty cup. "And now—a tour?"

He rose, took her hand, and led her out onto the back veranda and down the stairs to the white sand. The path, lined on both sides by rich beds of flowers, meandered past a picturesque palapa, outdoor fireplace, and stone patio with an old brick grill and an arrangement of weather-beaten teak furniture. From there the path wandered through a grove of buttonwood to emerge at a long, white beach. Gurumarra's cottage was just visible through the foliage. The sun glittered off the water, which whispered and lapped on the sand.

Diogenes had fallen silent, but his light step and graceful way of moving, and the glow in his eyes, told her how precious this place was to him. She felt awkward in her long, old-fashioned dress.

At the end of the beach, a cluster of mangroves blocked their way along the shore and the trail cut inland, winding up the low, sandy bluff, over the top, and partway down the other side; and there, suddenly, a most unusual structure appeared, hidden by the curve of the bluff, looking over the beach and out to the Gulf. It was built of weathered, dark marble and looked like a small, circular temple, but in between the columns were tall, mullioned windows, each pane a mysterious, dark-gray color, almost black.

It was so surprising a vision that Constance involuntarily halted.

"Come," said Diogenes in hushed tones, leading her around the structure. He grasped the bronze knob of a tall door, and it whispered open, disclosing the spare interior. He handed her inside and closed the door behind.

Constance felt overwhelmed. It was utterly simple, with a black marble floor, gray marble columns, and a domed roof. But it was the mullioned windows and the quality of light that made the interior unworldly. The panes were of some sort of smoked, glassy substance, infused or inflected with billions of little shimmerings of light, depending on how one moved one's point of view. The light that came through them had a strange, attenuated quality that rendered the interior absolutely colorless. And as she looked at Diogenes, and the rapt expression on his face, she saw that he and herself were both rendered in black-and-white tones, all the color sucked out of the air. It was a most uncanny phenomenon. But rather than being disturbing, she found it serene and spiritual, as if all unnecessary adornment, all vulgar embellishment, had been stripped away, leaving only simplicity and truth. The temple was completely empty beyond a black leather divan, which occupied a space somewhat off center.

They must have stood there for several minutes, in silence, before Diogenes spoke. But he didn't actually speak: he hummed a low melody that Constance recognized as the opening voice of Bach's Passacaglia and Fugue in C minor. And as he hummed the tonic voice, then switched to the second voice, and the third, the temple began filling with sound building upon sound, layer upon layer, creating a contrapuntal wonder of echoes.

He stopped but the sound continued for seconds, dying away slowly.

He turned to her and she could see a glint of moisture in his dead eye. "This," he said, "is where I come to forget myself and the world. This is my place of meditation."

"It's extraordinary. The effect of the light is almost impossible to believe."

"Yes. You see, Constance, the great horror of my life is that I can see only in black and white. Color has been denied to me since...the Event."

She inclined her head. *The Event*, she knew, referred to the tragic accident of his childhood that left him blind in one eye—among other things.

"I've clung to the memory of color. But when I enter *here*, in this monochromatic light, I can somehow glimpse the color that I so desperately miss. I can see, almost out of the corner of my vision as it were, ephemeral flashes of color."

"But how?"

He spread his hands. "These panes are all ground and polished from the mineral called obsidian. Volcanic glass. Obsidian has some singular properties when it interacts with light. In the past, I once made a careful and special study of the effects of light and sound on the human body—and this is one of the results."

Constance looked around again. The morning sun was hitting one side of the temple, the light diffusing in, cool and gray, seemingly coming from everywhere and nowhere at once. The opposite side of the temple was dark, but not black. Neither pure white nor pure black was present in the room—everything was in infinite gradations of gray.

"So this is your obsidian chamber."

"Obsidian chamber...you might call it that. Yes, you could very well call it that."

"What do *you* call it?"

"My Tholos."

"*Tholos.* A circular Greek temple."

"Precisely. This one is based on the dimensions of the small Tholos of Delphi."

He fell silent, and Constance was content to simply stand and absorb the remarkable serenity, the beautiful simplicity, of the space. It was silent, and she felt herself falling into the most peculiar reverie, a dream-like state of nothingness, her sense of self dissolving.

"Let us go."

She took a deep breath, returning to reality, and in a moment found herself outside, blinking in the bright light, overwhelmed by the tidal wave of color that engulfed her.

"Shall we continue the tour?"

Constance looked at him. "I . . . feel a little disoriented. I'd like to return to the library and rest. Later, if you don't mind, I'd like to explore on my own."

"Of course," Diogenes replied, spreading his hands. "The island is yours, my dear."

44

Diogenes, resting in his second-floor sitting room, heard Constance quietly descend the back stairs, open the rear door, and walk across the veranda. She moved very lightly, but his hearing was unnaturally acute, and he was able to follow her movements by sound alone. He rose and looked out the window, and a moment later saw her walking along the pathway to the south end of the island.

She was, he understood, in many ways like a wild animal: a tiger, perhaps, or a mustang. The taming of such an animal had to proceed with infinite patience, gentleness, and kindness. And as with the taming of a tiger by her handler, the forcing of any issue could be fatal. He was still amazed he had conquered her, at least in part, coaxed her out of the Pendergast mansion, where she had lived almost the entirety of her long life, and succeeded in bringing her down here. It was the fulfilment of what were now his dearest dreams, his most cherished fantasies. But the taming wasn't complete by any means. Now was the most delicate time—the point where, at the slightest thing, the animal might bolt.

The most important point with wild animals was to give them their freedom. Never corner or cage one. The taming was imposed from within, not without. It was a seduction, not a conquest. Constance would willingly weave her own bonds, her own restraints, and impose them on herself—that was the only way it would work. He did, of course, have the ultimate lure—the arcanum. When she began to feel its rejuvenating effects…that, he hoped, would be the turning point.

Now that she was out of the house, he turned to the platter Gurumarra had brought him, on which was placed a single letter that had arrived at the post office box he maintained in Key West. Taking up a mother-of-pearl letter opener, he neatly slit open the larger, remailing-service envelope and removed the smaller envelope inside. This he slit open in turn and removed a single page of cheap paper. The letter was written in a tiny, precise, spiky hand. There was no salutation, he was glad to see, nor signature at the bottom, nor return address—but he knew very well who it was from.

> I have taken care of everything for you. _Everything_. It all came off exactly as planned. You needn't feel any concern about the assignment you gave me, as I have accomplished everything you asked me to do, leaving no loose ends. Just a firmer touch than you'd authorized, that's all. I will go into the details when we meet, which I hope will be as soon as possible.
>
> When? Where? I am so anxious to tell you everything. Please let me know when we can meet.

Diogenes read the letter twice, a frown marring his face. The importuning tone of the letter was concerning, and it only reinforced an uneasy feeling he'd had for some time. He rose, taking the letter and envelope to the small tiled fireplace, tore it into pieces, struck a match, and set it to an edge of the paper. He stood, watching, as the pieces curled up and were consumed. When it was done he took a poker, stirred the ashes once, and then again.

*   *   *

Constance strolled along the sandy path through the mangroves, which fell away, opening up to a meadow on the southern end of the island. She had long since passed by the "gardener's cottage," Mr. Gurumarra's bungalow, tucked away in a grove of sand pines. It was a beautiful meadow, fringed by low dunes and palm trees, terminating in a sweep of white beach that ended in a curving spit at the key's southern tip. She could see some structures set amid the waving grass, clustered around a thick-limbed, half-dead gumbo-limbo tree.

They were old Victorian outbuildings, constructed of red brick, weathered and crumbling. One had a smokestack that went up perhaps twenty feet, choked in vines. Curious, she followed the path toward them. The first and largest building, the one with the smokestack, had an old sign set in the brick façade, much faded, in which she could make out the word DYNAMO. She approached a shattered window frame to look inside, and a group of swallows flew out the broken door with much noise. Peering in, she could see the remains of machinery, draped in vines. This, she realized, must have been the old power plant for the island, now long abandoned. Beyond that stood three rows of sparkling new solar panels, and next to that a new windowless building with a metal door.

Curious, she went to the building and tried the knob, found it unlocked, and opened it. Inside was a single room full of racks of batteries with thick bundles of wires—the island's new source of power.

Backing out, she closed the door. There was another small brick building nearby, very old, with a green copper-sheathed door. A slanting roof led into the ground—this door led to some subterranean chamber. She went over to it. Painted on the door was the word CISTERN. She tried it and found it locked.

Putting her ear to the keyhole, she listened and heard the faint hum of machinery and the distant sound of running water.

Walking past, she went to the point of the island. Here, two gorgeous beaches met in a long sandy spit that extended into the turquoise water. She felt tired from her walk, and curiously listless. A refreshing dip in the water might help revive her. She looked around. There was nobody about, of course, and the house was at the other end of the key, hidden behind mangroves, with only the tower poking above. There were no boats.

It was as if the water before her, all the way to the horizon, was her private bath.

Feeling a surge of independence, she took off her shoes, unhooked her dress, slipped it off, and in a moment was standing naked, her toes in the water. Again glancing around furtively, she waded into the water, going out quite a way before it became deep enough to immerse herself. She lay on her back, staring up at the blue sky, and trying to calm her mind and simply exist, with no thoughts, no misgivings, no fears, no yammering inner voice.

In the tower of the main house, his eye to the lens of a telescope, Diogenes stared at her white figure floating in the green-blue water. His breath came fast and he could feel his heart hammering in his chest, and with a great effort he tore himself away from the scope.

45

THE SPECIAL OPERATIONS Center took up almost half a floor of Federal Plaza. It was a rambling labyrinth of glass and chrome, illuminated a cool fluorescent blue, with countless workstations, monitoring devices, satellite tracking screens, flat-panel displays of all sizes, terminals for controlling Predator and Reaper drones, and breakout rooms used by field agents planning operations; spooks listening in on satellite communications or sifting terabytes of email data; and federal nerds disassembling cell phones or employing decryption algorithms on confiscated laptops. Everywhere was a low hum of noise: the beep of electronics, the whisper of servers, the murmur of a dozen conversations. Much of the present activity was focused on one thing: crunching massive amounts of data in an attempt to discover the whereabouts of Diogenes Pendergast.

In a glass-walled room in one corner of the center, behind a closed glass door, Pendergast and Howard Longstreet sat at a conference table. A white-noise machine masked their conversation from any passersby. Although this room served as one of Longstreet's numerous satellite offices within Federal Plaza, it was bare save for two laptops, a phone on the table, and a monitor on one wall.

"Your trip to Exmouth was instructive," Longstreet was telling Pendergast. "Thanks to the landlord, we have identities for both Diogenes and his female companion."

"I wouldn't put much stock in Diogenes's identity," Pendergast said. "I believe he has two types—long-term 'avatars' such as Hugo Menzies that he carefully cultivates and that will stand up to official scrutiny, and throwaway names like the one he registered in the Exmouth cottage under, and the one he used to charter the plane that—I'm assuming—my associate Proctor was chasing. Those aren't worth investigating. The long-term identities are what we need to concern ourselves with. I'm not sure how many he still uses, but after he lost the Menzies identity, and what happened at Stromboli, I would doubt he has many left. At this point, having to sustain double, triple, or quadruple lives might be a burden to him."

"Well," said Longstreet, "his accomplice is no question mark at all. Flavia Greyling is in fact her real name. She's got a long and disturbing history. There are a couple of law enforcement agencies that would like to chat with her. Interesting that she used her real first name during her time in Exmouth."

"It seems to speak to a certain disdain for the authorities."

"Agreed." Longstreet tapped some keys and an image appeared on the monitor: a young woman with blond hair, ice-blue eyes, and high, prominent cheekbones. The photo was evidently a mug shot and, judging by the height scale being measured in meters, had been taken in some foreign country.

"There she is," Longstreet said, waving at the image. "On one of the few occasions when someone actually managed to get her in custody." He consulted the computer in front of him. "She was born twenty-four years ago in Cape Town, South Africa. When she was eight, both of her parents were found beaten to death with what the coroner believed was a cricket bat. The weapon was never found, and the deaths were ascribed to a home invasion. Unsolved. After their deaths, she passed through a series of foster homes—never staying for more than a few months. Kicked out, one after the other, the families often citing fear of physical violence. Finally, she ended up a ward of the state—put in an orphanage. Reports from social workers who interviewed her there said she'd been the victim of sexual abuse by her father from an early age. They described her as maladapted, aggressive, manipulative, withdrawn, fascinated by martial arts and weapons—particularly knives, real or improvised, which were always being confiscated from her person—and prone to violence."

Longstreet used a mouse to scroll through the data on his screen. "It was not long before she was moved from an orphanage to a reformatory. Several instances of assault were noted during her residency there; in one case, she beat a fellow inmate almost to death. Ultimately, when she was fifteen, a request was made that she be transferred to a high-security prison, despite her age. The reformatory staff was simply unable to control her. But before the red tape could be completed, she escaped—stabbing a psychologist through the eye with a pen and killing him in the process."

He perused the screen a moment. "They tried to run her down, but she was a wily one. She left in her wake a trail of crime and violence. She evinced a hatred of men: one of her favorite tactics was to loiter around in seedy neighborhoods until someone either solicited her or tried to molest her, at which point she would castrate him and stuff his genitals into his mouth."

"Charming," Pendergast murmured.

"At around sixteen, her wanderings took her to Japan, where she got involved with a yakuza gang. After some kind of violent falling-out that the Tokyo police are still investigating, she apparently went to Canton, China, where she joined one of that city's triads. According to our intelligence sources, her natural affinity for violence helped her rise quickly through the ranks. Almost immediately, she graduated from a '49' to a '426'—a 'Red Pole' enforcer, whose specialty was managing and carrying out offensive operations. By twenty-one, she was set to rise still higher within the organization, when something happened, we don't know what, and she left China for the United States."

Longstreet looked away from the screen. "In the years since, she's made her home here, although it appears she left the country for Europe on a few occasions. Based on the crimes she's presumably committed, she appears to be an extremely highly functioning sociopath, who kills and maims primarily for her own amusement. She has shown a remarkable ability to hide in plain sight and to evade the authorities at every turn. That mug shot is the only one we have of her, taken in Amsterdam. She escaped the following day."

"An ideal accomplice for Diogenes," Pendergast said.

"Precisely." Longstreet sighed. "Having identified Greyling is a coup, without doubt—and yet, given her ability to successfully elude law enforcement in the past, I'm not sure how much material progress we'll make." He glanced at Pendergast. "I presume you searched the cottage where they stayed with particular care?"

"I did."

"And?"

"It had been meticulously cleaned."

Longstreet stretched, ran a hand through his long steel-colored hair. "We'll send a CSU there anyway."

"I doubt if they'll find more than this." Pendergast reached into his pocket, withdrew something in a plastic bag, and handed it to Longstreet: a small slip of robin's-egg-blue paper.

Longstreet took it. "Interesting."

"I found it wedged between two floorboards near an air vent."

As Longstreet turned the bag over in his hands, Pendergast continued. "It's a partial receipt for a piece of jewelry—a gold ring with a rare tanzanite gemstone. I would speculate it was a present from Diogenes to Flavia—a reward, perhaps, for a job well done."

"So, with luck, we can use this to trace the purchase back to Diogenes," said Longstreet. "If we knew where this ring was purchased. Too bad the name of the store has been torn off."

"But we *do* know the store. There is only one that uses that particular color as the face they present to the world."

Longstreet glanced at the receipt again. And then he smiled—a slow, triumphant smile.

46

Diogenes entered the library, carrying with him a silver bucket of ice and a bottle of champagne, with two glasses. He set them down on the side table and turned to Constance, who was sitting at the harpsichord bench, idly turning pages of sheet music.

"Do you mind," he asked, "if I enjoy a glass while listening to you play? If you're in the mood to play, of course."

"Certainly," she replied, turning to the keyboard. He could see the music on the stand: preludes from *L'Art de Toucher* by François Couperin. Uncorking the champagne, he filled his glass and eased himself back into a chair.

He was concerned; more than concerned. That morning, Constance had arisen at ten, which seemed to him very late, although he wasn't sure—some people did sleep excessively long. She had eaten very little at dinner the evening before, and hardly touched the magnificent breakfast he'd prepared for her. It had now been almost forty-eight hours since the infusion, and she should be showing its effects—strongly. Of course, this life was very new to her, and an adjustment was to be expected. What he was noticing could well be emotional rather than physical. Perhaps she was also having second thoughts.

While he was thus preoccupied, he heard the first notes of the Premier Prelude in C major, slow and stately. It was not a difficult piece of music from a technical point of view. But as her fingers moved over the keys, and the rich low sound of the harpsichord filled the cozy room, he heard that the notes were uneven, tentative; he winced at a wrong note, and another; and then Constance ceased playing.

"I'm sorry," she said. "I seem to be rather distracted."

Diogenes made an effort to disguise the strong feeling of dismay, even panic, that arose in him. He set down the glass, rose from his chair, and came over to her, taking her hand. It was warm—too warm—and dry. Her face was pale, and half-moon shadows had formed under her eyes.

"Are you feeling well?" he asked, casually.

"*Very* well, thank you," came the sharp retort. "I just don't feel like playing."

"Yes, yes, of course. Champagne?"

"Not tonight." She removed her hand from his.

Diogenes thought for a moment. "Constance, before dinner, if I could just have a moment of your time. I need to do a little routine blood work, now that the arcanum has been in your system for two days."

"I've been pricked enough, thank you."

Not nearly enough for my taste, thought Diogenes, but quickly removed that unworthy thought from his head. "Really, my dear, it's a necessary part of the process."

"Why? You never mentioned it before."

"Didn't I? I'm so sorry. Quite standard, I assure you. A routine follow-up to any drug infusion."

"What could be wrong?"

"Nothing, my dear, nothing! Just a medical precaution. Now, may I? Let's just get it over with."

She brushed the hair out of her eyes. "Very well. Be quick about it, please."

She began to roll up her sleeve. Diogenes went to the cupboard where he kept the infusion supplies, removed a blood draw kit, and came back. He laid a sterile pad on the side table, placed her white arm upon it, strapped the tourniquet, tapped her veins, inserted an extra-large Vacutainer needle, and drew thirty milliliters.

"Do you really need that much blood? That's enough to choke a vampire."

"All quite standard." It was indeed far more than the usual amount, but he needed plenty to work with.

He quickly withdrew the needle and applied a cotton ball, taped it, and folded her arm up. "Done!" he said as brightly as he could muster.

She gave an irritated sigh. "I think I'll go to bed early. I feel drained—literally."

"No dinner? I am preparing *brochettes d'agneau à la Grecque*."

The irritated look on her face softened a bit. "I'm sorry, it sounds lovely, but I'm not hungry."

"Perfectly fine, not a problem. Shall I see you upstairs?"

The look came back. "Please don't *hover* so. I can manage on my own."

She disappeared through the library door, and a moment later he heard her light tread climbing the stairs.

He waited, listening acutely to the extremely faint sounds of her movements; the water running; and finally silence.

Swiftly, Diogenes took up the vial of blood and hastened through the darkened halls to the basement door, descending to his laboratory. Now he gave full flow to his feelings of apprehension. He quickly began setting up the tests for her blood work, chemistry panel and blood count, fibrinogen, hemoglobin A1C, DHEA, C-reactive protein, TSH, and estradiol.

At a certain point later that night he found that his hands were shaking, and he took a moment to put everything down, close his eyes, fold his hands, center and empty his mind. Then he continued, maintaining focus. There could be no more mistakes.

It was after midnight when the final results came in. As the numbers reeled off and the picture became clear, Diogenes began to shake again. It was a disaster. Where had he gone wrong? But he already knew the answer. Because he'd had at his disposal material from only a single cadaver, he'd had to cut a few corners, and he had made a few minor and perfectly reasonable assumptions.

But medicine was never straightforward. He should have started with the material of *two* cadavers. It wasn't a fatal mistake; at least, not yet. But for Constance's sake it was a problem that needed to be solved—immediately.

As dawn broke over the ocean, Diogenes quietly made his way up from the basement. He briefly retired to his chambers, changed into his morning gown, wetted and brushed his hair, patted his cheeks to bring back some of the color, and descended to the kitchen. To his surprise, he found Constance at the espresso machine, preparing coffee.

"You're up early," he said, freighting his voice with good cheer.

"I couldn't sleep."

And she looked it. Dark circles, a gray tinge in her otherwise pale complexion, faint blue veins visible in her neck and bare shoulders, a sheen of perspiration despite the cool morning. Diogenes stopped himself from asking if she was all right.

"My dear, I hope you won't mind, but I have to rush off to Key West today, to purchase some botanicals and equipment for my lab. I'll be gone all day, overnight, and part of tomorrow perhaps. Will you be all right alone?"

"I'm never better than when I'm alone."

"Mr. Gurumarra will be here if you need anything."

"Very well."

Diogenes took her hand briefly, turned, and left.

47

PENDERGAST ENTERED THE great pink granite façade of the Tiffany & Co. flagship store on Fifth Avenue, sweeping through the revolving doors into the bustle of the main floor, the mahogany cases brilliantly lit, the carpeted floors freshly vacuumed, the black veined marble walls and doorways glowing. He paused, feigning a confused look, and instantly attracted a slender and attentive salesman.

"May I help you, sir?"

Pendergast removed the receipt he'd retrieved from between the floorboards of the Exmouth cabin. "I have a question about this piece of jewelry. Here is the receipt. It was paid for with cash."

The salesperson took it. "And what is your question, sir?"

"It's of a personal nature. I'd like to speak with a person in authority who has complete access to all the sales records."

"Well, most of those records are confidential—"

"Sir, *if* you please, enough idle banter. Take me to the person in question."

The salesperson practically jerked to attention, responding to Pendergast's icy, aristocratic tone. "Yes, sir, I'll just have to see if she's available—"

"Onward!"

Thoroughly cowed, the man led Pendergast briskly through the vast room to an elevator in the back, which they ascended to a series of offices. Coming to a closed mahogany door, they paused. On the door was a name in gold leaf, edged in black.

BARBARA McCORMICK
SENIOR VICE PRESIDENT

Pendergast looked intently at the name. In the faintest palimpsest underneath he could see the last name MCCORMICK had been recently changed from something else.

"Let me just check to see if she's available—" said the salesperson, but Pendergast already had his hand on the knob and was opening the door.

"Wait—you can't just go in, sir!"

He stepped in, the salesperson following right behind; but Pendergast turned, placed a firm hand on his chest, shoved him back out, and closed the door in his face. Seeing a bolt, he turned it and then swiveled back to the person in the office. A woman of about forty, sitting behind a large antique desk, stared at him with an astonished look on her face.

"What is *this*?" she asked.

Pendergast gazed at her for a moment. She was a very attractive, well-put-together woman dressed in a suit, with blond hair and a gorgeous but understated string of pearls around her neck. Fury and alarm were both gathering on her face. The salesman was knocking on the door, lightly but frantically. His muffled voice came through: "*Sir, sir, you just can't barge in like that! Ms. McCormick might not be available! Hello, Ms. McCormick, Ms. McCormick, should I call security?*"

Pendergast turned to the woman. "Do send him away."

"Who are you, barging in like this? And locking my door!" She reached for her phone.

Pendergast gave a little bow. "I'm simply a customer with a tiny problem that only you, my dear Ms. McCormick, can solve. Will you please, *please* help me?" He bestowed on her his most dazzling smile.

"*Ms. McCormick! Ms. McCormick!*"

McCormick rose, looked Pendergast up and down with a penetrating gaze, and then went to the door. "It's quite all right," she said through the wood. "No need for security. I'll take care of the customer. You may go."

Then she went back to Pendergast, and circled him, observing him curiously. The alarm had faded from her face. "And your name is—?"

"Aloysius Xingu Leng Pendergast."

Her eyebrows rose. "That's quite a name, Mr. Pendergast. New Orleans?"

"Excellent. Please call me Aloysius."

"Aloysius," she said, going back to the side of her desk but remaining standing. "And you have a little problem?"

"Indeed I do." He removed the dirty receipt from his pocket and held it up. "This is for a piece of jewelry that was purchased about five weeks ago. Cash was paid. I need the name of the person who bought it."

"As I'm sure you know, that information is strictly confidential. We're a jewelry store. Imagine how our customers would feel if anyone could just come in and find out the name of a buyer!"

"I understand."

"And if it was paid for in cash, we may not have the name anyway."

"It was a ring, and according to this slip he brought it back in to be adjusted."

"Well, in that case we *would* have the name. But...as I said, it's confidential."

"Here's why I've come to you. You see, my wife has been unfaithful to me. He bought her a ring. I want to know who he is."

McCormick's eyebrows shot up at this, and a mixture of amusement, schadenfreude, and pity began to play about her lips. "Ah, the old story. The old, *old* story."

"I'm just shattered to find myself in such a situation. I really don't know what else to do. Can you give me some advice?"

"Forget the name. Divorce her. It doesn't matter who she's sleeping with. Just get rid of her. That's my advice."

"But...I *love* her."

"Good Lord. Don't be a sap. You *love* her? Come now! The world is full of women to love. And full of jewelry to give them," she added, with a smile and a wink.

"I'm rather naive when it comes to these things," said Pendergast, his voice laden with sorrow. "It seems I don't know women at all. And...and the *humiliation* of it!"

"Well, I *do* know women. A gentleman such as yourself would have no trouble finding a woman who would love and cherish you. Now, I think you should ask: why do you want the name of the man who's cuckolded you? If it wasn't him, it would have been someone else. And perhaps there were others. My advice: don't go there."

"I only want the name as a matter of pride. To be ignorant of who he is, to go about oblivious when one's friends know, is shameful. All I want is the name. Then I can..." He faltered, leaned toward her, and spoke in a confidential whisper. "Well, let me be honest with you."

"Yes. *Do* be honest."

"If I had the name, then I could pretend to have known it all along, and simply dismiss it as a matter of complete indifference. That's all. I wish to...salvage what little pride I have left."

"I understand. Yes, I do. You're a wealthy man, I take it?"

"Very."

"And she's going to try and get your money?"

"Without doubt."

"No pre-nup?"

"I was *so* young and naive. Oh, what a fool I've been!"

A long pause. "All right. I understand precisely where you're coming from. I myself know that kind of humiliation, when all your friends are talking behind your back, the whole world keeping it from you. And you—*always* the last to know." A bitterness had crept into her voice.

Pendergast raised his eyes. "I'm so glad you understand. It means a great deal to me...*Barbara*." He tentatively took her hand, giving it a slight pressure.

She gave a little laugh, let him hold it for a moment, then withdrew it. "Now, Aloysius, let me just go into my computer here and see what we have. But mind you: don't approach him. Stay away. And you didn't get this from me." She plucked the receipt from his fingers, sat down, and hit the keys, rapid-fire. "All right." She pulled a piece of paper from a notepad on her desk, wrote on it, and handed it to Pendergast.

In a lovely, schoolgirl hand was written a name: Morris Kramer.

He felt her keen eyes on him. He put on a suitable series of expressions: shock, disdain, contempt. "*Him?* The bounder. The little shit. My old roommate from Exeter. Well, I should have known."

She held her hand out and he gave her back the paper. She crumbled it up, dropped it in a trash can, and looked at him intently. "As I said, Aloysius, the world is full of women to love." She glanced at her watch. "Oh, it's time for elevenses. There's a lovely teahouse just around the corner. Care to join me?"

Pendergast bestowed on her another smile. "Delighted," he said.

48

At thirty-five hundred square feet, the Grande Suite of Miami's Setai Hotel was, Diogenes reflected, larger than most houses. It boasted not only killer views of the Atlantic, but also a media room, expensive statuary, original framed oils on the walls, a walk-through Sub-Zero kitchen, and bathrooms with black granite appointments. But unlike most five-star hotel suites, it was decorated with impeccable and understated taste: a sensory barrage of refinement and luxury. Diogenes hoped that this would have the desired effect, because the object of the barrage did not always have much use for the finer things in life.

That object was at present sitting on the wraparound leather couch in one of the suite's two living rooms. As he entered, a glass of Lillet Blanc in each hand, he bestowed on her his warmest smile. Flavia Greyling looked back at him. She was dressed in torn blue jeans and a T-shirt, along with the omnipresent fanny pack, and she was not smiling. Instead, a look he couldn't quite parse was on her face: part uncertainty, he thought, mixed with hope, curiosity...and something bordering on anger.

"Here's your dividend," he said as he placed the glasses on a table before the sofa. "So: that was the last item on your agenda?"

Flavia left the drink untouched. "Yes. I sent you that note through the remailing service, then left Namibia and stowed away on a tramp steamer headed for Sierra Leone and the safe house there. Your arrangements for the plane ticket here all came together yesterday."

"Excellent." Diogenes took a sip of Lillet. For the purposes of his visit to the Setai, he was in his Petru Lupei identity, with the charming European manners, clean-shaven and scarless face, exquisite bespoke suit, faint trace of an unidentifiable accent, and the one contact lens concealing his milky eye. "But I must ask: was it necessary for you to handle the owner of that automobile dealership, Mr. . . ."

"Keronda."

"Keronda. Yes. Was it necessary to deal with him so, ah, definitively? Given the circumstances, I mean."

"Absolutely. He deviated from the script. *Your* script. Instead of business as usual, he left the auto agency in a bloody mess. This interested the police, which you said was the last thing you wanted."

"True; it was."

"We left no trace behind us. Keronda was the only loose end. He had panicked; sooner or later he would have talked. I didn't think you wanted that. Did you want that?"

As she said this, she looked at him, her expression abruptly piercing. Despite himself, Diogenes felt a tickle of concern. She had a way of staring at people that was almost like being physically stabbed by one of her many knives. He had seen her use it on others—and had noticed the effect it produced. He did not like having it used on him.

"No, of course not," he said quickly. "You did what had to be done." Diogenes reflected that this was another example of why he needed to get rid of this girl once and for all. Only too well did he recognize in her the sheer pleasure of killing. "I owe you my thanks," he said, in the warmest tones he could muster. "My deepest, most sincere appreciation."

The look on Flavia's face softened. And now she took a sip of her Lillet, replaced the glass, and tucked her legs beneath her in what—for her—passed for a feminine gesture. "So what now? You know, I really enjoyed Exmouth. It wasn't like the other assignments you've given me—we had a lot of free time. Free time to get to know each other. You're not like anyone else I've met. I think you understand me, understand why I do what I do. I think you're not afraid of me, either."

"Not at all, my dear Flavia. And it's true—we understand each other very well."

She flushed. "You've no idea how important that is to me. Because I think it means...well, that you're like me, Peter. The way you think, the things you enjoy...like what happened with that houseboy in Brussels last year! Remember how he tried the badger game on you? You, of all people!" And here she dissolved into laughter, took another sip of her drink.

Diogenes recalled the houseboy in Brussels—but not with nearly as much amusement as Flavia did. He concealed this with an indulgent smile.

"So what's next for us—boss?" Flavia added an ironic emphasis to the final word.

"An excellent question. And it's really why I asked you to come here. As I said, the job you did was masterful. I couldn't have asked for better work—or more complete. In fact, as a result, there's really nothing else to be done at present."

Flavia stopped in the act of picking up her glass. "Nothing else?"

"Nothing that I need your assistance with. I believe I told you from the start of our partnership, Flavia, that I work on a number of projects simultaneously."

"I remember. I want to help you do that."

"But you must understand: there are some things I have to do on my own. I'm like a conductor: I can't always step down off the podium and mingle with the orchestra."

"The orchestra," Flavia repeated. "Are you saying I'm just an instrument? One of many? To be picked up and played when it suits you, and then set aside?"

Diogenes realized that the simile had been a bad one. He also realized that he had misjudged the depth of her paranoia and obsession. She had been so aloof when they first met; so proudly alone and self-reliant. She was everything he'd been looking for in an "assistant": quick-witted, absolutely loyal, fearless, ruthless, and cunning. When he first met her, his strong impression had been that she hated all men. It had not occurred to him that she would fall in love with him. Thank God he had kept so much about himself—his true name and his other main identities, for example, or his estate at Halcyon—from her. The situation was intolerable. In an earlier incarnation he would have rid himself of her in the simple way. But that was no longer his way...especially in this identity, which, as the owner of record of Halcyon, he intended to occupy for the rest of his—very long—life.

"No," he said. "Flavia, I did not mean that—not at all. I expressed myself badly. You and I are a *team*. You're right—I *do* understand you. More than that—I think you're the one person in the world who would never judge me. And, believe me, there are many who have. It's important to me to know you won't do that."

Flavia did not reply. Instead, she played with the ring he had given her, twisting it back and forth on her finger.

"What are you saying?" she asked, her voice a little husky. "Will I see you again?"

"Of course you'll see me again! More than that—we'll work together again. *And* again. But now is not the time. There are just too many things going on in…that other part of my life that is separate from you."

For a moment, he feared that she would make some declaration, pour her heart out to him. But she said nothing.

"My dearest Flavia, it won't be for long. I'll soon seek you out. We've had downtime before, don't forget. And it will be just as you said—we'll have all the time to spend together, get to know each other better. And that's at least as important to me as it is to you."

Flavia, who had been staring at the floor, raised her eyes to his. "Do you really think so?"

"I know so. *Our two souls therefore, which are one, / Though I must go, endure not yet / A breach, but an expansion, / Like gold to airy thinness beat.*"

Flavia said nothing. The Donne quote bounced off her like a squash ball off graffiti-covered concrete. Diogenes realized it was another presumptuous tactical error on his part, and he resolved to make no more.

"Until we meet again, I'm going to make sure that you live in the comfort you deserve." He reached into his pocket and plucked out a fat envelope. "I've arranged for a new safe house where you can live until our next assignment. It's in Copenhagen. Very luxurious." He patted the envelope. "The address, and the key, are in here, along with a passport, fresh cell phone, first-class plane ticket on a flight leaving tomorrow, and Danish driver's license."

Still Flavia said nothing.

"And a down payment on jobs to come," he added quickly. He put the envelope on the sofa between them. Flavia made no move to pick it up.

"This is a princely gift, you know," he said. "Proof of just how much you mean to me."

"*How* much?" Flavia finally asked.

"How much you mean to me? I could never put a price on my regard for you."

"No: how much *money?*"

This was encouraging. "Five hundred thousand dollars."

"*That* much, Peter?" Her face went pale.

"Are you all right, Flavia?" he asked quietly.

No response.

"Flavia, now do you realize your importance to me? And do you understand why this has to be? And how you can rely on my contacting you again—very soon?"

Now, at last, she nodded.

"I knew you would understand—because we are, as you've said, so alike. Now, if you don't mind, I have to go. I'll contact you on that cell phone—probably within a month, at most." And he leaned over, kissed her forehead, then straightened up.

"Why?" Flavia asked suddenly.

Diogenes glanced back at her. "Why am I leaving?"

"No. Why, exactly, did we do that last job? My having to pose as that girl, the wig and the trench coat, the crazy fake kidnapping and death, all that work changing planes and bribing pilots and Namibian doctors and arranging for a dummy corpse and refrigerated coffin—and me leading a wild goose chase into Botswana. *And* Keronda. You promised you'd explain it someday. Well…?"

He waved his hand. "Of course. Now that's it's all over, I'm happy to explain. My best friend is a first-rate FBI agent, but simply a babe in the woods when it comes to women."

"So?"

"That woman—Constance, you saw her in that Exmouth shop and in the restaurant—was a fortune hunter of the worst sort, after his money and nothing else. She'd gotten him to sign over a million in family money, the witch. I just wanted to get his money back.

But…well, it all ended badly, as you may know. My friend drowned. But Constance still had the money. Hence the kidnapping, to lead her accomplice astray and get the money back by ransom. It worked beautifully—thanks to you."

"So what happened to her?"

Another dismissive wave. "You mean Constance? Once I got the money back, good riddance! She's undoubtedly gone on to con some other rich man."

"What about the money?"

"Well, my friend is dead and the money is of no use to him. Why shouldn't I split it with my closest associate, Flavia?" And he gave a slow, knowing smile.

She returned the smile. "I see."

Diogenes was vastly relieved. He was desperate to bring this whole conversation to an end. A lot could happen in a month or two. Perhaps she would find a boyfriend, or get into a car crash, or overdose on drugs. By the time she tried to find him—if she did at all—his trail to Halcyon, well hidden to begin with, would be that much colder. He rose. "Until we meet again."

He leaned down and this time gave her a kiss on the lips—very short and light—then straightened up, looking into her eyes. What was she thinking? She had become so pale and still. But she was still smiling.

"Now, Flavia, go enjoy Copenhagen! You deserve it. And keep that cell phone with you at all times: I'll be calling you soon. So for now: *à bientôt*, my dear."

And with a bow, he turned and left the room.

A moment later the front door to the suite closed with a quiet click. Flavia did not move. Even before Peter was out of the apartment, the smile had left her face. She sat there, quite still, recalling his words, recalling the things she had heard him say to others—things that he hadn't meant, that had been slick and clever and consummately manipulative. Most of all, she thought about the job they had just completed—the job at whose heart, it seemed, was the girl: Constance Greene.

Suddenly she stood up, walked across the living room and out onto the balcony of the suite. Briefly, she reached for her fanny pack—then had a different idea. She grasped the ring Peter had given her and tried to pry out the expensive gemstone. When it wouldn't budge, she banged it against the balcony railing—again and again and again, skinning her knuckles in the process—until at last it popped free. She picked up the stone, turned it around in her fingers for a moment, then hurled it out in the direction of the Atlantic. The carcass of the gold ring remained on her finger, the four gold prongs that had previously held the stone now empty and protruding.

Next, she walked into the living room and looked around, coldly sizing up the space. Walking over to a display case, she pulled it open, removed a marble statue, and—after studying it briefly—used it to smash the glass of the case into fragments. Then—still unnervingly controlled—she stepped into the kitchen and, one at a time, took the glassware pieces from the cabinets and dashed them to the floor. Next, she went through the entire three-bedroom suite, using the prongs of her ring to slash the artwork hanging on the wall to ribbons. Picking up a corkscrew from the wet bar, she went back into the living room and ripped to shreds the modular leather sofa on which she and Peter had sat together, just minutes before.

When she was done, she found she was panting ever so slightly. Retreating to the bedroom—the bedroom that, just half an hour before, she had held such different hopes for—she packed her small bag. Then, walking out of the suite, she rode the elevator down to the opulent lobby.

"I'm Ms. Lupei," she told the man behind the counter. "I'm afraid my husband has rather made a mess of the Grande Suite. Please put all damages on the credit card you have on file. I'm checking out."

And with that, she gave the man a grim little smile, turned on her heel, and walked toward the hotel exit, the occasional drop of blood dripping from her skinned knuckles onto the polished marble floor.

49

A<small>T THE TAIL</small> end of rush hour, it was a fifty-minute drive in heavy traffic from the Setai Hotel to Miami Baptist Hospital, one of the largest hospitals in South Florida. Petru Lupei parked his rental car in a dingy garage about a quarter mile away, pulling into a dark spot behind a steel column that blocked the view of the security camera covering the area. Inside the car, he changed out of Lupei's elegant suit, carefully folding it on the seat. Then he dressed in the clothing of Dr. Walter Leyland. He pulled on Leyland's casual khaki slacks and a blue shirt and polyester tie, knotted it sloppily, then pulled on his white hospital lab coat with his ID badge clipped to the lapel. He put Dr. Leyland's wallet into his pocket, with its Florida driver's license and credit cards, and slipped Dr. Leyland's cell phone into the other pocket. Taking two balls of cotton out of the doctor's bag that sat on the passenger seat, he inserted them into his mouth, wedging them up between his upper gums and his teeth, to give Leyland his characteristic pudgy face, and he removed Lupei's blue-colored contact lenses and replaced them with Leyland's brown ones. He brushed white stage powder into Lupei's hair, changing the light brown to salt-and-pepper.

As he morphed identities, Diogenes felt a certain sadness that the carefully created and lovingly nurtured Dr. Walter Leyland of Clewiston, Florida, would soon meet his demise. It was, in a way, like the death of a good friend. But sacrifices had to be made. And besides, he'd never given the Leyland identity the care and feeding he had to, say, Hugo Menzies, or in particular Petru Lupei. Lupei was, in fact, his masterpiece—totally impregnable, impossible to trace, absolutely authentic, real Social Security number, meticulously devised and constructed: the name he planned to hide behind for the rest of his life.

Leyland carefully placed Petru Lupei's clothes and shoes in the oversize doctor's bag. On top of them he put a slim stainless-steel container holding the good doctor's surgical instruments, a contact lens case, and the small bottle of actors' hair color, along with Lupei's wallet and glasses.

Beside everything else in the bag sat the small medical container for transporting human tissue.

The car would soon be of great interest to the police. It had been rented by Dr. Leyland and would have his DNA all over it. There was nothing he could do about that. A DNA swab in the car would match Dr. Leyland; so would the fingerprints. That was as far as the DNA and fingerprint database matching would go, as this was a case that would be very quickly solved. A second person in the world also had Leyland's DNA—by the name of Diogenes Pendergast—and that DNA was, most unfortunately, in the FBI database. But that secondary search would not likely be made once Leyland had been so quickly identified. Even if it were, Petru Lupei had assiduously avoided leaving any official record of his own—matching—DNA. Nothing in the car would connect with Petru Lupei.

Excellent.

He closed the valise and left the garage by a previously scouted route—a route that made sure the good doctor Leyland was adequately captured on security videos along the hospital's perimeter. Once again he mused that the quicker this was concluded, the better.

He walked down Southwest Ninety-Fourth Street, across the lush hospital campus, and soon arrived at the main entrance. Nearly two thousand doctors were affiliated with Baptist, so he had no fear of being challenged here. He had already arranged to have his ID authorized, a simple matter for any Florida doctor with credentials and minimal hacking skills. He swiped his badge with the magnetic stripe when he went through security, under the attentive but friendly eye of the guards, and entered the spacious lobby. Having previously memorized the hospital's layout, he walked briskly past more cameras to the elevator bank—looking like a doctor with a purpose—and took an elevator to the intensive care unit. This floor also contained a nearby suite of operating rooms.

Leyland knew that any unrecognized doctor going into the ICU was likely to be scrutinized and possibly even stopped by a nurse, albeit with a friendly *Hello, Doctor, can I help you?* To lessen that possibility, before entering the ICU he made his way to the operating suite and used his card to enter the doctors' locker room. There, across from the rows of lockers, he found what he was looking for: a scrub dispensing machine, the size of a gigantic filing cabinet. He swiped his card and the machine obligingly unlocked the glass panels on its front, allowing him to choose a bin containing sterile scrubs in his size. He quickly put them on. Now the possibility of being challenged by anyone was greatly reduced.

From there, he went down the halls to a pre-selected storage room. He had carefully choreographed the entire activity ahead of time. Again swiping his card, he gained access. There were no security cameras in this room or in the hall adjacent to it—that was crucial to his plan.

Removing the surgical kit, he placed his doctor's bag on a shelf in the back, hiding it behind some boxes, and shoved the kit into his waistband, hidden under the scrubs. Then he exited and headed for the ICU and swiped yet again to enter. He had to admit, the security at Baptist was comprehensive, due to the hospital's size and its location in a high-crime area, but in this case security was his friend. Assuming, of course nothing unexpected arose. One thing crucial to his plan: one always had to swipe on the way *into* a restricted area, but one never had to swipe *out*.

Moving with purpose, he checked his watch. He was aware of a rising, unhealthy excitement that he did not have time to fully check. *If t'were be done, t'were best done quickly...* While there were no security cameras within the ICU, there was an extremely high ratio of nurses to patients—one nurse to three patients—and he could not risk just going into a patient's room, because the assigned nurse would certainly follow him, wondering who he was and what he was doing. Thank God for union-mandated breaks; the nurse he needed to be gone had just taken hers—as he knew she would have.

He quickly walked past the nurses' station and went into a single room containing an eighty-two-year-old patient, Frederica Montoya, in the final stages of dementia and congestive heart failure. A "Do Not Resuscitate" order had been placed on her chart. Nobody would rush in when she coded, although they would of course come soon enough and he would have to work extremely fast.

The old woman was at death's door. Constance, even if she never knew what he was doing, could hardly protest his actions.

He entered the room, shut the door. The patient was on the bed, unconscious, on a ventilator. She was clearly dying, albeit taking her sweet time. Her vitals, recorded on the wall monitor behind the bed, were weak but steady.

He quickly laid out his surgical kit, removed a needle, and injected a carefully calibrated lethal dose of morphine into the drip. The effect of the anesthetizing agent would be practically instantaneous and he went to work immediately, not waiting for her to code. He stripped off her bedclothes, rolled her on her side, opened her hospital gown, and made a quick incision along her lower spine. He worked with extreme care and swiftness. Her vital signs started to become erratic as he worked, and about the time he removed the cauda equina she flatlined and a whole suite of beeping alarms went off. He quickly placed the CE into a sterile test tube and sealed it, wrapping it in the surgical kit.

But even before he could begin the second phase of his plan, the door opened—bloody hell that they couldn't be locked—and who should come striding in but a doctor, not a nurse. The man halted, taking in the scene—the dead woman on her side, the bloody incision—then gave a shout, rushing at Leyland with instinctual horror. "Doctor, what in God's name—?"

The doctor's cry was cut short by a long scalpel jabbed upward into his neck. Leyland leapt back and simultaneously skipped to one side, slicing open the throat as he did so, successfully avoiding the spray of blood. The doctor, gargling into silence, fell to the floor. Not wasting a moment, Leyland took a brief look at the doctor's name tag, went to the open door, and looked out. A nurse was hurrying down the hall, responding to the code.

"Dr. Graben and I are handling it, nurse—if you don't mind," he told her. "It's a DNR, it's almost over. Please—let us give her her dignity."

He eased shut the door.

Now here was an unexpected opportunity that he must not overlook. He rolled the doctor onto his stomach. Grasping the back of his white coat, he tucked the scalpel into the material and sliced it up, then did the same to his shirt, exposing the man's back. There was something about the lumpy whiteness of it, knowing he was going to cut into the flesh, that excited him. He palpated the spinal cord, found where he needed to begin the incision, pushed the scalpel in and drew it downward just to one side of the cord—as needed to access the cauda equina at an angle.

Blood flowed out of the incision, but not much. That made things easier. Opening up the very bottom of the cord, he teased out the cauda equina, the "horse's tail," so named because the massive bundle of nerve fibers looked like thousands of gray hairs.

This unexpected second sample would more than help. He hadn't meant to kill a young, healthy human being, but it couldn't have been avoided. Now he would have an excess of material to work with, and it would not only make the formulation foolproof, but also allow it to be accomplished in far less time.

Tucking the bundle of tissue into the test tube with the first, he now went to work on a tableau of murder. Using his scalpels, he first slashed the doctor across his throat a few more times, mutilated his face, then sliced his back to ribbons, disguising the incision. *Yet who would have thought the old man to have had so much blood in him…* He proceeded to slash the torsos of both victims with his scalpels, scoring them this way and that, being careful not to get blood on himself, but making the incisions look as much like the product of a madman as he could. The feeling of the scalpel in the flesh, the tug of it, the smooth resistance and then the sudden feeling of giving way, the sprays of blood that were already quickly ebbing—all this made him frustrated that he could not linger; that he had no time to enjoy it; that he was under such enormous time pressure.

All too soon he was done. Glancing at his watch, he saw he had accomplished all he needed in less than ninety seconds.

He scattered the scalpels about, then rose, examining the tableau with a critical eye. It was gloriously shocking, vile, and disgusting: blood everywhere, all over the snowy sheets, on the linoleum floor, splattered on the walls. Clearly the work of pure insanity. And not a drop of blood on himself. Remarkable.

Tidying himself, he went to the door, opened it, slipped out, shut it behind him. There was the nurse in the hall, uncertain and concerned.

"Nurse?" said Leyland. "Remain there and await Dr. Graben's summons. He's still with the patient and is *not* to be disturbed. He won't be long."

"Yes, Doctor."

He strolled through the doors, out of the ICU. The alarm would come at any second—not nearly enough time for Dr. Walter Leyland to get out of the hospital. But even if he could, he had been recorded already on a dozen video monitors.

A spring in his step, Leyland turned one corner, then another, and was just slipping into the storage room where Petru Lupei's clothes were awaiting him as the general alarm went off.

50

Pendergast stood in one corner of the two-bedroom apartment, still as a marble statue, watching the FBI's extensive crime scene team at work. They were wrapping up: photographic equipment was being put away; fingerprint kits were being closed and samples of lifting tape carefully archived; laptops were being shut down; evidence lockers, practically empty, were being stowed for removal.

As he stood there, his cell phone rang. He slipped it out, examined the number. It was blocked, of course.

"Yes?" he said into the phone.

"Secret Agent Man!" came the voice of Mime. "I'm calling with the promised update."

"Go ahead."

"Sorry it took so long, but your man Proctor has grown increasingly difficult to track. Especially once he reached Africa."

"Africa?"

"That's right. And off the beaten track, too. It took my entire gang, so to speak, to compile what he did. Okay, here's the skinny. I'll keep it short because I imagine you're busy, and I never like to spend more time on the phone—even this phone—than necessary. We managed to track him from Gander, to Mauritania, to Hosea Kutako Airport in Namibia. Whew, and what a job it was. But from there, the trail went cold."

"You have no idea where he went from the airport?"

"My best guess, based on local police chatter, is that he, um, *visited* a car dealership across the street from the airport and then headed east, maybe into Botswana. But that's it. Everything I've tried, every dirty trick and secret back door, has come up empty. We're not exactly dealing with the digital future in places like these."

"I understand. But there's no sign that he's dead?"

"No. A body would be something that would rise to the surface—digitally, that is. He's alive—but way the hell and gone somewhere."

"Thank you, Mime."

"Anything I can do to help my favorite fed. Now, how about the matter of my fee? That disguising cellular duplexer would really, really come in handy."

"I'm getting one appropriated for you. Naturally, you would only use it in a manner to assist law enforcement."

"Naturally!" There was a wheeze of laughter.

"Thank you, Mime." And Pendergast slipped the phone back into his suit pocket.

He watched the crime scene team finish up for a few more minutes. Then he walked across the living room—as clean and bare as the other rooms—to the nearest window. The Hamilton Heights apartment was in one of the neighborhood's newest buildings, a twenty-story structure on Broadway and 139th that dwarfed the brownstones and row houses that made up most of the surrounding streets.

The window looked west, toward Riverside Drive and the Hudson.

A barge loaded with cargo slowly made its way upriver, bound for Albany.

There was a sound behind him and he turned to see Arensky, the FBI agent in charge of the forensic team. The man was standing there deferentially, waiting to speak with him.

"Yes?" Pendergast asked.

"Sir, we've completed work. If it's all right with you, we'll go back downtown and begin logging the data."

"Is there much?"

Arensky shook his head. "Just the occasional print."

Pendergast nodded.

As Arensky turned and began gathering the teams together, the front door opened and Longstreet appeared, his tall figure filling the door frame. Seeing him, Arensky walked over quickly and they began conversing in low tones, Arensky gesturing this way and that, calling over various team members in turn, evidently to give Longstreet their reports.

Pendergast watched for a moment. Then he returned his eyes to the window. Gazing over the tops of the low buildings that stretched westward toward the river, he could make out—past the long lines of brownstones—the tall gables and crenellations of his own Riverside Drive mansion. Even without binoculars, he was able to make it out quite clearly: the front door, servants' entrance, service ports—even the shuttered windows of the library.

This apartment had obviously been chosen because it afforded an excellent spot from which to observe the activity at 891 Riverside.

Now he stooped to take a close look at the windowsill. Two sets of three holes each, at regular intervals, had been drilled into the wood of the sill, forming two triangles about six inches apart. Anchors, no doubt, for a telescope mount. The heavy weight of a sixty- or eighty-power, light-enhancing spotting telescope such as Diogenes would have used would make such anchoring advisable—providing extra stability for his study of that most private of domiciles.

As he straightened up, Longstreet came forward. In answer to Pendergast's unasked question, he nodded. "Agent Arensky's filled me in," he said. "It's more or less what we expected to find. The apartment was leased for a one-year term by a Mr. Kramer, about three months ago."

"No doubt one of Diogenes's throwaway identities. And was much seen of this Mr. Kramer?"

"We've interviewed the neighbors and the doormen. The next-door neighbor, a woman in her late seventies with very little to do, was particularly helpful. We've got a police artist in to make the facial reconstruction—not that it will do us much good. Mr. Kramer was seen with some regularity at the beginning of his tenancy, frequently in the company of a young woman."

"Flavia."

Longstreet nodded. "Several people identified her from the mug shots we provided. Diogenes, on the other hand, was not. He was here, though." Longstreet swept the room with a hand. "Even doing simple field matches with the forensic laptop, we've found prints from both of them all over the apartment."

"I see."

"There was a period when neither of them was seen. That, no doubt, corresponds to the Exmouth period. And then, around four weeks ago, 'Mr. Kramer' returned—this time without Flavia. He began to keep odd hours: leaving late at night, returning home around dawn. He was seen, off and on, by various doormen and the elderly neighbor...until about a week ago. And then, suddenly, he vanished—taking all his possessions with him." Longstreet frowned. "And this time, Flavia seems to have been more careful. There are no scraps of evidence to suggest where they, or more importantly he, might have gone."

There was a pause. "I'm afraid that's about the same story we've been getting down at Special Operations," Longstreet continued. "There have been no recent hits on TSA monitors, bank or credit card audits, or anything else. Cross-correlation of the security screen network has produced nothing. My teams in the field, and I've employed many, have turned up nothing. The trail's gone cold." He sighed. "I'm sorry, old friend. I know that finding that sales receipt, tracking him down to this bolt-hole, must have raised your hopes. I know it raised mine. But now, it's as if Diogenes has just vanished into thin air."

"I see," Pendergast said in a flat voice.

"I want to get him as much as you do," Longstreet said. "Believe me, this is going to remain my top priority. Although I'm afraid we're going to have to turn down the heat on our search for Diogenes temporarily. We're forced to take some men off the job and retask them to that crazy doctor-slasher murder in Florida. It won't be for long, though—I promise you that."

"Doctor-slasher murder?" Pendergast asked, turning away from the window.

"Yes. This doctor—apparently a doctor, anyway, I don't recall his name—just walked into a Miami hospital and killed an elderly woman. On death's door already, if you can believe it—dying of congestive heart failure. Slashed her up most impressively, Jack the Ripper would have approved. When another doctor walked in and, it seems, surprised him at his game, the lunatic killed him and slashed him to ribbons, as well. And then he just disappeared." Longstreet shook his head. "Craziest thing. All over the national press, which makes it a priority for us, as well."

Pendergast stood still for a moment. Then he looked back at Longstreet with a curious expression on his face. "Tell me more about this double murder."

Longstreet seemed surprised. "Why? It's just a distraction. We're obviously dealing with some sociopath—he'll be picked up soon and we can get back to the business at hand."

"The double murder," Pendergast repeated. "Humor me, old friend, if you please."

51

It was another glorious November day in the Keys as Diogenes eased his Chris Craft into the dock, cleated it, and hopped out. He plucked the small cooler out of the back cockpit, filled with ice and containing the two caudae equinae, and hurried along the pier to the house. He kept an eye out for Constance as he approached, but all was quiet.

He entered in a state of high nervous energy, avoided the library, and went straight to his basement laboratory, locking the door behind him.

Six hours later he emerged with a box tucked under his arm. It was now late afternoon and the house and island were awash in that soft golden light so distinctive to the Keys. He went to the library and there found Constance, sitting by the dead fireplace, book in hand.

"Hello, my dear," said Diogenes.

She raised her head. He was shocked by her distracted appearance, but he managed to keep his expression cheerful.

"Hello," she said in a low voice.

"I hope you got along well in my absence."

"Yes, thank you."

Diogenes was hoping she would ask about his trip, or why he'd shaved off the Van Dyke he'd begun to regrow, but she did not. He hesitated. This might be difficult. "Constance, there's something I must discuss with you."

She put down the book and turned to him.

"I . . . I have to confess I deceived you about that blood test. It wasn't routine. And it revealed something wrong."

Her eyebrows raised, a faint stirring of interest in her face.

"The arcanum I gave you failed."

He took a deep breath, let that sink in. He had rehearsed this scene a dozen times in his mind on the way back from Miami. He couldn't rush this; he needed to give her time to absorb the new information and think through the situation.

"Failed?"

"I imagine you are feeling the ill effects of it. I am so very, *very* sorry."

She faltered, looked away. "What happened?"

"The biochemistry is exceedingly complex. Suffice to say I made a mistake. I have now corrected it." He set the box down and opened it up, to reveal a three-hundred-milliliter bag filled with a violet liquid.

"Is that why you went to Key West?"

"Yes."

"To obtain more caudae equinae?"

Diogenes had been waiting for this very question. "Good Lord, no!" He shook his head vigorously. "Absolutely not. I've fully synthesized the drug, no need for more human tissue. It's just that the first synthesis was faulty because of a mistake I made. I've now synthesized a new batch, reformulated. A *good* batch."

"I see."

She looked so exhausted, she appeared almost more unwell than tired.

"I'd like to give it to you, now, to restore you to health."

"How do I know this batch isn't a 'mistake' as well?" A dryness had crept into her tone that Diogenes didn't like.

"Please trust me, Constance. I figured out exactly what went wrong and I've corrected it. This formulation will work. I swear to you on the strength of my love: *this will work.*"

She said nothing. He got up and walked to the IV closet, removed the IV rack, and wheeled it over next to her chair. He spread a sterile pad on the table, wrapped the tourniquet, located a vein, and inserted the IV. She watched him, apathetic, unresisting. Working quickly, he started her on saline, hung the bag with the arcanum, switched a valve, and in a moment the pinkish-purple liquid began to creep down the tube.

"I trusted you before," said Constance, her voice prickly with irritation. "Why should I trust you again?"

"The first time I was too eager, too much in a hurry to give you the miracle of extended life."

"You still look rather in a hurry."

Diogenes took a long, deep breath. "I am in a hurry because I love you and want you to be happy and healthy. But I have *not* hurried the preparation of this drug."

She was silent for a minute, a querulous air still clinging to her. "I'm not sure I care for being your guinea pig."

"My lovely Constance, you're a guinea pig only in the sense that the drug is formulated for one person only—you. There's no one else I could try it on."

"Except yourself."

"There isn't enough." *She's very quick, even now,* he thought.

She shook her head and he spoke fast. "Everything is so new. And you're sick. Give it time—please. That's all I ask."

She breathed out with evident irritation and brushed a hair from her face, saying nothing. Diogenes glanced at the bag. He had upped the flow to run it in as quickly as possible, and already about half was gone.

"Your bad humor is a symptom of the misformulated arcanum," said Diogenes.

As soon as he said this, he realized that was a mistake. "My *bad humor*," she said, "is due to your excessive solicitousness, your creeping about the house listening for my every movement. I feel like I'm being stalked."

"I'm sorry, I hadn't realized I was bothering you so. I'll give you all the freedom you wish. Just tell me how to act."

"For starters, get rid of that telescope in the tower. It makes me feel like you're spying on me."

Against his will, Diogenes found his face flushing.

"Yes," she said, looking at him keenly. "I see that you *have* spied on me. No doubt when I was swimming the other day."

Diogenes was flummoxed. He couldn't bring himself to deny it. He simply could not find an answer, and his silence was all the admission she needed.

"Everything was fine here while you were gone. I wish you hadn't come back."

This cut Diogenes to the quick. "That's not only cruel, but unfair. Everything I've done—everything—has been for you."

"Cruel? This coming from the maestro of cruelty himself?"

Diogenes felt this like another blow. He could feel a rising humiliation, and something else—the stirrings of anger. "You chose to come down here, knowing full well my history. It's wrong of you to throw it back in my face."

"*Wrong?* Who are you to decide what's right and what's wrong?" She issued a loud, sarcastic laugh.

This savage escalation left Diogenes reeling. He had no idea how to respond, what to say. The drug was three-quarters through. He could only hope to God it would take effect soon. Constance was talking herself into a rage.

"When I think back on what you've done," she said, "on all that history, when I recall how you made Aloysius desperately unhappy, I wonder how you can live with yourself!"

"Aloysius made me miserable, as well. Please, Constance."

"*Please, Constance,*" she said mockingly. "What a mistake I made, trusting you. Instead of making me better, you've poisoned me. How do I know this isn't more of the same?" She shook the IV stand with her free hand.

"Oh, careful! Careful!" Diogenes steadied the stand, protecting his precious drug.

"I should have known your promises would prove worthless."

"Constance, my promises are inviolate. All this anger of yours— that's your sickness talking. That's not you."

"Isn't it now?" She grasped the tubes. He lunged to stop her, but was too late—she ripped them out of her arm, the violet liquid spraying about, dotted with flecks of blood, the rack toppling to the floor with a crash.

"Constance! Good God! What are you doing?"

She flung the tubes at him and turned, running from the room. He stood there, frozen in shock, as he heard her feet hurrying up the back stairs, the door to her wing shutting and the bolt slamming home. He tried to get the pounding of his heart down so that he could hear; and he did hear, a faint, stifled sobbing from above. Constance, weeping? That shocked him more than anything else. He looked down at the floor to see the last of his precious arcanum drain out of the bag and onto the rug.

52

After spending almost an hour conducting a minute search of the hospital room in which the elderly female patient and a doctor had met their deaths, Pendergast—with Longstreet's tacit approval—had appropriated one of the doctors' lounges at Miami Baptist for a series of interviews. Longstreet looked on with detached bemusement. He'd been relieved enough to leave the scene of the crimes—although he was no stranger to blood, the extravagant Jackson Pollock–like sprays and spatterings that covered a remarkable amount of the room's surface area were a bit much even for him. Now he looked on, curious to see exactly what Pendergast was onto—if anything.

First, Pendergast spoke to the lieutenant in charge of the crime. He grilled the cop at great length about everything they had learned so far. There was, it seemed, no apparent motive. The killer had chosen a victim, apparently at random—a most bizarre choice of victims, too; one who was about to die anyway. The killer had been interrupted by an eminent young cardiologist, Dr. Graben, who paid for his discovery with his life. Both victims had been mutilated with scalpels in the most lavish way imaginable, basically sliced to ribbons.

The police had begun a careful investigation into the killer, about whom there seemed to be little question. He had been identified by security cameras, by witnesses, and by the doctor's badge he'd used to enter various areas of the hospital. He was a Dr. Walter Leyland of Clewiston, Florida. He was not affiliated with Miami Baptist and, as far as was known, had never previously met or had dealings with either of the victims. While the official inquiry had only just begun, it appeared that this Dr. Leyland spent a great deal of time abroad doing volunteer work with Médecins Sans Frontières and other such organizations, and that his patient list was very small—in fact, they were still trying to gain access to his office; there was no secretary or nurse to answer the phone, and a court order was in the works. In addition, it seemed Dr. Leyland operated, in a very limited capacity, as a state-appointed M.E., but once again the investigation into that was in its infancy. They would know more, the lieutenant said, in the hours and days to come. The doctor's car had been located and was still being swept and analyzed, along with his cell phone and credit cards. The biggest mystery, however, was why he should snap like he did and kill two people in such a savage way.

Next, Pendergast spoke with a nurse from the ICU, who corroborated the story that Dr. Leyland entered the room of eighty-two-year-old Frederica Montoya, who was just days, even hours, from death due to congestive heart failure. A few minutes later, Dr. Graben had entered the room. Puzzled, the nurse had been about to do the same when Dr. Leyland stuck out his head and told her to please leave matters to the two doctors. Five minutes later, Dr. Leyland had left the room and told the nurse that Dr. Graben was still with the patient and was not to be disturbed. When Dr. Graben did not emerge in another five minutes, the nurse became alarmed and investigated.

Dismissing the nurse, Pendergast called for the head of hospital security. The man said that they had not yet completed their examination of all the security tapes, but that—while they had numerous images of Dr. Leyland passing hospital reception, entering a doctors' locker room, and other places—they had yet to find any images of him leaving. No, the video tech could not explain the discrepancy.

Pendergast asked for an image of Dr. Leyland and the man complied with a grainy screen capture. Pendergast and Longstreet studied the image for some time: a salt-and-pepper-haired man with puffy cheeks.

"Doesn't look like your typical serial murderer," Longstreet said. "All the same, there's something familiar about him."

"Isn't there," Pendergast murmured.

Finally, he called for the chief crime scene investigator. The man had had two days to write up his findings, and he had a very interesting observation to make. While the old woman had died first, the violent slashings and stabbings had begun with the unlucky doctor who'd blundered into the room.

"How can you be sure?" Pendergast asked.

"Blood spatter analysis," the CSI said. "There were spatters of arterial blood from Dr. Graben on the lower walls, the bed, the monitoring equipment. But these were *overlain* by most of Ms. Montoya's blood."

"That makes no sense," Longstreet said. "If Leyland was interrupted in his murder of Montoya, you would expect the blood spatter analysis to show the opposite."

"Precisely," said the CSI. "Something else: there is much less of Ms. Montoya's blood on the walls than there is of Dr. Graben's."

Pendergast thought for a moment. "Thank you," he said at last to the CSI. "You've been most helpful."

As the man left the room, Longstreet turned to Pendergast. "Okay. I admit it's a conundrum. How did this Dr. Leyland get out of the hospital without being seen? And why did he commit this atrocious double murder, slash these two innocents to pieces? But more to the point: what on earth is *your* interest in it?"

"All excellent questions. Do you think you could arrange for us to see the bodies?"

"You mean, at the morgue? Of course—if I make some phone calls PDQ. They don't keep bodies on ice too long down here in Florida." Longstreet frowned. "Wait...you're not thinking that—"

Pendergast raised his eyebrows, as if waiting for the other shoe to drop.

But Longstreet shook his head. "No. It makes no sense."

"I *am* thinking that, and, yes, it would make no sense. That is, in fact, what interests me: the completely bizarre and inexplicable nature of these murders. That, and the screen capture of Dr. Leyland. I'm hoping an examination of the bodies will help shed further light on things." And Pendergast indicated the cell phone in Longstreet's pocket. "And so: if you wouldn't mind, H? You did imply time is of the essence."

53

Twenty-four hours had now passed with Constance locked in her room—twenty-four hours of absolute silence, save for the occasional running of water and the lightest of treads on the floor, which reassured Diogenes that at least she was still alive. She had made no appearance, not even to eat. Once, late the previous evening, he had gone to the door and knocked softly, carrying a tray of food for her, the most exquisite sweetbreads and foie gras in a red wine veal reduction. There had been no sound, no response, to his knock. And so he leaned in to the door panel and whispered that he had dinner for her. And the strangest whisper, just on the other side of the door, came back, startling him with its proximity and its crazy timbre.

"Go...away...now."

And now, as another evening approached, he sat in the library, his hands gripping the arms of the chair. He couldn't concentrate; he couldn't read; he didn't want to listen to music; he couldn't even think straight. What was she doing in her room? Had the arcanum taken effect? Had he made another mistake, despite the maniacally obsessive care he had taken with the new formulation? Her mental state had always been of a rather precarious nature. Had she, at long last, finally gone insane?

He had to get himself under control and put an end to this morbid brooding. The place to do that was his meditation chamber. He made for the back door, almost running; went down the stairs; and hastened along the sandy path that led to the bluff. Moments later he emerged into the saw grass. As he came around the bluff the temple emerged from behind the dune, gilded in the late-afternoon light, beckoning him with its sanctuary. He opened the door and entered, making his way shakily to the black leather divan near the center, where he lay down, exhausted and slick with sweat.

Immediately the magic of the place began to work on him: the coolness, the peace, the gray silence, the A minor light. He half closed his eyes and, yes! He could just see, obliquely, those little glints of color, like fleeting flecks of rainbow from a rotating piece of cut glass.

Yes, this was better. Constance would eventually emerge from her room—the requirement for food demanded it. And then he would deal with whatever happened, turn on the full wattage of his charm, and try as he had never tried before to keep her on his island, make her love him as he loved her. He had succeeded this far; he would not fail now.

Slowly, his breathing returned to normal as peace settled over him. The sun was low in the sky, and one side of the temple glowed pearlescent, while the other side, in shadow, was dark and mysterious.

He stretched out on the long divan, the leather buttery soft. He reminded himself that dealing with her was indeed like taming a wild animal. He could not, must not, press her or push things to a head. She had to come out of that room of her own free will. And then he would see if the arcanum had worked. He felt certain that, once she felt its surging effects, she would have a new outlook on life. That the outlook still included him, he hoped and prayed to the gods.

Suddenly a vague shadow passed over the panels of obsidian glass. Someone had just walked by. And there it returned: a dim outline, moving slowly toward the door. It wasn't Gurumarra; this part of the island was forbidden to him.

Whoever it was, was standing at the door. Waiting. And then he watched in a kind of chilling horror as the knob slowly turned and the door eased open.

And there, framed in the blazing light of the dying sun, was Constance.

He stared at her, as she stared at him. He rose to his feet. She was transformed, utterly changed: strong, radiant, glowing with health and vigor. She was wearing one of the old-fashioned dresses she had brought down from New York, but now, as she stepped into the temple and closed the door, he saw her white hands reach behind and unhook the top of the dress. It was like a dream. He watched, mesmerized. Slowly she worked open the hooks, one by one, and then she slipped her arms out of the sleeves. For a moment she held the top of the dress in place, and then she released it, letting it drop to the floor.

She wore nothing underneath. Her long, white body, slender yet voluptuous, with a hint of muscles moving under the pale skin, was like a vision.

She gave her head a little shake, loosening her hair. He couldn't move. She took a step toward him, and another, then a third, until she was very close, her face inches from his. Slowly she began to unbutton his shirt, and he saw she was breathing rapidly, her chest heaving with excitement, face flushed. It was extraordinary: the change the arcanum had wrought on her was nothing short of miraculous.

Ever so slowly, barely touching him, she removed his shirt, and then she knelt, taking off his shoes, unbuckling his pants—until the two of them stood there, inches from each other, naked. Only then did she reach out and lean toward him, giving him a long, lingering, delicious kiss before slowly pushing him backward onto the divan.

54

I<small>T WAS SHORTLY</small> before one in the morning when the dark figure piloting the airboat through the Great White Heron National Wildlife Refuge navigated past the final group of small, hump-like islands that obstructed the way to the larger landmass identified on the coastal classification atlas as Halcyon Key. The engine was kept low, to avoid attracting attention. It had been a difficult journey—the shallow water and labyrinthine channels were barely navigable, even in daylight—but the airboat's draft was almost insignificant. Now it approached a long pier. A speedboat was moored alongside: an antique wooden runabout named the *Phoenix*.

Flavia Greyling cut the airboat's engine and let it glide past the pier and come to rest on the long, sandy beach that ran away on both sides into clusters of mangroves. She got out of the boat and pulled it up under the pier, the crunch of sand barely discernible over the sighing of the wind in the palm trees. Then, crouching behind the little gazebo at the pier's end, she took stock.

Over a low bluff, she could see the roofline of a large house, surrounded by royal palms. Some distance away, she made out a smaller structure, half-hidden among the mangroves, that appeared to be the servant's quarters.

Flavia was dressed entirely in black, and wore the lightweight tactical research boots favored by SEALs. She had exchanged her blue fanny pack for an ebony one, and she wore black leather gloves of Italian design, chosen for their thinness rather than for style. She had not gone to the extent of blacking her face and dyeing her blond hair black, as she sometimes did on other missions she'd undertaken: after all, this was a different kind of job.

She moved forward, creeping cat-like up to the edge of the low bluff. Here, she took a small monocular from her fanny pack and examined the house and grounds. All seemed quiet. There were a few lights on—gas lamps or perhaps kerosene, judging by their flickering quality—but no activity that she could spot.

She returned the monocular to her pack and zipped it closed.

She had been beside herself with fury when Peter had left her in that hotel room in Miami; more angry than she liked to recall. It wasn't just that he was keeping part of his life private from her: it was the way he'd tried to jolly her with praise and then paid her off with that money and then left—as if money could somehow take the place of all the time they'd spent together, everything she'd done for him, like she was some kind of whore. Even though they hadn't done *that* yet, she knew he'd been tempted. She'd seen him looking at her.

What really burned her up was that she'd seen him pull the same slick shit on others, and it made her furious to think he believed she would swallow the same line. He obviously didn't trust her—and after all she'd done. Well, two could play at the deception game. He'd not be on his guard. He'd assumed he'd succeeded: he'd think she was spending his money in Copenhagen and waiting by the phone for a call that might—or might never—come.

Fuck waiting by the phone. She wasn't going to let him get away like that. So here she was.

She had his credit card number from the hotel. Easy to get as they'd checked in as husband and wife. Starting with that, she'd wasted no time learning more about Petru Lupei. It was investigative work of the kind she'd done many times before in tracking down her quarry, and she was very good at it.

Through a combination of social engineering, rudimentary hacking, rummaging through public data, and getting a billing address via the credit card number, she'd fitted the pieces together. It began with a PO box, which contained a few bits of helpful information. With these, and some phone calls to the hall of public records and related government offices, she picked up a bread-crumb trail that had been inadvertently—and very indirectly—left behind by Petru Lupei. It lead from one shell company to another, and ended, finally, in a corporation, Incitatus, LLC, that had only a single asset: an island off the southern coast of Florida called Halcyon Key, purchased almost twenty years before.

It was an hour's trip by motorboat from Miami.

On the dark beach, as she examined the house, Flavia smiled. Petru knew, of course, that she was good at her job. He was the kind of person who would never hire second best. It was becoming clear he didn't return the kind of feelings she had for him; at least, not yet. But he *was* fond of her, of that she was sure.

And now, here, she'd done him one better. She'd learned his secret. She had discovered his private hideaway. Not only that—she had managed to *find* it all on her own and make her way to it. And now, when she chose to reveal herself to him, he'd understand just how clever and accomplished she really was. She would surprise him. That surprise, she knew, would lead to a heightened respect, because Petru respected people who got the better of him—which happened almost never.

And that respect—she felt sure—could easily blossom into love. Especially in a place like this. He only had to see how perfectly matched they were in every way.

Making no noise, she rose over the bluff and made her way across the sand to the rambling house, almost ethereal in the moonlight. She stepped onto the veranda, tried the front door, and, finding it unlocked, quickly entered, closing it behind her. She wondered at the lack of security, but then surmised that the island's very remoteness—and difficult access—was its own best defense.

She stood in the front hall, cloaked in darkness and silence, and did a quick recon: openings to the left and right led into what appeared to be a library and living room, respectively, while a broad staircase ahead led to the second floor. Curious, she walked into the library. Moonlight streaming in the broad windows revealed it to be a two-story space, with expensive-looking rugs on the floor and walls covered with books and small framed paintings. A tiny, unfamiliar-looking piano stood in a far corner.

Flavia frowned. Something about this room did not feel like the Peter she knew. Somehow, it had a . . . feminine sensibility about it. She could almost smell perfume lingering in the air.

She crossed the hallway to the living room. This room, while equally beautiful, was rather different in feeling. The cut-glass chandelier, the heavy wing chairs, the plush fabrics of the sofas and cushions—everything had an old-fashioned elegance rather than the modern, almost clinically simple style that Petru Lupei had always favored.

At least, so far as she'd known.

In the far corner of the living room, a doorway led into darkness. Listening again to make sure her presence was not yet known—she'd surprise Peter in her own time, and in her own pleasant way—she pulled a tiny torch from her fanny pack, turned it on, and—shielding it with one hand—walked through the door. It led into another library-*cum*-office, this one much smaller than the one across the hall. She gazed for a minute at the books on the walls; at the framed paintings. The pack of tarot cards on the desk she recognized as being Peter's preferred Albano-Waite deck. The shelved books were on topics such as military strategy, torture methods of the ancient world, novels in what appeared to be Italian—now, this was more like the Peter she knew. The frown fading, she pulled down one book, Walter Pater's *The Renaissance*.

It opened to the flyleaf. To her surprise, an unfamiliar name had been written in ink: DIOGENES PENDERGAST.

She shrugged, replaced the book. Peter must have borrowed it and forgotten, accidentally-on-purpose, to return it. How very like him. She put the book back and took down another: Suetonius's *The Twelve Caesars*.

There it was again: the owner's name inscribed on the inside front cover, in the same handwriting—Diogenes Pendergast.

The handwriting looked familiar. And, with a sudden shock, so did the name. Pendergast. That was the name of the FBI agent they had been observing in Exmouth.

My best friend is a first-rate FBI agent but simply a babe in the woods when it comes to women . . .

She slid the book back with a savage thrust, but not so savage as to make any noise. Was this the secret life that Petru Lupei talked about? Was this "best friend" actually something more—a relative perhaps? A brother? Did Petru have another name: Diogenes Pendergast?

She knew, of course, that Petru used false, temporary identities in the work they did; he'd used one in Exmouth and another in New York. But it had never occurred to her until this moment that Petru Lupei *itself* was just another of those identities.

Embarrassment at her gullibility—and anger at being so used—rose within her. For the first time in her life, she had allowed her feelings for someone to bring down her guard.

More quickly now, but with consummate stealth, she crept upstairs. It was divided into two wings, each comprising a suite of rooms: bedrooms, morning room, bathroom. Both wings appeared occupied. One of them had several articles she recognized as belonging to Peter—a pocketknife, a money clip, an Hermès tie, carelessly draped over the back of a chair.

The other wing was occupied by a woman.

After very quietly and cautiously examining all the rooms—and finding them all to be empty—Flavia returned to the second floor's central hall. Her mind was a whirl of confusion. What was the meaning of this?

She descended the steps and left the house through the front door, once again closing it behind her. She glanced around, then walked stealthily along the beach, past the servant's quarters, to a trail that cut into the mangroves, heading inland.

She followed the trail over another sandy bluff, then stopped. Ahead lay a very odd building: a circular structure, almost like an ancient temple, that overlooked the Gulf. Between its marble columns were windows that—instead of being made of glass—were of some unusual dark-colored stone that gleamed like mercury in the moonlight.

Flavia stared at the structure for a moment. A strange feeling came over her, a most uncharacteristic apprehension, as if the building held secrets too terrible to learn. But, catching sight of a mullioned door between two of the columns, she took a deep breath and came forward, at the same time reaching into her fanny pack and pulling out one of the Zombie Killer blades she always carried. Not only was it useful for sticking, but she found it made an excellent lock pick and jimmy, as well.

But when she reached the door, she stopped. An odd, sick mingling of emotions came over her as she listened to the sounds from within. After a moment, she knelt to look through the keyhole. It was dark inside, barely illuminated, but there was enough ambient moonlight filtering through the smoked windows for her to see all too clearly what was going on. She froze, a surge of fury, hatred, and disgust welling up inside her.

So it was all lies—all of it. His "best friend," the "fortune hunter," the million-dollar theft and ransom. Not one thing he'd told her was true. And here he was, with *that* woman, making love to *her* with a passion that, despite herself, tore Flavia's breath from her lungs.

She staggered away from the door, then sank back against the cool wall of the temple. She wanted to raise her arms, stuff her fingers in her ears, shut out the sounds...but it was as if all strength had been leached from her limbs. All except for her hands: they kept playing with the Zombie Killer, passing it back and forth between her palms, as the sounds of lovemaking went on, and on, and on.

55

THE MEDICAL EXAMINER'S office of Miami-Dade County was located in a drab-colored modern building of indifferent architecture. The interior was as cold as sun-soaked Tenth Avenue outside was hot. In the basement, among the capacious walls of corpse lockers, it was even colder. Susceptible to chill as always, Pendergast buttoned his suit jacket, pulled his tie up around his throat.

The medical examiner who'd greeted them at the entrance to the morgue cooler, Dr. Vasilivich, was a cheerful, heavyset man with a tonsure like a medieval monk's. "It's a good thing you've got pull," he told Longstreet after the introductions had been made. "And that you were able to get here so early. Both bodies were about to be released to their families."

"We won't take up much of your time," said Longstreet, with a significant glance at Pendergast. Pendergast knew his old CO was growing tired of humoring him.

"What are you looking for, exactly?" Vasilivich asked.

"We aren't sure," Pendergast said before Longstreet could speak.

Vasilivich nodded and led the way down the room. To the left and right, the walls were lined from floor to waist height with stainless-steel doors. "Montoya first, then," he said. "Age before beauty." He chuckled.

Stopping before a locker near ground level, he grabbed the handle, then slid it out slowly. A draped form lay on the cold steel. "If you have any specific questions, ask," he said, pulling on a pair of latex gloves. "I'm afraid I'm the only one who can touch the bodies."

"Understood," said Longstreet.

"Prepare yourself," Vasilivich said as he grasped the concealing drape. "This makes *Hellraiser* look like Captain Kangaroo."

He pulled the drape aside, revealing the naked figure of an elderly lady.

"Christ," Longstreet muttered.

The head and chest were covered with dozens of deep, gaping wounds, the slashes strangely gray given the bloodless tissue. Lacerations seemed to cover every inch of the torso, and the face was so cut up as to be almost unrecognizable. The two agents looked on in silence.

"No autopsy," Pendergast said at last, referring to the lack of a Y-incision.

"The county coroner deemed it unnecessary," said Vasilivich. "Same thing for Dr. Graben." He paused. "Funny thing, though."

"What is?" Pendergast asked.

"According to the toxicology report, Ms. Montoya died of heart failure, most likely due to an overdose of morphine."

"These wounds weren't the cause of death?" Pendergast asked.

"The window of time between events is so brief that it's hard to be sure. But at least some of the lacerations were postmortem. There was as much blood on the bedsheets, you see, as there was on the walls—insufficient vascular pressure."

"Couldn't the death have been caused by the shock of the initial wounds?" Longstreet asked.

"It's possible. As I say, the overdose was only ruled the most likely causative factor. But given the violence of the attack, any number of elements could have brought on death—and probably did."

Leaving the body, Vasilivich moved down a few more rows, pulled open another cold locker, and rolled out another body. When the drape was removed, the corpse of a man was exposed. If anything, this body was even more lacerated than the elderly lady's had been.

"No question about cause of death here," Vasilivich said as they surrounded the body. "Exsanguination, resulting from transverse laceration of the aorta. That was probably the killer's initial blow. There are several others, however, that would have been sufficient to cause death—the severed femoral artery, for example, here."

There was a pause.

"What would cause an overdose of morphine?" Longstreet asked. "Could the drip have malfunctioned?"

"It's extremely rare, especially these days. Those machines are foolproof."

"So it was most likely intentional," Pendergast said. "But if an overdose was in fact the cause, it was still administered close enough to the time of the knife attacks to allow for a degree of arterial spattering."

"Why would somebody try to kill the old lady by overdosing her, then cut her to ribbons?" Vasilivich asked.

"Because he—or she—was interrupted," Longstreet answered.

"Yes," said Pendergast. "If the overdose theory is correct, perhaps the killer hadn't initially intended to slash the body. The woman was on a death watch anyway—everyone would assume she died of natural causes. But Dr. Graben stumbled upon the murderer in flagrante. The murderer slashed him to death—then killed Montoya in the same way, to make it look like the work of a lunatic."

"It's like no lunatic murder I've ever seen," said Vasilivich. "And I've seen more than my share."

"Why not?" Pendergast asked.

"Because of all the slashes to the backs as well as the torsos. Their backs are sliced to ribbons—they look as if they'd been whipped with a cat-o'-nine-tails. Okay, the wounds to the frontal sides aren't all that unusual—Graben even has some defensive wounds on his forearms—but what murderer bothers to slice up their victims' *backs*?"

"A particularly twisted individual," Longstreet murmured.

"Turn him over, if you please," Pendergast asked.

Vasilivich gently turned over the doctor's body. It was indeed a veritable checkerboard of deep slashes, particularly in the region of the lower back, over and across the buttocks.

Pendergast examined the corpse for a minute. Then he froze. After a moment he bent over the lower back, his hand coming forward.

"Agent Pendergast," Vasilivich warned.

Pendergast stopped. "Note this section of vertebrae here, from about L1 to S2."

"Yes?"

"Please inspect it. Wouldn't you say that the extensive shredding and tearing of the flesh along the spinal column is more than just the result of slashing with a knife?"

Vasilivich placed his gloved hands on the corpse's lower back and began gently pulling away the flesh, first at one spot, then another. "My God," he murmured. "You're right. There's been an excision."

"Can you identify the missing material?" Pendergast asked.

More prodding. "Yes," said Vasilivich. "It would appear to be—"

"The cauda equina," Pendergast finished for him.

The M.E. looked up at him, blinking in surprise. "How did you know?"

"Examine the old woman's body, if you please. See if it is missing its cauda equina, as well."

It was the work of two minutes to determine that this was, in fact, the case.

"Aloysius?" Longstreet asked in a strange tone. "What exactly is going on here?"

But Pendergast did not answer. *The cauda equina.* Very quickly, many things fitted themselves together in his mind. Enoch Leng and his elixir. Constance Greene and her sister, Mary. *And now Diogenes.*

So the killer *had* intended to slash his victim from the very beginning. The morphine was simply to dispatch her, to make his job easier. But once one knew where to look, all the lacerations, cuts, and slashes in the world couldn't hide the fact that a small excision had been made from both bodies.

"Why are you doing this?" he asked his absent brother, in a voice below the threshold of hearing.

At that moment, there was a loud knock on the cooler door. Vasilivich walked over and pulled it open. One of Longstreet's field agents was waiting outside. He quickly stepped in.

"Yes?" Longstreet asked.

"There's been a break in the Leyland case," the agent said.

"Go on."

"We already knew that, infrequently, he did work for the Hendry County medical examiner. But we've now learned that, even more infrequently, he assisted the M.E. in administering lethal injections to death row patients."

"And?" Longstreet urged.

"Just seven days ago, he supervised an execution at Pahokee. Single-handedly."

Pendergast quickly drilled the man with his gaze. "And who was executed?"

"Lucius Garey. He was buried the day before yesterday."

Just as quickly, Pendergast turned back to Longstreet. "You need to put through a request to have that prisoner's body exhumed. This morning."

"Not until you explain what's going on."

"I'll explain on the way to the grave site. Now please, make the call. There's no time to lose."

56

THE ENTRANCE OF the aptly named Gates of Heaven Cemetery in Lady Lake, central Florida, was chained and locked. Inside the small cemetery, a procession of cars was parked beside a single grave, around which yellow privacy screens had been erected.

Inside the enclosure were seven people: Special Agent Pendergast; Executive Associate Director Longstreet; a local public health official; a Lake County doctor named Barnes who had been court-appointed to supervise the exhumation; and two gravediggers, who were now hip-deep in an oblong hole of muddy earth. The seventh person—Lucius Garey—was for the time being belowground, somewhere under the feet of the diggers. He was anticipated to appear in the open air very shortly.

Pendergast and Longstreet stood aside from the rest, speaking in low tones.

"So let me get this straight," Longstreet was saying. "Your great-grand-uncle, Enoch Leng, perfected an elixir that could extend a person's life span by a prodigious degree."

Pendergast nodded.

"And one ingredient he needed—at least, at first—was a freshly harvested cauda equina, the bundle of nerves at the base of a human being's spinal column."

"Correct."

"He used this elixir on himself because he was working on a complex project that, he felt, would take more than a normal life span to complete. But before doing so, he tested it on his ward. Constance Greene."

Pendergast nodded.

"What, exactly, was this complex project?"

"It's not germane. Suffice it to say it ultimately was rendered unnecessary."

Longstreet shrugged. "But later, in the 1940s, modern science had caught up sufficiently so that he was able to create his elixir from purely synthetic sources. He no longer needed to kill human beings to acquire their caudae equinae."

"That's correct."

"And both he and Constance continued to take this new, synthetic version of the elixir until about five years ago, when the Riverside Drive mansion was broken into and Leng tortured and killed."

"Yes. He refused to divulge the secret of his elixir."

"What happened to the killer?" Longstreet asked.

"Again, not germane. He joined my ancestor, Dr. Leng, among the dead not long after committing the killing."

"And Constance?"

"I found the only remaining copy of the formula and burned it. After Leng's death, without the benefit of the elixir, Constance began to age normally."

"So she really was born in the 1880s."

"Yes."

"And you burned the formula. My God, what a decision..." Longstreet threw a sidelong glance at Pendergast. "It is remarkable,

Aloysius, how many things about yourself and your family you haven't told me."

"What would have been the point? And as you can imagine, many of them are painful or mortifying—or both."

For a moment, the two fell silent, watching the gravediggers at work.

Longstreet shifted, spoke again. "I'm assuming you believe that it was Diogenes who killed those two people in the hospital. Killed them for their caudae equinae."

"I believe it was Diogenes, yes. Although judging from the evidence, I would guess he planned to kill only the old woman. The doctor surprised him in the act; to escape detection, he killed the man and harvested his cauda equina as well, as a trophy of opportunity. And then he savagely slashed up the bodies in the hope of covering up his excisions."

"But why? You said you destroyed the last copy of the formula for Leng's elixir. Is he taking it himself? Or has Miss Greene decided she wants to remain young, after all?"

"I can't say," Pendergast murmured after a moment. "It is possible there was another copy of the formula, still in existence, that I did not know about. But recall: the formula Leng used for the last sixty-odd years of his life was *artificial*—it did not require using the cauda equina of a human being. Diogenes would appear to be using the *original* formula. Making his actions doubly confusing."

"Do you think it was somebody else—that this was just a freak coincidence?"

Pendergast shook his head. "I don't believe in coincidence." Then he glanced at Longstreet. "And after what happened to us, underneath that bridge in Thailand, I thought you'd stopped believing, as well."

Longstreet nodded slowly. "You're right. I did."

There was a hollow thud from the deepening hole, and a shout from one of the gravediggers. Pendergast and Longstreet came forward as the two men swept mud off the top of a flimsy coffin. Within minutes, ropes had been secured around the coffin and—with an effort—it was raised from its grave and deposited atop a plastic tarp on the nearby grass. The public health official stepped forward; examined a small plate screwed into the top of the coffin; examined the headstone; examined a piece of paper attached to a clipboard he held in one hand; then gave a nod. The gravediggers unsealed the coffin and placed the lid to one side.

Within lay the large form of Lucius Garey, wearing a dark suit and white shirt open at the collar. He had proven too large for the coffin, it seemed, and the mortician had bent his knees to one side in order to fit him in. His eyes were wide and staring, and in death the prison tattoos on his neck had turned a ghastly color.

The county-appointed doctor began pulling on gloves, but Pendergast beat him to it. Gloves already on his hands, he darted forward and—with a grunt of effort—flipped the body over indecorously within its coffin.

There was a chorus of protest. "Aloysius," Longstreet said, "what the hell do you think you're doing?"

Instead of replying, Pendergast merely pointed.

As was the way with cheap, potter's-grave-style burials, Lucius Garey's "suit" did not extend over his whole body. Instead, it merely covered his torso and the tops of his legs, like a sheet. His naked backside was now exposed to the sky.

At the lower end of his spinal column, a small incision was visible.

"Doctor?" Pendergast asked, removing his own latex gloves and tossing them into the coffin. "Would you mind examining that incision?"

After glaring briefly at the FBI agent, the doctor knelt at the graveside and scrutinized the corpse.

When he said nothing, Pendergast went on. "Would you say that the cauda equina of the deceased appears to have been removed?"

The doctor's only answer was a curt nod.

At this, Pendergast turned, ducked between the privacy curtains, and began walking briskly away from the grave site. Longstreet watched for a moment, then turned to the others. "Thank you," he said. "We're done here."

Back in the car, driving slowly toward the front gate, Longstreet cleared his throat. "So Dr. Walter Leyland—Diogenes Pendergast, that is—performed the state-ordered execution of Lucius Garey. In his role as acting medical examiner, he also certified him dead. And in so doing, he was able to extract the man's cauda equina without anybody being the wiser. Taken in a different sort of context, one might almost call the whole thing beautifully symmetrical."

"One might," said Pendergast.

They waited at the gate for the cemetery guard to unlock the chain and let them out.

"There's one thing that's obvious," Longstreet said. "Diogenes did not want anyone to know he was harvesting the cauda equina. Otherwise, he wouldn't have needed to go to such elaborate lengths as performing an execution." He glanced over. "Is there any chance Diogenes knows you're alive?"

Pendergast didn't answer for a moment. "I don't think so. I believe he's been too busy with…other matters. On the other hand, in my haste to track him down, I haven't made an effort to conceal my presence. That was an oversight on my part." He stirred in the passenger seat. "One thing, though, is crystal clear."

"What's that?"

"Whether my brother knows I'm alive or not, he is a transcendentally careful individual. There's only one reason I can think of why he'd go to such lengths to conceal his harvesting of these caudae equinae: *the chance* that I might still be alive. Because I'm the only person who would understand their real significance. And the only reason this would concern him would be if he was—and planned to remain— within a short distance."

"You mean—?"

"Yes. Diogenes, and Constance, are here in Florida...somewhere close."

57

THE ELECTRUM SUN rose into the late-morning sky, illuminating the myriad mangrove islands that dotted the shallow turquoise water, ending in the blue sea of the Gulf. Diogenes felt the warmth of the sun on the side of his face as he stood at the stove, cooking a breakfast of omelets with enokitake mushrooms, prosciutto, Gruyère and Brie, and fresh-chopped basil. He picked up the pan and slid an omelet onto a plate, which he whisked over to Constance, seated in the breakfast nook.

This omelet was in addition to the thick slabs of buttered toast and marmalade, half a dozen rashers of bacon, and fried green tomatoes he had already served. She was famished—and no wonder, when he thought back to the long, and wakeful, night they had spent together. My God, she was strong—and so daring, self-assured, and fearless! She had exhausted him many times over. He was spent; utterly spent.

Her face was unnaturally bright as she ate. Finally, omelet finished, she laid down her fork. "That will do, thank you very much."

"My dear, I've rarely seen such an appetite."

"I'd hardly eaten in days. And, of course, we burned a lot of calories."

"Yes, yes." Diogenes was curiously reluctant to discuss these sorts of things; it was his strict Catholic upbringing. He was glad Constance didn't do what some women did and go over such details in retrospect, discussing it as if it were as commonplace as driving a car or going sailing. But she did not; she was apparently as reticent as he to sully their shared experience with conversational vapidities. And yet he couldn't help recalling, with a frisson of electricity, the way her delicate fingers had traced the lines of his private scars...

She rose abruptly, pushing the plate aside. That same bright look was on her face—too bright, perhaps, but he supposed that's the way certain women were...

"Let us go for a swim," she said.

"Of course. But perhaps we should digest our meal, first?"

"That's an old wives' tale. Come."

He thought of querying her about bathing suits but realized that was not the point. He rose, kicking off his slippers, and they walked arm in arm across the veranda, through the buttonwood, to the pier. She headed down it at a quick walk and he followed; even before she reached the end she was shedding her bathrobe and, nude, dove into the water. He followed.

She swam straight out, at a fast crawl, while he came on behind. After several minutes, he stopped. "Constance? Don't go out too far!"

But she was still swimming intently, heading straight out into the channel. "Constance!"

She could not hear, it seemed, and kept on, making for one of the deeper channels. What was she doing?

"Constance!"

But now she was so far out all he could see was the little fluttering of white water as she swam. He felt a sudden grip of panic. Was she crazy? Was she going to kill herself? Such thoughts seemed absurd. Yet now he could barely see her—and even as he squinted, treading water, he realized he could no longer see her at all.

He turned and swam back, as fast as he could, for the dock. The Chris Craft was still cleated and he quickly pulled on his morning robe, untied the boat, jumped in, and started the engine. In a moment he was winging his way across the water, heading in the direction she had disappeared, his heart in his throat. The fast boat quickly closed the distance and soon he could see the splashing of her crawl. He throttled down, threw the engine into neutral, and drifted alongside her.

"Constance!"

She stopped swimming and looked over at him. "What is it?"

He tamped down his panic. He did not want her to think him worried. She had already expressed her irritation at his excessive hovering.

He gave her a forced smile and a wave. "Care for a ride back?"

"Don't mind if I do."

She kicked her way over to the side of the boat and hauled herself into the rear cockpit, her body covered with water droplets flashing in the sun. Diogenes reached under the console, found a towel, and handed it back.

"You are quite the seal," he said.

"I didn't learn to swim until I was an adult," she said, breathing hard and drying herself off, without the slightest self-consciousness. "But I caught up."

"Indeed you did."

Diogenes brought the boat in a broad arc, heading back to the island but not too directly. It was a glorious morning on the water.

"I have a little gift for you," he said. "Back in the library. Or rather, in an alcove off the library."

"Really? I don't recall any alcove."

"You shall see. Shall we say ten minutes?"

"Shall we say three hours? I'm rather fatigued from my swim."

"Three hours? What about lunch?"

"I'd just as soon skip lunch today, thank you—especially after that large breakfast."

"Very well, my dear."

He tied up at the dock and they went back to the house. Constance went immediately upstairs and so did Diogenes, each to their separate wings. Diogenes wondered how long these sleeping arrangements would last. Not much longer, he hoped.

58

DEEP IN A thick cluster of mangroves at the western edge of Halcyon Key, in the heat of early afternoon, Flavia Greyling stirred in her camouflaged sleeping bag. It was not a restless stirring—the restlessness had died away some time ago. It was more the languid movement of someone who had come to an important decision and was now just marking time, waiting to carry it out.

At first she had been angry—so angry that a red mist hung over her vision as she'd piloted a course away from the island, and more than once the airboat had become hung up in the shallow waters of the wildlife refuge. But by the time she'd reached Marathon, the red mist had receded and she once again felt the calm anticipation she always experienced before an operation, like good hard concrete beneath her feet. Oh, she was still angry, of course—but now she was stone angry, and she knew the feeling well.

There was only one way she'd found to get past it.

She had visited a survivalist store on Marathon and—using a bit of the money Diogenes had given her in Miami—purchased a week's worth of supplies: sleeping bag, waterproof tarp, plastic spade, drinking water, personal hygiene items, spare batteries, twelve-hundred-calorie Mayday snack bars in the inevitable apple-cinnamon, and two dozen MREs—chili mac, stroganoff, pasta fagioli—in individual Mylar pouches. At a gun shop down the street, she'd used her false identity papers to purchase a Glock 22, an extra clip, and two 50-round boxes of .40-caliber ammunition.

She'd gassed up the airboat, then—stealthily, approaching from the uninhabited side—returned to the island. Quickly, she'd found this heavy stand of mangroves, far from any structures save some maintenance buildings and an ancient smokestack. Here she had carefully hidden the airboat and made her bivvy. And then she had undertaken a protracted recon.

There was no further activity at the temple-like structure. Lights were on in the main house, but she had seen no movement. She felt certain, however, that Peter, or rather Diogenes, was inside. And so, too, was the bitch.

At first, her anger had been directed solely at Diogenes. All this time he'd lied to her, concealing his true identity, his secret life—this despite how close they'd become, how many dangers they'd faced together, how many challenges they'd overcome. Not only that, but he'd been with another woman—Constance Greene, no less, the one he had called a blackmailing slut that he'd nothing but contempt for.

All lies. But the more she thought about it, the more she realized it was unfair to pin this on him. Diogenes hadn't deceived her out of malice, or some streak of cruelty. He'd done it to protect himself. He was threatened in some way—she was sure of it. He hadn't told her much about his past, but she knew instinctively that something— some event or series of events—had hurt him terribly; had broken something inside him, something deep and fundamental.

This was something Flavia could understand.

It wasn't his fault that he couldn't trust her. The fact was, he *had* trusted her—with his freedom, with his life—several times. It was just that he hadn't been completely honest. Now that she knew his true identity, she could prove to him that there was no reason to hide anything from her; not anymore. She could help *protect* him from whatever it was that drove him to such secrecy.

But Constance Greene—she was a different story. Here was a woman who'd barged into his life, made herself comfortable in his most private of homes, and taken his love—the love that, Flavia knew in her heart of hearts, belonged to her alone. With Constance out of the way, the field would be clear. Oh, it might take time to win him over. But it would be worth it. Because Diogenes, she knew, was the one man in the world that she could ever feel anything for, save revulsion. They were soul mates; she knew it, and so would he—eventually. Once his head was cleared of that bitch.

But she had to be careful; she had to do this right. She could not allow Diogenes to view Constance as a victim, or—even worse—a martyr. Who knew what kind of web that girl had spun, what kind of mind games she was playing? And so she had to watch, and wait, and pick a time—a time of her own choosing.

Of course, there was still a chance things could go wrong. Diogenes might not understand what she was doing, or why, and come after her. She'd prepared herself—emotionally and physically—for the possibility. Hence the law enforcement magazines she'd purchased for the Glock—fifteen rounds in the magazine and one in the chamber. Sixteen rounds before she'd need to reload. If it became necessary, he'd fall in a hail of bullets.

But Flavia was pretty sure that wouldn't happen. She, not Diogenes, was the conductor now—and she would see that things played out right. Then the whore would be dead—and she, Flavia, would be the woman in that strange gray-black temple.

Once again, she stirred comfortably in the sleeping bag, then closed her eyes.

59

It was half past three, and Diogenes was in the library and waiting at the appointed hour, when Constance appeared. She was, as usual, wearing another Victorian dress. "You need a new wardrobe," he said. "Would you like to go shopping tomorrow? Key West has some lovely stores."

"Yes," she said.

"And now, a special present for you, my dearest. I was waiting for the right moment. I believe it has now come."

He walked over to the wall of bookshelves, grasped a small brass handle, and gave it a tug. A set of shelves swung out to reveal a secret room behind.

"What's this?" she asked.

Diogenes took a step inside and hit the light switch. It revealed a most unusual room, with a table in the middle, some strange old portraits on the walls, many multi-branched sconces holding candles, a tiny fireplace, and a very large and curious wooden case along one wall, with a silk curtain as a front.

"This is my special surprise for you. In this room you will find all the accoutrements of Victorian spiritualism, including a knocking or 'turning' table, Ouija board, candles, tambourine, bells, and a cage with an accordion in it that can be played remotely. There are poles, levers, wires, hooks, and funnels. That large case is what is known as a spirit cabinet. In short, this room contains everything necessary for holding a genuine Victorian séance, including all the devices used in tricks and frauds. Of course, you don't need tricks and frauds if you indeed make contact with the spirit world."

Constance went over to the collection. Diogenes was relieved and satisfied to see that she appeared completely entranced. He was pleased at himself for thinking of something she would love to have, but would never have thought of on her own.

"I might just add that this entire setup belonged to a famous British medium known as Estelle Roberts. Five days after Sir Arthur Conan Doyle's death, in 1930, in front of a massive crowd in the Royal Albert Hall, Roberts contacted Doyle's spirit—or so she claimed. No one of course has ever been able to refute, or confirm, this or any of her other séances."

"How did you acquire it?"

"When she died in 1970, her house in Monken Hadley was shut up and fell into disrepair. I've always had an interest in these things; as you undoubtedly know, magic and prestidigitation is a Pendergast family interest going back generations. Six months ago, the old house came on the market; I realized this might be something that would amuse you, so I bought the house, had all the accoutrements of the séance room removed and carefully restored—and brought here. I then sold the old house at a profit—London real estate is *such* a good investment these days."

He watched with delight as she explored the spirit cabinet, drawing back the curtain and looking at the strange devices within. She examined the turning table, peering underneath and poking around at its complex curves, corners, and carved decorations.

"I thought you might cherish this little collection," said Diogenes, softly. "In fact, I *knew* it. I know that your long life, and the way your family was taken from you at a young age, has made the past very dear to you. That's why I created this space: as a memorial to the past. With any luck, *your* past. When you feel ready, we shall have a séance. Perhaps, in time, you will be able to communicate with your sister, Mary. Or your parents."

A great stillness came over Constance as he spoke, and Diogenes realized he might have stepped over a line. This was a very private aspect of her life, and this construction of his might seem like presumption.

She rose rather stiffly, staggered a moment, then began walking toward the bookcase door. As she passed by him, he was shocked at the deeply troubled expression on her face.

But then, just inside the door, she halted abruptly. For what seemed a long time, she remained still, her back to him. And then she turned around. Her face, her entire being, radiated exceedingly strong and conflicting emotions: of boldness and dread, determination and hesitation.

"What...what *is* it?" he stammered, terrified by the look on her face.

She raised her chin and took a step forward, with an expression of hatred, malice—and triumph.

60

The special agent in charge of the FBI Miami Field Office, Vantrice Metcalf, was very curious about her two special visitors. She had heard vague rumors about one of them going almost back to her days at Quantico—a legendary and controversial agent who operated outside the rules with apparent impunity; whose collars often ended up dead; and who was sometimes spoken of as the sort of rogue agent the new FBI should no longer tolerate. And yet he was not only tolerated, but seemed to have the run of the Bureau.

The other one she had also heard about, but that was mostly due to his high position as executive assistant director for intelligence. He was eccentric in his own way, a rather shadowy figure, but known to be brilliant, tough, and fair.

And here they were, in her office, together, and what a contrast they made. Longstreet, with his craggy face, long gray hair, rumpled blue suit, remarkable height, and gravelly voice. And the other...the *other*. So pale, sleek, and cat-like, with a buttered-biscuit accent from the Deep South, antebellum manners and gestures: a genteel yet intimidating persona with glittering chrome eyes and a black suit. It was the first time she had seen an FBI agent in a black suit—it just wasn't part of the culture.

Metcalf was a sort of collector of people, and she prided herself on her ability to scope out a person by appearance alone. She *could* read a book by its cover, and that was one reason why she was the youngest SAC in the history of the Miami office, *and* the first woman, *and* the first African American. As she looked these two gentlemen up and down, she realized that nothing less than complete and total cooperation would be required—and that would bring to her side two very useful allies, who might be able to help her on the long road to her ultimate goal: FBI director.

"Gentlemen," she said. "What can I do to help?"

It was Longstreet who replied. "Ms. Metcalf, Special Agent Pendergast and I are on an assignment that is both confidential and unofficial. We have a rather unorthodox request."

"Very well." She wouldn't make it too easy on them. She couldn't be seen as a pushover—whatever it was they wanted.

"We'd like an hour, alone and unsupervised, in your PRISM system operations unit."

At this, Metcalf's eyebrows went up. This was a request so completely out of line that even she was momentarily astonished.

"We understand this is a rather unusual request," said Longstreet.

"Well, I'm sorry, gentlemen, but even coming from the executive assistant director for intelligence this request is beyond the beyond. You know you need to go through channels."

At this, the other one stirred. "Is that a no?"

The way he asked the question, so quietly, so politely, and yet so full of menace, was something Metcalf would have to analyze later and adopt herself.

"Have you heard the word *no* from me yet?" she said pleasantly.

"And I hope we won't," the man named Pendergast replied.

She waited, letting the silence build.

"Let me explain—" began Longstreet.

Pendergast laid a gentle hand on Longstreet's arm. "I don't think Ms. Metcalf is going to need—or want—an explanation."

That's very true, Metcalf thought. She let a second, longer silence build. To most people, Metcalf had discovered, silence was even more unbearable than pointed questioning.

"Ms. Metcalf," said Pendergast, "we never forget who our friends are. And we have long memories."

This was exactly what she wanted to hear, but she was surprised to hear it put so clearly. This was a man who valued directness. No weaselly beating around the bush. "When do you wish access?"

"Right now, if you please."

For a third time she let the silence build. And then she said, "Gentlemen, if you could have a seat, it'll take me about five minutes to clear the PRISM unit of extraneous personnel. I assume you'll need a technical support person?"

"Yes."

"I'll leave the best one in there, then."

When the room was ready, and as they were all leaving, Pendergast turned and offered her a hand as cool and clean as a fresh cotton sheet. "I'm so very glad we're friends."

Howard Longstreet followed SAC Metcalf down a series of hallways and elevators, until they reached the door to the windowless basement room, warm with the smell of electronics. It was small and awash in a bluish light from myriad computer screens. In this room, agents with special clearance could access certain of the NSA's relevant databases. He had been in PRISM rooms before, of course, and this one was no different. Except that it was now empty, save a single technician, lanky and nervous, with an unruly cowlick.

"Mr. Hernandez," said Metcalf, "this is SA Pendergast and Executive Assistant Director Longstreet."

"Um, hi," said Hernandez.

"They'll require your unfettered help for one hour," Metcalf said to the technician. "And of course what happens here is to remain confidential, even from me."

"Yes, Ms. Metcalf."

She retreated and closed the door. Longstreet glanced at Pendergast; there was a rare light of anticipation shining in those eyes. He wished he felt the same. This seemed like such a wild goose chase, a complete waste of time when they had so little time left. If it were any other agent he would have put an end to this detour right at the beginning. But he had known Pendergast far too long to dismiss one of his hunches out of hand. And the discovery of the missing caudae equinae, while extremely outré, was nevertheless telling. He just wished Pendergast was a little more forthcoming with his theories.

"Aloysius," said Longstreet, "would you like to explain to Mr. Hernandez what you want him to do?"

"Certainly." Pendergast brought out a large hard drive from somewhere in his suit and placed it on the table in front of Hernandez. "On this drive are twenty-four hours of video feeds from all the security cameras in the Miami Baptist Hospital. These cams capture every person who visits the hospital—without exception. They are comprehensive. It isn't possible to enter or leave the hospital without having your visage recorded multiple times."

Hernandez gave a nod of understanding.

"The hospital has about nine thousand visitors a day. There are approximately two hundred such cams."

"That's a lot of video. Is this about that slasher killing?"

Pendergast fell silent and a sense of disapproval filled the room.

"Sorry," said the technician.

"We believe an individual entered the hospital wearing one disguise and left it wearing a different one. He could have changed facial features, hair color, and perhaps other physical details as part of the switch."

"I see."

"So, Mr. Hernandez: how can we use your computing power and the NSA's databases to identify a person who *left* the hospital without ever *entering* it?"

"Why," said Hernandez, relieved, "that's a piece of cake. I thought you were going to give me something hard. The NSA has the best facial-recognition software in the world—better than Google's. I'll just ask it to match all the ingresses with the egresses and spit out the unique face that left but didn't enter."

At this, Pendergast broke into a rare smile. "And how long might this take?"

"How many gigs you got in that drive?"

"Three terabytes."

"Twenty minutes. Care to wait?"

Longstreet watched Pendergast slide himself into a chair, and he did likewise. Hernandez remained standing at the computer, typing on a keyboard.

As if timed by the clock, twenty minutes later the technician straightened up from his computer monitor. "Bingo! Got your man. At several angles."

Longstreet rose and followed Pendergast, who had leapt up like a cat and was scrutinizing a series of faces on a computer monitor.

"Let me put them up on the big screen," said Hernandez.

The faces popped up on a sixty-inch screen. They showed a tall man, dressed in an elegant brown suit, with brown eyes and brown hair, skin somewhat olive in tone, wearing fashionable titanium glasses. Longstreet stared with surprise and disappointment. It wasn't Diogenes—was it? The man looked so different.

Pendergast said, "Play some video, please."

Hernandez obliged, showing the man walking down a hallway; another image of him crossing the lobby; and a final image of him exiting. He was the right height and build, that was true, but a lot of people were slender and six foot two. Watching the videos, Longstreet felt disappointed. The man not only didn't look like the old FBI surveillance tapes he'd seen of Diogenes—he didn't *move* like him. In Longstreet's experience, the way a person walked was almost as identifiable as the way he looked. Everyone had a different way of walking, something that couldn't be disguised.

He glanced at Pendergast, only to see the man's face distorted by triumph mingled with anger.

"Surely that isn't Diogenes?" he asked.

"Most *surely* it is," came the answer. "I know my brother. That's him there, on the screen—I know it."

"But the way he moves?"

"My dear H! Naturally that would be the first thing he'd alter. The man doesn't walk like my brother, true—but doesn't the walk look the slightest bit artificial to you? He's playing up the difference—for the camera."

Longstreet turned to Hernandez. "Run that video again, please."

He scrutinized the feed once again. Damned if Pendergast wasn't onto something. "Aloysius," he said, turning away from the screen, "I've known you long enough to trust your hunches."

"This is no mere hunch," Pendergast replied. He turned back to

Hernandez. "I now have a second assignment for you: who is this man? Officially, I mean."

With a smile, Hernandez rapped on the keyboard. Within seconds, NSA facial-recognition software had come up with an identity and numerous details:

```
Name: Petru Lupei
SS# 956-44-6574
Place of birth: Râșnov, Romania
Date of naturalization: 6/15/99
Race: Caucasian
Height: 6'2"
Eyes: Brown
Hair: Brown
Identifying tattoos or marks: None
```

A lot more information scrolled past, but Pendergast ignored it. "Excellent," he said. "Now, Mr. Hernandez: I want you to look up this man's real estate holdings. And not just his personal holdings, but any real estate held by shell companies he owns, offshore companies, alleged relatives—in short, I want to know about any square inch of ground even remotely connected to him. With a focus on Florida."

"Of course." Another few clicks on the keyboard and a list appeared. Even with his vast experience, it still amazed Longstreet at how quickly the computer could connect a maze of carefully disguised shell companies. And then it occurred to him that the NSA had probably already done the work—for every registered company in the world. That would be like them.

Pendergast scrutinized the screen for a moment, then let out a most uncharacteristic cry of triumph. *"Right there!"* he said, stabbing a white finger at a listing.

Halcyon Key

Monroe County, Florida

Owned by: Incitatus, LLC

PO Box 279516

Grand Cayman

Registered to:

Aeolian Island Holdings, SpA, Milan, Italy

A fully owned subsidiary of:

Barnacle, Ltd., Dublin, Ireland

Director and sole shareholder:

Petru Lupei

"*Incitatus*," Pendergast murmured in a strange voice.

Longstreet felt something like a chill go up his spine. It was the one nugget of data they needed, he felt certain: that needle in the haystack, that faintest of lines in the sand, that—when found—led to Diogenes.

"Get the satellite imagery," said Pendergast. "Target that location."

"No problem." Hernandez called up another program, typed in a series of coordinates, and a moment later a satellite image popped onto the screen, of remarkably high resolution. It showed a medium-size island, surrounded by four smaller ones.

"Zoom in on the main island, please."

Hernandez complied. A large, sprawling house came into view, a pier stretching into the shallow bay, a smaller house hidden in the nearby mangroves, and, scattered around, some isolated outbuildings. A boat was tied up at the pier.

"When was this satellite image taken?" Pendergast asked.

Hernandez peered at the screen. "Eighteen months ago."

"The boat. Focus on the boat."

The image expanded until the boat filled the screen. It was an antique Chris Craft.

"That's it." Pendergast turned to Longstreet, his eyes feverishly alive. "That's where we'll find them."

Longstreet turned and stared at his friend. His head was almost spinning at the speed with which Pendergast had split the case wide open.

"H, we need to go in there—fast and hard," Pendergast said. "And we need to do it *tonight*."

61

W HAT IS IT?" Diogenes repeated.

"I wonder if you'd mind getting the boat ready," Constance said.

His mind went blank, as if he was unable to process what she was saying. The last few minutes had been so strange—her behavior had become so unexpected—that he could barely get the words out. "The boat? Why?"

"And then if you'd be good enough to take my things out to it." The conflict he'd read on her face, the hesitation, was now gone. "I did most of my packing earlier this afternoon—when I told you I was resting."

He passed a hand over his forehead. "Constance—"

"I'm leaving. My work is done."

"I don't understand. Your work?"

And now her voice was cool, even. "My revenge."

Diogenes opened his mouth, but no sound came.

"This is the moment I've been waiting for," Constance said. "It's not in my nature to gloat or tease. It is, however, in my nature to be brutal. So I'll make my explanation as concise as possible. This entire thing has been a charade."

"A charade," Diogenes managed to repeat. "What charade?"

"The charade of our love." And now he saw that, in one hand, she was holding her antique Italian stiletto—something he had not seen since the Riverside Drive mansion.

"But it's no charade—I love you!"

"I know that you do. How touching. And your courtship was, in all honesty, beautifully planned and exquisitely performed. It was all a woman could ask for." She paused. "A pity it didn't have its intended effect."

This had to be a nightmare. It couldn't be real. She couldn't mean this, *any* of this. Perhaps the arcanum had been flawed and, once again, she was not herself. And yet he felt a creeping, terrible uncertainty. "What in God's name are you saying?"

"Need I be more clear? Very well. What I am saying is: I don't love you. I never loved you. On the contrary: I *despise* you. I feed on my hatred of you morning, noon, and night. I cherish my hatred; it is now a part of me, indivisible and precious."

"No, please—!"

"When I first learned you were alive, down in the sub-basement, all I felt was fury. And then you spoke. You spoke with your honeyed tongue. Do you recall how, once you were done, I said I needed time in which to consider your proposition? I had become confused, uncertain. I was also angry—irrationally so—at Aloysius for disappearing, for drowning. And the prospect of becoming a mental vegetable was, of course, displeasing. But by the end of that night, I was at peace with myself. I was happy. Because I realized I was being given a unique opportunity: a chance *to kill you again*. Your supposed death in the volcano had been too quick. This time, I decided to do it right."

"You..." Diogenes took a step forward, then stopped. Never in his life—not even in the depths of youthful despair following the Event, or after the failure to steal the diamond known as Lucifer's Heart, or even during his recovery from Stromboli—had he felt so utterly devastated. "You took the arcanum..."

"The arcanum was an unexpected benefit. A happy circumstance, in that it not only aided me, but also helped convince *you* I was sincere— just as my knocking out Lieutenant D'Agosta helped convince you, although in that case I was saving his life, since you would almost certainly have killed him had I not intervened."

Diogenes staggered. "What about our night together? Surely that wasn't a charade!"

"It was the very climax of the charade. You were correct: your reformulated arcanum did restore my health and vigor. That restoration was...a most heady experience. And so now you can add your recollections of that night to your memory palace of pain. Remember how you once described our first night together? *An animal spasm.* This is my gift to you: one spasm for another. Yet I knew even then that the fleeting pleasure I gave you would be paid back in pain a thousandfold, every day, every night, for the rest of your life."

"It's not possible! The things you said, the expression on your face, your appetites, your smiles...That wasn't pretense, Constance. I would have sensed it."

There was a brief silence before Constance spoke again. "I must admit—when I saw Halcyon, when I saw your obsidian chamber— my resolve did occasionally waver. Seeing this room, in fact, was my greatest test. Ironically, that's how I knew I had to complete my work. And I remind myself how much *more* pleasure your suffering will give me than anything offered by the temptations of Halcyon."

Every word of Constance's, spoken matter-of-factly in that elegant, old-fashioned voice, was like acid in his ears. He barely knew what he was saying. "I don't believe it. This is some perverse joke. No one could deceive me like—"

"You deceived yourself. But I weary of this. Now you know the truth. And I wish to take my leave of this island of yours, leaving be-hind all your fine memories, hopes, and dreams...in tatters."

"You'll need the arcanum—"

"I'm content to join the rest of humanity in the march toward death. No, Diogenes, it is *you* who need the arcanum. Prolong your own life, so you can live in misery forever!" And now, at last, her voice broke out into a laugh: low, exultant, pitiless.

Hearing that laugh, Diogenes felt his knees buckle. He sank to the floor. A cold, baleful light seemed to spill over him. And with that light came a bleak realization, the bleakest he had ever known: this was no cruel joke. Her dismantling of him and his dreams was a masterpiece of vengeance, pitiless and awe inspiring in its comprehensiveness. Halcyon would be all the more lonely now that he had experienced their being to-gether. Constance knew that. She knew that she was leaving him here, a broken man, in a place she had made intolerable with memory.

His eyes were cast downward; a haze obscured his vision. "Is there nothing I can say, nothing I can do, to convince you that—"

"No," she said. "And please don't demean yourself by begging; it's unseemly."

Diogenes said nothing. The haze grew thicker.

"Actually, now that you mention it, I am curious about one thing. That door on the far side of the island; the only one anywhere that's locked. What's behind it? I know perfectly well you're hiding some-thing there. I might as well see everything before I go. That I should be at all curious suddenly strikes me as the height of improbability, but that in itself is probably the reason. I saw a key around your neck last night; no doubt it fits the lock. Give it to me, please."

Last night. As she spoke, out of nowhere he heard an echo sound in his mind. *Let her try to deny it—we were one.*

The mist receded. Diogenes looked up to see her standing above him, one hand outstretched.

A change came over him.

What's behind it? I know perfectly well you're hiding something there.

All hope might not be lost. He realized that he had just been given a chance—his last chance...

He staggered to his feet, did his best to collect himself.

"No," he said, his voice hoarse in his own ears. "No. *I* will show it to you. *I* will guide you through it. I will reveal to you...that part of my soul no one has ever seen before."

Constance withdrew her hand. Something unfathomable flashed in her eyes.

"Very well," she said.

A moment of silence passed. And then Diogenes—walking a little unsteadily—left the alcove, passed through the library, and headed for the front door. Constance followed a few steps behind him.

Moments later, a dark form detached itself from the deep shadows of the library where it had been hiding, listening, and—careful to keep out of sight—followed the two as they made their way across the sand toward the path leading into the mangroves.

62

PENDERGAST BOUNDED UP the stairs from the basement, Longstreet following more slowly in his wake.

"We can leave immediately," Pendergast said over his shoulder. "It's a hundred miles to Marathon by plane. From there, you and I can charter an airboat—the channels around that area of the Keys can be very shallow, I believe. We'll be in position shortly after nightfall."

"Just a moment," Longstreet said. And something in his voice made Pendergast stop and look back.

"What do you mean: *you and I?*"

"I should have thought it obvious. The two of us."

"A covert operation?"

"A surgical strike against Diogenes."

Longstreet shook his head. "We're not doing that."

Pendergast frowned. "What do you mean?"

"Do you remember what you said, back in my New York office?"

Pendergast waited.

"You said exactly this: *My brother must die. We must make sure—completely sure—that he does not survive apprehension.*"

"That's correct."

"You said something else: something equally true. *We owe it to Mike Decker.*"

Once again, Pendergast waited.

"As members of the Ghost Company, you and I both swore a solemn blood oath: to avenge the death of any compatriot to who died at the hands of another."

"*Fidelitas usque ad mortem.*"

"Precisely. And that's why it's not going to be you and me who go down to this Halcyon Key. It's going to be a massive strike force."

Pendergast took a step back down the stairs. "H, that isn't the way to prosecute this operation. I know my brother. The two of us, descending on the island in stealth, have the best chance of—"

"No. There are far too many unknowns. We don't know who else is on the island. We don't know what kind of security we might find. We don't know what steps Diogenes has taken to harden or fortify— or booby-trap—his domicile. And we don't have the luxury of time. You said it yourself: we need to do this tonight. We don't have time for more intel. Diogenes is too clever, and he's too unpredictable."

"And that's exactly why—"

"Listen, Aloysius. Ever since you returned to New York, I've let you play this your way. I've called in markers, burned through thousands of man-hours doing data and forensic analysis. I followed you to Florida on a whim. I held up the release of two corpses to their families, arranged for an emergency exhumation, watched you manhandle a body already at rest—"

"Discovering the whereabouts of my brother as a result."

"You had the inspiration. But the heavy lifting was done by PRISM. I've done a little more digging since you told me that Diogenes was still alive. He's responsible not only for Mike's murder, but also for that of a Dr. Torrance Hamilton; an artist, Charles Duchamp; the attempted murder of an ex-employee of the New York Museum, Margo

Green; the kidnapping of a woman I think you know, Viola Maskelene; the theft of the New York Museum's irreplaceable diamond collection and its subsequent destruction; the incitement to homicidal madness of several Museum employees; and a grand-scale plot involving the Museum's Tomb of Senef that I'm not exactly clear on. Not to mention the two recent slasher murders in the hospital here. And those are just the crimes of his that come to mind—I have no doubt it's the tip of the iceberg. We're to take down such a murderous, dangerous, psychotic fugitive by an—excuse me—covert operation? The two of us? No: now that we know the location of Diogenes's safe house, it's time to do things by the book. We'll spearhead the operation, for sure—but backed up by a massive federal SWAT presence."

"There's another variable to consider here: Constance. I've told you her story. She's a psychologically damaged individual whose mind-set we can't predict. She might be under Diogenes's thrall. Whatever the case, we can't risk injury to her."

"If she's under his thrall, she can shoot a gun just as well as he can. My men would be in danger. But, look, we'll do everything we can to avoid her getting hurt."

"If you send in a SWAT team, people are going to get killed."

"Of course. *Diogenes* is going to get killed. Do I have to remind you again of what you told me? *My brother must die.*"

"H—"

Longstreet held up a hand. "Sorry, old friend. I'm calling this one."

There was a brief, tense silence. Then Pendergast simply nodded.

The two proceeded up to the office of SAC Vantrice Metcalf, where Longstreet provided her with some very surprising information and asked for her assistance in planning and executing an immediate SWAT operation. Metcalf agreed. The Tactical Operations Center was activated on the second floor, and the three moved there. They were quickly joined by two, then half a dozen, and then a dozen more agents, and—under Longstreet's direction—plans for a night assault were quickly and expertly put together. And meanwhile Pendergast stood back from the group, still as a statue in his bespoke black suit, one arm folded over the other, listening as the op came together, neither his eyes nor his facial expression betraying anything about his inner thoughts.

63

The sun was just sinking into the Gulf of Mexico as Constance followed Diogenes out of the mangroves into the meadow at the far end of Halcyon Key. Diogenes had not said a word to her since leaving the house. He was holding himself more erect now, and his bearing was steadier. But Constance could make out no expression on his face. His heterochromic eyes seemed to be bottomless pools in which no spark of personality registered.

He walked toward the series of buildings at the far end of the meadow, passing the old, crumbling power plant and stopping before the copper-sheathed door labeled CISTERN. He reached up, took a gold chain from around his neck—from which hung a black key—and fitted the key to the lock. With a whisper of well-oiled hinges, the door opened outward.

Still without a word, Diogenes stepped inside, flicking on a series of light switches as he did so. Over his shoulder, Constance could make out a large, circular chamber of old brick. A red-painted metal box was set into the near wall. A stairway led down to a stone catwalk that ran around the outer wall in a semicircle, ending at an iron-banded door. Five feet or so below the catwalk was a smooth surface of black water.

She had won. Her revenge was complete: Diogenes was a beaten man. And yet she was conscious of a sudden, intense curiosity about this place. She sensed, rightly or wrongly, that there was a still-deeper level to him—a level she had not yet, despite everything, fully sounded. Why she would even want to, considering the sharpness of her hatred, she did not quite understand.

As Diogenes led the way down the staircase, he at last broke his silence. "Cisterns such as this are very common in the Keys," he said. "It is often the best way to collect fresh water." His voice was hollow, and distant, and utterly atonal, and it echoed strangely in that underground brick chamber, as if coming back from the realms of the dead.

Reaching the bottom of the staircase, he made his way along the lip of the catwalk. Again, Constance could make out the distant hum of machinery. As she followed, she glanced down toward the water. The cistern below had no rungs, steps, or other means of egress; if one were to fall in, there would be no way to climb out.

Where the catwalk stopped at the iron-banded door set into the cistern wall, Diogenes paused. He pointed at the door. "Beyond this lay the old machinery once used to pump water to the house. The machinery was remarkably large and extensive. Modern technology, of course, rendered it obsolete long ago, and it was disposed of. As you shall see, I have found a new use for the empty space."

Employing the key once again, he unlocked the door, pushed it open. Blackness yawned ahead. Stepping back, he made a small gesture, ushering her inside.

Constance hesitated. She could see nothing; there was no reflection from the central cistern. She could almost imagine taking a step forward and dropping into limitless empty space. But nevertheless, after a moment she moved past Diogenes and into the room.

Her heels rapped on stone.

Diogenes followed her in, closed the door behind them. For a moment, all was dark—a blackness so complete that Constance, who was no stranger to the dark, had never experienced its like. But then there was a faint click, and a light came on in the ceiling.

Her first impression was that she was floating in a black and silent void. Then there were additional clicks, and as Diogenes turned on light after light, she realized where she was. She was standing inside what appeared to be a perfect cube, with floor, walls, and ceiling of black marble. But then, as she looked more closely, she realized that the lights—which were spaced at regular intervals, a few feet below the ceiling—were actually placed behind very thin panes of some dark, smoky substance. The substance was of no particular color, but rather a shifting, shimmering grayscale, and the light that filtered from behind the panels gave the room a faint, strange, glittering luminescence, as if she were imprisoned within a smoky diamond of various shades of gray. And then she realized: the walls and ceilings of the room had been paneled entirely in obsidian.

As if on cue, she heard a bitter, mirthless laugh from behind her. "That's correct," came the same atonal voice. "This, not the meditation temple, is my *true* obsidian chamber. It is a shrine—if you can call anything that collects those things that bring shame and pain a 'shrine'—to my past life."

Looking around more closely, Constance now saw that a series of oblong frames were set into all four walls at intervals as regular as the lights. All were the same size—about eighteen inches by two feet. They were not flush with the walls, but extruded, at precisely the same distance from the floor as their brethren. They, too, were edged in obsidian, with fronts of clear glass. A small, hidden pinlight within each case gave their contents—in layouts reminiscent of the artist Joseph Cornell—a faint illumination.

"My museum," Diogenes said. "Please—allow me to act as docent. These displays are chronological, starting here, at your left."

He took a few steps from the door, stopping at the first frame. Inside, Constance saw a sketch, drawn on ruled school paper, of an old, miniature city. It was breathtaking in its scope and fine detail. It could only have been drawn using a magnifying glass and a technical pen with a tiny, tiny nib. Every microscopic house had been shingled; every cobble on every street had been lovingly shaded; every doorway had a microscopic number above it.

"I drew that at age seven," she heard Diogenes say. "I lived in that city, in my mind. Every day I would add more detail to it. I loved it above all else. I include it here as a reminder of what I might have become—had things been different. But you see, while I was still at work on this...something happened to me."

"The Event," said Constance.

"Yes. The Event. You don't know much about it, do you? I'm sure Aloysius never spoke of it."

Constance remained still. She was staring at the remarkable drawing. It was barely conceivable someone so young could have created something so detailed, so perfect.

"Aloysius and I were playing in the basement beneath the Maison de la Rochenoir, our old New Orleans house on Dauphine Street. We stumbled upon a hidden room full of props, created by our great-uncle Comstock for his magic show. One of them was called 'The Doorway to Hell.' Aloysius goaded me into it. It...turned out to be a device built for one of two purposes: to drive a person mad—or frighten them to death."

How horrible, Constance thought.

"It was some time before I could be rescued from its interior. It was so terrible, I tried to kill myself with a Derringer left there to offer eternal 'relief' to the person trapped inside." He paused. "The bullet went in my temple, but it was a small caliber and it came out my eye. There was a question as to whether I would survive. I did survive. But then, afterward, things were...different. I was sent away for a time. Color vanished from my world—leaving me only with monochromatic shades of gray. My ability to sleep was, and remains, impaired beyond remedy. When I returned, I was changed. Changed utterly."

He moved on to the next frame. Constance followed. Inside was a tiny crucifix, covered here and there in dark stains that appeared to be old blood. A legend at the bottom of the crucifix read: INCITATUS.

"I felt strange urges that I didn't understand. On the other hand, neither did I fear them. From time to time I...indulged myself in them. But as I approached maturity, one desire took preeminent hold over me: the thwarting, mortification, and ultimate destruction of my brother, Aloysius—who had visited this horror upon me."

He now moved slowly past several frames, pointing first at one tableau, then at another. Constance saw things she did not understand: a hair shirt made out of some organic substance; a hangman's noose; what looked like a thick bunch of poison sumac, wrapped tightly in fishing line.

"At first, my attempts to wreak vengeance on my brother were haphazard. Unfocused. But as I grew older, a plan began to take form. It would require years, even decades, to carry out. It would require all my time and attention. It would require the creation, and the loving curation, of several different identities. For example, that of the New York Museum curator Hugo Menzies."

They had by now rounded a corner and were halfway down the second wall. He stopped at a frame that held within its mercury-colored walls an ancient bayonet. "The weapon that killed Special Agent Michael Decker, Aloysius's close friend. Not the real one, you understand—that is still no doubt in an evidence locker somewhere—but an exact replica."

He moved to the next frame, which contained a copy of the magazine *Museology*; a museum ID, spattered with blood; and a box cutter.

"Margo Green," Diogenes said, by way of explanation.

The next frame held a handwritten letter, several pages long, signed "A. Pendleton." Beside it was an expensive-looking ladies' handbag.

"Viola Maskelene," Diogenes said in the same, strange, hollow voice. "That did not end well."

More quickly now, he steered her past other frames, rounding the obsidian space to the exhibitions on the third wall: a cut-glass crystal containing what appeared to be diamond grit; a memorandum from Herkmoor Prison—and then, Constance stopped. In the middle of the third wall was a frame containing a fragment of a bloodstained satin sheet and a half-drunk glass of greenish liquor, with a faint trace of lipstick on the rim.

She turned suddenly to face Diogenes.

"You," he said simply.

"I've seen enough," she said, and abruptly stepped past him and began making her way toward the exit without looking at the other displays.

Quickly Diogenes scrambled to keep up. He darted ahead, and—as she rounded the fourth and final wall—placed himself between her and the door, blocking her path.

"Wait," he said. "*Look.*" And he pointed at the frames.

After a moment, she complied. Save for the first—which contained an obituary, a bloody scalpel, and a decorative fan of Central American design—the frames on this wall were all empty.

"I've changed," he said—and this time, the voice was not entirely cold and hollow; there was an edge to it. "I've changed *again*. I've stopped. Don't you understand, Constance? Although that was not my original intention when I started keeping these trophies, this place has become—as I've implied—my Museum of Shame. It chronicles my misdeeds, both successful and unsuccessful, as a way of ensuring that I will never, *ever* go back to the old ways. But I created it for another reason, too: a safety valve. I realized that, if I ever did feel the old...needs resurfacing, all I would have to do was come here."

Constance turned away from him, not entirely sure whether she was blocking out his words or her uncertain reaction to them. She realized her eyes were resting on the final occupied frame: the one that contained a scalpel, a fan, and an obituary. The obituary was for an eminent cardiac surgeon, Dr. Graben, who had been the victim of a homicidal slasher. The obit bemoaned the incalculable loss to science and humanity this man's death heralded. It was dated only four days earlier.

"So you lied," she said, pointing at the obituary. "You *did* kill more people."

"It was necessary. I needed another sample to synthesize the elixir. But I don't need any more: you can see, feel, the results for yourself."

"And how is that supposed to make me feel? Others have died—died unnecessarily—so that I could live."

"The old woman was comatose, moribund. And the doctor wasn't supposed to die. His entrance was unexpected."

Once again she began to walk away; once again he interposed himself between her and the door. "Constance. Listen. This room is a perfect cube—but the space that originally held the pump machinery was not. I've created a room within a room. Did you notice that large box, at the top of the stairway? When I made this room, I filled the space between the walls of *my* obsidian chamber and the original stone of the pump room with plastic explosive. *Plastic explosive*, Constance—enough C-4 to turn all of this—the chamber, the cistern, everything—into a fine mist. That box at the top of the stairs is the trigger, set on a time delay. Once, as I said, this chamber had a different purpose for me. Now it fills me with self-loathing. As soon as I was secure in your love, I was planning to blow it up—to destroy forever my shameful and violent past."

Constance said nothing.

"I've bared my heart to you, Constance," he went on, his voice suddenly urgent. "You've seen everything now. I never told you, but it was always my hope that, in time, we could both take the arcanum, and keep on taking it. Now that I have the perfect synthesis, not only have I succeeded in reversing your unnatural aging—but I have the ability to keep you, in essence, forever young. We can *both* stay forever young, cut off from the world, reveling in each other. And not only that alone: our son could join us, here in this most special place. He *deserves* to join us. Despite what you said before, he's only a child. A little boy. He needs more than to be a figurehead, an item of veneration. He needs his parents. Here, we can forget our difficult, painful former lives and turn instead toward the future. Isn't that a beautiful vision?"

His pleading tones echoed through the dim room.

"If all that is true," Constance said, "if that life is really behind you, if this is nothing more than a chronicle of the past deeds of a former existence...why were you so quick to enshrine *this*?" She pointed to the obituary.

Diogenes looked from her to the frame. After a moment, he hung his head.

"I thought as much." And she turned to maneuver around him.

"Wait!" he said urgently, following her as she opened the door leading to the catwalk. "Wait. I'll prove it to you—the *ultimate* proof. I'll arm the device now, detonate the C-4. Turn this museum into a crater. You can see for yourself—from a safe distance."

She paused on the catwalk, looking down into the dark water. Behind her, Diogenes spoke again.

"What more proof can I give you?" he asked quietly.

64

CONSTANCE GAZED AT Diogenes a long time. She watched as perspiration beaded his face, and she absorbed the desperate yearning in his eyes. She saw the last, faint glimmer of hope in him, like the final coal in a dying fire.

Time to step on that coal.

"Proof?" she said. "You've given me all the proof I need of your *love*." She spoke this last word with heavy irony. "Please do set the timer. I would take great pleasure in seeing all this blown up."

"I'll do it. For *you*."

"I'm not convinced you could bear to have your precious mementos destroyed. You see now," she murmured, in a voice full of feigned warmth, "how well we understand each other? It is true—we are alike, so *very* alike. I understand you. And you, Diogenes—you understand me."

Diogenes went pale. She could see that he did indeed recall: these were the very words he had spoken to her at the moment of her seduction at his hands, four years before.

And then she recited, in Italian, the lines of poetry he had whispered in her ear as he'd eased her down onto the velvet cushions of the couch:

He plunges into the night,
He reaches for the stars

With the recitation of these words, his bicolored eyes seemed to drain of color. She had stepped on that last spark of hope, and she felt the metaphorical crunch of it under her heel.

His face now began to change, his features slowly twisting into a horrible grimace of mirth. A dry, dusty, dreary laugh issued from his lips; it went on and on, a whispery, throbbing thing.

"So it is not to be," he finally said, wiping his mouth. "I was duped. I, Diogenes, was completely taken in. It appears I am still searching for an honest man—or woman, as the case may be. *Brava*, Constance. What a performance. Your genius for cruelty exceeds my own. You have left me with nothing. Nothing."

Now she smiled in turn. "But I *do* leave you with something."

"And what is that?"

"The arcanum. Take it: and may you live a long, *long* life."

A silence ensued as they looked at each other.

"We're finished here," said Constance, turning away. "Take me to the boat, if you please."

"I'll meet you at the boat," Diogenes said, in a hoarse voice. "I have something to take care of first. In that—" and he laughed suddenly, giddily— *"in that vast perpetual torture-house. Let thine eyes stare . . . Let thine eyes stare . . ."*

Shutting her ears to this, Constance turned and walked around the edge of the cistern and up the stairs into the dusk.

He did not follow. She had no fear of turning her back on him—

despite everything, his love for her was still too great to allow him to do her harm. Besides, her own life held little value for her.

She hoped he was setting the charges. A museum like that, the physical embodiment of mental sickness the likes of which the world had rarely seen, should not be allowed to exist. She had destroyed his future; and now he himself would destroy his past. If in the end he had the intestinal fortitude to do it: that was still an open question.

She walked the trail through the buttonwoods and mangroves to the long beach. At its far end, the pier ran out into evening water, dark blue in the twilight. Now that it was over, she felt a deep catharsis—but at the same time an emptiness. Her burning hatred, her thirst for revenge, was over, and it left behind a yawning hole. What would be her life now? Where would she go? What would she do? She could never return to Riverside Drive; with Aloysius dead, that was out of the question. She was utterly alone in the world.

Her thoughts were interrupted by a sound of crashing vegetation. She turned and out of the mangroves came—inexplicably—the figure of a young woman, small, wiry, with streaming blond hair, coming straight at her, silent and focused, knife in one hand and gun in the other, face swollen with bloodlust.

Taken utterly by surprise, Constance tried to dodge the charge as the woman rushed into her, but it was too late and the knife came flashing through the evening light, catching her dress and cutting across her ribs like the scoring of a hot poker. Constance cried out and pivoted, raking her hand across her assailant's face as the girl skidded in the sand and came back at her, gun raised.

65

Once the sun dipped below the sea horizon, darkness fell rapidly. A small kayak, in dull olive, slid out from behind Johnston Key and embarked on the half-mile crossing of the shallow channel. A. X. L. Pendergast, paddle in hand, headed for the cluster of mangrove islands that lay off the southeastern end of Halcyon Key. The kayak glided over the water as Pendergast struggled with the paddle, trying to get into the rhythm of it, propelling the kayak forward without splashing or tipping over. It was a quiet November evening, herons flying low over the water, their wings making a sound like rustling silk.

He knew he had very little time; the two SWAT helicopters would be arriving from Key West Naval Station in less than twenty minutes. Pendergast had been unable to persuade Longstreet that his sort of massive response would not be effective against a man like Diogenes, that it would play to his strengths, and that it might well end in the death of Constance—whether she was hostage or participant. Pendergast was painfully unaware of her state of mind, but he felt certain she was—whatever else—unbalanced. For these reasons, during the staging process Pendergast had slipped away and "appropriated" a cigarette boat from the South Beach Harbor Marina. It had a carbon-fiber hull and twin engines that, in quiet water, could put out a thousand horsepower and do close to ninety knots. At Upper Sugarloaf Key, he'd exchanged it for a kayak and tropical wet suit from one of several kayak rental shops, now closed for the day. The problem was, he had never used a kayak before and not only was the bloody thing tippy and hard to control, but he kept catching the feathered paddles in the water as he tried to go forward.

Finally, though, he mastered the basic motion. And it was not much later when the little island cluster loomed into sight ahead. They were not actual islands, per se, but clusters of mangroves rising out of the shallow water, their roots forming a tangled mass. Pendergast drew the kayak into a hidden channel in the mangroves and tied it up. After a brief struggle he managed to extract himself silently and stood up in about two feet of water. He reached into the kayak's cargo compartment and took out a shoulder holster holding his Les Baer, strapped it on, then shrugged into a small black Osprey backpack.

Light was fading from the sky as he waded around the side of the mangrove island. The charts indicated the water was no more than three feet deep, and that proved to be the case as he moved forward, threading his way among mangrove stands. The lightweight black wet suit made him almost invisible in the gathering dark. Emerging from the cluster of mangroves, he kept low as he waded across an area of open, shallow water toward the main island, Halcyon. He emerged from the water at a small, sandy beach and paused there, listening. All was quiet. A trail wound inland, which he knew from satellite images led to the smaller house on the island; he moved along the trail until it opened up in the sandy area surrounding the house. It revealed itself as a caretaker's cottage, a light glowing in the living room window. Moving stealthily, he came up to the window, raised himself, and peered in. An elderly black man, seated in a wing chair, was reading a thick copy of *Ulysses*.

Pendergast considered that the gentleman's quiet evening was about to be disturbed—but not quite yet.

Moving past the window, he consulted his mental map of the island, and chose the trail that led to the big house. The path carried him through a shadowy buttonwood grove and a pair of old gumbo-limbo trees before the rear of the house came into view. The lights were off; it didn't appear anyone was at home. A black night was falling; the moon would not be rising for a few hours yet. Keeping to the shadows, he ventured onto the back veranda and tested the door. Unlocked. He let himself inside, made a quick reconnaissance of the first floor, then exited the front door, convinced no one was home but that the house was currently occupied. Diogenes and Constance were on the island somewhere; he was sure of that.

He paused. There was a distant sound: a high-pitched cry, echoing from far down the island. Drawing his weapon, he listened intently. And then he heard three shots fired in quick succession.

Seeing the handgun, Constance dove straight for her assailant's knees, tackling her as the shots passed overhead with a whiff of air. They both fell and rolled in the sand, Constance grabbing the girl's forearm in both hands and slamming it repeatedly into the sand, knocking the gun loose. But the woman was amazingly strong for her size and managed to wrench free of Constance's grip; they both lunged for the weapon, the woman dropping her knife in order to get it. They fell upon it at the same time, clawing and scrabbling in the sand, seizing it with all four hands at once. They rolled over and over in the sand, squirming and writhing, first one on top and then the other. The girl tried to bite Constance but she jerked her head away, then bit back, aiming for her face, her teeth sinking into the woman's cheek, the woman screeching in pain. They rolled again and Constance ended on top, trying to dislodge the gun, while the other woman keened, blood flowing from the bite on her cheek. Just as Constance began to prize the gun free, she left herself open and the attacker hit her in the solar plexus with one knee, knocking the wind from her, and in the same moment wrenched the gun away.

Swinging out with her arm, Constance knocked the gun aside just as the shot came, the round hitting the ground next to her with a thud and kicking up a gout of sand. Constance's head was turned, but the attacker got a faceful. The woman fell back, shaking her head to try to clear the sand from her eyes, firing wildly, again and again and again, the shots going wide as Constance, gasping for breath, jumped on her once more and—with the strength of a rising madness—grabbed the gun and tore it away, jammed it into the woman's forehead, and pulled the trigger.

Click.

The clip was finally empty. In that moment the girl—with remarkable presence of mind—took full advantage of her momentary astonishment, striking Constance across the face with a karate chop and then rolling out from under her, reversing their positions. Now she was on top, and had recovered her knife from the sand; she lunged downward, but Constance rolled and the thrust went through the heavy material of her dress into the sand. With a determined silence the girl slashed and tore with the knife, back and forth, but it had snagged in the fabric. As her adversary worked to free her knife, Constance managed to draw her own stiletto out of her bodice and instantly thrust it upward.

The woman jumped back, landing nimbly but giving Constance time to get to her own feet. They circled each other like scorpions, knives drawn.

"Who are you?" Constance asked. The young woman looked familiar, but she couldn't quite place her.

"Your worst nightmare," came the reply.

She thrust; Constance danced to one side.

That was when she saw movement out of the corner of her eye. *Diogenes.* He had appeared at the edge of the beach and was watching them. His arms were folded, just like a spectator's.

But Constance had to maintain focus—and with a cool opponent like this she could not afford to give in to homicidal anger. The two circled tensely. She could see from the way the girl held her knife, and her light and quick movements, that she was far more experienced with a blade and that Constance would lose any extended contest.

The woman lunged; Constance dodged, but just barely, the swipe tearing the fabric of her sleeve and nicking flesh.

"A hit, a very palpable hit," said Diogenes.

She jabbed at the woman and found only air, the woman leaping to one side with a spinning martial arts movement, capitalizing on Constance's miss by offering her own lightning cut, this one nicking Constance's wrist even as she pivoted to avoid it.

One of those jabs was going to find its way home, Constance realized, and soon. Her heavy dress, weighted down with her blood, was slowing her. Would Diogenes intervene? But no: another glance revealed him standing in place, a look of interest, even amusement, on his face. Of course this would be just the kind of spectacle he'd enjoy: two women fighting to the death over him.

The heavy dress... The masses of fabric could be to her advantage. But she had to move fast; any moment, the attacker would connect with a thrust.

Constance made her move: taking a running leap at the woman, she swung her legs up in a swirl of fabric, enveloping her opponent in the dress; the girl, taken completely by surprise, issued a muffled cry and slashed with the knife, but it rent only cloth as they both fell to the sand, Constance scissoring the woman tightly between her knees. The woman thrashed and struggled, keening with fury, but she couldn't get her knife arm out of the tangle of material.

Crushing the girl between her legs, Constance twisted around, picked up the gun, and slammed the woman in the side of her head with it, and then again, until the screaming turned into a gurgle and she felt the woman's body go limp. Now she pinned the stuporous girl's knife arm, wrenching the wrist around and forcing the blade from it. Snatching up the knife, she scrambled backward, then rose unsteadily, knives in both hands.

Her attacker lay on the sand, unable to rise, moaning and semiconscious.

Constance turned to Diogenes. He was flushed, breathing fast, a look of almost sexual excitement in his eyes. This was the old Diogenes; the one she remembered so well. He made no move to help her and said nothing; he was spellbound by what he had just witnessed.

She felt abruptly dizzy. She placed her hands on her knees and lowered her head to try to clear it, taking deep breaths.

After a moment she heard Diogenes speak: she looked up, but he was not talking to her. The look of libidinous gratification on his face had changed to one of utter amazement and consternation, as he stared at a dark figure emerging from the buttonwood. The figure stepped forward into the last glimmer of twilight, dressed in a sleek black wet suit.

"*Ave, frater,*" came Diogenes's rasping salutation.

66

Constance stood on the sand, the semiconscious girl moaning at her feet, and stared in utter disbelief. Pendergast—*is it really him?*—was approaching, gun in hand. He was like a vision; she could hardly comprehend what she was seeing.

"Aloysius," she breathed. "My God. *You're alive!*"

She started to rush toward him, but something in his expression stopped her dead in her tracks.

"*Ave, frater,*" Diogenes said again. He was weaving in place slightly, almost as if he were drunk.

Pendergast raised the gun. At first, he aimed it somewhere between Constance and Diogenes. Then, after a moment, he trained it squarely on his brother. His eyes, however, were on Constance.

"Before I kill him," he said, "I need to know: do you love him?"

Constance looked at him in shock and disbelief. "*What?*"

"The question is clear. Do you love him?"

She felt movement at her feet. The girl, having regained her senses, had taken advantage of the standoff and made a shambolic run for a nearby cluster of mangroves. Pendergast paid no attention to her.

Now Constance was beginning to recover from the shock of seeing

Pendergast standing, alive, before her. A hundred questions rose in her mind: *What happened? Where have you been? Why didn't you reach out to me?* But the look on Pendergast's face made it clear this was no time for questions.

"I *detest* him," she said. "I always have—and always will."

"*Love lives on hope,*" Diogenes said in a singsong voice. "*And dies when hope is dead.*"

Pendergast ignored this, his gaze fixed on Constance. "Then perhaps you could explain why you left our Riverside Drive residence with him of your own free will—injuring Lieutenant D'Agosta in the process."

Constance took a deep breath. Her head was clearing from the fight, and she felt that amazing strength returning. In a calm, steady voice, she told him how she'd believed him to be dead; how she'd been wooed by Diogenes with confessions of love and the revelation that Leng's synthesized arcanum had begun to backfire—and of her own secret plan: how she hated Diogenes and realized his reappearance was her opportunity to wreak a vengeance on him more terrible than death. "You must trust me, Aloysius," she concluded. "I will explain it all, in full—in due time." She gestured at Diogenes, standing there, listening. "But meanwhile, you can see the result for yourself. Look at him: a broken man."

Pendergast listened to the entire recitation in silence, gun lowered. "So you were lying to him? From the very beginning?"

"Yes."

"And you do not love him," Pendergast repeated, as if unable to quite comprehend.

"No. *No!*"

"I'm so glad." And he repointed the gun at Diogenes's head.

"Wait!" Constance cried.

Pendergast looked at her.

Diogenes stepped forward, grasped the muzzle of the gun, pressed it hard against his own temple. "Go ahead, *frater*. Do it."

"Don't kill him," she said.

"Why not?"

"Much better to spare his life—to force him to live with his loneliness, with the memory of his wrongdoing. And..." She hesitated. "I learned something about him."

"Which is?" Pendergast's voice was cool, clipped.

Constance glanced back at Diogenes, who was still standing there, swaying in the moonlight, muzzle held against his head. "I didn't want him to hear me say this—but now there's nothing for it. He's not totally responsible for what he's become. You, of all people, know that. And there's a small seed of good in him—I've seen it. I believe he truly did want to reform, to start a new life. What he wants now, I can't say. Looking at him in this condition, my thirst for vengeance is thoroughly slaked. If you let him live, perhaps—just perhaps—he'll nurture that seed." Then she added, bitterly: "Perhaps he can water it with his tears."

As she spoke, a change came across Pendergast's face. It lost just a little of its marble-like hardness. But it was still impossible to know what was going on in his mind.

"*Please*," Constance whispered.

In the distance now, over the low whisper of wind among the palm trees, she could hear the sound of helicopter blades—faint, but growing ever closer.

67

Longstreet sat in the jump seat of the lead chopper as it thundered across the Keys, heading for a small cluster of islands north of Upper Sugarloaf Key. There were two SWAT teams coming in: Team Blue would land on an LZ near the main house on the northern end of the island, and Team Red, his own, would land in an open area by a few old outbuildings at the southern end. In addition, he had a Zodiac inbound, with more waiting in Key West on high alert, ready to shuttle in additional backup and shuttle out any casualties. He believed that, by employing a textbook pincer movement, they could land, secure the island, and capture Diogenes in less than ten minutes, provided it did not devolve into a hostage situation. That was always a possibility, although an unlikely one: he was fairly certain this Constance Greene was Bonnie to Diogenes's Clyde and that both would go down in a quasi-suicidal blaze of gunfire. But he also had a carefully worked-out alternative plan, just in case, with two experienced negotiators as part of the team.

He wondered once again what the hell had happened to Pendergast. He knew the man hadn't liked the SWAT approach and wanted to go in covertly. That was damned foolish, Longstreet knew; nothing was better than a blitzkrieg of overwhelming firepower. Back in their special forces days, there were times when Pendergast had disappeared just like this—no word to anyone—only to reappear later with some important objective accomplished. It had happened often enough that their team developed a slang term for it—*Don't pull a Pendergast* meant "Don't disappear without explanation."

Well, he couldn't worry about that now. If the man had indeed "pulled a Pendergast," he would be reappearing soon enough. Longstreet just hoped to God he hadn't gone rogue and prepared to do something stupid, triggering a nightmare of paperwork, questions, and hearings.

As they came in low and fast, he could see Halcyon Key loom into view through the open door of the chopper. Only a trace of light remained along the western horizon, on the edge of a dark, moonless night. Off to his right he could see the chopper conveying Team Blue, keeping good formation with them.

He murmured into his headset: "Blue, separate north and go in for a landing. We're landing south. Both teams on the ground at nineteen hundred twenty, to the minute."

"Roger that."

The chopper turned and slowed as it came in. Below, in the faint light, Longstreet could see the outbuildings and plenty of open area in the form of saw-grass-carpeted sand.

"Check weapons, body armor, and activate night vision," said Longstreet while checking his own equipment and 9mm Beretta, and lowering his night-vision goggles.

A moment later, he said: "Take us in."

The pilot came around and brought the helicopter down, streamers of sand blowing away in the downdraft, saw grass thrashing. The chopper settled on the sand and the team leapt out, weapons at the ready, spreading out, running for the cover of the outbuildings and the bushes, following Longstreet's predetermined plan to the letter. Longstreet was the last out, and he headed directly toward the beach.

Pendergast had stripped off Constance's heavy dress, leaving her in her slip. She was trembling all over. He doctored her knife wounds using supplies from his medical kit, cleaning them with a disinfectant, applying a topical antibiotic, and closing them as best he could with bandages—all the while keeping his gun trained on Diogenes, whose hands he'd cuffed behind his back.

He heard the throbbing of Longstreet's choppers.

"The cavalry approaches," said Diogenes tonelessly.

He ignored his brother. The wounds were not dangerously deep, but they were not shallow, either, and would require stitches. Constance had lost a lot of blood and was, he feared, about to go into shock, although she seemed strangely alert. Beyond that, her psychological stability at the moment remained very much an open question.

She had to be removed from the island as quickly as possible.

"Well, *frater*," said Diogenes. "If my life is to be spared, what now?"

Pendergast put an arm around Constance, bracing her and keeping her upright. He could feel the strange animal trembling that had taken hold of her form. She had fallen silent: vibrantly, glowingly silent. A strange state that he did not understand; but then, he realized, he had never fully understood her.

"Can you walk?" he asked.

She nodded.

"Put your arm on my shoulder, use it as a brace."

She grasped his shoulder, her body leaning against his.

Pendergast gestured toward his brother with the muzzle of the gun. "Let's go."

"Where to?"

"Keep quiet and follow my orders."

"And if I don't? You'll kill me?"

"*They* will kill you," said Pendergast.

"*They* are in for the surprise of their lives," said Diogenes. And then he chuckled, low, as if in response to a private joke. The chuckling went on.

At that moment, Pendergast heard the sound of a two-stroke engine out on the water and looked over to see the dim form of a Zodiac approaching the pier at the far end of the beach.

"Into the woods," he said.

Diogenes obeyed, chuckling and cackling under his breath, and all three went into the darkness of the buttonwood grove.

"That way," he said to Diogenes, gesturing with the gun.

His brother moved through the darkness, down a faint path among the trees. Pendergast supported Constance, who clung to him like a child.

"What's this surprise?" Pendergast asked.

"You shall know very soon. About now, in fact—"

An enormous explosion erupted behind them, a huge fireball rising into the darkness, weeping flaming debris and sparks; a split second later the pressure wave hit, pressing down the trees and generating a blast of wind. The explosion caused an instant reaction from the southern SWAT team, with the sound of gunfire, shouts, a couple of smaller explosions from RPGs being fired: a burst of frenzied activity that, Pendergast could hear, was rapidly approaching.

"What have you done?"

"That was perhaps the coincidence of the millennium. It wasn't intended for you or your compatriots, I assure you—it was a strictly personal demolition job. Typical of the FBI to be in the wrong place at the wrong time."

"What demolition?"

"My personal cabinet of curiosities. *O soul, be chang'd into little water drops, and fall into the ocean—ne'er be found.*"

Pendergast glanced from Diogenes to Constance and back again. He merely said: "Let us go south, parallel to the beach. With the utmost quiet."

They moved on, keeping to the trees and bushes behind the beach, as the sounds of battle continued behind them.

68

Flavia rose from the prone position she had dropped to at the sound of the explosion. She wasn't sure what was happening, or why, but what she did realize was that the sudden chaos was very much to her advantage. Chaos was going to be her cover, her friend.

Slipping along the edge of the island, just inside a band of mangroves, she approached the area where the explosion had gone off, which was now burning brightly, leaving a glow in the sky above her bright enough to navigate by. She heard the brief rattle of gunfire off to her left. As the mangroves ran out toward the northern end of the island, she crouched, staying behind them, and looked out at the scene of destruction.

A great crater had been blasted in the open, sandy area, dull flames flickering from it as if from the maw of a volcano. A hundred yards away, a chopper lay tilted on its side, afire, flames leaping up into the sky. Several bodies lay not far off, with two men—medics?—bending over them. She cast about and saw, just fifty feet away, in the open, another man lying on a stretcher, bandaged and moaning. He had already been taken care of, it seemed, and left temporarily while the others were triaged.

She couldn't begin to fathom what was going on here, or why helicopters full of armed men had landed, but she didn't care. She had only one aim: killing that bitch, Constance.

Keeping low, Flavia scurried out into the open, across the saw grass, leaving the cover of the mangroves. In another moment she stood over the man on the stretcher. His head and one arm were bandaged and his eyes were open, staring at her in dull surprise.

She quickly examined him, and there it was: a .45 in his holster. She slid it out, ejected the magazine, saw it was fully loaded, slapped it back in.

"What...are you...?" the man began, speaking painfully.

"Taking your weapon."

He sputtered, shaking his head, his body trying to move. "No..."

"Relax. Nothing you can do about it."

She saw he had an extra magazine in a magazine pouch on his belt; she took that, too.

"Nooo..." he said in a louder voice.

"See you later." She turned away. Then she hesitated, thought better of it, and turned back to the man, pulling a Zombie Killer from her fanny pack.

The job took only ten seconds.

Now she scurried back into the darkness of the mangroves, stopped for a moment to examine the weapon—a nice model 1911 Colt—and then she shoved it into her waistband and headed south to find the woman.

Longstreet, on the beach, was far enough from the explosion to be merely knocked down by it, but left unhurt—though it shocked the hell out of him. The three closest men were down; he rushed to their aid as the others in Team Red came back; and then the chopper, which had been knocked on its side, caught fire and there was a second, fuel-fed explosion. Everyone was in a panic, believing they were under a massive assault, firing at everything that moved. Longstreet himself had believed the same for a moment, but when he saw the deep crater, he realized it must have been a preset explosive device. Diogenes had set a bomb in the island's most obvious LZ, and they had fallen right into the trap. It was one of the scenarios Pendergast had warned him of. He realized he had badly underestimated the resistance they would meet, and he burned with self-reproach.

In his headset he could hear the confusion and consternation among the men, both his team and Team Blue. He immediately called in three more Zodiacs from Key West with extra men and medics to take out the wounded. But Key West lay eight miles southwest; at thirty knots the boats would take fifteen minutes to reach the island's pier.

Longstreet had an immediate decision to make: call off the assault or finish it, full-court press. He chose the latter. If they retreated now, it could turn into a weeks- or months-long standoff, another Ruby Ridge or Waco. It was pretty clear they were dealing with a deranged individual; as horribly as the op had begun, if they didn't finish what they'd started it would be even worse. They were too deep in it to abort now.

Longstreet rallied his men by radio. They were spooked and at the edge of control. He talked them down from their initial confusion, ordered them to stop shooting, and got them refocused. He gave the requisite orders to evacuate the wounded and ordered the two teams to proceed as planned. Team Blue, still in full force, was to go in and take the house. He and the remainder of Team Red would sweep north, clearing the island. The pincer movement would meet at the main house, where he hoped Diogenes would make his last stand. There, they could tear-gas, flash-bang, and, if necessary, burn him out.

Moving along the beach, Longstreet remained in continuous contact with the rest of the team, listening to the chatter on the channel. One of his men suddenly spoke through the comm, his voice at a whisper: "Red one, there's someone here. In the bushes."

"Red two, wait for backup. I'm on my way."

Longstreet scurried toward the GPS location, night-vision goggles lowered. It was another dense, overgrown cluster of buttonwoods and palmettos. He moved fast and soon connected with his teammate. The man had taken cover behind a dense stand of bushes.

"Through there," Red two said. "I heard someone moving. I ordered him to come out. No answer."

Longstreet listened. They were close to the shore and a maze of mangroves, which extended far into the water.

He called: *"FBI! Come out now!"*

No answer, but he heard the faint splash of someone moving in shallow water. He searched the dense tangle of vegetation with his goggles but could see nothing. If this was Diogenes, and he was pretty sure it was, he'd better be careful; the man would likely fight to the death.

He gestured for Red two to loop in from the right to try to cut off the person, and with a similar gesture indicated he would go in straight.

The man nodded. As they cautiously emerged from behind their cover, two shots rang out. Longstreet and Red two immediately dropped to the dirt.

"You okay?" Longstreet muttered on the comm, his head down.

"I'm good," came the whispered reply.

"Move in diagonally through that dense cover. I'm going in straight to get the fucker."

Longstreet crawled forward on his belly. He had to take out the shooter and he believed he had an advantage in the night vision, although he couldn't be sure Diogenes didn't have goggles, as well.

As he moved, he heard another faint splash—the man was retreating. From his prone position he aimed at the sound and fired twice.

That stirred the shooter into retreating faster, and he heard more splashing, which gave him a better fix. He fired twice again and thought he heard a grunt of pain.

Leaping up, he ran toward the sound, entering the water and wading fast through a tiny, winding channel in the mangroves, firing once, and then again—widely spaced shots to keep the shooter in retreat and to suppress return fire. It was very dark in the mangroves, but with his goggles he could see well; he hoped to God the shooter could not. Red two was behind him to the left, looping around to cut the shooter off. He had set up their approaches to make sure there was no chance of a friendly-fire accident. But Longstreet wanted to get to him first. If it was Diogenes, he was going to kill the man himself, and this setup provided the perfect way to do so with complete justification.

He stopped, listening. There was a blur of motion in his goggles, but it was too quick to get a bead. He pressed on, firing once again, pushing through narrow channels in the mangroves. The pressure of his approach was spooking the shooter; he heard louder crashing as the target moved hard and fast, trying to get away.

Another shot came tearing through the mangroves, clipping a branch by his shoulder, and Longstreet dropped into the water. It seemed the bastard wasn't as spooked as he'd assumed. Two more shots, coming in high, and then more thrashing through vegetation as the target continued retreating. He wasn't far away, and the noise made a fine target.

Longstreet rose, aimed carefully at the sound, and fired. There was a short cry and a final crash—and then silence.

Moving quickly, he bashed through a screen of mangroves—and came upon the shooter. He stared, incredulous: it was a young woman lying on her back, chest covered with blood, eyes open. For a second he thought it must be Constance Greene—but this was certainly not the woman whose picture had been in the briefing book. In fact, with a sudden shock, he knew who this was; the face was recognizable from mug shots and security videos he'd viewed. Flavia Greyling stared back at him with glittering, hate-filled eyes and, with her strength fading, tried to raise her gun, but he reached down and pulled it out of her hand. She held a wicked-looking knife with a green handle in the other. Grimacing with pain, she raised it as if readying it for a throw...and then collapsed back into the water.

His teammate came up behind him. "What the hell? A *girl*?"

"Yeah." What the hell she'd been doing here on Halcyon, Longstreet couldn't begin to imagine. This was turning into an absolute clusterfuck. Pendergast had been right, after all.

"She's not target two, is she?"

"No."

"Where'd she come from?"

"No idea. You get her out of this crap and to the pier, evac her on a Zodiac."

"She's dead."

"Maybe. Just get her out and do your best. I've got to meet up with Team Blue at the main house."

Longstreet pushed out of the mangroves and headed up the beach.

69

Longstreet jogged up the beach and soon arrived at the main house. It was already surrounded by Team Blue, and a hostage negotiator was on a megaphone telling everyone to get out, last warning. They were coming in and any resistance would be met with deadly force.

"Anyone in there?" Longstreet asked, coming up to the Blue leader.

"We don't know. No shots fired, no sightings, no sounds. Could be empty."

Longstreet nodded. Diogenes wasn't in there, he knew it the minute he saw the house—a rambling wooden structure that would burn in five minutes, that offered no cover anywhere: a 9mm round would go straight through the entire building.

"Hit it with flash-bangs and go in."

"Yes, sir."

"I'm moving on—I've got a special assignment to do." Longstreet turned away. Diogenes and the woman were somewhere else. The assault on the house would be a perfect diversion, allowing him to track them down when they least expected it. As he moved away, he heard the man on the megaphone announcing that their last opportunity to come out had expired; and a moment later came the sound of shattering glass and the muffled booms of the flash-bangs.

Moving stealthily through the mangroves, away from the main action, Pendergast supported Constance while keeping Diogenes in front, at gunpoint. His brother moved slowly, as if in a fog. They proceeded with stealth, maintaining the deepest cover. Ahead, he could see a second fire through the trees; it was, he knew, the caretaker's cottage. A moment later he peered into the clearing surrounding the house. It was indeed on fire, having been cleared and taken. The fat copy of *Ulysses* now lay in the sand, along with numerous footprints. The SWAT team had moved on, leaving the area empty.

"Keep moving," Pendergast said, gesturing toward the trail that led from the cottage to the beach.

"Where are we going?" Diogenes asked.

Pendergast did not answer. They moved along the trail and, a few moments later, came out at the edge of the beach. Pendergast paused to reconnoiter. It was empty. An FBI Zodiac was tied up at the pier, opposite the main house. He could see two people loading the wounded on stretchers into the boat. Shortly the boat's engine fired up and it left the dock, speeding southwest. The rest of the activity now seemed confined to the main house.

They walked on, keeping to the deepest shadows of the trees hanging over the edge of the sand. About two-thirds of the way up the long beach, Pendergast halted. Just offshore lay the string of tiny mangrove islands dotting the shallows.

"Aloysius."

To Pendergast's astonishment, a figure of a man emerged from the edge of darkness. Longstreet. A gun was in his hand.

"After our last conversation, I should have figured you'd find your own way down here," Longstreet said.

Pendergast remained silent.

"I'm not sure what you're up to," said Longstreet, "but I'd feel a hell of a lot better if you dropped that 1911 of yours into the sand."

Pendergast dropped his gun.

"You may have forgotten honor, and our oath, but I haven't." Longstreet stepped forward and pointed his gun at Diogenes. "Now is the moment," he said. "Prepare to die, you bastard."

There was a long silence.

This seemed to unnerve Longstreet. He glanced at Pendergast. "He killed Decker."

More silence.

"I'll drop him, we'll get our stories straight, and nobody will be the wiser."

Constance spoke. "No."

Longstreet ignored her. His finger tightened on the trigger.

"*No!*" Constance cried, suddenly lunging at Diogenes and pushing him sideways just as the gun went off, the round missing. She placed herself in front of Diogenes.

"For fuck's sake, get her out of my way," Longstreet said to Pendergast.

Pendergast looked at him. "My answer is also . . . *no.*"

"What the hell are you talking about?"

"You will not kill him."

"We swore an oath! *He murdered Decker.* You yourself said killing him was the only way!"

"He's my brother."

Longstreet stared at him, speechless.

"I'm sorry," said Pendergast. "It's . . . family."

"*Family?*"

"You have to be a Pendergast, perhaps, to understand. I'm guilty of terrible crimes against my brother. I'm the reason he is the way he is. I realize now that if I'm party to killing him, I won't be able to live with myself—and I mean that in the most literal way possible. I'll have no choice but to end my own life."

Longstreet looked back and forth between the brothers incredulously. "Son of a bitch, if this doesn't take the cake."

"H, please. Don't kill my brother. He'll disappear and you'll never hear from him again. You have my word."

At this, Diogenes laughed sarcastically, grotesquely. "For the love of God, don't listen to him. Kill me! I *want* to die. Oh *do* man up, *frater*, and tell your pal to pull the trigger!" A choking sob escaped his lips, even as his laugh continued.

"He's a serial killer," Longstreet said. "You expect me to just let him go?"

"*Ko ko rico!*" Diogenes said abruptly, spewing Longstreet with saliva. "*Ko ko rico!*"

"Believe me—allowing Diogenes to live will bring him far more pain than anything our criminal justice system could mete out." Pendergast paused. "And he isn't going to kill again—I know that now. But it's your decision. I put his life—and mine—in your hands. Constance, please step away."

Constance hesitated a moment, then complied.

An unbearably tense minute passed. And then Longstreet slowly lowered the gun. "I can't believe I'm doing this," he said. He stared at Diogenes with open hatred and spat into the sand. "If I ever see you again, motherfucker, you're a dead man."

Pendergast moved quickly, uncuffing Diogenes, who had abruptly gone silent, staring.

"Wade out to that cluster of islands," Pendergast spoke to him quickly. "In the outermost one, you'll find a kayak in the mangroves." He held out the Osprey pack. "In here is food, water, money, and a chart. Head for Johnston Key. Lie low. When things have died down, make your way back to civilization. I've no doubt you can come up with a good story and a new identity. And, I hope, a new outlook as well. Because Diogenes Pendergast died here—in the explosion. Metaphorically *and* literally."

After a hesitation, Diogenes took the pack and slipped it onto his back. He stepped forward, bent sharply, moving slowly, as if under a far heavier load than the pack could account for. He began wading out into the dark waters. But then he turned. His dim form wavered in the murky gloom, like a disembodied ghost. "Died, you say? *Frater*, you're quite right. *I am become death.*" And then he turned and vanished into the night.

After a long hush, Longstreet turned to Pendergast. "That was a big one to ask. *Too* big. You've caused me to break both my oath *and* my sworn duty as a federal officer." He glanced around. "I think we're done here—and you and I, brother, we're also done." He turned briskly. "What about her?"

Pendergast spoke with quiet meaning in his voice: "You're referring to the kidnap victim? Thank God we managed to rescue her. Constance, Agent Longstreet will take care of you now and get you to a hospital. There will be a debriefing, of course, in which you'll tell the FBI all about your *kidnapping*."

"I understand, but... what will you do, Aloysius?" asked Constance, staring at Pendergast.

"I will go home. And await you there."

As they spoke, two more Zodiacs came roaring in over the water toward the pier, followed by a third. They were filled with men. A fire was now leaping up above the trees—the main house was going up in flames, as Longstreet knew it would from the flash-bangs. The men piled out of the Zodiacs and came running down the pier, some heading toward the burning house, a few peeling off and running up the beach toward them. Longstreet quickly replaced his headset and switched it on.

"Is everything all right?" one cried.

"Fine," he said. "We rescued the kidnap victim. Constance Greene. She's hurt: evacuate her in a Zodiac, take her straight to Lower Keys Medical. Assign two agents for her protection."

"And the target? Any word on him?"

Longstreet hesitated for a second, jaws working. "Took the coward's way out," he said brusquely. "At our approach, he blew himself to kingdom come in a massive detonation. I doubt we'll find so much as a fingernail. Gentlemen, the operation is now over."

EPILOGUE

Mrs. Trask walked briskly across the marble floor of the grand reception hall of the Riverside Drive mansion, feather duster in hand. It was one of those deceptively warm late-November days that seemed to promise that spring, rather than winter, was imminent. Sunlight filtered down through the antique skylights, gilding the brass fixtures of the mahogany display cases and illuminating the objects within. Mrs. Trask found many of these objects to be peculiar, even disturbing, and she had long ago learned to dust the cases without examining their contents.

The room looked far different than it had when she'd first returned from Albany with a glad heart, despite her grief over Mr. Pendergast's death: her sister's mysterious illness, which had at first seemed to be getting increasingly worse, had suddenly vanished in a way the doctors described as little short of miraculous. But imagine: arriving home at 891 Riverside meant discovering not only an empty house, but yellow crime scene tape strung across this very room! A quick call to Mr. Pendergast's friend Lieutenant D'Agosta had fixed that, at least: the lieutenant had come over the very next morning and supervised in person the removal of that dreadful tape. He'd also given her the surprising and wonderful news that Mr. Pendergast was all right; he had not drowned after all, and was now simply—as was his wont—off on one of his cases. No doubt he would show up in his own good time, probably sooner rather than later.

The lieutenant had not, however, answered her other questions. Where was Proctor? And where was Constance? She couldn't tell if the man knew nothing, or was hiding the truth from her.

Just before she left for Albany, Mrs. Trask had heard Constance announce her intention of moving to quarters in the sub-basement...a place she herself never entered. But it seemed that, in her absence, those plans had changed. Suitcases were missing from Constance's room. Proctor, too, was absent, and it appeared he'd left in a hurry: his room was disordered—something most unusual for a man as finicky about neatness as he was.

No doubt when Mr. Pendergast returned he would explain all. It was not her place, he had made clear many years ago, to concern herself with these endless and strange comings and goings.

Mrs. Trask moved from the reception hall to the library. Here there was no cheerful November sunlight: as usual, both the shutters and curtains were drawn, leaving the large space lit only by a single Tiffany lamp. Mrs. Trask bustled about, dusting and straightening, but in fact the room was already spotless—she'd gone over it every day since she'd returned—and her cleaning was more from habit than necessity.

She was used to Mr. Pendergast's frequent absences, of course, but it was much rarer for Constance or Proctor to be gone. With all three of them away, things felt queer indeed. The mansion seemed even bigger than usual, and it was full of a lonely, ambient emptiness that made Mrs. Trask rather uncomfortable. Upon retiring each night, she locked not only the door to her rooms, but the door leading into the servants' quarters, as well.

She'd thought of trying to telephone, but realized that she knew neither Mr. Pendergast's nor Proctor's cell phone number. Constance, of course, had no phone and didn't care for one. Really, once they were back, she was going to have to make sure to...

At that moment, a hollow knock resounded on the front door.

Mrs. Trask paused in her dusting. Visitors to 891 Riverside were rare—almost unheard of. Except for Lieutenant D'Agosta's recent appearance, which she herself had requested, she could only recall two such knocks on the door in the last twelve months. The first had proven most distressing indeed, and the second had precipitated the sudden visit of Mr. Pendergast and Constance to Exmouth that—until just recently—she believed to have ended in tragedy.

The housekeeper stayed where she was.

A few seconds later the knock sounded again: so loud it seemed to reverberate through the house.

It was not her place, she told herself, to answer the door. Nevertheless, something told her that—in the absence of anyone else—Mr. Pendergast would want her to do so. It was a bright, sunny morning, after all; what was the chance of it being a robber, or some other ne'er-do-well?

Exiting the library, she crossed the reception hall once again, passed through the long, narrow refectory, and entered the front hall. The massive front door stood before her like an ominous portal, monolithic, with no door viewer set into its grim lines.

As she stood there, a third knock came. She jumped slightly.

This was silly. Taking a deep breath, she unbolted and unlocked the door, then—with some effort—pulled it open. And then she stifled a scream.

A man stood on the stoop before her: a man who looked to be in the very last stages of debility. His shirt was stained and torn almost to ribbons; the inside of the collar was almost black; half-moons of dried sweat darkened the armpits. Despite it being November, he had no coat. His pants were, if anything, even more rent than the shirt. One cuff had come undone, billowing out over the bare and impossibly dirty foot below; the other trouser leg had been cut or, more likely, ripped off at the calf. The cloth of one shoulder and one leg were heavily matted with dried blood. But it was the man's gaunt and hollow face that most distressed her. His hair was plastered to his head like a skullcap. Dirt, mud, blood, and dust coated his skin so thickly that she had a difficult time distinguishing his race. His beard was a tangled rat's nest that ended in several spiky points. And then there were his eyes: two burning coals set deep, so deep, into sockets of purplish black.

She seized the door and was about to slam it closed when she realized that the specter standing in front of her was Proctor.

"Mr. Proctor! My goodness!" she said, opening the door wide. "Whatever happened to you?"

He took one tottering step forward—then another—and then collapsed to his knees.

Quickly, she knelt, helping him to his feet again. He appeared to be beyond exhaustion.

"What happened?" she repeated as she guided him through the refectory. "Where have you been?"

"It's a long story." His voice was faint, barely a whisper. "Can you help me to my room? I need to lie down."

"Of course. I'll bring you some broth."

"Constance—?" he murmured.

"She's not here. I don't know where she's gone. I think that Lieutenant D'Agosta might have some idea. You should ask him."

"I will."

"But I do have wonderful news. Or did you already know? Mr. Pendergast is alive. He didn't drown, after all. He was back here, briefly—then left again, about a week ago I understand."

For just a moment, those coal eyes brightened even further. "Good. That's good. I'll call Lieutenant D'Agosta first thing tomorrow."

They were halfway across the reception hall when Proctor abruptly stopped. "Mrs. Trask?"

"Yes?"

"I think I'll rest right here, if you don't mind."

"But let me at least get you to a sofa in the library, where you'll be—"

Yet even as she spoke, Proctor released his hold on her and slid slowly onto the cold marble floor, where he lay, unmoving, in a dead faint.

ONE WEEK LATER

December 3

Pendergast laid aside the thick book he was reading—Douglas Hofstadter's brilliant if at times recondite *Gödel, Escher, Bach*—and looked over at Constance Greene. She was sitting opposite him, ankles crossed demurely over a leather footrest, drinking Hediard Mélange tea with milk and sugar and gazing into the fire.

"Do you know what I just realized, Constance?" he asked.

She glanced back at him, eyebrows raised in mute inquiry.

"The last time we sat together in this room, Percival Lake paid us a visit."

"You are right. And therein—as the saying goes—hangs a tale." And she went back to sipping her tea and looking into the fire.

Mrs. Trask and Proctor appeared quietly in the library doorway. The housekeeper had long since recovered from her shock, and was simply glad to have the household together again. Proctor, too, looked like his old stoic self, and the only remaining sign of his ordeal was a slight limp—the result, he'd explained, of a lion bite and a hike across almost two hundred miles of trackless desert.

"Excuse me, sir," Mrs. Trask said to Pendergast. "But I just wanted to know if we could do anything for you before we had our supper."

"Nothing, thank you," Pendergast said. "Unless you need anything, Constance?"

"I'm perfectly fine, thank you," came the reply.

Mrs. Trask smiled, curtsied, then turned away. Proctor, the eternal cipher, merely nodded and followed her back in the direction of the kitchen. Pendergast picked up his book and pretended to resume reading, but privately he continued observing Constance.

She'd spent the last week in a private Florida clinic, recovering from the wounds she'd sustained in the fight with Flavia, and tonight was her first night back in the Riverside Drive mansion. Although they had spoken at some length over the week—and while each had told in detail their stories of how they'd spent the last month apart, and any lingering misunderstandings were now fully cleared up—she did not seem herself and, truth be told, had not—as far as he could tell—since leaving Halcyon. All evening she had seemed restless and brooding; she would start to play a piece on the harpsichord, then leave off in the middle of a passage; she would pick up a book of poetry and stare at it, but for half an hour not a page would be turned.

Finally, he lowered his book. "What's troubling you, Constance?" he asked.

She looked over at him. "Nothing is troubling me. I'm perfectly fine."

"Come now. I know your humors. Is it something I've said or done—or not done?"

She shook her head.

"It was unforgivable of me to leave you defenseless like that in Exmouth."

"You couldn't help it. You nearly drowned. And as you know, I managed to—how should I put it?—entertain myself in your absence."

Pendergast winced inwardly.

After a minute, Constance shifted in her chair. "It's Diogenes."

"How do you mean?"

"I can't stop thinking about him. Where is he now? What's his frame of mind? Will he seek out the good in life—or will he prove a recidivist?"

"I fear that only time will tell. I hope for all our sakes it is the former—I gave Howard Longstreet my word on the matter."

She picked up her teacup, then put it down again without tasting it. "I hated him. I loathed him. And yet I feel that what I did was too cruel—even for somebody as wicked as he was. Even...given what he'd done to me. And to you."

Pendergast considered a variety of answers, but decided that none of them would be satisfactory.

"You made him the way he was," she went on, her voice lower, eyes still on the fire. "He told me about the Event."

"Yes," Pendergast said simply. "It was a stupid, childish mistake—and one I regret every day. Had I known, I would never have forced him into that terrible device."

"And yet that's not what troubles me. What troubles me is that, despite everything, he *tried* to come back from the dark place in which he'd spent so many years. He created Halcyon. It was to be his retreat from the world; his place of safety. Also, I think he built it to make sure the world would be safe from *him*. But then he made the mistake of falling in love with me. And I—I was consumed with a thirst for revenge."

Suddenly she looked directly at Pendergast. "You see, we're two sides of the same coin, you and I. You, at least in part, made Diogenes into the monster he was. And now, I've unmade the good man he tried so hard to become."

"Do you really believe he was telling you the truth?" Pendergast asked gently. "That he loved you? That he had left the sick and evil part of him behind?"

Constance took a deep breath. "He *had* left the evil part of him behind—as best he could. I don't think he'll ever be free of it; not entirely. But yes: he loved me. He cured me; he saved my life. He would have done so even if I hadn't agreed to stay at Halcyon. Those days we spent together...he couldn't have said such things—done such things—if he hadn't been utterly in love."

"I understand." Pendergast hesitated. "And, forgive my bluntness—just what, ah, *things* did you do?"

Constance went quite still in her chair. For a moment, she didn't reply. When she did, it was in a very quiet voice.

"Aloysius, I hope you'll understand if I ask for your solemn promise never, ever to ask me that question again."

"Of course. Pray forgive my indiscretion. The last thing I want to do is pry, or to cause you mortification in any way."

"Then it's forgotten."

Except that it wasn't. If anything, Constance seemed now to grow more restless, more agitated. She went back to looking at the fire, and the conversation died. And then, after several minutes, she glanced over at Pendergast again.

"There's something that Diogenes told me—shortly before you arrived."

"Yes?"

"He observed that my son—our son, his and mine—needs to be more than a figurehead; more than the nineteenth Rinpoche, the venerable figurehead of a distant and secret monastery. He's a boy, as well: and a boy needs his parents—not just acolytes to worship at his feet."

"You've visited him before," Pendergast said.

"Yes. And do you know what? The monks wouldn't even tell me his religious name. They said it was a secret, to be known only to the initiated and never spoken aloud." She shook her head. "He's my son; I love him...and I don't even know that name."

She was breathing more quickly now. "I've made up my mind. I'm going to stay with him."

"Another visit?"

"I'm going to *live* with him. In the monastery."

Slowly, Pendergast laid the book aside. "You mean, leave Riverside Drive?"

"Why not?"

"Because—" Pendergast was nonplussed. "Because we have—"

Constance stood up abruptly. "*What* do we have exactly, Aloysius?"

"I care for you deeply."

"And I—*I love you*. But you made it very clear, that night in the Captain Hull Inn, that you don't return my love."

Pendergast began to stand up, as well. Then he sat back down. He passed a hand over his forehead slowly, and he felt his fingers trembling as he did so. "I…I love you, too, Constance. But you must understand—I cannot let myself love you in that way."

"Why not?"

"Please, Constance—"

"Why not, for God's sake?"

"Because it would be wrong; wrong in many ways. Constance, believe me: I'm a man; I feel the same things you do. But I'm your guardian. It wouldn't be proper—"

"Proper?" She laughed. "Since when have you cared for propriety?"

"I can't help the way I've been brought up, the system of values and morals inculcated into me my entire life. Then, there's our age difference—"

"Are you referring to our *hundred years* age difference?"

"No. No. You're a young woman, I'm a—"

"I'm *not* a young woman. I am a woman who has already lived far longer than you ever will. I've tried to tamp down those needs, those desires, that every person feels." Now her voice was quiet again, almost pleading. "Don't you understand that, Aloysius?"

"Of course. But..." Pendergast felt overwhelmed with confusion, unable to order his thoughts. "I'm not very good at this. I fear that should we...have the relationship you suggest, something will go wrong. I would no longer be the person you look up to, that you respect, as your guardian, your protector..."

This was followed by a long silence.

"That's it, then," Constance said quietly. "I can't stay here. Knowing what I know, having said what we've said—continued living under this roof would be intolerable." She took a deep, shuddering breath. "There's an Air France flight to Delhi that leaves at midnight. I checked earlier in the day. If you'd be so good as to make the arrangements, I'll ask Proctor if he would drive me to JFK."

Pendergast was stunned. "Constance, wait. This is so sudden—"

She spoke over him, quickly, her voice trembling. "Please just make the arrangements. I'll get my things together."

An hour later, the two stood beneath the porte cochere, waiting for Proctor to bring the car around. She was wearing a vicuña coat, and her Hermès Birkin bag—a gift from Pendergast—hung on one shoulder. Headlights striped the façade of the house; a minute later, the big Rolls came up. Proctor, his face a taciturn mask, emerged and put Constance's things in the boot, then opened the rear door for her.

She turned. "There's so much I want to say. But I won't. Good-bye, Aloysius."

Pendergast had a thousand things he wanted to say, as well, but in that moment he couldn't find the words. It felt, somehow, that a part of himself was leaving—and yet he seemed powerless to do anything about it. It was as if he had set an engine in motion that, once started, could no longer be stopped.

"Constance," he managed. "Isn't there anything I can say or do—?"

"Can you love me the way I wish you to? The way I need you to?"

He did not reply.

"Then you've answered your own question."

"Constance—" Pendergast began again.

She put a finger to his lips. Then, taking it away, she kissed him. And without another word got into the Rolls.

Proctor closed the door, then got back behind the wheel, and the car began making its way slowly down the drive. Pendergast walked after it as far as Riverside Drive. He watched as the vehicle merged with the northbound traffic. He watched as its lights slowly became indistinguishable among myriad others. And as he watched, a silent shadow clad in black, a light snow began to fall, covering his pale hair; he remained unmoving for a very long time as the snow grew heavier, his figure slowly fading into the blur of the white winter night.

The authors wish to thank Patrick Allocco and Douglas Child for their assistance with various aircraft-related aspects of the novel.

ABOUT THE AUTHORS

The thrillers of **DOUGLAS PRESTON** and **LINCOLN CHILD** "stand head and shoulders above their rivals" (*Publishers Weekly*). Preston and Child's *Relic* and *The Cabinet of Curiosities* were chosen by readers in a National Public Radio poll as being among the one hundred greatest thrillers ever written, and *Relic* was made into a number one box office hit movie. They are coauthors of the famed Pendergast series and their recent novels include *Beyond the Ice Limit*, *White Fire*, *Blue Labyrinth*, and *Crimson Shore*. In addition to his novels, Preston writes about archaeology for the *New Yorker* and *National Geographic* magazines. Lincoln Child is a former book editor who has published six novels of his own, including the huge bestseller *Deep Storm*.

Readers can sign up for The Pendergast File, a monthly "strangely entertaining note" from the authors, at their website, PrestonChild.com. The authors welcome visitors to their alarmingly active Facebook page, where they post regularly.